Books by Lois Greiman

UNZIPPED
UNPLUGGED
UNSCREWED
UNMANNED
ONE HOT MESS

Unscrewed

Lois Greiman

A DELL BOOK

UNSCREWED
A Dell Book / February 2007

Published by Bantam Dell
A Division of Random House, Inc.
New York, New York

Book design by Susan Hood

Dell is a registered trademark of Random House, Inc., and the
colophon is a trademark of Random House, Inc.

ISBN 978-0-440-24361-8

Printed in the United States of America
Published simultaneously in Canada

www.bantamdell.com

OPM   10   9   8   7   6   5   4   3

To Sagacious Sage, who is like a son to me . . .
except hairier, and larger, and oh yeah, equine

1

I'd trade every last one of you for a moment's peace
and a dog that don't pee on the carpet.

> —Glen McMullen, arbitrating
> his progeny's latest dispute
> regarding favoritism

DON'T WORRY ABOUT me. I'm only your mother,"
said my mother.

But I was unruffled. It was 7:17 on a fine spring
Saturday, and I'd had a rejuvenating yet relaxing afternoon at home.

I smiled beatifically into the phone, found my fabulously placid center, and refused to be dragged into a
McMullen skirmish, or Weirdsville World, as I like to call
it. I was past all that now, a grown woman, my mother's
equal.

"I'll call you tomorrow. I promise," I said. My tone was
as smooth as a dove's dulcet coo.

Maybe it was the years of higher education that had finally allowed me to overcome my clinging blue-collar roots. Maybe it was the framed Ph.D. that hung in my office in Eagle Rock, where I counsel the poor unfortunates of the greater Los Angeles area . . . or maybe it was simply my innate classiness shining through. But regardless, I was serenely anticipating a quiet evening with a gentleman caller.

"Tomorrow!" Mom's voice dropped to a boxerlike baritone, a sound reminiscent of my acne-infested adolescence. But I was uncowed. I was, after all, a licensed psychologist . . . and there were a couple thousand miles of windswept prairie and inhospitable desert separating us. "Tomorrow? This happens to be your brother's life we're talking about."

I tilted my head at the image of myself in the full-length mirror that was anchored to the back of my bedroom door. Not bad.

"I'm well aware of that, Mother, but Peter John is an adult now and must learn to work through his own self-imposed life crises." His current crisis involved a woman. Her name was Holly. In point of fact, Pete's last five dozen life crises had involved women. But this one had the added drama of an impending infant. My idiot brother was about to procreate.

"Don't you get uppity with me, Christina Mary."

"I assure you, I am not getting uppity," I said. "I'm simply suggesting—"

"I know what you told Holly."

My clever rejoinder withered on my lips. "I don't know what you're talking about," I said.

"You call that girl back," Mom warned. "You call her back this instant and tell her you're just a bitter old pill and that Peter John will make a fine daddy."

My lungs felt too big for my rib cage. It was the same feeling I'd had when I'd come home late smelling of boy and Boone's Farm's finest. "I'm sorry ... um ... bad reception," I rasped.

"Don't you hang up on me, missy. I talked to Holly just last night and she said—"

I rubbed the phone frantically against my skirt, then brought it back to my ear. "Sorry ... going ... tunnel."

"... tell you this much, nobody's going to be talking about my grandbaby behind my back. It's a McMullen and it's gonna have the McMullen name if I have to cart that girl down the aisle on my back. I'm not just going to—"

"I'll ... you ... soon," I said, then frantically clicked the phone shut, tossed it into my underwear drawer, and closed my eyes.

It was 7:21 and I didn't feel quite so serene anymore.

I stared at myself again. My skirt was the approximate size of a Post-it Note. And my push-up bra, though religiously true to its promise, squeezed out a little roll of fat beneath the black elastic. I looked pale and a little bit like I was going to throw up.

But that was ridiculous. I am, after all, a secure, intelligent woman. Comfortable in my own skin. Independent and happy to be so. Well educated and ...

Closing my eyes again, I bent at the waist and refused to barf. Secure, intelligent women who are comfortable in their own skin do not hurl just because they're about to embark on a date. Secure, intelligent women greet their escorts with secure, intelligent smiles then make secure, intelligent conversation.

I straightened with firm resolution, tugged the abbreviated skirt toward my distant knees, and cringed. Maybe I should change into something less...naked. I turned toward my closet but stopped abruptly, remembering one basic truth.

Life is short.

Crap! My brother was going to have a baby. A baby! Which probably meant that I wasn't getting any younger.

And life is unpredictable. That singular fact had been proven to me with startling clarity some months earlier.

I'd been counseling a fellow named Andrew Bomstad. He was wealthy, attractive, and famous. Turns out he was also deceptive, perverted, and dangerous. Which was unfortunate. Even more unfortunate was the fact that he thought it amusing to chase me around my desk like a Doberman after a pork chop, then drop to the floor, deader than kibble.

A few weeks and a police investigation later proved that I had not been involved in the Viagra overdose that contributed to his cardiac arrest. But by then I had already banged heads with a dark police officer named Lieutenant Jack Rivera.

Rivera was LAPD down to his short hairs. He had the instincts of a pit bull and a sense of humor to match. He'd accused me of murder on more than one occasion...and he was going to pick me up for dinner at eight o'clock.

I felt my stomach bunch up like cookie dough gone bad. True, I thought, I'd dated some losers, but usually my beaus didn't threaten me with ten to life.

I looked at myself in the mirror again and began madly running facts through my head. Fact 1: Life was zipping past me like a streaker on speed. Fact 2: Rivera was hot. Fact 3: I hadn't had a date in . . . well . . . a while. Fact 4: Rivera was *really* hot. Fact 5: Life is short.

Maybe too short to be a chickenshit. Maybe too short to bow to fear. Maybe too short to spend every night like an aging nun with gonorrhea.

Perhaps I should slip out of the mini and meet the grim lieutenant at the door in nothing but a smile. And a cold sweat. I could feel the perspiration crank up already, creeping out from my underarms like frosty dew.

Better stick with the clothes idea. Even if I hadn't had sex for eighteen months, one week, and four days, I would probably remember the wheres and hows if the opportunity presented itself. Maybe it was just like riding a bicycle. Then again, Rivera wasn't like the little three-speed I'd pedaled down the back streets of Schaumburg, Illinois, as a kid. He was more like a Harley. Bad-mannered and snarly but with a tailpipe that made you want to drop-kick your inhibitions and hang on for the ride of your life.

Not that he was my type. My type used words like "sesquipedalian" and had an intelligence quotient somewhere in the range of the national debt. But my type hadn't come knocking much lately. Instead, my type had picked the lock, walked right in, and threatened my life with a butcher knife, after which point I had struck my type in the cranium with a telephone and screamed bloody murder. But that's another story entirely.

The point is, maybe it was time to take a chance on another type.

Besides, in a manner of speaking, I'd been dating Rivera for weeks already. Okay, maybe "dating" wasn't quite the right term. We'd been...sparring. And sparring with Rivera can be pretty much deadly.

But at least he was currently convinced of my innocence. Probably. Then again...maybe secure, intelligent women don't fantasize about boinking a guy who thinks they're capable of murdering their most illustrious client. On the other hand, Rivera had an ass like a plum ripe for the picking and—

Damn it! No. I wasn't some martini-toting cocktail waitress anymore. I was a high-class psychologist, and it didn't matter what kind of fruit the lieutenant's derriere resembled. What mattered was his intellect, his education, his sensitivity.

Good God, I had to cancel my date!

The thought hit me like a cartoon anvil. I spun around on my heel and gallumped toward the telephone on my nightstand.

Harlequin huffed and lifted his bicolored head from my coverlet, where he'd probably been drooling. Harlequin's a dog. The vet said he might be half Great Dane. The other half's up for grabs. Smart money's on something in the bovine family. He tracked me droopy-eyed from where he sprawled beside my new (well, new second-hand) ankle-strap Guccis. They had three-inch stiletto heels and sexy silver bows at the ankle.

I lifted the receiver, stared at my newly purchased footwear, and thought hard.

The truth crept insidiously into my consciousness and went something like this: One doesn't buy shoes with three-inch stiletto heels and silver bows at the ankle to wear while discussing the theory of relativity with balding microbiologists who wear bow ties and tube socks. One buys them for guys with fruity body parts. I chewed on my lower lip. Sometimes it helps me think. This time it only made me hungry. For beefcake in plum sauce.

I settled the receiver carefully back in its cradle. Eighteen months, one week, and four days stretched behind me like a mirage-inducing drought. Eighteen months, one week, and four days is a long time for anything that doesn't produce acorns.

Harlequin whapped his tail against my bedspread like a Major Leaguer testing his bat and tilted his boxy head at me.

"Very well, then," I told him, using what has been referred to rather unkindly as my nose voice. I don't like dogs. They stink and they take up too much room on the bed. Of course, the same can be said of men, and I've been known to forgive them on occasion. "Don't give me that look. I'll go out with him." The tail whapped again, picking up tempo. "But I'm not going to sleep with him." He huffed a sigh. "And a guy like Rivera's not gonna wait around long. So don't get your hopes up." Rivera had brought Harlequin to my door a few months earlier. He'd been just a pup, but had still been the size and color of Aunt Mavis's prize Holsteins. He's gained a good twenty pounds and three inches since then. "But I don't care." I was shaking my finger at him. The textbooks don't list this behavior as one of the signs of insanity. But they've missed other benchmarks, too, such as dating men who name their body parts things like "Dreammaker." "He's not my type anyway. I'm a licensed psychologist. He's a . . ." There was a good half inch of pink inner lid visible below each of the dog's eyes. He made Eeyore look as giddy as Goofy. If I liked dogs, I would have spent half my day trying to put a smile on his lopsided face. "Well, never mind what he is. I know how you feel about him, so I won't cancel, but I'm going to dress casual . . . classy, but casual."

Harlequin plopped his slack-lipped snout back on the mattress with a groan.

Thirty-odd minutes and five pairs of pants later, I was back in the skirt and bra. But I'd added the Guccis, six fat hair curlers, and a layer of makeup.

"The shoes didn't match the pants," I said. My tone wasn't defensive. It's never defensive when I talk to dogs. That would be pathetic.

Harlequin tilted his head and gave me a loopy expression that may have suggested canine approval.

But why wouldn't he approve? My skin was clear and I was wearing a damned nice bra.

My legs looked pretty good, too. Little bows really add something to the overall appearance of an ankle. And it probably didn't hurt that there was a quarter of a mile between them and my rarified hemline.

"You chew these up and I'm sending you to live with your dad," I warned, slanting my head to get a straight view of my legs. Harlequin did the same. "Yeah, he spoils you now, but—"

Perking his wind-sail ears, he turned his head toward the door and emitted a bark deep enough to vibrate the floorboards.

I jerked my attention toward the offending portal. The cookie dough ball bounced from my stomach to my knees.

I wasn't ready for Rivera. My hair was still in hot rollers. My earrings didn't match my nail polish. And my tires needed rotating.

Another woof rocked my world.

Snatching my blouse from its place on the chair, I raced toward the bathroom, wildly assuring myself that Rivera wouldn't come early. He might be a hard-ass know-it-all cop who habitually accused me of heinous crimes and threatened me with incarceration, but he wouldn't be so cruel as to show up at my door a full . . . I glanced at my watch. It was 7:57. Damn it!

Harlequin barked again. I could hear his nails clicking on the curling linoleum as he frolicked in a circle near my front door. I yanked the hot rollers from my hair and tossed them into the sink.

My stomach roiled, but I ignored it, chanting, "Life is short. Life is short. Life is—"

The doorbell rang. Harlequin bayed. I froze like a dumbfounded mannequin. My stomach did a double flip, threatening to expel its contents by any means possible. The doorbell rang again.

I struggled into my blouse, buttoned madly, then opened the bathroom door a fraction of an inch. "Just a minute!"

Harlequin was hyperventilating. I was doing the same. I closed the door, braced my back against it for an instant, then used the toilet before it was too late.

It sounded like a freight train when I flushed, but I was beyond caring.

The doorbell rang again.

"Be right there."

Harlequin was barking nonstop. Barking and bounding. I could feel his euphoria in the soles of my sexy shoes every time he hit the floor.

My hair looked like it had been slopped on my head by a mad Impressionist. I had planned to wear it up when I'd vowed to go casual but classy. I wasn't sure what to do with half-naked and sweating like a water buffalo.

Maybe I shouldn't answer the door. Maybe Rivera hadn't heard me yell. Maybe if I was really quiet he'd go away and—

The toilet gurgled. I glanced toward it. Toilet paper was swirling madly toward the rim. My heart flipped inside out.

"Holy crap!" Rummaging madly between my vanity and stool, I jerked out my plunger and torpedoed it into the bowl.

Water spilled over the edge like toxic waste.

I whimpered something between a prayer and a curse.

Knuckles rapped on my front door. "McMullen. You in there?"

"Just a minute!" I didn't sound so congenial anymore. A little breathless. Kind of nuts.

My plunger slurped at the toilet contents, then won the battle with one victorious glug.

Water sluiced down the drain. My shoulders slumped, the exhausted victor.

"Damn it, McMullen. What the hell's going on in there?"

"Nothing." My voice was raspy with post-traumatic exhaustion.

"Open the door or I'm breaking it down."

I peeked past the bathroom door to where Harlequin was having some sort of ecstatic seizure in my entryway.

"McMullen."

"Just wait!" Damn barbarian. He didn't deserve a push-up bra. Should have worn a horned helmet and a pelt. "I'm coming."

A moment later Rivera was pushing his way past Harlequin into my vestibule.

"You okay?" His voice was clipped. His eyes scanned my house, expecting desperados behind every table leg. If he pulled out a Glock, I was going to kick his plum-shaped ass onto Opus Street, but apparently all was safe, because he shifted his devil-dark attention back to me with slow deliberation.

I resisted squirming like a pubescent tuba player.

"Of course I'm all right," I said.

His lips hitched up a quarter of an inch. He has a scar on the right corner of his mouth. I don't know how it got there but there have been more than a few occasions when I've fantasized about giving him a matching one on the other side.

"Of course," he repeated, and reached down to absently fondle Harlequin's ears. "It's not as if a high-class broad like you would get yourself into some kind of trouble."

I resisted rising to the bait. "The dog missed you," I said. It just so happens I *am* a high-class broad, even if we were standing two millimeters apart and the smell of him was reminding me that I needed more fruit in my diet. USDA orders.

He straightened, still watching me with undiluted attention. When Rivera focuses, it sometimes seems like the rest of the world has taken a sabbatical. "I thought maybe there was some maniac with a shoe bomb and a mother complex holding you for ransom or something."

"I try to keep maniacs confined to the vestibule," I said.

He laughed with those Spanish black eyes. I felt weak in the ovaries. Harlequin was pressed up against his thigh like a love-starved groupie. For a second I wondered if there was room for two of us.

But before I could determine the answer to that age-old dilemma, Rivera raised a hand to my face. I held my breath. Was he going to kiss me? Was I ready? I could feel my temperature shoot off the charts. My mind was racing. It was too early. Or maybe too damned late. And I didn't want to faint. Or seem too easy. In which case I probably should have worn a skirt that was bigger than my thumbnail and a blouse made of some sort of opaque material instead of—

Holy crap, he was leaning in. His dark charisma hit me like a hot wind.

"Is that toilet paper?" he asked.

My mind slammed to a halt. I stumbled backward, slapped my hand to my left ear, and felt the filmy tissue on my fingertips. It did indeed seem to be toilet paper. I just managed to refrain from sliding under my linoleum.

"I cut myself shaving," I said, backing away. "Make yourself comfortable."

"In the vestibule?" he asked, but I had already retreated to the sanctity of my bathroom.

My face was as red as Mexican hot sauce when I looked in the mirror, but at least there was no more toilet paper adhered to my ear. I patted my cheeks with a little cold water, calmed my breathing, and took a look at my hair. It wasn't as bad as I had feared. I plied it with a pick just to give myself some time to think. Maybe it wasn't too late to change back into pants . . . and a parka. Something to assure Rivera I had no intention of sleeping with him, that I hadn't even noticed that he smelled like something you'd spread on pancakes. Or . . . I could barricade myself in the bathroom and slide a note under the door.

Go away. I'm working toward the celibacy world record.

I closed my eyes and paced. Water, or something similar, splashed against my shoe.

Shit!

Probably.

Luckily, or possibly because my toilet rebels with the regularity of Old Faithful, I keep a bucket and rags under my sink. Squatting was not a simple task in the Post-it-Note skirt, but I managed.

I could hear Rivera mumbling something to Harlequin, who seemed to be concurring in a series of hums and whines.

Two seconds later I was running water into the plastic pail. Cramped from squatting, I put the bucket near the toilet, spread my legs, and bent from the waist to clean up the floor.

"McMullen—"

I squawked and spun around.

Rivera was standing in the doorway, brows raised, gaze pinned to where my ass had been, half exposed in my cleaning lady imitation. He skimmed his eyes down the length of my legs. It took about half an hour.

"What?" I rasped.

A smile twitched his lips. Then he stepped inside and closed the door firmly behind him.

2

If they really wanted us to resist temptation, they shouldn't a made it so damned tempting.

> —James McMullen, Chrissy's
> most astute and
> philosophical brother

I FELT AS if the oxygen had been sucked out of my lungs by a Power Vac. The world seemed to waver a little around the edges as Rivera stepped close.

My bathroom wasn't big enough for a pair of pimentos. He was bigger than a pimento. I hoped.

Harlequin whined from the far side of the door. I may have done the same.

"What are you doing?" Rivera's voice was deep and smoky.

"I just . . ." I nodded toward the bucket. "I had a little . . . trouble . . ." Breathing. What the hell? I was a trained professional. A licensed psychologist. And he looked as tasty as a raspberry truffle.

"You trying to seduce me, McMullen?" he asked.

"Whaa—" My huff sounded like I was clearing a blow horn, but he was still gazing at me, chocolate eyes bedroom-soft and felonious grin off-kilter. "No. I . . . No. My toilet- –"

It occurred to me through a foggy sort of unreality that no sentence should begin with the words "my toilet" when a man was looking at me like this man was looking at me, but I couldn't seem to stop myself, to catch my breath, to function with a modicum of normality. I love normality.

I cleared my throat and reached for my professional voice. "My toilet overflowed."

"I missed you," he said, and shifted closer. Our thighs brushed. His were hard.

"I was just . . ." My hormones were jumping like Mexican beans and had begun shouting obscene suggestions. But the last time I listened to my hormones I'd been accused of petty theft and threatened with a restraining order. Long story. ". . . cleaning up," I said.

"Looked like you were practicing for a pose-off."

"My septic system is . . ." I felt light-headed and over-heated. Maybe I was wearing too much clothing. He sure as hell was. "Ummm . . . somewhat out-of-date."

He shifted a half inch closer. I wouldn't have thought it possible. "Legs look good, though."

Maybe I would have commented, but I was concentrating on breathing. And there was a commandment I was trying rather desperately to recall. It went something like . . . thou shalt not covet thy neighbor's ass. "I didn't want to get it on my shoes."

"Shoes look good, too. I like the bows." He propped a hand against the wall behind me. He was so close I could taste him. My insides twisted up like silk undies.

"Hope I didn't . . ." Drooling would be bad. I shouldn't drool. ". . . get them dirty."

"Damn things should be registered as lethal weapons."

I was beginning to pant. "The shoes?"

"The legs." He was so close I could feel his breath on my face. Jesus God, he was going to kiss me. The last time I'd kissed a guy . . . Ahh, hell, I couldn't remember the last time I'd kissed a guy.

"Rivera!" I gasped.

"McMullen . . ." he murmured.

I tried to be strong, or conscious. "I don't think we should—"

He kissed the corner of my lips. Something below my waist whimpered. Might have been the dog. Kinda doubt it.

"Let's skip dinner," he said.

I opened my mouth, but even my stomach failed to object. Maybe I was temporarily dead. This was heaven. The celestial toilet rested against my left knee.

He slipped his hand behind my neck. My brain went limp.

"Damn," he said, "you've been driving me crazy ever since you killed Bomstad."

A few cerebral cells bumped around, trying to work out the meaning of life, or how to remain vertical. "I didn't kill Bomstad." My voice sounded kind of breathy.

"Used to believe that," he murmured, eyes half-closed, head tilted the slightest degree. "But one look at you in this alleged skirt probably stopped his heart." He shimmied his hand down my back to the skirt in question. I shivered to my toenails and let my head rest against the wall behind me.

"How's *your* heart?" I asked. I sounded funny, like someone had taken sandpaper to my larynx.

"Last physical said my heart was pretty good."

I swallowed. "What'd they say about your other stuff?"

The left corner of his mouth hitched up a tad. "Other stuff's feeling pretty good, too."

I couldn't argue. It was pressed up against my thigh.

"Kinda out of practice, though," he said.

"Yeah?"

"Use it or lose it."

I was so damned weak. Even the memory of my past seventy-six beaus couldn't convince me to kick and run. "Wouldn't want that."

"I could make dinner . . . afterward." One of his thighs was between mine, kind of cradling me. "If I live that long," he added, and kissed me.

I kissed him back. He had one arm on each side of my head, holding me up, locking me in. If this was torture . . .

His hand moved to my breast. I locked my knees to keep from falling into the toilet, or climbing him like a spider monkey. He kissed my neck. His lips were firm and warm. I was vibrating with need just like the heaving-breasted women in the romance novels I'd been reading since I was old enough to hide under a blanket with a flashlight. His chest felt like sun-warmed marble against my palm—just like a romantic hero, all brawny and sexy and . . .

The vibrating near my crotch was joined by a tinny, almost recognizable melody.

Now, that was something different. Even Danielle Steel hadn't thought of that. I pushed him away, glanced down. "Is your . . ." I began. I was hardly panting at all. Excellent. "Are your pants singing?"

He chuckled. "Cell phone," he said, and slipped his hand around my waist.

"And here I thought you were just happy to see me."

"Believe it," he said, and shifted so I could feel the full length of him against my hip.

"Shouldn't you . . ." I might have gasped a little. ". . . answer it?"

"No." His hand was under my shirt. His phone was still ringing. Either that or my thighs had started to harmonize.

"Catchy tune." I couldn't quite identify it, but it seemed wise to fixate on it lest I take him down like a grizzly on a salmon and swallow him whole. "Carly Simon?" I guessed.

He drew back with a scowl, paused as if dragging his mind past the stark banks of lust and back into sanity. Then he dipped his hand into his pocket. Flipping open his phone, he pressed it to his ear, eyes searing mine. "Yeah."

I couldn't hear the voice on the other end of the line, but his expression darkened toward dangerous. I was still leaning back against the wall.

"All right," he said, and snapped the phone shut. The

bathroom was as silent as my bedroom had ever been. A tic bounced in his jaw. His eyes were blacker than hell. "I've got to go."

My ovaries growled. I may have done the same. "Now?"

"Yeah." He shoved the phone into his pocket. It was matched by a bulge on the other side. Maybe he kept his nightstick there. "Sorry."

I straightened, but I didn't grab him by the shirtfront and demand favors of any sort. Instead, I smoothed out my skirt. "Everything all right?"

He glared at me from beneath heavy brows, but I'm not sure he really knew I was still there. "Trouble with the senator."

"The . . ." I shifted my weight more securely over my three-inch heels. "Senator?"

He opened the door. Harlequin sprang inside, but Rivera didn't seem to notice him, either. You've got to be pretty far gone to ignore a dog the size of a refrigerator.

"Dear old Dad," he said, but even in my current state it would have been difficult to misread the sarcasm.

I opened my mouth, but nothing came out. My brain was tumbling around in my skull like a sun-dried raisin. Seems like all my body fluids had been called to the front lines.

"Listen." His voice was rough and deep, his dusky gaze fire-quick as it shot toward the front door and back, impatience stamped like a tattoo on his brow. "I'll have to take a rain check."

"No problem," I said, drowning out the strident protests from belowdecks.

"You sure?"

"Of course." I managed a nod. "Familial matters come first. You must attend."

He stared at me for an instant, then kissed me once, quick and hard. After that he was gone, striding across the floor like RoboCop on steroids.

It took me a full minute to marshal my senses. But finally I teetered atop my heels, wobbled out of the bathroom, and traipsed into the kitchen. The freezer handle felt nice and solid beneath my hand. I refrained from ripping it off and pulled out a carton of Freaky Deaky Fudge ice cream. Frozen moral support.

I shoveled a spoonful into my mouth. It hit my overheated system like a garden hose on a forest fire ... optimistic but ineffective. It didn't matter, though. I wasn't some teenybopper bent on steaming up the windows on my boyfriend's T-Bird. I am woman. Hear me roar. Or moan.

Harlequin whimpered, possibly in sympathy. Possibly because I was eating and he wasn't. I flicked him a chunk of Freaky. He caught it, swallowed, made a face.

I grinned at his expression. Everything was fine. So Rivera had left prematurely. It was no big deal. If I was ever going to have a grown-up relationship, I would have to learn to rise above minor frustrations and petty inconveniences.

I ate some more ice cream.

Rivera had issues to work out with his father. I knew that much from past conversations. Thus, it was really quite commendable that he was attempting to do so now ... at 8:20 ... on a Saturday night ... during the first viable date I'd had since the Clinton administration.

Another bite of Freaky Deaky made me feel a bit calmer. I didn't want to rush this relationship anyway. We were adults. We both had obligations, careers, pasts. And I'd made the mistake of moving too fast before. A tsunami was mild compared to the catastrophic results of those disasters.

And it wasn't as if Rivera wasn't attracted to me. I had hard evidence to the contrary. I gave myself a Freaky Deaky salute for my cleverness and reminded myself there was no hurry. He'd be back. We'd talk things through like intelligent adults. Maybe I could help him unravel his tangled emotions regarding his father. Men often have mixed feelings concerning the patriarchic head of their adolescent years, especially ....

" 'Like a Virgin'?" The song title sailed from my lips on a glycogen wave. Rivera's phone had been playing one of Madonna's megahits.

I stood, spoon still loaded, glaring numbly at nothing.

Oh, yeah, I was all for talking things through, self-actualization, getting in touch with one's inner child, and all that crap.

But what the hell did a *virgin* of any sort have to do with Lieutenant Jack Rivera? Wasn't that particular song far more likely to herald a call from an old flame out of his sordid past than from the illustrious senator he hated like a father?

But maybe I was being overly suspicious. Maybe *all* the grim lieutenant's calls were preceded by sexually suggestive songs that whispered breathily of being touched for the very first time.

Yeah. Sure. Made sense.

And maybe if Colin Farrell propositioned me with his crooning Irish accent and his soulful fuck-me eyes I'd tell him to take a hike. 'Cuz that's just the way the world works.

3

It's not as if I don't like men, I just have more respect for my washing machine.

—*Hannah Greene,*
Peter John McMullen's
first disenchanted wife

SOLBERG," I SAID by way of greeting. I was gripping
the phone in both hands, holding on like a sun-welted
businessman reeling in a tiger shark.

"Babekins."

The Geekster's voice was as nasal as ever. I remembered
to be strong, because even though he was a stunted little
techno nerd with a retarded sense of humor and a laugh
like a wild ass, he had a world of knowledge at his geeky
fingertips.

"You busy?" I was trying to sound casual, but my mind
was bouncing.

"I was just about to make Angel here some popcorn."

"Elaine's there?" Elaine, aka Angel, was my best friend. And it was my fault she'd hooked up with an electro-dweeb. That knowledge can still bring tears to my eyes.

"Yeah. She's a hell of a— Sorry, sweetums," he told her, ineffectively covering the mouthpiece. "A *heck* of a Scrabble player. You wanna talk to her?"

"No." Ignoring Laney's presence gave me a chance to pretend she was touring the Louvre with Johnny Depp instead of being holed up with a vertically inadequate myope. "Listen, Solberg, I need a favor."

"Shoot."

It was just a turn of phrase. I reminded myself not to get excited. Taking a deep breath, I jumped in. "I need Rivera's home address," I said.

There was a pause, maybe the sound of some eye-popping. "Jesus! I mean, geez, Chrissy." I could hear him shuffling his feet. They were size 12, huge for his five-foot-seven frame. I refused to contemplate what that meant in the dimensional scheme of things. "The grim lieutenant don't exactly have me on his short list of friends now. If I—"

"Not the lieutenant," I said. "The senator."

There was silence for seven heartbeats. I counted them in my head, but they were almost drowned out by Madonna's crooning lyrics. *"Like a Virgin," my ass!*

"Senator Rivera?" he asked.

"Yes."

"The grim lieutenant's prestigious sire?"

"Yes."

"Uh-huh." He sounded ultra-controlled, as if he were on the edge of a precipice and didn't want to make any false moves, lest he teeter into the yawning abyss. But I was already in the damned abyss, wasn't I? And Madonna was down there with me, singing up a storm. "What's going on, babekins?"

"A lot of unnatural shit, that's what!" I snapped. There may have been a bit more vitriol in the statement than I had intended. But Solberg was as charming as a bald lab rat and he was dating Brainy Laney Butterfield, possibly the most beautiful woman in our stratosphere. What did that mean for the rest of the female population?

Growing up together, I had always fantasized that she and I would marry matching brain surgeons and take high tea with the queen at Buckingham Palace. But if the royal guard heard Solberg's hee-hawing guffaw, they'd shoot him from the parapets and feed him to the Celts.

"Unnatural?" he repeated, but I wasn't quite cruel enough to tell him there was nothing so aberrant as he and Laney existing in the same solar system.

"Get me the address," I said instead, "and I won't tell Laney what you did when I drove you home in your Porsche."

I could feel his mind whirring on the other end of the phone line. He'd been as drunk as a frat boy when I'd dropped him off in his neo-riche neighborhood one hot summer night. If I said he'd danced the mambo with Shamu while wearing his boxers on his head, he'd believe me. And he doesn't even wear boxers.

I can't begin to tell you how sad it makes me to know that.

Still, for one elongated moment of silence I thought he might argue.

"Gonna take me a couple minutes," he said instead, and excused himself.

I hadn't even finished off my carton of Freaky Deaky when he called me back, rattled off an address, a warning about messing with powerful politicians, and a plea not to tell Laney anything that might alter her high opinion of him. But he didn't have to worry. She'd seen his scrawny frame decked out in swim trunks and still hadn't called the pound. Knowing that, there seemed little I could do to change the unpredictable tides of fate. "I'm a changed man, babe," he whispered. "I wouldn't do nothin' to—"

I hung up on him and crumpled the scrap of address in my palm—3430 Tramonto Drive, Pacific Palisades. A ritzy part of town. Real estate there runs into the bazillions, and houses hang suspended over the bay like crystal chandeliers. It would take me nearly an hour to get there. Not that I was planning to spy on Rivera. That would be beneath me. Sophomoric and suspicious. If the lieutenant and I were ever hoping to get past the heavy breathing stage, I was going to have to learn to trust him. Trust, after all, is the cornerstone upon which all secure relationships must be constructed. The very bastion . . .

" *'Like a Virgin'!*" I gritted, and tossed the empty ice-cream carton in the trash.

Ten minutes later I was chugging up the 210, systematically berating myself the whole way. From what I had heard, Rivera's relationship with his father was prickly at best. I should give them a chance to work things out. On the other hand, I wasn't intending to interfere. I was simply going to see if he was there.

Relatively comfortable with that justification, I followed my trusty MapQuest directions and turned onto the 405, then merged onto the I-10 and traipsed northwest along the Pacific Coast Highway. During daylight hours the spectacular view can take your breath away. At night it's more likely to take your life. Fog was just beginning to creep in from the bay, flowing like tattered, gauzy sleeves toward the rugged bluffs.

My thoughts were just as threadbare, worn at the seams, frayed at the edges.

The fact that Rivera was willing to lend a hand when his father called was a good sign, I reminded myself. A sign of healing, perhaps. As a therapist and a friend, it would be wrong of me to resent his efforts. In fact, when next I spoke to him I would commend him for his attempt to mend familial fences and . . .

A police cruiser streaked up behind me, flashing lights cutting through the ragged mists, siren sounding eerie in the muffled night. I checked my speed. Seventy miles an hour in a sixty-five zone. Damn it to hell. I worked up a full head of steam as I crunched onto the shoulder of the road. Wasn't like I was stealing old ladies' life insurance policies or—

The cruiser zipped past, taking Sunset Boulevard and heading west.

I wilted with relief and gave myself a mental shake. There was no need to rush. Nothing to worry about. The wheeling lights had already disappeared by the time I turned onto Los Liones, but I could still hear the siren.

Or another siren. I glanced in my rearview mirror. The

cop car behind me barely slowed for the turn, careened around me, then sped into the encroaching fog.

I scowled. Seemed like an awfully good neighborhood for such goings-on. But maybe some rising starlet was serving pretzels and Heinekens, incurring the rush.

It was difficult to see my directions even with my interior light on. I missed a turn, made a U-ey in a cul-de-sac, and took a right onto Tramonto Drive. An ambulance pulled in behind me.

Something balled up in my stomach. It might have been the Freaky Deaky, but Edy's and I have a working relationship. I keep the company in business, and it doesn't mess with my gastric system.

Up ahead, it looked like Christmas. Red and blue strobe lights were rotating in their plastic casings atop cop cars. A tall, rough stucco house was caught in the crisscross beams of the cruisers, the terra-cotta roof scalloped against a blue velvet sky, the front door open as if to invite all comers. Apparently, Senator Rivera lived in a hopping neighborhood.

An officer in blue stepped into my headlights, hand raised as he walked toward me.

I managed to brake before plowing him down like roadkill. My curiosity was roiling as I powered open my window. "What's going on?" I asked, giving him a smile and a glimmer of cleavage.

He bent slightly at the waist, but he was either gay or distracted, because he barely noticed the display. I gave him a quick appraisal. Good-looking, young, attractive in a narrow, academic sort of way. "I'm sorry, ma'am," he said, his voice amazingly devoid of emotion despite his age or lack thereof, "you'll have to turn around here."

But I had almost reached my destination. In less than a minute I would know whether Rivera's Jeep was parked in front of his father's manse. And if it was, well, then I could get on with that trust thing, couldn't I?

"I'm afraid I'm unable to do that, Officer," I said, lowering my tone an octave and trying to imbue it with sincere intelligence. I retracted the smile and wished I could do the same with the cleavage, but the cleavage was pretty much out there. "I have an appointment. But it will only take me a—"

"I'm sorry," he interrupted. I hate being interrupted more than I hate Brussels sprouts. But growing up with three perpetually adolescent brothers can do that to a girl. "You'll have to come back—"

"That's impossible." Interrupting other people, however, doesn't bother me in the least. "But I can park here, if you prefer, and walk—"

"Like I said, ma'am, you'll have to turn around."

I also hate being called "ma'am."

"I have an important engagement with—"

"What kind of—"

"It's a private matter." I could feel my adrenaline start to blend with the estrogen in my blooming system. It mixed a heady brew. "Between myself and my client."

His brows lowered a quarter of an inch. "Are you counsel?"

Counsel? I let the question swirl around in my head. "Mr. Rivera's expecting me," I said. "His house is just up ahead. If you'll let me . . ."

There was a moment of terse silence, then, "Did he call you?"

Umm. "Yes." Sometimes the truth's as good as a lie, but I didn't want to take any chances.

"What's your name, ma'am?"

"McMullen."

He glanced toward the house, impatient. "Pull over to the curb. Wait in the car," he said, then strode purposefully toward the front door of the stucco castle.

Weird. Backing up a little, I cranked the Saturn's wheels toward the lawn. Maybe I should just turn around and go past Rivera's house from another direction, I thought, but in that moment I caught the number written in black metal scroll against the pale stucco—3430, Senator Rivera's address. A little bit of vertigo struck me.

The car door seemed to open by itself. There was a mob standing on the sidewalk, five men and two women crammed together like people do in times of tragedy and excitement.

"What happened?" My voice sounded hoarse.

"Don't know." The guy who turned toward me was pure yuppie. Perfect hair, perfect teeth, and a perfectly ironed dress shirt in mandarin orange. If I could have seen his hands I was pretty sure his nails would have shone with a fresh buffing. "The police showed up about half an hour ago. But they won't say what's going on."

"Somebody's dead." The second guy was a few pounds heavier but just as yuppie.

"You don't know that, Dave," said Mr. Perfect.

"It happens just like this on *CSI* and somebody's always—"

"This isn't—"

My mind tuned them out as my attention wandered toward the street. And there, parked across Tramonto Drive, was Rivera's Jeep. A wave of nausea curdled my stomach.

And something hit me in the back of the head. It might have been a thought. Or a premonition. Sometimes they come at me like disoriented bats.

"You Ms. McMullen?"

I turned.

A man in a tan tweed jacket and blue jeans strode partway down the winding stone walkway that led toward the house, the officer who'd stopped me at his elbow. Their heads shifted together. A few words were spoken. Maybe they were too quiet to hear. Maybe it was the swelling waves in my head that kept the world at bay.

"You Ms. McMullen?" he repeated. The suit was medium height, square-jawed, no-nonsense. I lurched back in time, to another place, another crime scene, another officer. I felt off balance. Maybe it was the three-inch heels.

"Yes."

"I'm Detective Graystone. Officer Bjorklund said you had an appointment with Mr. Rivera."

"What happened?" I asked. Dread was a greasy ball somewhere just south of my esophagus now.

"We're still attempting to determine that, ma'am." His blond hair was thinning and gleamed in the wheeling lights. "At approximately what time did the lieutenant call you?"

The lieutenant! They weren't looking all grim-faced and hard-eyed about the senator at all. They had assumed

I was there on the younger Rivera's behalf. Why? The possibilities made me feel dizzy, sick. "I have to talk to him," I said.

Graystone grinned, but his eyes were hard. "Now, here's something new, Bjorklund. They don't usually lawyer up *before* they're charged. When did you last speak to him, Ms. McMullen?"

"Listen," I said, "I know my rights." I didn't really, but I was starting to consider reading up on that. "And I'm fully aware that I don't need to address any questions until—"

"When?" he gritted, and stepped up close. His eyes were silver blue in the eerie lights of the cruisers. Fog shivered past. The crowd behind me seemed eons away, leaving me alone in a sea of uncertainty.

"Just a couple hours ago," I said.

His expression didn't waver, but his eyes flashed in the surreal lights. "Bjorklund!" He grabbed the younger officer's arm, drew him close, murmured something short and quick.

"But—"

"Get your ass in there and do it."

Then Bjorklund was gone.

"Is someone dead?" My words came by themselves. No thought processes involved.

"How long have you been his attorney?"

My attention snapped to him. The lights on the cruisers turned crazily. The world whirled with it. "What?"

He narrowed his eyes, a freight train slowing down, taking stock. His gaze didn't shift, but he seemed to assess me just the same: the filmy blouse, the ridiculous skirt, the heels. He gave me his friendly face and drew a careful breath. "What's your given name, Ms. McMullen?"

"Christina," I said. What had happened? Where was Rivera?

"And your relationship to Mr. Rivera, Christina?"

Good question. Excellent question. "I'm a psychologist," I said, straightening to my full height, just over six feet in the silver-bowed Guccis. "I'd like to see him."

"You're his psychologist?"

I had a friendly face, too, but I wasn't about to waste it on him. "Is he in trouble?"

"Has he ever spoken to you of a Ms. Martinez?"

The name rang a tinny little bell in my brain but I couldn't recognize the tune. "Not that I can recall."

"She was . . ." He paused a second. His eyes gleamed as they skimmed toward my cleavage. ". . . a friend of his, too."

The world felt suddenly cold.

"She was also the senator's fiancée," he added.

"I don't . . ." Reality was a hard glacier pressed up against the world I wanted to have. "Was?"

Something feral gleamed in his eyes. "Was," he repeated.

The earth seemed to be dropping away from me.

His gaze slipped lower, down my exposed legs to the little bows at my ankles. "Were you on a date, Christina?"

"What's going on?" It was all I could manage.

"I'd like to ask you a few questions if—" he began, but at that instant hell exploded inside the house. Something shattered. Someone yelled.

And suddenly Graystone had a gun in his hand. He spun around and sprinted up the walkway to the house.

I went with him. I don't remember ascending the front steps. Don't remember passing the threshold. But suddenly I was there and no one stopped me. Like a feather on Graystone's coattails.

The air smelled of taut nerves and melted chocolate.

The entry seemed hollow and empty. Marble clattered beneath my heels. The living room was vaulted, arched stucco doorways, Persian rugs, crowded with people. Lieutenant Jack Rivera lay facedown on its pale hardwood floor. Two men dug their knees in his back. His forehead was bleeding, a bright stain of crimson over crusted black, but he never saw me. His eyes glowed with rage. Veins stood out like swollen tributaries in his dark forearms.

I didn't realize until sometime later that I had pressed my back up against the rough plaster of the wall behind me.

"Get the hell off me," Rivera snarled, like a wild animal netted but not yet tranqed.

"Calm down. Just calm down." The nearest standing cop had a gun trained at Rivera's head. There was a bruise developing over the officer's left eye. Another uniform was wiping blood from his nose with the back of his hand.

"What the hell's going on here?" A man entered beside me. I cranked my head to the right, taking him in in strange blurps of frozen time. Big man. Black. Huge hands. Tired eyes. "Graystone?" he queried.

The blocky suit stepped forward. "Dispatch got a call at nine-twelve. Said there was trouble at this address."

"Who called?"

"Don't know that yet, sir."

"Christ!" The big man's gaze, thunderbolt-fast and midnight-dark, snapped to Rivera's.

"Get these assholes off me," the lieutenant snarled.

"Shut the hell up!" ordered the officer in charge, but his eyes were beyond tired when he turned them back to Graystone. "What time did we arrive?"

"Nine twenty-eight, sir."

"Who came?"

"Tebbet and Irons."

The big man's gaze swung sideways, probably to the two officers in question, who were standing out of my line of vision. "And?"

"Front door was open when we arrived, Captain Kindred." The man who stepped forward to answer was short and squat, back straight, expression cranked tight, just starting to perspire. "We knocked. No one answered. House was quiet. I announced us. LAPD. Tebbet notified base of our intentions to enter said residence, then we went around back." He swallowed. "The light was on in the hallway, as was the light in the kitchen. Unsure whether there were lights—"

"Get to the damned money shot," growled the captain.

Irons nodded snappily. "The lieutenant was lying just to the left of where Tebbet is standing. He seemed unconscious."

"Fucking hell." Kindred ran his fingers through nappy hair cut short. "And the girl?"

All eyes turned toward something I couldn't see. The

captain took a step forward. The crowd parted like grains of sand, opening my view like a panoramic picture.

And then I saw her—sprawled on her back, half in the living room, half in the hall. She was barefoot. Her toenails shone bloodred against the hard marble tile and matched her long, tapered fingernails to perfection. A white satin bathrobe was belted at her waist. Her head was turned just so, her lips as red as her nails, her smooth ballerina's neck flawless, flowing gracefully into her shoulders and half-exposed breasts. Her eyes were wide and staring, liquid amber, shocked and unblinking as she gazed through a sable net of glossy hair. It flowed like a blue-black river over the slick fabric of her robe and onto the blond basswood floor beneath.

She was extremely beautiful, I thought, and found myself sliding down the wall onto my near-naked ass, legs spread wide and head reeling.

Extremely beautiful and absolutely dead.

4

In my experience, "what the hell" is generally the most interesting decision.

—*Eddie Friar, who had agreed to Chrissy's brainstorms more times than most*

I WAS RUNNING, running and falling. Crying and screaming. But I couldn't get away. Death was squeezing my lungs, stealing my breath. I thrashed wildly, trying to break free.

"Mac? Mac."

I heard my name through layers of cotton batting. I jerked, found I was free, sat up, and blinked. My heart was hammering at my ribs. It was dark all around me, but light streamed from some sort of opening. An apparition stood in the center of it.

"Mac." The apparition rushed at me. A horse thundered

along beside it. I scrunched back in terror. "Are you all right?"

I think I shook my head. My bumbling thoughts cleared a little. "Laney?" I guessed.

"What's wrong with you?" Her palm felt cool against my forehead. "What happened?"

I blinked, tried to take a deep breath. The horse morphed into a dog the size of a Hummer. It licked my hand.

"Are you okay?" Laney pushed the hair back from my face. Her fingers felt soft against my cheek. The dog's tongue was rough. Harlequin. His name was Harlequin. Where was I? "I tried to call you after you talked to Jeen."

Jeen. Solberg. A few more facts filtered lethargically into my cranium.

"But you didn't answer your phone. Or your cell. You must have let the battery run down again."

"Battery," I said. The filtering was pretty slow going. I can't dance worth crap, and I'm like the anti-Christ in the kitchen, but I'm a world-class sleeper. I'm not quite such a champion at waking up, however.

"Mac, what happened? Are you high? Did Rivera drug you or something?"

"Rivera." The filtering turned to a sudden flood: Shock on a dead girl's face. Rage in Rivera's eyes. "Laney." I snapped my gaze to hers and grappled for her hand. "I think he killed her."

"What?" The question came from the doorway. I jerked in that direction. Solberg jittered there, short, skinny, be-spectacled. I hoped this wasn't my bedroom, considering his presence.

"What are you talking about?" Laney was holding my hand between both of hers, squeezing gently. "What's going on?"

"The senator was dating his ex."

"Slow down."

"Creepy." I shivered. "And she was..." I felt breathless, shaky. "So beautiful. Like the statue of Madonna in Father Pat's office. You remember?"

She nodded, but she might have been humoring me. I've noticed that people do that with the mentally deranged.

"Her skin..." I shook my head. My memories were vivid. Her skin had looked flawlessly smooth, as if she'd never suffered a day of acne. Never struggled through manic brothers and adolescent boyfriends. But it was her eyes that snagged me. Eyes wide with shock and dismay, wondering how her perfect life had come to this. "I think *she* called him. Not his father," I rambled. "But from his house. *'Like a Virgin.'* Dead. And I thought—"

"Jeen, turn on the light, please." Laney's voice was firm but soft.

Light splashed all around me. Reality seeped in a careful inch. We *were* in my bedroom. But at least Laney was here, too.

She squeezed my fingers in hers. Her eyes, as green as the hills of the old country, looked naked and troubled. Harlequin's looked droopy and sad. Maybe he's not great at waking up, either. Sometimes I think we have a disturbing number of characteristics in common. "Start at the beginning," she said.

I drew a deep breath, thought back, let my tension ease

a notch, and did just that. I remembered the hazy shock that had enveloped me, Graystone's tight-lipped questions, my own monosyllabic answers, Officer Bjorklund's silent presence as he drove me home. Somehow my little Saturn had followed us. Magic maybe. Maybe not.

Two hours and a pot of coffee later, I felt scrubbed clean of emotion. Drained, beaten, sandblasted. Laney and I were sitting in my living room. Solberg had left some time before. Harlequin had happily taken his place, sprawling across the end of the couch with his head on Laney's lap and his tail curving toward the floor. Light seeped cautiously between the slats of my blinds, illuminating every sparkling dust mote in its path.

Elaine and I stared at each other.

"So what now?"

I wasn't sure for a moment if it was her question or mine. But I didn't think I had spoken, so I shrugged a response.

"You know . . ." I was sitting in my La-Z-Boy, balancing a mug atop my knees and wrapping my arms around my shins. The coffee had long since gone cold. "I think my taste in men is actually getting worse."

She fondled Harlequin's ears. He grinned drunkenly. Elaine always affects guys that way. "I think you've forgotten Ace."

I glanced at her, unsure, but then the memory struck with sudden rudeness. Ace had been the man's actual, given name. He had used my credit card to hire prostitutes for my surprise twenty-second birthday party. Three prostitutes.

"He only paid them," I mused. "He didn't murder them."

"Mac—"

"Listen," I said. Snapping the mug from my knees, I jerked to my feet. "I don't think I ask too much. All I want is a normal guy. One who doesn't murder anyone. Who doesn't hire call girls for my entertainment. Who doesn't steal my underwear. Who doesn't—"

"Who stole your underwear?"

"Warren," I said, facing her. "You remember Warren."

She scrunched her face. She was only moderately more adorable than usual when she did so. If I had a grain of pride I'm pretty sure I would hate her for that and a thousand other irresistible attributes. "I don't recall a Warren."

"Please tell me that even in my list of loser beaus an underwear-stealing hypochondriac is unforgettable."

There must have been something pathetic in my expression, because she said, in something of a monotone, "Oh, yes. Warren."

I stared at her. "You are the worst liar I've ever known."

"No, really, I re— Am not," she said, changing course and looking offended.

I closed my eyes and sank down beside her, scrunched between her and the armrest. "What the hell's wrong with me, Laney?"

"Nothing." Her answer was quick and solid.

"Worst liar ever," I said, and dropped my head back against the cushion. It smelled a little like dog. I hate dogs. I reached out and stroked Harlequin's muzzle. He snored happily.

"Really, Mac," Laney said, "there is nothing wrong with you, except . . ."

I lifted my head and blinked at her. We've been best friends since fifth grade, bonded by serious adolescent ugliness and boys who stink. And in all that time I couldn't remember a single instance when'd she found fault with me.

Well, maybe once. No, twice. No . . . Well, she found a lot fewer faults than most people.

"What?" I said.

She glanced toward the window. Dawn was becoming more aggressive.

"What?" I repeated.

She shifted her gaze back to mine. "I think you're intentionally looking for flaws."

I stared at her.

"In the men you date," she explained.

I kept staring. "Laney," I said. "When a guy commits murder, it's called a felony, not fault-finding."

"You don't know he killed her."

Memories were rushing in again, revving up my heart rate. "I don't know he didn't kill her, either."

"You could say that about—"

"Who?" I challenged. "Who? Solberg?"

She gave me a smirk.

"How many people has your little cabbage possibly killed, Laney?"

"That's not the point."

"That's exactly the point. Solberg is normal compared to the guys I date. Solberg! That hurts me," I said, clutching my mug to my chest. It said "I Hate Mondays" in red letters, with "Monday" crossed off and every other day of the week scratched in. It had been a gift from a guy I'd dated five years before. I'd gotten rid of him but kept the cup. One of my better deals. "It hurts me right here to say it," I told her.

She grinned. "Careful, Mac, your jealousy's showing."

"Oh!" I flopped back onto the couch, free hand pressed to my chest. "*Et tu,* Brutus?"

"What are you going to do now?"

" 'Do'?" I rolled my head toward her. "What can I do? I'm going to cross the dark lieutenant off my list of possibilities and move on."

"You have a list?"

"I didn't say it was long."

"How many?"

"Don't be cruel."

"Maybe he's innocent."

"Of what? Murder or lying?"

She opened her mouth, closed it, opened it again. "Okay, he maybe lied about his father calling."

"Either that or he thinks his father's a virgin."

She ignored me. "But that doesn't mean you can't give him another chance."

"You're sticking up for him?"

"I just think you're being hasty."

"You're sticking up for Rivera. You remember that he accused me of murder, don't you?"

"That was . . . unfortunate."

"He stole my blouse so he could test a cherry stain. A cherry stain, Laney."

"I'm not saying he's well adjusted. But then . . . he's a cop. Maybe you can't expect—"

"Threatened me."

"They call you a ballbuster," she blurted.

I stopped, mouth agape. "What?"

She cleared her throat and lowered her brows. They formed perfect twin arcs, like canopies, over her Emerald Isle eyes. "Jeen thinks men are afraid of you."

I shook my head at her. "What the hell does that have to do with anything?"

"You put them on the defensive."

"So you're saying Rivera lied to me about his dad calling, drove over to his father's house, and killed Martinez because he was afraid of me?"

"I'm saying . . ." She pushed Harlequin's head gently from her lap and rose to her feet with the grace of a dancer—which she is. Men make pilgrimages from as far away as Poughkeepsie to see her in tights. "You're going to get up." Reaching for my hand, she pulled me to my feet. "Get dressed." She turned me around like a windup toy, then pushed me toward my bedroom. "And go talk to him."

I stopped dead in my tracks and pivoted slowly back around. "What?"

"You've got to give him a chance. Ask him what happened. Get his side of the story."

"I do not."

She stared at me, her eyes wide and solemn, like the preacher's daughter she would always be. "Someone Rivera once cared about is dead, Mac. He's hurting, and whether he had anything to do with her death or not, he's in trouble. The Chrissy McMullen that I know . . . that I love . . . is going to do something about that."

She could instill guilt in a rock. But I'm harder than a rock. "You don't know me as well as you think you do."

She stared at me. I have never once beaten her in a stare-down. I glanced at the floor.

"I'll drive you to the police station," she said.

5

There is not a single gene pool entirely free of toxic waste.

—*Dr. Candon, psychiatrist,*
professor, and brother of a
cross-dressing kleptomaniac

I'D LIKE TO speak to Lieutenant Rivera," I said.

The man behind the counter had teeth the size of small rodents and a comb-over. The thing some men tend to forget is that hair is required in order to achieve a successful comb-over. But regardless of the state of this guy's coiffure, his fingers were quick on the keyboard in front of him.

"I'm sorry," he said, not glancing up. "Lieutenant Rivera isn't on duty today."

"Not on duty," I said, then paused, scowled, and held on to my patience. "I was told he would be held here overnight."

Confusion zipped across his face, but he kept his gaze on the computer screen and tapped a few keys. I watched his eyes widen. Apparently, it was early in his shift and he hadn't yet gleaned the precinct gossip. "Sorry," he said finally, "but the lieutenant is not allowed visitors at this time."

"I'm not a visitor. I'm a . . ." He was already shaking his head. "Psychologist."

"Sorry. I can't—"

"Excuse me." Laney squeezed in beside me at the counter. My arm pressed against hers, which pressed against her left boob, which made Comb-over Guy's eyes water.

Twenty seconds later we were ushered into the guts of the precinct while Comb-over put a call in to the powers that be. I sat hunched in a plastic chair like a palsy victim. My eyeballs felt like they'd been scrubbed with steel wool and my hair was greasy. I was wearing faded running pants and a white zip-up hoody over the fuck-me blouse I'd donned the night before. I was picking at a broken thumbnail when Laney elbowed me. I glanced toward her, but we never made eye contact because her gaze was welded elsewhere. I followed her line of attention toward a man conversing with a female clerk. His hair was silver, expensively shorn, and swept back from a regal, high-boned face. His skin was the color of a high-calorie cappuccino and spoke of blood that was ancient long before my own antecedents began filching sheep. His nose had a noble bow to it, his stance was relaxed yet perfectly straight, and he wore an Armani suit like most men do weekends. Casually, as if he had no one to impress. His dove gray shirt was accented by a burgundy tie, and not a wrinkle showed in the crisp fabric that stretched across his chest and beneath the broad shoulders of his dark, double-breasted suit coat.

A glass office opened a few yards to his right, and a towering man stepped out. It took my stuttering mind a minute to recognize him. Captain Kindred, still weary-eyed and guarded.

"Leighton," said Armani, and leaving the flushing clerk to stare after him in shiny-eyed admiration, he stepped forward to take the captain's hand in both of his own. "How's Lilah?"

"She's fine." Kindred nodded once, tension tight across his massive shoulders as he crunched his hands to fists and zipped my memory back to the roiling emotions I'd felt from his men the previous night. Admiration, nervousness, fear. Captain Kindred was not a man to be trifled with.

"And the kids?" Armani continued. "Maria must be, what? Seventeen now?"

"This May."

"Still playing the violin like a gifted angel? Some hot-blooded vaquero hasn't swept her into matrimony, has he?"

"God forbid!" The captain relaxed a little, almost smiled. "She's been accepted to Juilliard."

"Ahh . . ." Armani shook his head, eyes growing misty, as though the revered daughter were his own. "That's grand. Just grand. You must be very proud."

"Yes." Kindred nodded, shuffled oversized feet, fisted

oversized hands. "Thank you for your help in that regard."

"I was happy to do it," said Armani, and everything
about him suggested it was true. "It was nothing. Nothing
at all. It was Maria who plied the horsehair. And your
Lilah who carried out the threats. *Si?*" He nodded. "It is
not a simple task to raise a successful child in these days.
This I know." A trifle of sadness shaded his stately features, firing his rich liqueur eyes, forcing his back a little
straighter.

"Listen, Miguel," said the captain. "I'm sorry about this
damned circus. I wouldn't have—"

"I know." He interrupted easily, sweeping away the
emotion with an elegant hand and two simple words. "I
am certain you're doing everything in your power to set
things right."

The captain's gaze snapped to me, then away. "Come
into my office. We'll—"

"No." Armani shook his head. "No. I've nothing to
hide, Leighton, and the same, I am certain, can be said of
my son."

"I wouldn't have locked him up, but he was scaring the
shit out of my . . ." Kindred paused, deepened his scowl so
his eyes were almost lost beneath the cliffs of his brows.
"If the press catches a whiff of a cover-up, the mayor will
fry my ass."

"But he is well. He is safe?"

"Yes. Absolutely."

"What happened?"

The big shoulders tensed again. "I'm sorry, Senator. I
can't tell you any more than I did on the phone."

Senator! Reality zapped me like a Taser. Mr. Armani was Rivera's father. Elaine and I turned toward each other like ventriloquist dummies. Seconds passed in wordless silence as my mind seized every scattered piece of rumor I'd ever heard about the former politician.

". . . maybe tell you more than I can."

I glanced to my right. Both men were staring at me. I squelched a weak-kneed desire to scrunch back in my chair like a cornered rat. Captain Kindred had turned toward his office. Miguel Rivera was already making his way across the floor toward me, his handsome features solemn, his eyes like eagle lasers.

That's right . . . eagle lasers.

"Ms. McMullen." He had a rich, graceful accent that made plain English sound pale and wobbly by comparison.

"Yes." My voice squeaked like a poor soprano's. "Yes." I stood up. The chair teetered against the backs of my knees.

He reached for my hand. Our fingers met. His were slightly calloused, long, perfectly groomed. I wished to hell I'd made time for a manicure . . . and taken a shower, washed my hair, worn matching shoes.

"I am told you are my son's psychologist."

I opened my mouth, blinked, adjusted my thinking. "No. I'm his . . ." What the hell was I? "I'm not his therapist."

"No?"

"I'm just a . . . just a friend," I stammered.

The glimmer of a smile shone in his eyes. He leaned in

a bit and tightened his grip slightly. "Ahh, not *just* a friend, I think. A Rivera could not be so foolish as that."

"I . . ." I could actually feel myself blush. Holy crap. Paint me with acne, squeeze me into a tuba, and I was back in high school.

Laney shifted beside me, exuding a double dose of moral support and blatant curiosity.

"And this is?" The senator glanced to my left.

"Elaine Butterfield," she said. Her voice didn't warble one iota. But why would it? She was wearing real clothes. And she was Elaine Butterfield.

"It is very good to meet you," he said. Releasing my hand, he reached for hers, but neither his fingers nor his gaze lingered. Didn't rest on her cleavage. Didn't slip to her legs. Like a miracle, he turned back to me.

"So you were there, at my house, this past night?" he asked.

The question seemed to squeeze the breath from my lungs.

"Yes, sir. I was," I said. "For a short while."

"And my son, he was there also."

I remembered the snarling rage on Rivera's face as they pinned him to the floor. "Yes."

He drew a deep breath, fortifying himself. "And my Salina . . ." He paused, fought for strength. "She was already dead?"

A crappy day had just turned worse. "I believe so. I'm sorry."

He nodded, lifted his chin a small degree. "So tell me, Ms. McMullen, in your educated opinion, what do you believe happened last night?"

"You were there. You tell me."

The words were a growl from my left. The three of us turned in stunned unison. Lieutenant Jack Rivera stood not five feet away, hair rumpled, eyes sparking.

"Gerald." The senator straightened. His lips pursed. "They have released you as promised. I am glad."

"So what went wrong?" Rivera took a step closer. His face was unshaven, his shirt untucked. "She threaten to leave you again?"

I saw tension in the senator's body language for the first time. "I think it would be unwise for you to make a spectacle at your place of employment, Gerald."

"Unwise?" The word was a snarl. Around us, every living soul stopped, breath held, listening in gleeful horror. "You sorry son of a bitch. What'd you do?"

"I thought perhaps you had learned to control your temper," said the elder Rivera. "But I see now that you have not. Not last night, and not this morning."

"Control?" Reaching past me, Rivera snatched up a chair and slammed it against the wall. Half the room jumped. Captain Kindred's door sprang open.

"Lieutenant!" His voice cracked like a whip.

A muscle jumped in Rivera's stubbled jaw. His gaze skipped to me, rested a heartbeat, then turned toward the captain.

"What the hell do you think you're doing?" Kindred's voice was a low rumble, barely audible in the sweating silence of the room as he strode toward us.

Rivera shifted his gaze back to his father. His fists tightened on the chair, veins bulging beneath the folded cuffs of his sleeves.

"You wanna lose your badge? That what you want?" Kindred asked. His voice was a raspy threat.

The muscle jumped in Rivera's jaw again.

"Look at me," the captain snarled, thumping a hand against Rivera's chest. " 'Cuz I'm the man that can make it happen."

Rivera gritted his teeth, eyes blazing. Their gazes clashed. Dark on dark, sparking with rage and frustration and regret.

"We been through some shit together, Lieutenant," Kindred said, stepping up close, blocking the senator from Rivera's sight. "But I'll do what needs doing. You can damn sure bank on that."

The chair trembled in Rivera's hand. He set it aside, straightened, then shifted his gaze to me, smoldering hot with tight-coiled frustration.

I opened my mouth, but if I had any fabulous verbal plans, I have no idea what they were. He was Rivera, as volatile as meth, as unpredictable as a schizophrenic. Maybe he was innocent. But maybe he was guilty as hell.

Our gazes fused for one elongated moment as he probed my soul, and then he nodded grimly, turned, and walked out the door.

The captain closed his eyes and eased his big hands open. Around me, people began chattering like startled chipmunks.

The senator spoke first. "I am sorry." Kindred turned toward him. "I very much hoped he had matured."

"He'll be all right," said Kindred. "Just needs to blow off some steam. He'll come around."

But the older man shook his head. "I fear our past

stands between us. His mother and I . . ." he began, then smiled sadly. "But these are not your troubles, are they? Thank you for your efforts, Leighton. I shall not forget them."

The captain turned with a scowl toward his office.

The senator focused on me, gave a slight bow. "Ms. McMullen." He reached for my hand with both of his, drawing me close, holding me with his gaze. "He needs a friend now. Someone who believes in him."

I tried to step back. If there was one thing I knew for sure, it was that Rivera had read every rabid doubt in my head, every raging fear in my weak-bladdered soul. "I don't think I'm—"

"If not you, then who?" he asked, smiling gently. "Go to him. Give him the comfort only a beautiful woman can give a man," he said, and patting my hand, he turned to leave.

Beautiful? I stood like a dumbfounded monkey, staring after him in bewilderment and wondering if he'd noticed my mismatched shoes.

6

Marriage is like a toothbrush. It starts out smooth
and gets kind of prickly toward the end.

—*Howard Lepinski, who
brushes twelve times a day*

IT WAS A long night, during which I did a lot of tossing.
I would have turned, too, but Harlequin took up most of
the available turning space. By Monday morning I felt like
my brain had been rolled in sawdust and deep-fried in
pig fat.

The clock said 8:42. My first session was at ten. Time to
rise and shine. Well, no time to shine, just to rise.

I remained where I was.

The memory of Rivera's dead-set eyes seared me to the
bone. He'd looked at me as if I were somehow culpable.
As if he could blame me for doubting him, when the truth
was, I didn't know him. Had never been given a chance to

know him. All I was sure of was that he was as unstable as nitro . . . and a liar. He was lying nitroglycerin. Well, at least he was a neglecter of the truth. He'd never mentioned Salina. Not one word. Not one damned syllable. What was I supposed to think? That his presence during her death was simply coincidental? That he was as innocent as a kiwi? That he'd walked into his father's living room, found her dead, and decided to take a nap on the hardwood?

Well, none of it mattered. It wasn't my concern. If Rivera had wanted a real relationship, he would have made some sort of effort toward that end. Would have told me about his past. Or at least about his present. Holy crap! His father had been engaged to his ex, who happened to look a lot like a slinky version of Salma Hayek.

I slapped my hand over my eyes and moaned. How did I keep making the same mistakes? Well, okay, not *exactly* the same mistakes. My boyfriends weren't generally accused of manslaughter. So I had to get points for originality. I mean, it wasn't easy constantly coming up with all-time lows in my history of less-than-romantic entanglements.

But this time I knew one thing for certain.

I dropped my hand from my eyes and sat up like a toy soldier. My days of living stupid were over. I didn't need a man anyway. I had a good job. Well, I had a job. And a nice house. Well, I had a house. I had a good life. Well . . . anyway, from now on I was going to concentrate on nothing more grandiose than keeping all three.

And if I dated—*if* I dated—it would only be with pedigreed men. Men with taste, men with substance, men who neither accused me of murder nor were accused of murder themselves.

I rolled out of bed. Eeyore's tail wiggled on the back of my pajama top. My silk nightie had gone AWOL again.

I wandered into the bathroom, used the toilet, then eyed the scale near the sink. It stared back, cocky as a Frenchman. But this was a new me. A confident me. The scale was not the enemy. Striding up to the plate, I stepped boldly onto the smooth white surface, and winced.

Ten minutes later I was laced into my running shoes and stepping out the front door. Harlequin looked dashing in his red nylon leash. Controlling him was kind of like trying to box up the wind, but after the turmoil of the past six months, there was something comforting about having a rhino-size carnivore on a string. And there was the added bonus of his tendency to pull me up the hills.

The jacarandas were capped in purple blossoms and blooming early on Opus Street. Had I not been sure my lungs were about to explode I would have stared in awe. Dr. Seuss couldn't have conjured up anything more outrageous, but I turned my back to them and chugged up Oro Vista. True to form, Harley did his part to tow me along. Downhill was like trying to water-ski behind a Zamboni. By the time I reached my own slanted stoop, my right arm was two inches longer than my left and I wasn't sure which of us was panting harder.

Sloshing water into Harlequin's dish, I set it on the floor near the kitchen counter. He slopped it up while I retreated to the bathroom. No water for me. Instead, I stripped off every thread of clothing, gritted my teeth, stepped back onto the scale, and glared. Maybe it wasn't the enemy, but I sure as hell wasn't going to invite it over for pizza and beer. Stepping off, I slipped off my watch and removed my hair binder. Then, picking up the scale, I placed it on a cushy portion of the carpet in my pencil-sized hallway and gave it another chance.

One hundred and thirty-two pounds.

Not bad. If I didn't eat for a week and shaved my head, my weight would be perfect.

I was inspired to eat light. Breakfast consisted of seven raisins and a glass of water. Not because I wanted to look good for men. The new Christina McMullen didn't care about such outdated considerations.

Jack Rivera might have bone-melting eyes and an ass like a hot cross bun, but that only mattered to the old Chrissy. The new Chrissy was playing it smart. Living right. Keeping her nose to the grindstone.

Where the hell did one find a grindstone?

I pondered that on my drive to work and studiously did not think about buns of any kind. When a guy in a Chevy truck with license plates that said BOSSMAN cut me off, I ground my teeth, bided my time, and returned the favor at the first possible opportunity. Huh. The new Chrissy seemed to be almost as vindictive as the old one.

Eleven minutes later I was sitting across from my first client. Jacob Gerry was thirty-one, attractive, and successful. Luckily, he was also as gay as a bluebird. Ergo, no temptation to fraternize. Fraternizing with clients is a big no-no and tends to jeopardize one's career. After the debacle with Andrew Bomstad, mine didn't exactly need jeopardizing. Not that the new Chrissy would have been tempted even if Gerry fought fires in his underwear while simultaneously curing cancer. The new Chrissy was grinding her nose.

"Do you believe everyone really has a soul mate?" Jacob's voice was quiet and earnest, his eyes solemn. He worked in advertising, dressed like a Macy's mannequin, and probably made enough in an hour to pay my mortgage. But he was short one mate for his soul.

"What exactly do you mean by a 'soul mate'?" I asked.

He smiled, showing teeth just a little shy of perfect. Somehow it only made him more appealing. "Is this a clever ploy to induce me to discuss the meaning of life?"

Actually, no. I just honestly had no idea what a soul mate was. But I was pretty sure it wasn't a guy who ate the center out of my birthday cake or used my e-mail address to converse with girls who had names like Satin and Honey.

The new Chrissy shrugged enigmatically. "Perhaps," she said.

Jacob glanced out the window, smile fading. The view was less than awe-inspiring. Unless you were inspired by the sight of the Sunrise Coffee House. Which, by the by, had darn good scones. The old Chrissy had sometimes been inspired.

"I used to think I needed someone . . ." He paused, thinking. "Right."

" 'Right'?" I repeated, clever as a fox.

"You know. The right image. The right apartment. The right friends."

I steepled my fingers. "And now?"

"Now . . ." He looked wistful and tired when he turned back toward me. "Now I think I might be an ass."

By the time Jacob left, the new Chrissy was a little confused. Weren't we supposed to be fussy? Weren't we supposed to aim high? By lunch she was only hungry. Turns out raisins don't stick to your ribs like, say, . . . food.

So I trekked to the coffee shop early, obsessing over a Bacon Brava sandwich on a croissant with extra mozzarella and potato chips. I ordered a turkey on rye and returned to the office feeling smug and a little resentful. Damn freakin' poultry.

I saw four clients back to back without even coming up for air.

At 5:51 I heard Howard Lepinski talking to Elaine in the reception area. I finished updating Peggy Shin's records and dutifully set the rest aside. The old Chrissy wasn't real concerned about punctuality. Five minutes late was spot on time as far as she was concerned. But I was different now. I opened the door at six o'clock on the dot.

Lepinski settled onto my couch like a little old lady protecting her pocketbook, knees pressed primly together, back straight as a pin.

I said hello. He managed the same. A few seconds ticked away in silence before I decided to give the proverbial ball a shove.

"So how was your—"

"I'm thinking of going back to my wife." The words sped from his lips like 220 sprinters.

I sat dumbfounded. If I had been Lepinski's mistress this might have been bad news. Or maybe if I had been his wife. As things stood, I wasn't sure what to think.

Mr. Lepinski was a little man with a twitch, a mustache, and eyeglasses thick enough to render them bulletproof. I'd been counseling him for almost a year.

"Are you certain that's what you want to do?" I asked.

Lepinski shrugged and blinked twice. He was extremely fond of blinking...and shrugging. Sometimes it was a little disturbing, like watching a palsied zebra finch. Maybe that's why Mrs. Lepinski had, some months earlier, decided to do the Mattress Marengo with the guy who sold her pork ribs on Tuesdays and Thursdays. But there may have been other reasons.

"She's not seeing *him* anymore."

I assumed when he said "seeing," he actually meant screwing, but neither Chrissy was too excited about asking. I nodded and refocused. Lepinski had problems, but compared to some men, most of whom I've dated, he's got his pencils all in one box. "Did she tell you that?"

"Yes." He glanced up, twitched. "She says it's over."

I couldn't help wondering if the missus had called it quits with the pork-rib guy because she desperately longed to return to the connubial bliss she'd once shared with her beloved spouse, or because Porker had belatedly come to his senses. I'd met Mrs. Lepinski. She was marginally better-looking than a rump roast, but not quite as charming.

"So you miss her," I said. It was not quite a question, but left the door open for a response. Sometimes I surprised even myself with my spectacular cunning. Go, new Chrissy!

Lepinski's myopic gaze flitted toward the door and back. "She's my wife."

I sat in intelligent silence. Sometimes I sat in idiotic silence, but I tried to avoid it at the office.

"I mean, of course I miss her." He was looking defensive and fidgety, darting his attention from my framed Ansel Adams to my nearly empty desktop. It boasted one photograph, a magnet thingie with geometric metal pieces stuck to it, and two files aligned just so.

"You're living alone since the separation, aren't you, Mr. Lepinski?"

"Yes."

"In an apartment?"

He twitched. Maybe he saw where I was heading and didn't like the direction. "So?"

"I was just wondering how you like your new space."

"Space?" He snorted. "It's the size of a thumbtack. Don't even have a toaster."

"I couldn't live without English muffins," I said.

He shot his gaze back to mine. "What?"

I smiled and leaned forward to rest my elbows on my knees. They were stylishly garbed in dove gray Chanel trousers. Secondhand, but still classy as hell. "Tell me what you miss most about Sheila."

"Well . . ." He scowled, looking angry—or constipated. "She, uh . . . I don't understand the question."

I shrugged. "Does she make you laugh? Do you like the way she smells? Is she a master chef?"

Definitely angry, but maybe constipated, too, and more than a tad defensive. "She doesn't like the kitchen."

"Oh." I leaned back and *uh-huh*ed. "How does she feel about the bedroom?"

He froze. His mustache twitched and he darted his gaze away as if he hoped to do the same. "What?"

"We haven't spoken much about your relationship with your wife, Mr. Lepinski. I'm wondering what makes it special. Is it . . . say . . . sparkling dialogue, a mutual love for buffalo nickels, or something more intimate?"

"*Intimate?*" He said the word as though it were being dragged out of his throat with a garden trowel.

"You were intimate, weren't you?" I asked, and smiled to break the tension. No go.

"Of course. Of course we were . . . intimate."

The room went silent. I waited. Nodded. Waited some more. He didn't expound, leaving me to wonder, what kind of person doesn't like to talk about sex?

History and personal experience immediately suggested that it's the kind that's not getting any. Just about then, *I* could think of forty-seven subjects I'd rather discuss. Forty-eight if you count asphalt. I do.

"How often?" I asked finally.

His Adam's apple bobbed. "That's between Sheila and me."

"Is it?"

"What?"

"Listen, Mr. Lepinski, I'm not a voyeur." And if I were, I sincerely hoped I could find a better subject than a little man who favored rainbow-colored socks and considered collecting coins as exhilarating as skydiving. "I'm just wondering if, perhaps, you've misplaced your affections."

"Huh?"

"Might it be possible that you don't miss your wife so much as you miss . . . warm toast?"

"I don't eat white flour anymore."

I refrained from grinding my teeth. "Then perhaps it's something else associated with Sheila that you long for. That is to say, your own home . . . comfort." I paused, daring myself to terrify him again. "Sex."

For a moment I thought he might actually launch himself out my window and thwap into the coffeehouse next door. But he remained where he was, clawed hands holding his knees in place lest they skitter across the room like south-of-the-border fleas.

"Have you been seeing anyone?" I ventured, cautious now, for fear he'd do himself bodily harm in his haste to escape.

"Seeing . . . ?"

"Dating," I explained.

His eyes went round with panic. I'd like to say I found his reaction ridiculous and melodramatic. But the new Chrissy's no idiot.

"No!" he said. "No. I mean . . . I'm married. I can't. I wouldn't know . . . how. . . ." His voice trailed off.

"It's just a thought, Mr. Lepinski," I said. "You don't have to run right out to a singles bar or anything."

"Singles bar?" For a moment I thought he might burst into tears, which, from my perspective, was the most normal reaction I'd ever seen him exhibit. Anyone who doesn't want to cry at the thought of a singles bar is either a hopeless masochist or just . . . hopeless.

"That is to say, I think it's important that you examine

your true feelings for your wife before you make any firm decisions."

He twitched and glared. The clock ticked. He twitched again.

"Perhaps returning to her will make your life a living Utopia—or perhaps it will only further degrade your self-esteem."

He said nothing. I carefully abstained from jumping to my feet and roaring at him. The woman had cheated on him . . . while wearing his pajamas . . . with the *meat* guy.

"Hence, you must determine what you truly miss, then decide if the pleasure of her company, or the return to your former life, is worth your efforts."

He bounced his knees up half an inch and shot his gaze toward the window. I waited to the count of five.

"Tell me, Mr. Lepinski, how does your wife make you feel when you—"

"What about sex?" he croaked.

I paused. "Pardon me?"

"Is it worth degrading my self-esteem for sex?"

"Uhhh—"

"I mean . . ." His face was as pale as a full moon. People get damn freaky during full moons. "It's not like we did it all the time or anything."

"You and Sheila."

"Not much more than four times a week."

I felt my proverbial jaw hit my proverbial knees. "Four—"

"But it was better than nothing." He was whispering now, a secret. "Don't you think?"

"Four times—"

"She wasn't very nice sometimes." He paused, agonized. "Called me a weenie little sliver of a man and . . ."

Four times a week? I hadn't had sex four times in the past . . . Holy shit, I wasn't sure I'd had sex four times.

". . . a waste of oxygen," he said.

I clicked my mind into gear. "Well, as I'm sure you're aware, people sometimes say things they don't mean when—"

"A germ turd."

All right. All evidence suggested that the woman was a first-rate bitch, but I had to give her top scores for imaginative insults. "When people fight they often—"

"We didn't fight." His brows were beetled over his magnified eyes and his voice sounded musty. "Or talk."

I cleared my throat. "Just, ummm . . . just the sex, then?"

He nodded dejectedly. "Pretty much." He glanced up, straightening abruptly. "But even that's better than nothing, isn't it?"

"Well, that would be . . ." My mouth felt a little dry. I reminded myself not to squirm in my chair. Squirming was for oversexed teenagers who played the tuba and couldn't get a date for the prom. I'd been a hell of a tuba player. "That would be for you to decide."

"Life is short, you know, but . . ." He seemed to be searching his soul. It looked painful. "I suppose there should be more. Maybe I could find someone who didn't call me names and would still be willing to sleep with me."

Four times . . . a week. "I've heard it's been done." My own voice sounded kind of scratchy.

"Yeah," he said, then stronger, "Yeah. Hey." He glanced up, giving me a hard look from behind his Coke-bottle glasses. "You busy Saturday night?"

7

Friends are nice. You can tell 'em stuff, but you can swear like a gangster at an *enemy*. And that's all right, too.

—Angela Grapier, one of Chrissy's more insightful clients

THE NEW CHRISSY felt a lot like the old Chrissy by the time she got home. Tired, beaten, and kind of mucky.

I'd been tempted to stop at McDonald's for some deep-fried fat, but had, in honor of the new me, gone to the supermarket instead. By eight o'clock I was trudging up the sidewalk with a bagful of organic vegetables and free-range chicken. The new Chrissy was going to learn to cook nutritious, low-fat meals. In fact, it might be fun. Just Harlequin and me, laughing in the kitchen, experimenting with avant-garde recipes, eating off the same spoon.

I fumbled around the grocery bag, shoved my key in

the lock, and proceeded inside. The new Chrissy had a decent security system, 'cuz people kept trying to kill the old Chrissy. You'd be surprised how motivating death threats can be, even when you can't afford the Sunday paper. I punched in my code, turned . . . and issued a soundless scream.

Rivera stood not three feet away.

My stomach dropped to floor level. He remained absolutely still. His eyes were dark and brooding. Hell, his hands were dark and brooding.

"It's Monday," I warbled. It's strange what you'll say when your stomach is lodged somewhere in your right ankle.

He leaned a shoulder against the wall of my vestibule and stared at me like I'd lost my mind.

"You work late on Mondays," I said, trying to reestablish my intellect.

"You must have known I was here."

"What?" My mind was chanting, *"It's just Rivera, just Rivera, he's a cop."* But my memory kept projecting a dead girl with staring eyes. The grocery bag jiggled a little in my hands.

"Jesus, McMullen." He pushed away from the wall, looking tense and angry. "How many damned death threats do you need to get before you start taking precautions? My Jeep's parked across the street. You must have noticed it."

"It was dark." And I'd been thinking about the sauce Chin Yung's puts in their hun sui gai. It tasted like liquid ambrosia. I kind of doubted if even the new Chrissy was capable of concocting liquid ambrosia.

"What about the dog?" he asked.

Harlequin, I noticed, was circling him rather madly, hind end wiggling like an earthworm.

"Dog?" I repeated, thinking it sounded better than "What?"

"Doesn't he usually greet you at the door?"

"Not always. Sometimes he's—" I paused, gave myself a mental smack, and launched a belated attack. "What the hell are you doing in my house?" My tone was justifiably angry, but my skin still felt a little creepy. The last time I'd unexpectedly discovered a man in my living room there'd been a lot of screaming, a good deal of scrambling, and a bit of blood. I was hoping to avoid all three in this instance.

He titled his head, watching. "You scared of me?" he asked, and took a step closer.

I resisted backing up. Backing up wouldn't help. A .45 might be handy, though. "How'd you get in?"

"You didn't answer my question."

I raised my chin like a flyweight ready to take it on the chin . . . well, maybe a lightweight. "No, I'm not scared of you. I'm—"

He scoffed at me, tossing back his head a little, cocky as hell.

"Okay, I'm scared," I snapped. Pushing him aside, I stomped through to the kitchen. If he was going to kill me at least I was going to get one last meal. In which case I should have bought fudge and a couple dozen cartons of cigarettes. "Why wouldn't I be scared?" I plopped the groceries on the counter and glared. "We were supposed to be on a damned date. A date." I may have snarled at him as I slapped the celery onto the yellowed Formica. "You get a call. Say it's your father. Fine, I say." Broccoli joined the celery. "Fine. All understanding. All trusting. So you march off. And voilà!" I made a poofing motion with a bunch of green-topped carrots. "Two hours later a woman's dead and you're lying on the floor with some guy's knees—"

"Sounds more like pissed."

My lips moved. No sound came out. The carrots drooped between us. "What?"

"You sound more pissed than scared," he explained. Reaching into the bag, he pulled out the chicken and glanced at the label. "Jesus. Free-range organic? What the hell does that mean?"

I tried to snatch the package from his hand. He tightened his grip. "They're humanely treated."

"They're chickens."

"Humanely treated chickens."

"Christ! Seven forty-nine a pound. That's not chicken that's a fucking felony."

I made another grab at the meat, came away the victor, and slapped it on the counter.

We faced off. He crossed his arms. He was wearing a ribbed charcoal V-neck sweater. It was stretched smooth over his shoulders, pulled away from his wrists, and laid loose where his belly should be. Rivera's too ornery to have a belly.

"Go ahead and ask," he said, voice low.

I stared at him, mind spinning, eyes almost tearing up at the sight of him. Maybe the old Chrissy had kind of liked him. Had kind of hoped he was the one. The new

Chrissy turned and set the carrots primly beside the other veggies. "I don't know what you're talking about."

"I wasn't sleeping with her."

I resisted turning toward him. Resisted . . . everything. Silence echoed around us, lonely and cold.

"Not anymore," he said.

I turned. Resistance was futile. "Not anymore?"

"No."

"Since when?"

A tic jumped in his jaw. "It's a long story."

I stared at him, fighting hard, then turned and pulled a bottle of extra-virgin olive oil from the bag. The sight of it didn't exactly make me want to burst into song, but I couldn't help remembering the tune Rivera's phone had played. The memory didn't do a lot of good things for my mood. "I bet it is."

"Don't get so pissy," he said, and grabbed my arm.

For a second I actually considered braining him with the oil bottle. It was glass. The new Chrissy was determined to avoid contact with polycarbonates. "*Pissy?*" My voice sounded a little like Satan's. "You lied to me."

"I didn't lie. I just—"

"Your father! You said you were going to see your father. She didn't look like your father, Rivera."

"I didn't say I was going to see *him*. I just said there was trouble with him."

I jerked my arm from his grasp, yanked open the refrigerator, and shoved the olive oil inside.

"Jesus, McMullen, what the hell's wrong with you? A woman's dead. And you're worried about semantics."

I closed my eyes. The air from the refrigerator felt good.

I considered crawling in. There was plenty of room. Beside the olive oil sat a can of coagulating sweetened condensed milk and some green cheese. "Were you in love with her?"

"Listen—"

"Were you in love with her?" I turned slowly in the open doorway.

He glanced toward the window. The muscle worked in his jaw again. "Not anymore. Maybe never."

I drew a careful breath, thoughts jumping like sautéed shrimp. "How'd she die?"

Emotion flashed across his face. Anger, frustration, things I couldn't identify. "You think I killed her?"

My stomach felt crappy. Which sucked, 'cuz if this was going to be my last meal, I wanted like hell to enjoy it.

His eyes narrowed from dangerous to deadly. But I wasn't feeling so jolly myself anymore. "You think I'm capable of that?" His voice matched his expression.

Silence again, heavy as death. I pursed my lips and reached into the grocery bag. "In my line of work, you learn pretty early that people are capable of a great deal, Rivera. The complexities of personalities are so vast and—"

"God damn it!" He slammed his palm against my counter.

Harlequin and I jumped in unison. Rivera moved in close. I could feel his breath on my face, crowding me into the fridge. "Fuck your cock-assed psychobabble. Do you think I killed her or not?"

Fear stung like an icicle in my soul. Maybe he had murdered her. Maybe he was insane. Maybe I'd be a moron to risk upsetting him further. If I had a brain in my head I would soothe him, calm him. Lie to him. "I don't know," I said.

He stared at me for half an eternity, and then he nodded, moved away, looked out the window above the sink.

I stepped out of the refrigeration, legs a little squiggly.

"She said she needed to talk."

So I'd been right, but somehow that knowledge didn't make me feel a whole lot better. "That was her personalized ring tone."

"Madonna was her favorite. Sali . . . she liked to make people think she was born with a silver spoon. Made everything look easy. But she scraped for everything she got. Maybe she related to Madonna." He shrugged, grinned crookedly. "She was a wizard with technology. Got the song off the Internet. Somehow programmed it into my phone. Laughed when I couldn't figure out how to change it back." He shifted his gaze, his expression, looked at me, eyes dark as sin. "She sounded scared when she called. She didn't scare easy."

He seemed fairly rational for a nutcase. I chanced a question. Could be I'm the nutcase. "What was she doing there?"

"At Dad's house? Funny story," he said, but his tone suggested that it might not really be hilarious. "She lived with him." He drew a breath, carefully, as if to keep things from boiling past the lid, from seeping out of control. "For the past few months."

"You never told me." Childish. Childish response. The new Chrissy was ashamed and reached for the carrots to cover her feelings.

"I always thought he was just seeing her to fuck with me. Get under my skin. Then Mama calls." His voice had dropped half an octave. "Says he plans to marry her." He huffed a laugh. "Marriage! And she's, what? Half his fuckin' age."

"And that disturbed you."

"Disturbed me?" He leaned in, tilted on the edge of anger. "Christ. You're a piece of work, McMullen. Sometimes I don't know who'd like to see me fry more ... you or Graystone."

Oh, yeah, he was mad. But I wasn't so tickled, either. I stowed the carrots in the fridge. "Would now be the time to tell you that love is ageless? Like granite and ..." I gave my hand a cleverly flippant twist. "... diamonds."

Rage warred with something else in his eyes. It might have been humor. Then again, I thought, it might have been insanity. "I think I'm beginning to understand why Hawkins wanted to kill you," he said.

The hair lifted on the back of my neck. Doctor David Hawkins had been one of L.A.'s premier psychiatrists, and my mentor. There had been a time not so long ago when I'd thought he was the cat's pajamas. That was before he tried to kill me in my own kitchen with a butcher knife. "Professional jealousy?" I suggested, and pulled a bottle of stevia from the bag.

Rivera snorted and turned away.

"How long did you date?" I asked.

"Salina and me?" He ran his fist along the countertop. Thinking back. "A year or so. She worked on the senator's first campaign. God, she was young. Not long out of high school. I thought I had seen it all by then. Nineteen, just applied to the police academy." He stopped, glanced at me, drew a heavy breath. "She looked so fragile. I should have known better. Even then. But she was so damned pretty. Not dumb pretty. Smart. Savvy. Not taken in by his crap. God, I loved that about her."

"Whose crap?"

His eyes took me apart, analyzed me. No need for the Rorschach test.

"You probably think he's a saint," he said.

"I *am* Catholic," I agreed. It would have been nice to pinpoint his mood, to know exactly which way the wind was blowing, but so far I was feeling buffeted from every direction.

"And *he's* an asshole," he said.

I didn't mention the fact that his old man also looked great in Armani. "Why do you resent him with such fervor?" I opened the cupboard and shoved the sweetener inside.

He shook his head. "Go do your therapeutic mumbo jumbo somewhere else, McMullen. I'm not in the mood."

I watched him. "Okay. What makes your dad an asshole?"

"Murder."

I felt my eyes pop, my heart stop. "You think he killed her?"

He didn't answer. It was answer enough.

"Do you have proof?"

He laughed.

My mind was humming, dredging up shards of memories. "You said he was there. At the house."

"Did I?"

"Yes." Maybe. Or maybe my mind was muzzy from lack of sleep and junk-food deprivation.

He shrugged. The movement was stiff. "Could be I was imagining."

"Imagining what?"

He stared at me for a lifetime, then spoke, voice low and hard. "On my way there I thought I saw . . ." He shook his head, closed his eyes for an instant. "Him."

"Where?"

"Los Liones."

"Alone?"

He glared.

He hadn't been able to tell. A pet rock could deduce that much. "It was dark," I said, reading his eyes.

The corner of his mouth jumped. "I realize that, McMullen."

"He was inside a vehicle. Could you see what kind of car?"

He said nothing.

"You were on your way to his house, geared up for a confrontation. Maybe you—"

"I know it doesn't make sense," he gritted.

"Okay." I rested my butt against the counter and stared at him, trying to look casual, but my nerves were cranked up tight. "What's his motive?"

"You sound like a fuckin' whodunnit."

"Why would he want to kill her?"

Emotion crackled in his eyes. "The senator likes to call the shots."

I blinked, trying to align my mental picture of Miguel

Rivera with his son's. They were miles apart, shifted at odd angles. I searched for a question. "What shots?"

"It wouldn't have been the first time she threatened to leave him."

"Is that what she said? On the phone? That she was leaving him?"

"She said she needed a change. That things were going to be different."

"What did that mean?"

He shook his head. I could see the grating uncertainty in the way he held himself. It didn't fit the image I had of him.

"You think she was leaving your dad for someone else?"

"I don't know what the hell to think." He paced the tight confines of my kitchen. "When I heard her voice, the strain in it, I should have asked. Should have . . . Damn it." He drew a careful breath. "I should have been thinking."

But he had rushed off instead, rushed off to the woman he'd maybe once loved, maybe still loved. The thought blistered my gut, but his eyes did worse. They burned my soul. I don't like it when eyes do that. "You wanted to help," I said.

"Did I?" He stopped pacing, huffed a laugh. "I remember thinking, *This is one the old bastard can't win.*"

"Salina, you mean."

"Maybe I was just going to gloat."

I considered denying it, but he would see through that. Hell, he was a soul burner. "Maybe that was part of it," I said.

He narrowed his eyes at me. "You feeling sorry for me, McMullen?"

"I can be nice if I want to."

"Hasn't happened before."

"Yeah, well..." I reached into the bag again. "I'm scared, remember? Maybe I'm just trying to keep you from strangling me."

I realized in an instant that I wasn't the least bit funny and cranked my eyes toward him. But he snorted and leaned his hips against the edge of the counter, relaxing marginally.

"Old man is as rich as Judas," he said. "And he'll be richer yet when his stocks take root." He shook his head.

"Stocks?"

"Computers, pharmaceuticals, makeup. The senator is everywhere. Bastard can smell money before it's even minted. Always gets what he wants."

"Always?" My hand closed mindlessly around a can of something.

He turned toward me. "Maybe not always. There was my birth, not to mention some petty theft in middle school. But joining the police academy..." He shook his head, almost laughing at his own thoughts. "I think that was the one that really burned his ass."

"He didn't want you to be a cop."

He laughed. The tension was beginning to creep back in. "I was Miguel Rivera's son."

"What did Salina see in him?"

The tendons in his wrists tightened as he gripped my counter. "What do you see?"

"Besides money and power?"

His eyes crackled. I was going to have to quit being honest.

"You think he's for real?" he asked. "You think the face the public sees has anything to do with the living, breathing Miguel Geraldo Rivera?" He laughed. "Fuck it, he can seem like a peach, can't he? Hell, if it were all a lie, I'd marry him myself."

"That's illegal. Even in L.A.," I said, and stuffed whatever I was holding in the top cupboard.

He stared at me. The noose of tension tightened a notch. "You actually fell for it, didn't you?" he asked.

I felt itchy. "Fell for what?"

"Oh, yeah." He laughed. "You swallowed his act whole. Hook, line, and fucking Evinrude."

I stayed calm. Go, new Chrissy. "Was he instrumental in your release?"

He stiffened, and he hadn't exactly been Mr. Softy before. "He's a charming bastard, isn't he? Well dressed, manicured, articulate?"

Funny, but that was almost exactly what I'd been thinking. "It must be in the genes."

"You like him." It was nothing short of an accusation, tantamount to high treason. Possibly punishable by death. What did I really know about this guy?

"Maybe if you'd define 'asshole' for me—"

"She's dead. That definition enough?" His voice was clipped. I kept mine charmingly melodious. Taming the wild beast and all that.

"You didn't see anyone at his house when you got there?"

He shook his head, brows scrunched over brooding

eyes. "Door was unlocked. Security disarmed. I went in." He was reliving it in his mind. "Called her name. No answer." He drew a slow breath, seeing her. "Fuck."

"She was already dead?"

There was a moment of horrible silence, then, "I don't know. I'm a damned cop and I don't know. Funny, huh?" He didn't look amused. "She was lying there. I could see her from the hallway, looking at me. Eyes so big they could swallow a man whole. I thought maybe she was still breathing. Maybe there was a chance. Ran toward her." He closed his eyes, exhaled carefully, shook his head. "That's the last I remember. After that, nothing."

"What? What do you mean, 'nothing'?"

"Nothing. One minute I was moving toward her, the next I was surrounded by cops yelling at me to stay down. Hell, I didn't even know I *was* down."

"Nothing in between?"

"I think I hit Trank in the eye. Might have busted Pensacola's nose."

I gave him a look, but he didn't continue. "Any particular reason?"

He shook his head, scowling, lost. "I just . . . I don't remember coming to. I just remember . . . ."

"What?"

"Her eyes. Dead. I think I went a little crazy."

"Before or after?"

"What?"

I swallowed the question, reached back into the bag, blindly searching for normalcy. It wasn't in there. Just a bottle of something or other. "And you don't remember anything else, before you went unconscious?"

"No."

"There must have been something. A noise, a shadow . . ."

He gritted his teeth. "I don't know."

"Did someone hit you?"

"I don't know."

"Then—"

"I don't know! God damn it!"

The room echoed into silence.

He crunched his hands into fists and paced. "I should have used my head. Should have called for backup. Should have . . ." He breathed deeply and let his shoulders droop.

I fought the effects of his vulnerability. I didn't want to see him this way. Didn't want to empathize with him. Didn't want to like him. "You couldn't have foreseen the circumstances," I said. "No one can blame you for—"

"Don't say it, McMullen." He turned slowly toward me. "Don't say no one can blame me, 'cuz I'm pretty damned sure you might be wrong."

The guilt was there, throbbing in his eyes like a raw wound.

I shook my head, searching for words. "People react differently when they're emotionally involved."

"I don't get emotionally involved."

Feelings ripped across his face like an electrical storm.

"Good to know," I said, still holding the forgotten bottle. "Does he have an alibi?"

He tried to force himself to relax, failed, laughed. "He's Miguel Geraldo Rivera, McMullen. An alibi comes with the name."

"I don't know what that means."

"It means he'll come out of this smelling like a flower garden. Hell, he'll probably make a fortune on it."

"But you think he did it." I watched him, waited, breath held. He didn't answer.

"And you're sure he's innocent," he murmured.

"I didn't say that."

"Because he wears silk ties and pays a hundred bucks for a haircut."

"You're putting words in my mouth."

"Looks good in Armani."

I turned toward the cabinets, controlling my temper with stunning aplomb. "I never said—"

"Has a nice fucking tan."

"God damn it, Rivera, grow up!" I said, and slammed the cupboard door with all the force of terrified frustration.

The noise reverberated through the room as I stared at him.

Rivera raised a lazy brow. Romance novelists would call it sardonic. I call it his arrogant, son of a bitch expression. "Grow up?"

"Okay, so you hate him. Half the men in the known universe want revenge on their fathers. Long to live out their adolescent fantasies of retribution. That doesn't make their dads murderers. Ever hear of Oedipus?"

He turned toward me and suddenly, in the flash of a thought, I was pinned against the counter, my back bent over it.

"Oedipus?"

"Greek," I said. My mouth felt like it had been scoured

with beach sand. My larynx was frozen, but I managed to babble. "It's when a man falls in love with his mother and—"

"What do you call a man five times older than his fiancé?"

He wasn't actually touching me, but I was curved away from him like a Bowflex machine. "Well preserved?" I murmured.

Uncertainty shone through the anger on his face.

"You've got to admit, he looks pretty good for a hundred and fifty," I rasped.

If I'd been attempting to reduce the tension, I maybe should have tried another tack, but he eased away an inch. I straightened the same amount, daring to breathe.

He nodded, drew back, inhaled a breath. "Maybe *you* should marry him, McMullen. Now that there's an opening," he said. Then he stalked out of the house, leaving the door open behind him.

8

Opportunity may only knock once, but temptation'll knock down the damn door and drag you out by your hair.

> —Lily Schultz, Chrissy's first employer and lifetime mentor

I ATE THE CARROTS raw, stowed the celery, burned the chicken, and delved beneath the crystallized sweetened condensed milk to carve out the bottom with a spoon. The old Chrissy was firmly back at the helm. But who could blame her? She was obviously dealing with a deranged personality. Rivera's, not mine. And his was very possibly deranged and murderous.

I felt jittery and confused. The clock on my nightstand said 12:48 when I got out of bed, paced into the bathroom, and peered under the sink. But I'd gotten rid of my Virginia Slims stash weeks ago. Pattering into my office, I checked the bottom drawer of my desk. That was empty too. So I plopped into my swivel chair and stared at the blank screen.

"Why don't you marry him, McMullen?"

It was like a taunt from my childhood. *"If you like peanut butter so much, why don't you marry it?"* Rivera had officially reverted back to grade school.

But, to be fair, lots of people did when they were thrust into familial turmoil. I, for instance, broke out in acne when I got within a fifty-mile radius of my roots.

On the other hand, maybe Rivera had some grounds for his accusations. If I remembered correctly, there had been a scandal involving the good senator, something about a young intern. But it was a big step from fornication to felony.

Absently clicking on my computer, I tapped into the Internet. As far as I knew I was the only person in the civilized world still using dial-up, but it saved me five dollars a month. I could buy half a gram of free-range chicken for that. Or a buttload of fun-sized Snickers.

The thought of all that peanutty goodness brought me up short.

Swiveling my chair about and stepping over Harlequin, I paced into the kitchen and opened the freezer. It contained two black bananas, a Mars bar, and a bag of green beans harvested before the new millennium. I took out the Mars bar. I'd already eaten a gallon of crystallized sweetened milk. A little candy was just hair of the dog.

Masticating thoughtfully, I leaned back against the counter and ruminated on the last two days. Okay, so Rivera was a jerk. No surprise there. Most men are jerks. So I still found him attractive. That didn't mean anything.

I found Spider-Man attractive, too. And pirates. Damn, I love pirates. Didn't mean I was going to delve into their family histories, try to figure out why they despise their fathers, and expose their former love lives. That would be asinine. And I was through being asinine. Well, except for the sweetened condensed milk debacle. I felt a little sick to my stomach as I finished off the candy bar, but starting tomorrow, the new Chrissy was going to be firmly back in charge.

Tonight, though, I craved cigarettes like a death row convict. Toddling back into my pea-size office, I sat down at my desk and sighed.

By 1:15 I knew that the senator looked good in a tux and hobnobbed with the rich and famous. He was also a major stockholder in half a dozen companies that were out to change the world as we know it. Mindtec, for instance, was working on a computer small enough to adorn its owner's wrist. New Age would soon have a product on the shelves that cut UV rays while allowing your skin to tan, and a company called Sharpe Pharmaceuticals was perfecting a revolutionary cure for baldness.

By three in the morning, I'd read enough business news and political garbage to make my head feel as sick as my stomach. By 3:04 I was dead to the world, dreaming of pirates and politicians, with a dog the size of a minivan drooling on my sleeve.

Running three miles the next morning was like doing chin-ups with my tongue. Not easy. A smutty haze was trapped between the San Gabriels to the north and the

Santa Anas to the south and east, keeping the air quality just above lethal.

By the time I reached home I felt like throwing up. Might have been the distance, or maybe it was the fact that I'd eaten my weight in complex carbohydrates the night before. Dropping Harlequin's leash, I bent at the waist and watched him bound up the stairs like Tigger. I'd obviously worn him out.

Ten minutes later, the shower was spritzing erratically against my backside. When I won the million-dollar SuperLotto, I was going to have the plumbing redone. That'd leave me a couple thousand to spend on free-range chicken.

The drive to work was unusually civil. If you don't count the guy in the convertible who was sporting pencils in his nostrils and belting out show tunes at the top of his lungs, the trip was completely uneventful.

By the time I reached the office, I couldn't get "Oklahoma" out of my head. Elaine was standing behind the reception desk.

"Greetings!" she rumbled.

I stopped to stare at her. I wasn't particularly surprised by the guy in the convertible, but this was something new. "Is that a broadsword?" I asked, eyeing the weapon at her hip as I tossed my purse onto a nearby chair.

"Rest assured, I shall stow it behind the file cabinet before Master Fennow arrives, my mistress," she said.

I narrowed my eyes. Elaine's an aspiring actress, which is why she left Illinois for L.A. My reasons for following were a little foggier and had to do with adolescent bastards who fornicate in the backseats of Buicks with other women. Unfortunately, after three plus years in the City of Angels, my boyfriends were still adolescent bastards, and Laney still couldn't act. But she was tenacious, and there was always Pamela Anderson's unlikely rise to fame to keep her optimistic. "Xena: Warrior Princess?" I guessed.

"Close," she said, using her own voice and slamming the file drawer shut. "Queen of the Amazons. I should really have a longbow instead, but Jeen didn't have one of those lying around his house."

Maybe I should have wondered what Solberg was doing with a broadsword, but the question that surfaced was "You were at his house again?" The thought made me feel a little queasy. It might have been my sugar binge from the night before, but I didn't think so. I mean, if Brainy Laney Butterfield was settling for the Geekster, I might as well hang up my diaphragm.

"Let's focus here," she said, spreading her fingers on the desktop and scowling. "What do I need to change to become Hippolyta?"

"The ummm..." I took a stab in the dark. "The Amazon queen?"

"Yeah."

"Well..." I shuffled my purse aside and sat down beside it. "What's she like?"

"She's tough. Aggressive. Hates men. In fact, I think she might eat them."

"Eat them? Literally eat them?"

"And some legends suggest that Amazon women removed their right breast so as to leave their bowstrings unimpeded."

"I'm not sure that's what's meant by suffering for your

art." I glanced at her boobs. Thirty-four D. They're unenhanced. Whoever said life is fair should be shot in the ass with an Amazonian arrow.

"I don't think they'll ask me to go that far."

"Probably not," I guessed. When Laney put on a swimsuit, men in the next county fainted. Hollywood is weirder than ape shit, but I was pretty sure they had figured out that sex sells. "What does Hippolyta wear?"

"I'm not sure. What do you think I should audition in?"

"Have any deer-hide thongs?"

"Not on me."

"There's a load off my mind," I said, and rummaged in my purse for lip gloss.

"What do you think a man-eating Amazon woman would be like?"

"Why are you asking me?" I asked, abandoning my search. A penny was stuck to the lining of my handbag by something I didn't care to contemplate.

She grinned sheepishly.

I scowled. "Solberg's an idiot," I said. "And he's wrong. Men are not afraid of me."

"He is."

I snorted. "Me and dust?"

She laughed. I'd found over the past few months that she was impervious to insults on his behalf. I figured that meant one of two things: Either she didn't give a crap about him, or she was so infatuated she didn't care what I thought. I had a bad feeling which one it was.

"Showtime," she said, and suddenly the sword was gone, disappearing without a noise under the desk. She straightened, smiled. The door opened behind me. The first client of the day stepped inside. He was five foot nine and weighed in at well over two hundred pounds. His hair grew in wispy little tufts out of his shiny pate. He had fat mumbly lips, and in all the time I've been counseling him, I've never understood more than three consecutive words.

Elaine beamed at him like he was the king of Prussia. "Good morning, Mr. Patterson."

He mumbled something under his breath, not quite able to meet her eyes.

"Is that a new jacket?"

Another mumble. It sounded like "Rasum frazzle muddle pump" to me.

"Really? At Burlington's. Well, you have great taste. It brings out the color of your eyes. You look like a young Paul Newman."

Mr. Patterson straightened slightly, and in that moment some sort of strange metamorphosis seemed to take place, because for an instant I could actually see the resemblance.

Rising to my feet, I turned on my heel and slumped into my office. The truth was out. I would never be the therapist Laney was. No matter how many diplomas I treated to hundred-dollar frames and hung on my wall, she had a gift that neither education nor psychotherapy could reproduce. It might have been called kindness.

*N*early three hours had passed when Elaine opened my door with a snap. "Mistress." The sword was missing, but the attitude was not. "There is a person of the male gender wishing to converse with you."

"A man?" I'd seen three clients since I'd spoken to her. The last one was prone to washing his genitalia in bleach three times a day. Laney's rumbling accent and odd phraseology seemed apple-pie normal in comparison.

"On the calling horn."

"The . . . Oh." I glanced toward the phone. "Who is it?"

"He claims to be Miguel Rivera."

"Miguel—holy crap!" My brain did a somersault in my head. "The senator?"

She closed the door behind her and hurried to my desk, making a face and whispering as if she didn't want her alter ego to catch her out of character. "I think so."

"What does he want?"

"I didn't ask. Thought I'd act casual. Should I ask?"

"Yes. No. I . . . What do you know about this guy?"

"Not much. He only served two terms, so he was still relatively young after his twelve years. There was a bit of scandal about him and an aide. But the press loved him, good projection, photogenic, that sort of thing. Still, he only won the second term by a sliver. And then there was talk of a payoff. I think he's got a horse running in the Derby."

"Seriously?"

"And stock in Fablique."

"The lingerie company?"

"That's what I heard. I might be wrong."

I stared at her. She had boobs like missiles and brains like a Rhodes scholar. Life sucks. "I did a two-hour search on the Internet," I whispered. "All I know is that he looks good in a tux and maybe our children's grandsons won't have to worry about male pattern baldness."

"Should I tell him you're otherwise occupied?" She grinned. "Counseling a shvetambaras or something?"

"If I knew what the hell a shvetambaras was, I might say yes. As it is, I think I'm going to pee in my pants."

She looked at me. "You don't have to know what it is, Mac," she said. "You're Christina McMullen."

There was something about the way she said it with such devout conviction that almost made me believe, too. I felt myself straighten and wondered foggily if I looked like Mr. Patterson.

"Marry me, Laney," I said.

She laughed.

The front door dinged. "Answer the phone," she countered. "And take notes." She disappeared into the lobby. "Mr. Granger. Great pumps."

Mr. Granger had come out of the cross-dressing closet a few months earlier. He stands six-two in his stocking feet and gets a five o'clock shadow at high noon. I'm pretty sure there are more than a few who would like to see him go back in. Mrs. Granger included.

"Are they Phyllis's?" I heard Laney ask.

I closed my eyes and concentrated on the conversation ahead. But really, how does one prepare herself for a hot ex-senator who might just be a murderer?

I cleared my throat and picked up the receiver. "Hello?"

"Ms. McMullen." His voice was exactly like I remembered it, as if he'd waited his entire life to talk to me.

"Yes. Is this Senator Rivera?"

"Miguel. Please."

Miguel. Please. Like poetry from the mouth of Zorro.

Geez, I'm a child. I straightened in my chair and amped up my nose voice. "What can I do for you, Senator?"

There was the slightest pause, then, "As you may well guess, I am concerned for my son."

Because he's a nutcase? I wondered, and couldn't help but remember how the lieutenant's eyes had smoldered as he'd bent me over my stained Formica. "Is there any news? How is the investigation progressing?"

He sighed heavily. I imagined Zorro doing the same. "Slowly, I fear, as is so often the case."

Uh-huh. Say something else.

"Thus I am hoping to assist."

I paused a moment, trying to catch up. "With the investigation?"

"I am not completely without influence in this city of angels, Ms. McMullen. Toward that end, I thought perhaps you would dine with me so we might share information."

Yeah, he sounded like Zorro, but maybe he wasn't Antonio Banderas, with his smoky voice and love-me eyes. Maybe he was Anthony Hopkins, who also happened to be Hannibal Lector. My nerves were jumping. Salina had been very dead. "I'm afraid I wouldn't be very helpful, Senator." Especially if I were also dead.

"There I am certain you are wrong, my dear. My son thinks very highly of you."

I was probably just about to say something fabulously witty, but I can't remember what it was, 'cuz his words shut my mind down. I like to think I'm all grown up. But I lie to myself about other stuff, too. Caloric consumption, for instance. "I would be happy to help you, Mr.

Rivera. Really I would. But my schedule is terribly tight. In fact—"

"I would not take up so very much of your time, Ms. McMullen. An hour. No more."

"I'm—"

"You do not have another appointment for some while after Mr. Granger."

"That's true, but . . ." I paused, temporarily stunned in spite of my mature realism. "How do you know—"

"Please." His voice had dropped a little, making it a rich, dark blend of regret and concern, and almost causing me to forget he knew more about my schedule than I did. Zorro was tricky. "For an old man's only son."

It was the third time he'd interrupted me in a three-minute conversation. It might be the only thing the old man had in common with his only son. Well, that and the fact that they were both murder suspects. At least in my book.

The hair at the back of my neck was getting a workout lately.

"I shall pick you up at one o'clock. You may choose the restaurant."

"No!" I didn't want to seem jumpy, but I'd gotten into cars with murder suspects before. It hadn't gone so well.

"Then I shall choose," he said. "Gennaro Rosata sets a fine table."

My nerves jangled. I fiddled with a pen. It slipped out of my hand and onto the floor. I tried speaking again, keeping my words carefully slow so that they wouldn't jumble together like an upset Scrabble board. "I meant, no, I can't meet you, Senator. As I was about to say, I've a great deal of paperwork on which to catch up. I'm afraid . . ." No kidding. ". . . I will be forced to forgo lunch today."

"Oh, but you must not. You shall waste away to a shadow."

Hmmmph? "I assure you—" I began.

"Gennaro's entrees are all *fatto en casa*."

I was prepared to be impressed. But it was difficult since I had no idea what the hell he was talking about.

"Their cannelloni melts in your mouth."

Cannelloni! Holy crap.

"Do you like tiramisu?"

My mouth was starting to pool with saliva. Sometimes I dreamt about tiramisu. But wait a minute. That was the old Chrissy. The new Chrissy eats broccoli and free-range chicken. I calcified my resolve and slurped the saliva down my throat. "I'm sorry. Truly I am. But—"

"I shall be waiting outside your office in my Town Car."

"Town Car?" Did Town Cars have tinted windows? Bulletproof glass? Soundproofing? I wondered, but then my stomach rumbled, drowning out all those mundane considerations.

"You needn't divulge any information that makes you uncomfortable," he said.

The old stomach whined again. I covered it with one hand. Well, almost covered it. "Like I said—"

"Please, Ms. McMullen, it is of the utmost importance."

Elaine stepped in, eyes wide with un-Amazonian interest.

I gave her the eyes back and made a throat-slashing motion with the edge of my left hand.

"Very well," I said, hating myself and my weak-assed salivary glands. "I'll meet you outside my office in one hour. But I'm telling my secretary where I'm going and with whom."

He laughed. "You are cautious. That is wise. Gerald would be pleased if he knew."

I had an idea he might be wrong. I had an idea Gerald might piss in his pants if he knew.

"If it would make you feel better, I could give you Captain Kindred's direct number," he said. "You could inform him of your whereabouts as well."

Call Rivera's superior? I would have laughed out loud if I weren't still having that saliva problem. "Why not just inform the president?" I asked.

He laughed. "We could do that also if you like."

The funny thing was, I had no idea if he was serious.

"I'm looking forward to meeting with you, my dear."

"Yeah," I said, fresh out of intelligent conversation.

9

Maybe in fairy tales you're only as old as you feel, but here in L.A. you're every second as old as your pores.

—*Tess Langley, makeup artist*

Ms. MCMULLEN." Senator Rivera bowed over my hand. Behind him the Town Car stretched on for a couple city blocks. "It is very good of you to join me."

His eyes looked shadowed and tired, but it didn't do much to detract from his overall attractiveness. In fact, it may have added a weary monarch kind of appeal. "Come." He made an elegant gesture toward his vehicle. I think I had seen the prince do the same in *Cinderella* once—but come to think of it, it might have been the footman...who, in reality, was a rat. Something to think about. "You must be famished."

As I slithered inside, the leather seat sighed almost loud enough to muffle the groaning agreement of my stomach.

The senator settled in gracefully beside me. Not a groan to be heard. His driver shut the door.

"What did you wish to discuss?" I asked. I rather think I sounded like Cinderella herself. Or maybe one of the stepsisters. I hoped I wasn't the fat one.

"Salina's death . . ." He paused, drew a breath, shook his head. "It is a terrible shock."

"I'm very sorry."

"As am I."

We pulled decorously into early-afternoon traffic, no honking horns, no rude gestures—like Des Moines without the pig stench.

"She was an incredible woman."

I tried and failed to think of something to say in reply.

"A beautiful woman." This seemed to be a recurring, and possibly tiresome, theme. "It is difficult," he said. "Tragic beyond words." His back was very straight, as though he supported the weight of the world on his capable shoulders. "But nothing I can do will bring her back. Therefore I must live with the pain."

I opened my mouth, hoping something intelligent would fall out, but he held up a palm, saving me from myself.

"I have not been completely honest with you, Ms. McMullen."

The same could be said of every man I had ever met. But they usually didn't admit it right off the bat. I was flabbergasted.

"The truth is this . . . though I am convinced of my son's

innocence, there is little I can do to help prove it. But perhaps . . ." He paused, looking weary. "Perhaps I can prove my love for him."

I scowled. After talking to Rivera Junior, this wasn't exactly how I'd expected the conversation to proceed. Maybe my surprise showed on my face, because he smiled grimly.

"I see by your expression that Gerald has told you something about me, Ms. McMullen."

I searched again for something to say. Nothing.

"I know he paints me as something of a monster," he continued, "but perhaps I am not the ogre he thinks me to be, yes?"

A shrug didn't seem sufficient. Neither did absolute silence, but I went with it anyway.

"I want nothing so much as to overcome the bad blood that has come between us."

I carefully formulated a question. But nothing sounded great. "About that bad blood?" seemed a little vague. And "You were boinking his girlfriend" a bit accusatory.

He watched me, seeming to see into my soul. His smile was flickering, sad. "I did not seduce Salina away from my son, if that is what you believe."

He seemed to be waiting for a response. "I'm not sure what to believe," I said, which was oh so true.

"Perhaps I should start at the beginning." He glanced out the window. Palm trees lined the boulevard. As the story goes, they'd been transported from Florida in the '40s, hoping to convince folks that California was the tropical paradise Palm Beach was currently thought to be. Sixty years and ten million cantankerous citizens later, and voilà . . . L.A. was a shining example of political spin. "Salina is . . .

was . . . the daughter of an old friend. Luis Martinez." The senator's expression was solemn, aged, wise, introspective. I had to remind myself that he was talking about his late fiancée, a woman younger than his only son. "She and Gerald became friends. Indeed, we had hopes they would someday wed, combine our families. It would have been an advantageous arrangement."

"So her family was wealthy?" I realized suddenly that I wouldn't have been surprised to learn Rivera had lied to me. What did that say of our relationship?

"Wealthy?" He shook his head. "Not in the usual manner. But she had all the makings of greatness. Strength, beauty, ambition." He tapped the side of his head, not disturbing a single hair. "Brains." He sighed. "Her mother died when she was yet young. Luis, he was beside himself with grief. I thought it best that he leave Mexico, put the memories behind him. I finally convinced him to come to California. I did not have much influence at that time, but I managed to secure him a job on a ranch—the Mañana Estrella. It was no more than manual labor, but he did well there. And Salina . . ." He sighed. "She looked much like her mother." He shook his head. "Perhaps the pain was too great. Perhaps that is why Luis could not seem to appreciate her as he . . ." His voice trailed off. "I've no wish to speak poor of the dead. Luis was a good man, a fine man. He did the best he could. And Salina, she loved the horses. Took to them like a bee to honey. I can see her still, black braids bouncing as she rode. Bareback. Always bareback, and fast as the south wind. She was fearless. Even then. It was something my son did not understand."

"Her fearlessness?"

"*Sí.* I believe he thought he must protect her."

"From what?"

He looked into my eyes. "From me. But he was wrong. I had no interest in her. Not in that manner. Not even when she first worked on my campaign. I thought for a time that she would have been good for my son, that they would wed, but Salina..." He drew a deep breath through his nostrils, leaning back slightly. I could imagine him smoking a Cuban cigar and playing poker with the heads of state. "She was not one to take a backseat to another."

"A backseat?"

"Gerald...Well..." He lifted a hand as if in resignation. "He will always be a Rivera, whether he wishes to admit it or not. And he was young."

"How young?"

"Young enough to look at others." Ageless, then. "And Salina..." He smiled fondly. "She did not take any slight lightly."

"He cheated on her?"

"Cheated?" He made a surprised expression, as if he did not quite understand the word. "No."

Maybe there was no such thing as cheating in his world. Maybe it was flirting or loitering, or tripping into someone's bed. "He was forthright with her. Said that he thought they should see others."

"You know that for a fact?"

"If you are wondering if Gerald told me, the answer is no. But I worked very closely with my volunteers, Ms. McMullen. And Salina was the daughter of a special friend.

I knew she was troubled even before she came to speak to me of her concerns."

"And that's when you started seeing her?"

"Oh, no." He gave me a paternal smile. "My wife and I had our problems even then, but Salina was far too young."

Unlike two days ago when she was in her dotage. I remembered the baby-soft skin, the whiskey-bright eyes.

"It was some years later that my affection for her became interest in her as a woman. Some years after the death of her father. After Gerald's marriage, in fact. You see, regardless of what my son has told you, I never intended to hurt him."

"So you didn't know he would be upset if you married his ex-girlfriend . . . who happens to be half your age?"

He watched me in silence for a moment. His eyes wrinkled a little, an older version of the younger Rivera, no less appealing, perhaps, certainly no less powerful, but craftier. "You are not one to mince words, I see. I should have known that would be the case. My son would not cohabitate well with a woman of weak resolve."

I felt an almost overwhelming need to inform him that I wasn't cohabitating with his son. In fact, we might not even be speaking. But after a moment of silent reflection I had a strong suspicion the senator already knew. After all, he knew Mr. Granger was my last client until evening. He probably knew what size pumps the poor guy wore.

I said nothing. There are few things that make one seem more intelligent than silence. I'd learned that from shrink school and three garrulous brothers.

The senator was still watching me. He drew a deep breath, as if reaching into his reserves for strength. "To the best of my knowledge, Gerald and Salina hadn't seen each other for more than a decade when I began seeing her. He had been married and divorced. I believed, at the time, that he was through with her, that he had moved on," he said.

My stomach cramped. "You *believed*?"

He sighed. "Salina is not an easy woman to forget."

Tell me how gorgeous she was again, I thought. *'Cuz that's never going to get old.* "Was he still in love with her?" My tone was, I thought, beautifully casual.

The senator watched me, gaze hard and steady. "What do you know of Salina Martinez, Ms. McMullen?"

I resisted squirming. This wasn't exactly where I'd hoped the conversation would go. I mean, I wasn't thrilled to be locked in a Town Car with a possible murderer, but it seemed preferable to telling Rivera's father that I'd never heard of Salina until I'd seen her dead on his living room floor. It might suggest that my supposed boyfriend had been less than completely forthright with me.

"That she can ride horse bareback?"

He laughed. "What else?"

"What should I know?" I asked, hedging.

"That Gerald did not kill her."

Silence echoed in the car, like secrets wrapped in darkness.

"You must believe that," he said.

I went with the intelligent silence idea for a moment, then, "Where were you at the time?"

Surprise showed on his striking features. If he faked it, he was as talented as he was handsome. But then, he'd spent more than a decade in Washington and no small amount of time in L.A. What isn't faked? "Tell me, Ms. McMullen, do you think I may have killed her?"

I didn't say anything. Not so much for intelligence's sake as to keep myself from cutting my own throat.

He dropped his chin as if to study me more closely. "So that was the reason for your hesitation over lunch," he said. "I assumed it was a wise woman's usual reservation about seeing an unknown man alone."

He watched me in silence. I waited for his denunciation.

"How brave you are," he said instead.

Huh?

"To think I may have had a hand in a woman's death and still accompany me here."

Umm . . .

"You must care a great deal for my son."

"You didn't answer my question," I reminded him.

Outside the tinted windows, the world seemed strangely quiet.

"I was on a plane, Ms. McMullen, and I did not harm my fiancée. Nor shall I harm you."

I refused to fidget, but it was a close thing.

He smiled wryly. "My driver would never allow it." He flicked his gaze toward the front seat. "Would you, Roswald?"

"No, sir," came the answer.

"There, you see. He is very old-fashioned that way.

The last time he had to clean blood off the seats, he said . . ." The senator made a halting gesture with his palm. ". . . absolutely no more."

My breath caught in my throat and he laughed.

"I joke," he said, then, taking my hand between his, he sobered handsomely. "I would never have harmed my Salina."

He was probably telling the truth, but how the hell was I supposed to know for sure? Was his act a little pat? A little too well cued? The woman he had planned to marry had just died on his hardwood floor. Shouldn't he be inconsolable?

"Indeed, I loved her quite desperately."

"And she you?"

He smiled mistily. "It is difficult to guess the heart of another, is it not?"

It was a corny statement, and I would have liked to mock the sentiment, but he was right. I once had a boyfriend who convinced me of his undying adoration three days before sleeping with the stripper from his best friend's bachelor party. His name was Karl. Hers was Tinsel. I might have been able to forgive him if she'd been a Martha or a Louise. But Tinsel? A girl's got to have some pride.

"Rivera . . . Gerald," I corrected myself, "said she called him just before he drove to your house. She was nervous."

The senator drew a deep breath, seemed to be looking inward. "Salina was a complicated woman. Complicated, passionate." He glanced out the window and cleared his throat. If he was acting, he should be in the movies. But he'd have to do it for love of the arts, because, from what Laney had said, he didn't need the money. "Opinionated. We argued," he admitted.

"When? On Saturday?"

"Every day," he said, and turning back, he gave me a tremulous smile. His eyes were dark and soulful. "The truth is this, Ms. McMullen: Salina often threatened to leave me. As often as not I said she should go. Perhaps I harbored some . . . uncertainty . . . guilt even, regarding our age difference. Perhaps I tired of the confrontations. But she and Gerald . . ." He shook his head. "I had no fear on that account. No matter the feelings he still . . ." He scowled. "That is to say, they were not meant to be together."

I kept a lid on my emotions and my face expressionless. "But he saw it differently."

He shrugged and bravely hid away the worry. "For a time after his marriage failed, perhaps. But he and Salina were not compatible. He knew that as well as I." He put a fist to his chest. "In his heart."

How about in his dick? I wanted to ask, but I didn't. That's where the Ph.D. comes in. "And what about Salina?" I asked.

"Your pardon?" he said.

I breathed carefully. "How did Salina feel about . . . Gerald?"

"That fire was long since extinguished."

"Who was the fireman?"

He stared at me a moment, then laughed. For reasons I can't quite explain, I considered hitting him. Like father, like son. But then he stroked my hand.

"So . . . your feelings run deep. This knowledge warms

my heart. My son will need a strong woman in his corner."

"Why would she call him?"

"I beg your pardon?"

"If Salina was no longer interested in him, why the phone call? Surely there was someone else she could have—"

"Ahh, here we are," he said as the car pulled to the curb. The driver exited, opened our door. Miguel got out, reached for my hand, drew me into the sunlight.

Now, the truth is, I've been known to exit a vehicle without assistance, but I didn't exactly despise the attention. Senator Rivera was tall and sophisticated, and smelled like . . . well, kind of a meld between smooth charm and old money.

Once inside the restaurant, the maître d' greeted us like we were demigods, nodding solemnly and motioning us toward the hushed interior.

The lighting was dim, the upholstery plush, the menus as heavy as lead.

We discussed luncheon options for a moment. The lasagna was good, the rigatoni mediocre, he said.

The prices made free-range chicken look like a bargain. I'd have to sell my shoe collection to pay for a bread basket. But even designer footwear is overrated in the face of really first-rate focaccia.

As it turned out, Rosata's was good enough to convince me to go barefoot for the rest of my natural life. The wine was mouthwatering, the salad tossed tableside. I don't even like salad. But one taste assured me I would have gladly given an ovary for it.

I glanced up. Miguel Rivera was watching me. I stopped the wild masticating. He smiled.

"It is refreshing to see a woman enjoying her food so."

Oh, shit. That meant I was eating like a starved porker. I stopped myself just short of apologizing.

Instead, I cleared my throat, leaned back, dabbed at the corner of my mouth with a starched napkin, and refused to remark on the fact that it was real linen and I had missed breakfast.

"I did not mean to make you self-conscious," he said.

And I didn't mean to eat the tablecloth.

"It's quite good," I admitted.

"Yes. One of Salina's favorites. She had excellent taste."

And probably didn't drool on the menu.

Our entrées arrived. If my waistband wasn't already feeling tight I would have thought I had died and gone to heaven.

My first incision into the cannelloni was careful, lest I swoon. I followed up with a little light conversation.

"What do you think happened to Salina?" I asked. Okay, maybe not too light.

The senator swirled his wine and gazed into the glass. "That I do not know."

"What are the police saying?"

"Very little at this time. At least to me."

"Did she have enemies?"

The whisper of a smile lightened his conquistador face. He'd barely touched his manicotti. Was that the sign of a murderer or simple derangement? "What beautiful woman does not?"

"Who were they?"

"Discounting my wife?"

I stopped eating, glanced up.

"Forgive me," he said, and gave me a grim smile. "That was but a poor joke."

"Your wife knew Salina?"

He sipped his wine, fingers long and tanned against the pale, sparkling beverage. "From the time she was a child," he said, and shook his head. "In retrospect, I see that Rosita's resentment is somewhat understandable."

No shit, Sherlock. "Resentment?"

"Ms. McMullen," he said, and lifted his hand the slightest degree. A waiter appeared like a pop-up in a children's book. A motion of the fingers, and the senator's plate was removed and we were alone once again. He leaned forward. "I have a confession to make."

Wouldn't that be convenient?

"I knew a good deal about you even before we met."

"I don't always eat this fast," I said. "I skipped breakfast."

He smiled.

I didn't say anything. In my world this kind of observation is usually followed by a farewell speech involving phrases like "see other people" and "someone younger."

"You are a unique woman," he said, "interesting, amusing . . . and, if I may say, quite beautiful."

Hmmmm?

"But those are the reasons my son is fascinated by you. I am interested for an entirely different purpose."

Beautiful?

"You have wisdom."

Quite beautiful?

"I know of your ... encounter with Andrew Bomstad," he said.

My mind snapped back to business. "Oh?"

"It was you who deduced the identity of his killer."

"I—"

He raised a hand. No waiter popped up. I wondered how they discerned the difference between animated conversation and gastric demands.

"My son is a fine police officer. But even with all the men and equipment at his disposal, he could not determine the culprit was actually your colleague."

I felt the blood leave my cheeks at the reminder. I liked to think I'd put the pieces of my past behind me. But some pieces were farther behind than others. "David showed up in my kitchen with a grudge and a butcher knife," I said. "It made detection simpler."

"You are modest."

What I was was lucky to be was alive, and I damned well knew it. In fact, this little conversation was serving as a reminder that I'd rather like to stay that way.

"I also know of the threat to your secretary's life," he added.

I felt a little sick to my stomach. I was pretty sure it wasn't the entrée. I'd defend Rosata's cannelloni to the death. "It's been an interesting year."

"It was you who saved her and foiled the plot to steal her boyfriend's invention."

Foiled? "I'm not sure what you're getting at, Senator."

"You are an intelligent woman, Ms. McMullen. Intelligent and well educated. But there is more to you than that. You have strength. In your head and in your heart." I watched him. He watched me back. "You were a waitress once, were you not?"

I shuffled in my seat. It would have been nice to deny my former occupation, since any connection with an establishment called the Warthog was unlikely to do my rarified reputation much good. But I figured he already knew the truth. "A cocktail waitress, actually."

He nodded. "So you have education and you have the smarts."

"I—"

"They are entirely different, you know."

"Senator Rivera, I'm afraid—"

"Police departments are not unlike marriages."

Huh? "I beg your pardon?"

"They are filled with emotion. Trust and love, yes. But also disappointment, bitterness." He made a fist and gritted his teeth. "Jealousy."

I stared at him.

"Believe me, I know this to be true."

"I've never been married."

"My son is innocent," he said. "Of this I have no doubt, but I am not certain how diligently his colleagues will attempt to clear his name."

"Why is that?"

He paused, thinking, then, "Some years ago, Gerald had a young informant who was instrumental to an ongoing investigation. The young man was found dead in the

San Gabriel River. Gerald was understandably upset and blamed his partner."

"His—"

"Nathaniel Graystone."

I remembered the blocky, sharp-eyed detective who had questioned me outside of the senator's house, but kept my cursing to myself. "Rivera thinks Graystone killed his informant?"

"Not with a gun or a blade, but with words. Gerald believed the detective had leaked information about the boy. And as you know, my son is not one to keep his ideas to himself, no matter how far they might be fetched."

My mind was making little loops in my cranium.

He leaned back in his chair, watching me, fingers still wrapped around the elegant stemware. "So you see, Ms. McMullen, there is reason to believe his contemporaries, some of them at least, may not wish to prove his innocence."

"What does this have to do with me?"

"I believe you have a deep understanding of people. Thus, I wish for you to tell me all you can."

"About what?"

"My son."

"I don't—"

He smiled and held up his hand. "As you know, there is a rift between us. I hope to mend that rift, for he will be in need of a friend."

The meaning of his words sunk in slowly. "You think he'll be found guilty?"

He said nothing for a moment, then, "Tell me of my boy."

I felt breathless. "Listen, Senator, I appreciate the fact that you hope to reacquaint yourself with your son, but I assure you, I am hardly his confidan—"

"I am certain you know more than you realize."

I had to think there wasn't much evidence to substantiate that. "Such as?"

"His dreams." He shrugged. "His friends, his enemies."

The truth dawned on me with ferocious suddenness, or belated lethargy. "You think someone set him up."

"I do not know." His eyes were hard, his gaze steady. "But I will learn what I can, and you will help me."

"I'm afraid—"

"That is not what I have heard."

"What?"

"I do not think you are easily frightened, Ms. McMullen."

He was wrong. I was about ready to pee in my pants and we hadn't even ordered dessert. "Maybe you've gotten the wrong impression, Senator. I don't believe I know your son nearly as well as you think. In fact, we only met—"

"When he accused you of murdering the man who intended to disgrace you."

Disgrace? An old-world euphemism for a crime committed by cowards and perverts.

"My son is not always tactful," he said. "This I am certain you already know."

I didn't agree. But I sure as hell didn't disagree, either.

"Who else has he insulted, I wonder?" he mused.

Nearly everyone, I assumed. He was Rivera. "I have no way of knowing," I said.

"This Dr. Hawkins. He was a powerful man, was he not?"

"David?" I still got a lump in my throat when I said his name. I had considered him one of my closest friends before he tried to kill me. Since then, there's been some tension between us. "He's in prison," I said.

"Because of, or partly because of, my son."

I let that information soak into my brain.

"Perhaps he holds a grudge," the senator said. "Perhaps he wants nothing more than to see Gerald incarcerated with him."

"If you're looking at old cases, don't you think there could be hundreds of possibilities?"

"No," he said, "I do not. If someone killed my Salina—"

"If?"

He shrugged. "There was no weapon found. No forced entry."

"I thought the police hadn't told you anything."

He smiled. "Information is power, Christina. May I call you Christina?"

I nodded numbly.

"Hence, *if* someone killed her, he was extremely clever. He was able to breech my security, to get inside, to make it look as though my son was the culprit. I do not believe I know anyone so clever . . . or so devious."

Maybe that was because his son *was* the culprit. Or maybe the senator was lying through his teeth. I felt sick to my stomach. "Who knew your security code?"

He smiled grimly. "We had not lived there long. I could barely remember it myself."

"So no friends knew?"

"No."

"How about family?"

He said nothing. I waited a beat and continued. "Did your ex-wife know the code?"

"I am not so foolish as that, Christina." He poured me more wine. "Indeed—"

"What about your son?"

The bottle clicked against my glass. His gaze met mine.

"Did Rivera know the code?" I asked.

"No."

"Are you sure?"

"Absolutely," he said, and motioned to the waiter, who appeared in a heartbeat with the dessert tray.

"My guest would like one of your wonderful treats, I think," he said.

"I really shouldn't," I argued, but I would have been more convincing if I told them my head was made of cheese.

He smiled. "You must try the tiramisu. It was Salina's favorite."

"Are you having some?"

"I have never been fond of sweets," he said, "but please, be my guest."

Not fond of sweets? Did that make him a murderer, or just damned weird?

I ordered the tiramisu and watched him as the waiter hurried away.

"Did Salina have any health problems?" I asked.

"Not that I am aware of."

"And yet you believe she may have died of natural causes?" It seemed ludicrous.

"As I said, I do not know what to believe, except that my son is innocent."

Yeah, I thought, he'd mentioned that, but I wasn't about to tell him that methought he was protesting too much. At least not until I'd had my dessert.

10

Love may be blind, but lust is just damned stupid.

—*Megan Banfield, Peter*
McMullen's second
disenchanted wife

I'M A NEW WOMAN. Too smart to get involved," I said, and panted up Wildwood Hill. I was out for a bit of a jog with Elaine. Which is like saying *"I'm doing a little biking with Lance."*

"Are you sure you're not already involved?" she asked. As far as I could tell she hadn't started breathing yet that morning.

"Absolutely." I was wishing I hadn't left Harlequin at home, 'cuz sometimes he sniffs things out and yanks me to a halt. There were only so many times I could stop to tie my shoes without Laney getting suspicious. "If Rivera had wanted me involved in his life he would have told me he was dating Salma Hayek. He would have said his father was currently sleeping with Salma Hayek and confessed that he was still infatuated with Salma Hayek."

"Are you trying to tell me Salina looked like Salma Hayek?"

"Salma Hayek with brains, according to Rivera."

"Which is assuming two things. One, the real Salma doesn't have brains . . . which, when I met her, didn't seem to be true. And two, the lieutenant's still infatuated with her, which certainly didn't seem to be true."

"Well . . ," My respiratory system was threatening revolt and my stomach was starting to chime in. My lungs can collapse at the slightest provocation, but my gastronomic system has been given a five-star rating by the Belly Association. I can run five miles before my gut starts to act up. I wish like hell I hadn't found it necessary to prove that. "I saw her," I said.

"And she looked like Salma Hayek?"

"How'd you guess?" I was beginning to pant like a retriever.

"I'm psychic. So Senator Rivera thinks his son is innocent?"

"That's what he said."

Laney was quiet for a while. Still no breathing. Pretty soon I was going to tackle her and check for a pulse.

"But you don't believe him."

We rounded a corner. Two guys on skateboards stopped to watch us jog past. Their jaws were somewhere around their waistbands . . . which, in a bow to the fashion lords, was just about knee level.

Laney was wearing a sports bra and shorts. I was wearing the same. I could have been wearing a Dutch oven and dancing the cancan. I doubt if they would have noticed.

"Of course I do," I said. "Why wouldn't I?"

"You don't believe him," she said, arms swinging rhythmically. Mine had lost the tempo about five million steps back.

I stumbled to a halt at a stop sign. Thank God for traffic. I didn't have an appointment until eleven o'clock. If people weren't impeding our progress by rushing off to work, I'd have to feign a broken ankle . . . again.

"I didn't say that," I huffed, squinting gratefully at the passing cars.

Elaine loped onto the street. Seems like the traffic had suddenly stopped in both directions. Like Moses at the Red Sea. Only it was Brainy Laney at Riverton and Stagg.

"You don't believe him," she repeated.

I lurched back into a shambling limp and panted up beside her. My feet hurt and my bladder was starting to whine. "He admitted that *Gerald* was still infatuated with her."

"Gerald?"

I shrugged at the nomenclature. Rivera looked more like a gerbil than a Gerald.

"He actually said that his son was in love with his own fiancée?"

"Not in so many words."

"So you're psychic, too?"

"Yes." Monosyllables were my friends. "And he doesn't believe she called him."

"How do you know?"

"He hedged when I asked."

"Ahhh."

I took a few moments to huff up a mogul-size mountain. "I think Rivera had their security code."

"And went in uninvited?"

I scowled.

"Is that what his father thinks?"

"Yes."

"Did he say as much?"

"His eyes did."

She gave me a look. "What did his mouth say exactly?"

"That Gerald knew that he and Salina were incompatible."

"And by that you determined . . ."

"Who did Salina look like?" I panted.

"Salma Hayek?"

I managed a nod. "Have you ever known a man who'd consider himself incompatible with Salma Hayek?"

"Besides Jeen, you mean?"

I stopped beside a row of oleander and bent double. "I think I'm going to ralph."

She laughed. Elaine has a nasty side. Sometimes I forget that, until I'm stupid enough to exercise with her again. "So you think he believes his own son killed his fiancée?"

"Yes. No. I don't know." I gritted my teeth and straightened, scrunching up my face and holding my guts in with my hand. "There was a crapload of mixed messages."

"Is he interested in you?"

"What?"

She shrugged, did a few stretches. Twenty feet away,

tires squealed. Someone honked, long and angry. It must have been a woman. Men don't get angry when Laney's stretching. "I think it's been established that he's not above stealing his son's love interests."

I forgot about the pain in my side. "That's crazy."

"Hmm?" she said, all innocence.

But I knew what she was doing. I'm a trained professional. "He is not trying to make me believe Rivera is guilty so I'll transfer my supposed interest to him."

She shrugged and jogged in place. I thought the old guy walking by with his Lhasa apso might swallow his teeth.

"He's not." I started off at a slow jog, hoping all my viscera would stay inside where they belong.

"And what has led you to this conclusion?"

"First of all, I'm not Rivera's love interest."

"What are you?"

"Wish I knew. Secondly, Miguel had Salma Hayek."

"Maybe he thinks he can upgrade to Christina McMullen."

There's a reason I put up with Elaine's perfection. It's because she's perfect.

"Ph.D.," she added.

I scowled. Mostly 'cuz it was the only expression I was still capable of performing that far into the run. "Discounting the mixed messages, the senator seemed like a decent enough guy."

"He probably is, then."

"He wouldn't intentionally cast suspicions on his own son."

We trooped along. She didn't comment.

"On the other hand " My mind was working about as efficiently as my body. If I was lucky I'd survive long enough to die on Laney's walkway. "He is a politician. In which case, it's lucky he didn't *eat* his own son. But . . ."

"But what?"

"But it doesn't matter to me, does it?"

"Because you're not getting involved."

"Absolutely not."

"I'm glad to hear it, Mac."

I turned toward her. Her voice sounded funny.

"You make a lousy hero," she said.

"Do not," I countered, but she was right. Last time I'd tried it was when her boyfriend had gotten himself in big-ass trouble and had inadvertently pulled her in after him. It had taken a full SWAT team to save the lot of us.

"Do, too," she said. "Besides, you don't even like him."

"That's true." We trotted along side by side. Some people say they get their second wind after a mile or so. I was still waiting for my first one. "And God knows he doesn't need my help."

"He's a police lieutenant," she said, apparently by way of agreement, but it got me thinking.

"The senator thought that might be the problem."

"What do you mean?"

"He thinks Rivera has made enemies."

"I believe I remember *you* threatening to kill him."

"Yeah, but I didn't have anything against Salina. Not until I realized she looked like—"

"Salma Hayek," she said.

I tried a "There you go" shrug. Only one shoulder still

functioned. "And she was already dead when I first saw her."

"So you're pretty sure you didn't do it?"

"Almost positive."

"How about the senator?"

"I'm less sure about him."

"Where was he supposed to be when it happened?"

"On a plane."

"To where?"

"I don't know."

"Because you're not involved?"

"And because he didn't tell me. How'd your audition go?" Life is too short for proper segues.

"Which one?"

"For the warrior princess."

"Amazon queen," she corrected. "I don't know." Both of her shoulders seemed to be functional. "Okay, I guess. But I haven't heard from them. I think they wanted some-one..." She searched for the word. I watched her face. When I run I sweat like something in the porcine family. She glows. Honest to God. If she ever gets pregnant her husband won't need a night-light.

"With only one breast?" I guessed.

"Sexier."

"Are you kidding?"

"The woman after me wore a string bikini and stiletto heels."

"I didn't even know Amazon queens had stiletto heels."

"And she could sing."

"Wow."

"And the girl after her must have been six-one in her bare feet."

"Can she find the square root of six-digit numbers in her head?"

"I forgot to ask."

"Missed opportunity," I said.

"I'll remember next time."

We turned onto Keswick and headed downhill. It was only half a mile before I could die in peace by Laney's front door.

"Do you think I should throw in the towel?" she asked.

"What?" I turned toward her in mild surprise. I was pretty sure I had heard her wrong, but I'd been fantasizing about Magnificent Mint Julep ice cream, so it was difficult to be certain.

"Should I quit acting?"

"Seriously?"

She sighed. Apparently, both lungs still functioned, too. Bitch. "I'm tired of rejection."

"What are you talking about? Didn't the producer give you his phone number last time?"

"Yeah, but—"

"And his cell, e-mail, and firstborn?"

"Look at you," she said. "You accomplished what you set out to do."

"What are you talking about? Do you see ice cream in my hand?"

"I'm thirty-three years old and still hopping from audition to audition, begging for menial parts."

"That's because men are idiots."

"Some of them are women."

"They're jealous idiots."

"That's what Jeen says."

"Oh, crap."

"Yep," she said, and grinned. "You're thinking like the Geekster."

We jogged along as I ruminated on that sour news.

Three blocks from our beloved destination, we dropped down to a walk. I was chanting *"Thank you, Jesus"* in my brain.

"So you haven't heard from the dark lieutenant lately?" she asked, hands on hips as she swayed toward home.

"Not since he stopped in to terrorize me."

"Then you don't know if he's on active duty or not."

"Could have been voted king, for all I know."

"You haven't called him?"

"No."

"Because the new Chrissy's too smart to get involved?"

I gave her a stiff head bob. "Because the new Chrissy's too smart to get involved."

||

And thanks to Christina McMullen, who has taught me that common sense and intelligence need not have any correlation whatsoever.

—*Sister Celeste, during her retirement speech*

GOOD MORNING-TIDE, Sensei."

It was neither Elaine's garbled twist of Middle English and Japanese nor her husky accent that stopped me dead in my tracks. It was her ensemble. "Is that...alpaca?" I asked. I had seen her only a few hours before, during our run, and wasn't quite prepared for the metamorphosis.

She glanced down at herself. Some kind of multi-colored fur covered her chest...almost. Below that her midriff was bare. Taut with muscle the color of clover honey, it swept in a shallow valley down to a silk wrap-around skirt.

"I got a callback," she said.

"No kidding? For Xena."

"Amazon queen."

"That's fantastic. When do you go in?"

"This afternoon. I'm crazy nervous."

"Nervous! Don't be ridiculous. One look at you in that"—I motioned to her chest—"dead thing, and they'll be handing over their babies wrapped in movie contracts."

"You think?"

I tossed my purse onto a chair and gave her another once-over. "Absolutely. Is Amazon Xena from the Orient?"

"I don't know. I thought I inferred an intriguing Asian bent to the dialogue, but I'm flying blind here. I couldn't— Whoops. Client at two o'clock," she said, and suddenly Amazon Xena was gone, replaced by a smiling Brainy Laney dressed in conservative silk.

Ten minutes later I was sitting in the day's first session. Bonnie Reinhart was forty-six years old, a kleptomaniac, and lots of fun. In fact, I couldn't find a single reason she might feel the need to steal, except of course that she enjoyed it. After five weeks of therapy, that's all I had discovered.

My next client wasn't quite so enjoyable. He'd been baptized Jeremiah Denny, but I'd been informed that his friends called him Jenny. His parents were concerned that it was because he was uncertain about his sexuality. But judging by his unrelenting concentration on my boobs, I was pretty sure they could rest easy on that count. They might have wanted to consider the fact that he was obsessed with sex and lacked any sort of social skills, however.

Angela Grapier entered my office not four minutes after Jeremiah shambled off. Angie's been my client since her dad decided she'd be better off without drugs and the certifiable boyfriends that went with them.

"Who's the perv?" she asked, tossing her backpack on the floor and curling up in the corner of my cushy couch. Angie's one of those people who can sum things up pretty quick. It had cost Jeremiah's parents a few hundred bucks for me to come to the same conclusion Angie had made for free in fourteen seconds.

"Can't tell you," I said, and refrained from adding *"Na na na boo boo,"* even though Angie tends to bring out the kid, and the tuba player, in me. "How's school?"

"Got an A in French. He always stare at boobs like that?"

I considered being coy. It hardly seemed worth it. *"Oui,"* I said.

She shrugged. "Hope you get paid good," she said, and moved on to concerns about her upcoming college plans and guys who thought they were funny but really weren't.

Five minutes after she left, the doorbell tinkled. Thirty seconds later, Elaine rang from the reception desk.

"Bonjour," I said.

"Ms. McMullen." Elaine was using her professional voice. It rarely precedes good things. I wondered vaguely if she'd had time to stow her broadsword behind the file cabinet before the latest arrival.

"What's up?" I have a professional voice, too, but I don't like to risk wearing it out.

"Two officers are here from the LAPD to see you, Ms. McMullen."

I gripped the receiver a little harder. True, the boys in blue were bound to arrive sooner or later. Still, I felt my blood run cold. There's nothing like a personal visit from a professional crime fighter to make you feel as guilty as sin.

"Tell them I went home," I said. "I'll hide under my desk." This wasn't an original idea. We'd tried it with Lieutenant Rivera once, in fact. It hadn't worked out real nifty. But Father Pat of Holy Name Catholic High School had been a big believer in the theory that practice makes perfect. It was one of several reasons I kept sneaking boys into his rectory for heavy-petting sessions. When I had justified my sins by saying that kissing "don't always come natural," he'd been less than amused.

"Let me check the appointment book," Laney said.

I could hear her shuffling pages and scowled at nothing in particular. We both knew I had squat going on for the next three hours. We could get in a seventeen-course meal and five games of Parcheesi before my next appointment. I'm not particularly fond of Parcheesi, but it sounded better than being accused of murder one and crammed into the backseat of a cruiser that smelled like hookers and alcohol-infused urine.

"You don't have a client until five o'clock, Ms. McMullen," Laney informed me, "but you mustn't forget about your dental appointment."

To Laney there's a fine line between lying and acting. Fictionalizing is what she did. I love Laney. "How do they look?" I asked.

There was the slightest pause. "Yes," she said. "With Dr. Beckett."

"Dr. Beckett" was code for "smart and sensitive." After her emancipation from braces, acne, and terminal shyness, Laney had been inundated with every possible type of proposition, but we had kept a standing date to watch *Quantum Leap* every week until the powers that be lost their minds and cancelled the show in 1993.

"Does he have Bakula's soulful eyes?" I asked.

"Definitely," she said.

"If I let them in, you have to promise to get them out of here in ten minutes."

"Certainly, Ms. McMullen."

"Thanks, Laney. Wait," I said, on the verge of hanging up. "Are they both Becketts?"

"One moment." I heard her flipping papers again. "That's Father Overmeir," she said. "At six o'clock."

Father Overmeir had taught freshman Algebra. I believe I'd once told Laney I wanted to lick his earlobes and/or bear his children. Father Overmeir was good-looking, tall, and amusing. Two years after graduation I could have sworn I saw him at a club called Master Blaster. He'd been doing the grind with a girl in pigtails who had size 11 feet and the beginnings of a five o'clock shadow. But that didn't make him any less entertaining.

"Soften them up," I said. "I'll be there in a minute."

Five minutes later my lip gloss was fresh and my hair firmly in place. I didn't want to look like a bag lady for Dr. Samuel Beckett.

"Officers," I said, standing very tall in my heavily discounted sling-backs. I was wearing a jungle green skirt that ended just shy of my knees, modest yet stylish, and accented with a bone-colored sleeveless shell. "Oh," I said, recognizing the scholarly officer from Senator Rivera's house. "Hi."

They were both holding their hats in their hands and seemed momentarily at a loss. "Ms. McMullen," said the nearest, rising to his feet. "I don't know if you remember me. I'm Officer Bjorklund. This is Officer White."

Laney had worked her magic. Bjorklund, aka Beckett, appeared to be composing poetry in his head, while Officer White looked happy but flushed beneath his milk chocolate complexion.

"Come in," I said, motioning magnanimously toward my office. "I'm sorry I haven't more time."

They trooped in, barely stumbling at all as they tried to pretend they weren't sneaking one more glance at Laney. I closed the door firmly behind them. On my desk, I have a photo of a good-looking guy holding the reins of a leggy red horse and smiling. His hair is tousled and streaked with silver. Sometimes clients assume he's my husband. In actuality, the picture came with the frame. But I can honestly say I respect him more than most any guy I've dated.

"Have a seat. Would you like some coffee?" I asked. This is me being hospitable. Yowsa.

They declined.

"Cold water? I've got Fiji." Personally, I risk my life on tap water on a daily basis, but Laney insists on impressing clients with designer fluids.

"I'll take a bottle," said White. Bjorklund held out. I think I may have been interfering with his rendition of "An Ode to Laney's Eyes." He probably would have been crushed if I'd told him it had been done a dozen times

before we were juniors, so I handed over the bottled water and sat down, crossing my legs at the ankle and tuck-
ing them demurely beneath my swivel chair. "I imagine
you came about Salina Martinez," I said.

"Yes. Just a few follow-up questions," said White.

"Very well." I sounded so damned polished, I wished
I'd had myself recorded for posterity.

"On the evening of Ms. Martinez's death, you were at
home. Is that correct?" asked Bjorklund.

"Yes."

"Were you there alone?"

"Some of the time." I already found that I wanted to expound, but I kept my answers concise. I've seen *Law &
Order.*

"You had company?"

"Lieutenant Rivera visited."

"For how long?"

"A short while."

"What were your plans?"

I raised a brow. As long as playing nice was advantageous, I was all for it. But I had to stop short of the full
truth here. Because the plans I'd had for the dark lieutenant on that particular night may not have put me in a
very positive, or moralistic, light.

"My plans?" I repeated.

"For the evening," he said.

"We had hoped to dine out."

"Anywhere specific?"

"A barbecue establishment in Rosemead," I said.

"What was the name of the place?"

I didn't want to say Big Bill's Big BBQ for fear it might

make me sound less than classy, but going anywhere else for ribs would simply make me look naïve, so I admitted the truth.

Bjorklund scribbled madly. "Did you have reservations?"

"I believe we did."

They glanced at each other. It seemed like simple enough information, which made me wonder why they didn't already know it. Certainly Rivera would have told them this much. "Did you call in the reservation, Ms. McMullen, or did the lieutenant?"

"Lieutenant Rivera said he would take care of those details."

"But you never made it to . . ." Bjorklund glanced at his notes. "Big Bill's Big BBQ?"

I played along, still wondering. "Lieutenant Rivera received a phone call before we left my house." But not before I'd found myself plastered up against the bathroom wall like human linguini.

"Do you know who called him, Ms. McMullen?"

"No, I don't."

"He didn't tell you?"

Seemed pretty obvious. "I'm afraid he didn't."

"But you must have had an idea."

I tilted my chin down, gave them a long-suffering glance through my lashes, and crossed my right leg carefully over my left. Laney had done a good job revving up their guy hormones. I could tell because they watched my movement like tick hounds tracking a beef bone. "All he said was that there was trouble with his father. I didn't know at the time that the senator was on his way to Seattle."

"Boston," Bjorklund corrected distractedly.

White looked mildly peeved, like he was just coming out of a trance. I'd seen it happen a thousand times before. In high school we'd called it "Laney Land."

"Yes, of course," I demurred, and hid my wily smile as I packed away the info.

"How long have you known Lieutenant Rivera, Ms. McMullen?"

"Since August twenty-fourth," I said.

They scowled in unison. I could feel their mental wheels spinning. I refused to help them turn.

"Was that your first date?"

"No." I knitted my fingers in my lap and watched them. Cool as pastrami, hardly remembering the dead body that had lain between us the first time I'd met Rivera.

"But you are dating him."

"I wouldn't refer to it in those terms."

"How would you refer to it?"

Stupid. "We're . . . acquaintances."

"Did you know he was once engaged to Ms. Martinez?"

I kept my mouth firmly closed, so the scream I heard must have come from inside my head.

The bastard had been *engaged* to her? Engaged to his father's fiancée, and he'd never said a word about it?

"No, I wasn't aware of that," I said.

White checked his notes. "Almost thirteen years ago."

"It's good of you to tell me," I said, and wondered rather wildly why he had. "But Lieutenant Rivera and I only know each other casually."

White glanced toward my door. Bjorklund nodded. "At approximately what time did he leave your house on Saturday night?"

"Eight-nineteen."

"Exactly?"

"I think my kitchen clock is two minutes fast."

"You're very precise, Ms. McMullen."

"One has to be in my line of work." What a bunch of monkey doo-doo. I was a psychologist. It made cocktail waitressing look like a cross between brain surgery and deep-sea diving.

Officer White looked as if he was about to ask another question, but at that moment Elaine popped her head into my office and the interview came to a jolting halt. She was wearing the dead thing again, which meant that she'd bared her midriff. But she'd added a longbow to her ensemble. The string sliced across the melon of her left breast and underscored her right.

"I'm not sure," I said.

No comment. Bjorklund looked like he'd just been struck by writer's block in the middle of his sonnet. White's eyes were the size of ripe tomatoes and his mouth was agape.

"Your mother eats raw sewage," I intoned. Neither of them even glanced my way.

"I'm sorry to bother you, Ms. McMullen," Laney said, ignoring my statement. "But it's three-ten, and traffic is going to be considerable."

"Yes, of course. My root canal."

"Dental appointment," she corrected.

"Right," I said, but it wouldn't have made a difference if

I'd told them I was going for bullfighting lessons which I took every Monday and Wednesday without fail from an aging matador in Madrid. "And you obviously have to morph into a warrior princess."

"Amazon queen," she said.

"Holy God," someone mumbled. I think it was Bjorklund. His lips had gone white.

"Well..." I stood up. "I'm sorry to rush off, Officers, but my bicuspid has been killing me."

"Uh-huh. You're an actress?" They never turned toward me. I was vacillating between reminding them to breathe and kicking them in the gonads, which might, actually, have had the same effect.

"Aspiring," she said, and smiled.

I thought White was going to wet his pants.

"You going to an audition now?" Bjorklund asked.

"I got a callback."

"Which studio?"

"NBC."

"The one-oh-one's going to be a parking lot."

"And I can't be late." She gave them another smile. Bjorklund looked like he couldn't take much more. "This is my first callback in months."

"What's the title?"

"*Amazon Queen.*"

"You playing the lead?"

She crossed her fingers. I'm not sure why even that was sexy. "Hoping."

"Would you..." White cleared his throat. "Would you be wearing that?"

"I'm afraid not," she admitted. "The producer said something about a thong."

Bjorklund grabbed the couch's armrest for support. I stared at Laney and made a shoveling motion with both hands. It was getting deep enough to swim. But her eyes were laughing like a mad monkey's.

"Tell you what," White said. I think he might have been holding his breath. "We're going back that way. We could give you a ride. Don't you think, Ted?"

"Ride." Poor Officer Bjorklund was down to monosyllables. I wasn't impressed. I'd once seen Laney strike a district attorney absolutely mute, and she'd been fully dressed at the time. What if she'd lost a shoe or something?

"Thank you," Laney said, "but if I hurry I can—"

"We don't want to hear you've been speeding," White said.

"Speeding," Bjorklund echoed.

"Might have to get out the handcuffs."

"Handcuffs." Bjorklund was a goner. Holy crap. He looked like he was going to keel over on my carpet. I gave Laney the throat-cutting sign, and she laughed out loud.

"Thanks again," she said, "but I'll be fine."

They wouldn't leave. So I stood up, trying to shoo them along like lost lambs. They rose shakily to their feet.

"Well, if you have any more questions for me, be sure to shove them up your nose," I said.

"It wouldn't be any trouble," White was saying as they toddled into the hallway after Elaine. She grabbed her purse from the desk, gave me a smile, and opened the door. They trundled after her, still talking.

I considered locking up and getting into my car to continue the ruse, but it hardly seemed worth the effort, since they were already leaving the parking lot, sirens screaming, as Laney pulled sedately into the siphoning traffic behind them.

12

There is no feature so attractive as a well-exercised intellect.

> —Professor Wight, six months
> before proposing to a
> cheerleader with a double-
> digit IQ

$\mathcal{B}$IG BILL'S."

"Yes." I had agonized over how to find out whether or not Rivera had ever made dinner reservations. After thirty-five minutes it had occurred to me that I could simply ask. "Can you tell me whether Jack Rivera reserved a table for March third?"

"The third?"

"Yes."

"Last Saturday?"

I was too nervous to answer.

`"No, ma'am," she said finally. "I have no one by that name."

"How about Gerald Rivera?"

She checked and sounded a little peeved when she finally told me, "No."

I chanced her wrath and tried every other name I could think of. Still nothing.

By eleven o'clock I felt sick to my stomach, raw and fidgety and desperate to know the truth. Bolstered by the success of my last call, I picked up the receiver again.

"Infinity Air." The voice on the other end of the line was male, probably middle-aged, and bored.

"Good day," I said. Back in '88 I had taken two semesters of French. When I graduated I could say "Where's the bathroom?" and "Yes, the woman is wearing a pink hat." Now I can only say "Yes." But I had developed a kick-ass accent, which I was currently implementing. "My name is Antoinette Desbonette." The original Antoinette had been a countess in one of those paranormal romance novels. She'd been elegant and witty. Of course, her lover tended to morph into a wolf at unexpected junctions. But he'd been sexy as hell. Wish I could find me a nice werewolf. "May I speak to the person in charge?"

There was a slight pause, then, "One moment, please." Elevator music played in the background. I waited. It wasn't as if I was getting involved in Rivera's problems. But I couldn't help being curious. Why the hell had his father asked me to lunch? I had been about as informative as a slug, and it was fairly obvious he had un-slug-related means of gathering information.

So why had he spent a small fortune to inform me his son was innocent? Yes, Rivera Junior was an unmitigated pain in the ass, but that didn't mean the senator should automatically assume I would think he was guilty.

"Can I help you?"

I found my sexy center, introduced myself again, and launched into my spiel. "Yes. I most fervently hope so. I am calling from the Boston Convention Center. We are hosting a seminar at which Senator Miguel Rivera is scheduled to speak. We sent a car for him, but he has failed to appear. Can you tell me if, perhaps, he missed his flight?"

There was a pause, then, "I'm sorry. I'm afraid we're not allowed to give out that information."

Damn it! "*Non?*"

"No. Company policy."

"But I cannot reach him by telephone. And we are quite concerned. Perhaps this once you could make an exception?" I put a little purr at the end of the sentence, but I might as well have saved my feline imitation.

"Like I said, I'm sorry. We can only give out that information to authorized individuals."

"Such as?" I put my utmost into sounding blonde.

"Police officers and the like."

An idea clicked into my head. I forced a little laugh. "So if I had introduced myself as *Detective* Desbonette, I would now have the information I so eagerly seek?"

He was neither amused nor charmed. "That and a badge number."

"Ahh, well . . ." My mind was racing. "I shall speak to the authorities, then. Perhaps they will call you in my stead."

A moment later I plopped the receiver back and cursed a blue streak.

Where was I going to get a badge number? I mean, sure, I could call Infinity back and give them a phony name and a bunch of digits, but I didn't even know how many digits they needed. I could imagine the conversation. *"Yes, this is Officer Petty, badge number . . . ahhh, four?"*

I glared at the phone, tapped irritably on my kitchen counter, and paced five times across my living room, mind boiling.

Twenty minutes later I was whipping west on the 210 at eighty-five miles per hour. An old lady in a silver Lincoln passed me like I was standing still. I refrained from flipping her off and leaned on the accelerator.

By the time a trooper stopped me, my little Saturn was rattling like a can of loose pebbles. I crunched onto the shoulder, heart pounding, gearing up for my performance.

The officer who sauntered toward me was tall and lean. He wore the regulation uniform and reflector sunglasses with a macho arrogance that made my feminist hackles rise. This might not be as difficult as I had anticipated.

I said a prayer for fools and psychotics and powered down my window.

"Damn it!" I said. "What the hell's wrong with you cops? Can't you see I'm in a hurry?"

For one bladder-quivering moment I thought I had overplayed my hand. I imagined him reaching through the window and fishing me from behind the steering wheel by the nostrils. But apparently that's a no-no—even in L.A.

Fifteen minutes later, after a performance that would have earned me an Oscar on the big screen, I had Officer Caron's full name and badge number. I also had a two-hundred-dollar ticket and an ulcer. But it was worth it.

I repeated that seventeen times as I crept shakily into the parking lot of the nearest Marriott. My legs felt a little bit gelatinous when I trekked into the lobby. It was nearly empty. A mulatto supermodel with a five-million-dollar smile manned a desk the length of my living room. But I was still too shaken to feel inferior. I asked for a pay phone and was directed to an area near the Nevada Ballroom.

Once there, I picked up the receiver, deposited a handful of quarters, and punched in the numbers I'd scribbled on a discarded envelope. By the time I was connected to the proper person at Infinity Airlines, I felt like I was going to pass out from sheer nerves. What if they knew Officer Caron personally? What if they had a photo of him? What if they realized he was a baritone instead of a quivery-voiced alto?

As it turned out, they neither knew him nor, apparently, cared to know him. A badge number was enough. Their asses were covered.

I remained lucid long enough to get my information.

The senator had indeed been on flight 237 from L.A. to Boston on the evening Salina Martinez was murdered. First class. Seat 1A.

13

Old age sucks, but the alternative doesn't look that great, either.

—*Ella McMullen, Christina's paternal grandmother and the only living creature Chrissy's mother has ever feared*

I SPENT THE REST of the afternoon trying to talk myself out of being stupid. No luck. No surprise.

Salina's memorial service was held at Ventura Mortuary at seven o'clock in the evening. I paced around my office like a gerbil in a maze while reviewing the myriad reasons it would be idiotic for me to attend.

There were eighteen of them. The first and most poignant was that Rivera might decide to kill me. The last and most practical was that my favorite panty hose had a run in them.

At 7:27 I parked in the lot behind the funeral home and walked the half block to the front door. I had dressed conservatively in black—black skirt and black blouse. Even my hose were black, partly because it was a funeral, but mostly in concession to the demise of my nude pair. I stopped short of wearing a black hat. Some people look classy in hats. I look like a bobble head.

The music was the first thing to strike my senses. Muted and low, it had a vampirish tone to it and immediately lifted the hair at the back of my neck. Some distance from the front door, a young couple stood apart from the muffled crowd, signing the leather-bound register. When they headed for the exit, blond heads tilted in quiet conversation, they looked like nothing so much as Ken and Barbie come to life, both tall, slim, and so beautiful it made my self-confidence sting.

The polished teak coffin stood near the south wall, surrounded by a forest of neon-bright flowers and polished greenery. I approached with some misgivings. After all, I wasn't really Salina's friend. Hell, I wasn't even an acquaintance. But morbid interest drew me like a red ant to a picnic. Truth is, I'm not all that comfortable with the living. The dead make my throat close up.

Once there, however, I couldn't seem to look away. Salina Martinez was stunning even in death. Her hair shone sapphire black in the fluorescent lights and her face, high-boned and tight-skinned, looked serene and youthful.

"Christ, she's even gorgeous postmortem."

I turned slowly, hoping to hell I hadn't said the words out loud. The woman next to me didn't glance up. "Never had a bad hair day in her entire goddamn life," she added.

"I . . ." I glanced around, wondering rather numbly if

she might be talking to someone else. No one was within hearing. It occurred to me that that might be a good thing. "I beg your pardon?" I said.

She gave me an assessing glance and thrust out her hand. "Rachel Banks." Several years my junior, she was blond, lean as a boxer, and pretty in a hungry tigress sort of way.

"Christina McMullen." Our hands met. Her fingers felt strong and sharp-boned. I could smell liquor on her breath. Bourbon. Noah's Mill maybe.

"You work for the senator?" she asked.

"No. I'm just . . . a . . . a friend."

She gave me a glance from beneath her lashes. Perhaps it was supposed to be knowing. It looked a little like she was going to nod into oblivion at any given second. Alcohol was not good to her. "She had a shitload of them."

"What?"

Her expression suggested she didn't think I was the brightest star in the heavens. Pretty perceptive considering her alcohol level. "Salina," she said, and nodded jerkily toward the casket. "She knew everyone. All the right people." Her lips drooped a little at the corners, but she was still smiling, a strange mix of expressions and emotions. "All the wrong people."

"She had a lot of friends?"

"Friends." Her eyes looked runny. "Enemies."

I glanced about, feeling like a voyeur, but unable to stop the question. "Who were her enemies?"

She stared at me a moment, then laughed out loud. The sound was low and throaty. Still, it echoed like a banshee's howl in the cavernous room. Beside the register, a woman in a navy blue pantsuit turned to scowl at us, while near the east door, two gentlemen stopped their conversation to glance our way. I cleared my throat and stared at my shoes as if they were the most fascinating things in the universe.

"You're kidding, right?" she said.

I glanced back at her. "I didn't know her well."

"Then I guess you're not on the list of people who hate..." She paused, scowled at the coffin. Her face contorted. "*Hated* her."

I was momentarily speechless. It doesn't happen often. "Are..." I paused. Some people think I live dangerously, but I'm generally not foolish enough to speak poorly of the dead. At least not until the body's cold. "Are *you?*" I said finally. "On the list?"

Her lips twitched. For a moment she didn't speak, then, "I started the damned thing."

I took an involuntary step back, but suddenly there was a hand wrapped around my biceps.

I jerked, glanced up, froze.

Lieutenant Rivera was standing not three inches away. His eyes were as dark as hell, his body stiff with what I could safely presume was anger. He only has a couple of emotions. Anger is the safest of the two.

"Ms. McMullen." His voice was low. A muscle danced unhappily in his jaw, and I realized a bit distractedly that this might be the first time I had ever seen him clean-shaven. His suit was black, well tailored, handsome. His shirt was gray, the exact same color as the slim tie that bisected the V made by his jacket. "What are you doing here?"

A fair question. My mind tried to come up with an answer that wouldn't get me killed. My mouth did the same. Neither was wildly successful.

"Aren't you even going to say hi?" Our stare-down was broken.

He turned slowly away, hand still banded tightly around my arm. "Rachel," he said, and I thought for a moment that his fingers twitched a bit. It was difficult to say for sure, though, since my arm was beginning to go numb.

"I haven't seen you in . . ." She narrowed her eyes. Her similarity to a hunting cat increased tenfold. "How long has it been, Jack?"

The muscle jumped again in his fresh-shaven cheek. "I heard you were in D.C."

"I got back day before yesterday."

He nodded.

"And you didn't call."

"Listen," I said, trying unobtrusively to tug out of his grip. "I can see you two have a lot to talk about, so I'll just—"

Rivera turned back toward me, eyes sparking fire, stopping me in my verbal tracks.

"If you'll excuse us, Rachel, I have something to discuss with Ms. McMullen."

"I bet you do," she said, and I was turned away from the casket like a recalcitrant hound. I shuffled along beside him, not wanting to make a scene, but not crazy about our respective positions, either.

"She seems nice," I said.

"What the hell do you think you're doing here?" His words were a snarl through clenched teeth. I realized in that moment that his clean-shaven jaw was the only thing ready for prime time. The rest of him looked jungle crazy. Well, except for the clothes. The suit was kick-ass perfect.

"I'm just paying my respects," I said, and managed to pry my arm out of his grasp.

"Respect?" He choked an almost silent laugh. "You've got no damned respect, McMullen."

Anger was working its way through the chinks in my fear. "I've got every right to be here, Rivera."

He gritted his teeth, glanced about the room, eyes hungry and dark before they grabbed me again. "Did you enjoy your little luncheon with the senator?"

"That's none of your . . ." I paused, catching my breath, feeling anger meld madly with the terror. "So you've stooped to spying on me, Rivera?"

"Spying?" He laughed. The sound was ultra-low and made the hair on my arms stand at attention, but not a head turned toward us. "Why? Was it a secret meeting, Chrissy?" he asked, and moved a quarter inch closer.

"Listen, Rivera, I don't know what the hell you're thinking, but I didn't do anything wrong." And yet I felt strangely guilty. "I didn't contact your father behind your back or anything. He called me and—"

He laughed again. I ground my teeth. "Is something funny?" I asked.

"Of course he called you, McMullen." He took a step closer, swallowing my personal space, breathing my personal air. Reaching out, he pushed a strand of hair behind my ear. Like we were lovers, like he had a right. Which he didn't, and yet his touch was electrifying, a strange blend of danger and affection. "How could he resist?"

"I don't know what you're talking about." My voice sounded funny, kind of breathy, like a porn star's.

He lifted his hand again. Maybe I should have backed away, but I was frozen in my tracks.

"You're female," he said, and skimmed the back of his fingers down my cheek. His thigh felt ridiculously hard against mine.

My stomach squeezed up tight into my chest, leaving plenty of room for my spleen to wrap itself in knots.

"And you're crazy about me," he added.

My mouth opened. I hope I was going to object, but he was standing awfully close, his lips inches from mine, his fingers warm against my skin.

"Gerald," someone said.

He froze at the sound of his name. Our gazes locked for a fraction of a second before he drew a careful breath and turned slowly toward the speaker.

The woman next to us was small and striking, with eyes as dark as my thoughts. Life sparked from her like fireworks. Her hair, an intense shade of black, was pulled demurely back at the nape of her neck. But it was her dress that caught my attention in a stranglehold. Canary yellow, it hugged her curves with the intimacy of a banana peel.

"Mama," Rivera said, deadpan.

My mind popped. My eyes did the same, then skittered from her to him in a wild attempt to determine whether he was joking.

"Gerald . . ." She pronounced the "G" with a rolling H sound. "You must introduce me to this friend of yours," she said.

I waited for him to say something rude. He didn't. Which spurred the weird realization that she really was his mother. Holy shit.

"Christina McMullen," he said, "this is my mama, Rosita Rivera."

She watched me, perfect brows arched over tell-all Spanish eyes. "Christina. How did you meet my Gerald?"

I opened my mouth.

"Ms. McMullen's a psychiatrist," Rivera said.

"Psychologist," I corrected.

A muscle jumped in his jaw. "She helped me with a couple cases a while back."

I would have liked to object just for the hell of it, but I could feel the tension radiating off him like a toxic cloud. Besides, his mother didn't need me to tell her what to think. She was assessing body language like a speed-reader. Her carefully groomed brows rose a little. Her red lips curved up. This woman was nobody's fool. "You were a friend of Salina's?" she asked me.

"No, ma'am," I said, mind whirling like a top-of-the-line bidet. "I'm afraid I never got a chance to meet her."

Even in strappy, wedge heels, she had to tilt her head back to look into my eyes. "You are more lucky than some, then," she said.

"Mama." Rivera's voice held dark warning, but it was careful, contained. "A little respect."

"Respect?" She snorted. "I do not respect that *barato*—"

But in that moment we were interrupted.

"Gerald," said a deep voice. I lifted my focus, feeling dizzy.

The newcomer was well into his seventies and stood

just behind Rosita. At one time he had been tall. Now he was stooped and broadening across his middle, which was cinched by tooled leather and accented with a belt buckle the size of my head. It sparkled silver in the overhead lights. He removed his bone-colored cowboy hat with a hand that was narrow and blue-veined. The other held the ivory grip of a fine-grained cane.

"Mr. Peachtree," Rivera said grimly, but his mother was more effusive as she turned toward the newcomer.

"Robert!"

"Rosita," he said. "I didn't recognize you." Taking her by the arm, he kissed her cheek. "Thought you were some teenage girl your boy here was wooin'. You age like a cactus flower, just keep getting prettier and prettier. But dang, it's good to see you." He had an accent strong enough to wrestle steers.

She smiled. "This is Christina McMullen, a psychologist." Her eyes were sparkling. "And Gerald's special friend."

The muscle jumped in Rivera's jaw again.

"A psychologist, eh?" Peachtree gave me a quick once-over and a lopsided Texas grin. Age, I had to deduce, had not yet diluted his Lone Star personality.

"She helps Gerald," added Mrs. Rivera.

I couldn't take it anymore. If there's one thing I didn't need, it was to feel like Rivera's damn lackey. "Actually, I have my own practice," I said. I could feel the grumpy lieutenant's impatience, prompting me to ramble on. Some people think I have an ornery streak. Some people are extremely astute. "Over in Eagle Rock."

Rivera's scowl was burning a hole through my fore-head.

I smiled merrily. "Not so far from here. Forty-five-minute drive maybe. I'm the only therapist, but—"

"I'm sure Mr. Peachtree has people to see," rumbled Rivera, and took my arm again.

"So you're pretty *and* smart. You look like just the kind of filly that could lasso Miguel's boy here, too," Peachtree said. "You ever think of doing corporate work?"

"What?"

"I've got me a little business. We're thinking of hiring someone like you."

I was floored . . . and flattered. I'd never been offered a job that didn't somehow involve cleaning up vomit.

"I suspect this ain't the place to discuss such things, but you think about it," he said, and turned back toward Rivera's mother. "So what about you, Rosita? You've been good, I hope."

"*Sí*. Yes. And you?" She leaned back, taking him in with her snapping eyes. "What are you doing in Los Angeles?"

"Just here on business. Straightening out a few snarls."

"Nothing serious, I hope."

"No, no." He shook his head, negating her concern and glancing around the room. "Thought I might see Danny here, though."

"I believe he just now left." She smiled. "It has been too long since I have seen you."

"Since Boston."

"Ohh." She made a sound of exasperation. "The most tedious meetings I have ever yet attended."

"You want tequila that'll peel the hair off yer head, you

come to Dallas. You want somethin' to put it back on, you point your bronc east, huh?" His grin was as wide as the prairie.

She laughed. "I thought Dottie was no longer allowing you tequila."

"What she don't know . . ." he said, and winked.

"Is she here?"

"Dottie? 'Course she is. You know I can't go nowhere without my blushing bride. Come on. She'll want to see you." He jammed the hat on his balding pate and leaned in conspiratorially. "I tell you, it was hell tearing her away from the great-grandbabies. She's knitted blankets from here to the moon. Baked enough cocoa cookies to feed the Dodgers. And the little buggers don't even sit up yet. But with Danny out of the nest, she's got to bake 'em for somebody else, I guess. 'Course, I'm the only one gettin' rounder by the minute."

"So little Anna got married?"

"No. No. Anna's still in school. Might be until they put me in the ground, too. But Barbara come through. Gave us a pair of twins."

"How wonderful."

"Bald as cue balls and ugly as Beelzebub, but don't go tellin' Dottie I said so. She'd trade five of me for the two of 'em, but she'll want to tell you herself." He turned toward us, gave me a nod, then shook his head at Rivera, seeming unsure of the protocol appropriate for the death of an ex-fiancée/future stepmother. "It's a shame. A damned shame. I only met Salina once, but she seemed like a real plum."

Rivera said nothing.

We watched them walk away. The top of Rosita's head barely reached the old man's chin, despite his bend and her high heels.

"What are you doing here?" Rivera's tone was no more chatty than it had been before the interruption.

I turned back toward him, cool as a cosmopolitan. "You didn't tell me you were engaged to her," I said.

A muscle worked in his jaw. "Why were you talking to Rachel?"

I gave him a smile. "You'll have to be sure to give me a list of people to whom I'm disallowed to speak, Lieutenant."

"Swear to God, McMullen, if I find out you've been snooping around this case, I'll personally—"

He stopped and swore under his breath. I followed his line of vision. It took me a moment to recognize the man making his way toward us, but the worst memories are often the clearest. I wasn't likely to forget Detective Graystone anytime soon. He was as solid and intimidating as he'd been when he'd interrogated me on the senator's walkway.

"Jack," he said, eyes hard and gleaming. "I didn't expect to see you here."

Rivera said nothing, but I felt emotion shiver through him on the very air I breathed.

"Thought you'd be too broke up about your girl's death." He paused. "Or was she your stepmama?" He shrugged his blocky shoulders. "Could be she was both, I suppose."

"Get the hell out of my face, Graystone."

"Or maybe you're disobeying orders and investigating

the case, huh? Could be you think the bastard that killed her is nearby. Right under my nose." He was standing close, blond head tilted back, seeping accusations.

"Don't push your fucking—"

"Ms. McMullen." He turned toward me. "I'm sorry you were shortchanged on your date the other night. Heard you had reservations at Bill's." He nodded. "Good barbecue. Great beer. Funny thing, though, Jack here never made reservations." He scowled, thoughtful. "Almost like he had other plans at the get-go."

Rivera stepped forward with a snarl. "You got something to say, Graystone, why not—"

"What the hell's going on here?"

I swiveled my head to the right. Captain Kindred stood not two feet away. Tall, black, dressed in a charcoal suit and a maroon tie the width of his head, he looked as comfortable as a rhino in a flowerpot.

"I asked a question," he growled.

"A young woman is dead," Graystone said, voice casual, not turning from Rivera. "I thought it might be a good idea to find out how it happened."

"Stay the hell out of this," Rivera snarled.

Kindred swore under his breath.

"That a threat, Jack?" Graystone asked.

"You bet your ass it is."

"Know what, Lieutenant, I don't give a goddamn if your daddy's the fucking shah of Iran, I'm gonna prove—"

"Shut the fuck up or I'll take both your badges," Kindred hissed.

They fell sullenly silent, still glaring.

"You think we need more press on this?" Kindred's

broad, black face was shiny with perspiration and emotion. "Is that what you think? That the LAPD is sitting so pretty with the damned media that we need some play?"

Graystone smiled grimly. "I don't care if the media—"

"Well, you'd better goddamn care, Detective," Kindred growled. "Or you'll find your ass sitting in the property room from here to the second coming." He gritted his teeth, sharpened his glare. "There were no signs of a struggle. No bruises. Until the tox reports come in, we've got nothing." He pressed half an inch closer. "You hear me, Graystone? You've got nothing."

The world seemed hushed around us.

Kindred eased his big hands open, shifted his wide stance. "Until you do, you keep your mouth shut. You understand me, Detective?"

"Yes, sir." The words were clipped, contemptuous.

"Then get the hell out of here."

For a moment I thought Graystone would refuse, but finally he turned toward me. "A pleasure to see you again, Ms. McMullen," he said, and left, sauntering through the crowd toward the door.

"You got fifteen minutes," snarled Kindred.

I turned back, breath held.

Rivera's eyes were flat and hard.

"Fifteen minutes," repeated the captain. "After that, I throw your ass in jail just for the hell of it."

Rivera nodded.

Kindred swore under his breath and made his way toward a boxy woman in an expensive silk suit.

"I want you to leave."

It took me a moment to realize Rivera was talking to me again.

"What?" When I turned back toward him it seemed as if we'd never been interrupted. Near the center of the room, a bevy of budding executives huddled together—a meeting of the young and the beautiful.

"You're out of your league, McMullen," he said.

I caught my breath. "I didn't know I had a league."

"You think I'm joking."

"I don't even think you know how, Rivera." I watched the mob of young Republicans. Not a hair out of place. Not a pimple to be seen. "What's with the beautiful bunch?"

The tic jumped in his jaw. I wondered vaguely if it was always there or if I just brought it out to play.

He glanced toward the clique. Even now the senator was making his way across the room toward them. The tic bulged in Rivera's cheek, but whether the anger was aimed at his father or the meeting of the young and lovely, I couldn't be sure.

I turned back, watching the reunion in fascinated silence. The mob looked orgasmic, shaking hands, lending condolences, leaning in close as if to catch the old man's merest scent. As for the senator, he appeared like a wizened lion, wounded but indestructible in the face of adversity.

"Damn bastard can smell it from across the globe."

"What? What can he smell?"

"Old money. Young blood," Rivera said.

"Maybe he's just being hospit—" I began, but just then

an unidentifiable noise issued from him. I turned, but his gaze was locked on his father.

"What was that?" I asked, but he was already pressing past me toward the crowd.

"Rivera." I grabbed his sleeve. "Wait a minute. Rivera!"

He stared at my hand for a full five seconds, then shifted his live-ammo gaze to mine. "What the hell do you think you're doing, McMullen?"

"Listen, Rivera." I was holding on like a hyena to an impala's leg. "Maybe this isn't a great idea."

He narrowed his eyes and his lips simultaneously in a parody of a smile. "You sacrificing yourself for the good senator?"

"Sacrificing." I laughed, and glanced around, scouting for reinforcements. My conservative sling-backs were planted firmly in the plush ivory carpet, and my fingers were curled tight in the crisp fabric of his sleeve, but I really wasn't sure I could hold him back if he decided to do something stupid, which I was pretty sure he was planning on doing. "What are you talking about?"

His grin sliced up a notch. It looked a little cannibalistic. I've never been that fond of cannibals.

"The senator," he snarled, leaning close. "You willing to take a bullet for him, too?"

"You're not a bullet." I chuckled. It was a stupid thing to say. I admit it, but it was a small miracle my mouth worked. I couldn't expect as much from my mind.

He snorted and tugged. I went with him, still hanging on for dear life.

"Where the fuck do you think you're going?" Captain Kindred appeared from nowhere. For a man the size of a small country, he could move like an elf. He grabbed Rivera's free arm in a hand the size of a catcher's mitt.

Anger roared across Rivera's face. "This is none of your business, Captain."

"The hell it isn't. You want to act like a goddamn idiot, you do it when the mayor's not standing around taking notes."

Rivera straightened slightly, stiff with rage. "You taking the senator's side, too, Kindred?"

"Taking sides?" the captain snarled. "What the fuck do you think this is, Rivera? The damned prom?"

"I think it's a fucking joke."

"You see me laughing?"

I personally wondered if he'd ever laughed.

"I'm only going to tell you this once, Lieutenant." Silence thrummed between them for a second. "Leave this room now, or don't bother showing up at the station tomorrow."

Tension cranked up tight. The two stared at each other, darker than sin, madder than hell.

Then Rivera drew a breath, shifted his shoulders. "I'll be at the funeral," he said, and turned away.

Kindred watched him leave, then blew out a heavy breath before turning toward me. "You with him?" he asked.

"What?"

He jerked his head toward the door. "You two together?"

I breathed a laugh. "No. I—"

His scowl darkened to dangerous.

My lips stuttered to a halt. It was like lying to God. "I have no idea," I said.

He watched me. I fidgeted like a scolded crossing guard. "The lieutenant's got some troubles," he said. "But there are reasons he . . ." He shifted his brooding gaze to the senator, then slowly back to me. "Just watch yourself," he warned, and walked away.

I stared after him in stunned silence.

"Are you in love with him?"

I turned numbly toward the voice. Rosita Rivera was back. It was like a revolving room, tossing people at me at erratic intervals.

"What?"

"My son," she said. "He has the hot head, but you love him nevertheless, sí?"

"Mrs. Rivera . . ." Was now the time to demure? Faint? Bolt? "I think you have the wrong—"

"We must get to know each other better."

"What?"

"Come to my house. Tomorrow, for dinner."

"I don't think—"

"I am the wonderful cook. My Gerald has told you that, no?"

"Yes." Actually, he really had. "But I'm . . . I . . . I don't . . ." Her arched brows were raised high, her painted mouth pursed. "I'm busy," I said.

"Nonsense. You must eat. I live in Sierra Madre." She rattled off an address, then spotted someone through the crowd and hurried away.

I stood staring like a beached whale.

Someone laughed. I was pretty damn sure it wasn't me. "You are so screwed."

That wasn't me, either. I turned. Rachel stood beside me. "What?"

She glanced toward the senator. He was watching us over the heads of his adoring fan club.

"The Rivera trifecta," she said.

"I don't know what you're—" I began, but just then someone roared in fury.

I jerked toward the door.

Something struck the outside wall, seeming to shake the very floor beneath my feet.

I stood in stunned disorientation, but Kindred was already streaking past me, gun drawn, dark face intense.

Lucidness struck me like a blow. "Rivera," I whispered, and leapt after him.

The door ricocheted against the wall. It was dark outside. Two bodies were tangled half on the concrete, half on the grass, arms and legs thrashing wildly.

Kindred cursed. He was holding his weapon in both hands.

I hissed a prayer.

"Get the fuck off me or I'll kill you!" someone snarled, but I couldn't decipher who it was. They were breathing hard, cursing and scrambling.

"Like you killed Legs?" The words were guttural, all but lethal.

"Not my fault your friends keep dying, Rivera."

"You fucking son of a—"

"Shut up, the both of you!" Kindred snapped. "Graystone, toss out the gun."

Gun! Terror held me motionless for an instant, but suddenly I was snatching my phone from my purse. My hands were shaking. I don't remember dialing.

"Throw it out, Detective. Jack . . ." Kindred's voice was almost soothing. "Let him up. It's not too late to salvage this. Get up nice and slow. We'll talk things through."

"Nine-one-one, this is Colleen." The voice in the phone startled me.

"Colleen!" I squealed, but just then the world exploded. A bullet zinged through the air. Shards of plaster rained over me, spattering on my head.

I screamed. The phone bounced from my hand as I ducked behind a nearby tree.

"Fucking bastard," one of the men growled.

"Goddamn—" answered the other, but the words were interrupted by the meaty sound of flesh against flesh.

Heavy breathing rasped the night air. I chanced a peek around the tree trunk. Someone was staggering to his feet. The other body lay still.

"What the hell do you think you're doing, Lieutenant?" Kindred snarled.

A gun dangled from Rivera's fingers. I could recognize him now, could see the sharp-etched outline of his face, the feral light in his eyes.

"Put the piece down."

Rivera said nothing. His chest was heaving. His jacket sleeve had been ripped at the shoulder, exposing the dove gray shirt underneath.

"Lieutenant." Kindred enunciated carefully, as if he were speaking to a child. "Put the—"

"I didn't kill her, Captain." Rivera's voice was almost too low to hear.

Silence echoed through the crowd of mourners who had gathered outside, then, "You think I'm an idiot?" Kindred's voice was lower still. "You think I'm a goddamn moron?"

Rivera shook his head, like a small boy being chastised. I could see now that blood was dripping down his forehead. It was diverted by his left eyebrow, then flowed in a dark eddy along the hollow of his cheek.

"Then give me the gun." Kindred sounded tired suddenly, like a father who's missed too much sleep.

"Put me on the case."

"This case?" Kindred laughed. It was little more than a weary snort. "Are you out of your fucking mind? I'll be lucky to keep you out of jail. Just hand over the gun before someone blows this so out of proportion I can't—"

But just then a cop car careened around the corner, lights wheeling, sirens suddenly full blast. Another came from the opposite direction, spraying colored lights across Rivera's face and gleaming off the gun that dangled chest-high from his fingers.

14

You don't really know a person till you've spent some time in their panties.

—A client, who, for obvious reasons, would just as soon remain anonymous

*H*OLY CATS!" Laney said. She was perched on the edge of her desk, peeling an orange.

I nodded and paced the narrow length of my reception area. It was empty except for Laney and myself, and her longbow, of course—ever vigilant.

"So they took him away in the squad car?"

"Yeah." The memory still made the hair on the back of my neck stand on end.

"Front seat or back?"

I shook my head. It had all happened in an instant. One minute he was there, the next he was gone. Kindred had wasted no time removing him from the scene. But what had happened after that?

"What happened after that?" Laney was reading my mind again.

"I don't know. I grabbed my phone and took off before anyone could decide it was my fault."

"Did you try calling him?"

"No answer."

"How about his dad?"

"The *senator*?"

"Does he have another dad?"

"I can't call the senator."

"Why not?"

"Because . . ." I did a jittery thing with my hands. I'm not normally a jittery person, but I'd dreamt about Rivera the previous night. He'd found out that *I'd* made the 911 call, and he hadn't been happy. Then he'd morphed into an alligator. Which was odd. I'd always figured he'd turn into a wolf if he were a shape-shifter. He'd be all dark and bristly and kind of sexy in an animalistic kind of way. "Because he's the senator," I said, then paused, scowling. "And his number's unlisted."

"His mother?" she asked.

I closed my eyes and did a full-body sigh, trying to relax, but my nerves kept jumping. I would have sold my hair for a pack of cigarettes and a get-out-of-lung-cancer-free card. "She invited me to dinner."

Laney's perfect brows shot toward her hairline. "Mrs. Rivera wants to have dinner with you?"

"Or to have me for dinner," I said. "I'm not sure which."

"I haven't actually heard that the Riveras are cannibals."

I stopped pacing. "What have you heard?"

"About Rosita Rivera?"

"Yeah."

"I don't know. Not much. There was that scandal about the senator and his aide, like I mentioned before. When I saw him with his wife at the premiere, everything seemed fine, though. But maybe that was just their public image and didn't reflect—"

"You saw them?"

"Uh-huh." She continued peeling her orange. Laney doesn't eat real food like Doritos and cheesecake and the kind of stuff that makes life worth living.

"Together?"

"Yeah."

"And you didn't tell me?"

"That was months ago, Mac. That's a long time in Mac Land. Andrew Bomstad hadn't dropped dead at your feet. The brooding lieutenant hadn't accused you of murder. You were just another nonfelonious citizen of L.A. Updating you about the Riveras would have been like telling you I met Grayson McCouch."

"Who?"

"Exactly. Anyway, I think the Riveras still attend some social functions together."

I pondered that while I munched on a section of her orange. It was organic. And not bad for something that hadn't been processed to within an inch of its life.

"Was that before or after the senator was engaged to Salma Hayek?" I asked.

"I'm not sure."

"Did Mrs. Rivera look as if she wanted to kill Mr. Rivera?"

"It's hard to say." She was still masticating on the first section of her orange. Give Laney an environmentally friendly lettuce leaf and she's busy for half an hour. "Viggo Mortensen was signing autographs."

"Holy crap!" I remembered Viggo from *Lord of the Rings*. The hair, the attitude, the body.

"I know."

"Was he wearing chain mail?"

"Blue jeans and a fringed leather jacket. He's an equestrian."

"Of course."

"And a poet."

Despite my jumping nerves, I drooled a little. I'm pretty sure it wasn't the orange. Viggo had made one hell of an Aragorn. When I was a kid, I'd imagined myself as a hobbit. After seeing the movie, I'd wanted to become an elfin princess, or a royal codpiece.

"Screw Rivera," I said.

"A little late for that," she said. "He might be in the slammer."

"Laney!" I scowled and ate another orange slice. "What would your dad say?" Her father is a Methodist minister, which may have prompted the dearth of swearing and fornicating and other all-American activities on Laney's part. But now she just laughed.

"I think what you should be concentrating on is that the Riveras travel in the same circles as the king of Middle Earth," she said.

I tried to focus, but the thought of Viggo in leather,

writing haiku, was almost more than I could bear. Which made me realize a sobering point: "He was right," I said. "I *am* out of my league."

"What are you talking about?"

I shook my head. "I'm not royalty, a codpiece, or a politician."

"Uh-huh."

I glanced out the window, giving the parking lot a glare. "So what am I going to do about Mrs. Rivera's invitation?"

"Don't go."

I snapped my attention back to her. "What are you talking about? I have to go."

"Then why did you ask?"

"Because you're supposed to talk me out of it."

"When have I ever talked you out of anything?"

"There was that time I was going to do a three-day liquid fast."

"You'd already opened the Lay's bag before I intervened."

"I was planning to pulverize them and drink them like a shake."

"You're sick."

"What am I going to do about Mrs. Rivera?"

"Don't do anything stupid, Mac."

"Like fasting?"

"Like getting yourself killed."

"Damn, I never thought of that. I should have talked to you before the Bomstad fiasco."

"I'm serious. Salina Martinez is dead. There's no reason to assume Mrs. Rivera wasn't involved."

I gave that some sagacious consideration as I finished

off her orange. She wasn't going to eat it anyway. "The same could be said of a hundred other people."

"Just be careful."

"Yeah, I could tell a police officer where I'm going. Or a U.S. senator. Oh, wait, they're both murder suspects."

"Just bring some protection."

I eyed her up. "The longbow's kind of bulky. And it doesn't go with my pants."

"I was talking about your Mace, genius."

A car pulled into the parking lot. My first client, spot on time. "I've got to find out what's going on."

She scowled.

"I'll be okay, Laney. I promise," I said, and wandered into my office.

*N*ine hours later, as I trundled east on the 210, I wasn't feeling so cocksure. My mind was racing like an overloaded freight train and my stomach felt queasy.

I don't know what I expected from Rosita Rivera's house, but I was surprised from the first moment I spotted her address. It was written in scrolled numerals on the ceramic-tiled pillars that formed the ends of her wrought-iron fence.

It was a simple home, not huge, but certainly not small. The most striking thing about it was the roses. They grew in wild abundance, a mixed rainbow of colors mingled in riotous harmony. They nodded behind the green iron fencing and smiled beside a pond where koi flitted about in the dappled sunlight. They lined the cobbled walk that marched to an arched front door, looking tumbled but graceful against the muted adobe.

I couldn't help but think about the lone cactus that overlooked the rock in the dust I call my front yard. Had it not been for Rivera, I would only have the rock.

I rang the doorbell, my heart doing a masterful tango in my throat.

"One *momento*." The yell came from deep inside the low-built hacienda.

I waited, holding a bottle of Veuve Clicquot like a dagger in my right hand. I had spent a full hour standing in Fuhrman's Liquors deciding on the brand. Veuve's had looked the classiest. But in actuality I had no idea how it tasted or if Veuve was the name of the champagne, the vineyard, or the guy that gave samples in little plastic cups. My stint at the Warthog hadn't exactly familiarized me with fine spirits. But I knew how to belch the "Star-Spangled Banner" backward. So far that skill hadn't come in as handy as I had hoped.

The door opened a few scant inches, then, "Christina!" Mrs. Rivera suddenly appeared in the doorway, clapping her hands together like an ecstatic schoolgirl. "You have come." She was dressed in a pair of white capris that hugged her like a second skin. Her hips were generous but shapely, her thighs slim. The capris were embellished with a multicolored sash at the waist. Strings of cheery garnets dangled at her dark-skinned calves. Her blouse was red, sleeveless, and showed a good deal of smooth, mocha cleavage. Her sandals had two-inch platforms and braided leather thongs that disappeared between her scarlet-painted toes. In comparison, I felt as big as a hot air balloon and as dull as dirt. "I am so glad. Come in. Come in."

I did so, towering over her like a lumbering penguin and wondering how long to wait before inquiring whether her son had been incarcerated. Or if he was guilty. Neither seemed to be the perfect opening gambit to cement a congenial relationship. "Thank you for inviting me."

"No, it is I who must thank you for coming. My son, he does not tell me about his loves as he once did. I must learn about them on my own."

"I, uhh . . ." I was stumped already and I hadn't even left her vestibule. "I'm not really . . . That is to say, I'm afraid your son and I aren't exactly . . ."

I was sweating like a running back. It was the first time in my life I was hoping to be interrupted. She let me stumble along, brows arched over black coffee eyes.

"Jack and I are just friends," I sputtered.

She threw back her head and laughed. I stared. She calmed finally, still smiling as she caught me in her sparkling gaze.

"You think I have no eyes, yes? Come along. Come along." We passed a living area. It was stuffed full, packed with cushy chairs, leather couches, colorful pillows, and two cages housing tiny birds as bright as fireflies.

I wandered after her.

"I, umm . . . I didn't know if you liked wine." After the riotous laughing, I was a little chagrined. "I brought you a bottle of . . ." I glanced at the label but couldn't remember how to pronounce the name. "Wine."

She turned toward me, scowling slightly. "Did Gerald not tell you? I do not believe in hard drink," she said.

"Oh!" I felt immediately guilty. "I just . . . I'm sorry. I didn't—"

She laughed and clapped her hands again. "I joke," she said, and traipsed into the kitchen with a wave of her hand. The walls were lined with iron racks from ceiling to floor. Bottles filled the metal circles like eggs in a nest.

"Well, hurry along. Open it," she said, and snatched a corkscrew from a counter covered with . . . everything. It had been nestled between a pair of orange peppers and the rest of the universe. If there was something missing, I couldn't guess what it was. There might not have been an orangutan.

Seven seconds later I was pouring wine into long-stemmed blue crystal.

Mrs. Rivera took a generous swig and gave an approving nod, either for my efficiency or my choice of wines. I wasn't certain.

I took a classy sip.

"So," she said, pulling a butcher knife from a cutlery block beside the sink. "Tell me, Christina, have you yet slept with my husband?"

15

He who laughs loudest has a high probability of being extremely inebriated.

—Topless magician's
assistant and premed
student Gertrude Nelson,
better known as Athena

THE WINE EXPLODED into my trachea. I coughed, sputtered, thought I might drown, momentarily hoped I would, then gazed at her with streaming eyes. "What?"

"My husband," said Mrs. Rivera, holding out her glass for a refill. "Have you bedded him?"

"I . . . I mean . . . I . . . just met him five days ago."

I replenished her drink. The bottle tinkled against the crystal.

She stared at me, wineglass in one hand, knife in the other. I missed Laney's longbow something fierce.

"Is that a yes or is that a no?" she asked.

"No!"

"No?"

"No!"

She paused for a moment, still watching me, then nodded. "Ahh, that is good," she said finally. Draining her glass, she plopped the crystal onto the tile counter. "Hand me that cutting board, will you, Christina?"

I lowered my gaze with an effort, searching hopelessly amidst the clutter.

"Right there." She waved the knife. Light glistened along the serrated edge. "By the books."

I found it buried beneath a half-embroidered dish towel and a pair of Harlequin romance novels. It was shaped like a pig. My hand only shook a little as I handed it over.

Her knife thunked like a guillotine through the first pepper. It sprang in two, seeds flying in every direction. "You know, Christina..." She pointed at me with the knife. "...it is possible that you and I are the only two women in this city who have not slept with him recently." She plopped some carrots on the board and whacked off their tops before waving at me with the weapon. "Drink your wine."

I considered arguing, but my mouth felt dry and she was armed. I took a sip. "He, ummm... I'm sorry."

"Sorry?" she said. Staring wordlessly into space, she finally shrugged. "*Sí*, I suppose I was, too. Sorry he is a *chancho*, huh? Here." Turning, she opened the oven and pulled out of pan of triangular somethings. "Sprinkle them with cheese, *sí*? It is in the refrigerator."

The fridge was reminiscent of her counter, loaded to

overflowing. I found the shredded cheddar after a safari into its frosty depths and pulled it triumphantly into the open air.

"How much?" I asked.

"You are not..." She waved the knife distractedly. I watched the light glimmer on the blade, mesmerized. "What is it called?"

"Scared?" I said.

"What?"

"What?" In retrospect, I think that I may have been feeling the effects of the wine already. One glass and I can usually be found facedown on the nearest horizontal surface, but sometimes fear for my life can keep me erect for a good hour or two.

"Lactose intolerance," she said. "You are not that, are you?"

"Oh. No." I drank again. "I'm not anything intolerant." Except for knife wounds. I was pretty sure I was knife-wound intolerant.

She laughed. "Good. That is good. Go ahead, sprinkle. Sprinkle."

I sprinkled.

"Those are quesitas. Miguel's mother made them the first time I ate at her house."

"Where was that?"

"Satillo. In Mexico. I was sixteen." She stared into space, momentarily forgetting the severed pepper and newly decapitated carrots. "We had not yet been dating four weeks when he asked me to marry him."

Holy crap. Sixteen! "And you said yes?"

She shrugged. "He was a fine catch," she said, still staring. "Ambitious. Courteous. Had a *culata* hard as a Spanish onion."

I coughed on my wine. I didn't know what a *culata* was, but I wasn't too drunk to make an uneducated guess.

"Of course . . ." She shrugged and made a face. ". . . he was also a slimy bastard. But I did not know that at the time." She resumed chopping. "My mother did not wish for me to marry him. We ran away to Mexico City without a peso between us, but, oh, the wedding night, huh? His hands were like voodoo." She glanced up, eyes bright. "More cheese."

I shut my mouth and sprinkled madly.

"Good. That is good. Now put them back in the oven. You know what is needed?" she asked, propping her fists on her hips.

A cold shower? A lobotomy? A bullet in the brain pan? A—

"Margaritas."

Whoa. "I really don't think—" I began, but she was already taking the cover off the blender.

"Get the ice, Christina."

I did. She used half a pint of tequila. Some of it made it into the blender, but most of it washed across the counter. Sugar was added, inside and out.

"This will hold us over until our marvelous dessert, yes?"

"I—"

"Which I cannot complete yet, for I do not have the brandy."

"Ahh . . ."

"But do not worry. It will be delivered soon."

"They do that?"

"*Sí*. I have a good relationship with Manny from Pablo's Spirits. Now, about the margaritas . . . the trick is in the fruit, huh?" she said, and added a banana, a boatload of strawberries, and the juice of a lime. She hit a button. The blender buzzed raucously, chewing up ice and fruit. A slice of orange came next. Liquid spattered the wall. She slapped on the lid. "If you add fruit enough, you will not become the drunk."

"Really?"

"That is what Miguel told me on our first time together." She shook her head and punched the OFF button. Silence exploded around us. "Gerald was created that very night."

When she was sixteen and drunk as a sailor? Did she resent the senator for that? Enough to think him guilty of murder? Enough to kill his fiancée?

"We decided to marry a week later. Mama did not know I was with child. But I was well aware." Padding across the tiled floor, she opened a cupboard and gazed up at the top shelf. "Fetch those glasses, will you, my dear?"

I towered over her, reached up, and came away with glasses the size of birdbaths.

She filled them to the brim then made a kind of salute.

I was compelled to drink. We had served margaritas at the Warthog. They'd tasted a little like battery acid. This one didn't.

"I knew I would give birth the moment Miguel filled me," she said.

I gripped the fat stemware and refrained from choking.

"I know these things. It is a gift." She shrugged. "And a curse."

I drank again. She seemed relatively well adjusted, but then again, so had David Hawkins, up to the moment he'd threatened me with a butcher knife, at which point I'd classified him as mentally unstable. Thank God for that Ph.D.

"So you knew you were pregnant when . . ." I cleared my throat. "You knew . . . right away?" I asked.

"Sí," she said, "but the truth is this, I would have married him anyway. He had magic in his hands." She wiggled her fingers. "And in his *pene,* too, huh?"

Jesus save me, I thought, but either Jesus was busy, or he'd heard this kind of talk before.

"I knew also that he would someday be important," she added. "I knew it in my heart. And my family . . . we were as poor as empty corn husks. Still, Mama cried when she found out we had been wed. Perhaps she had the gift, too, and saw things to come. I do not know, for I did not get a chance to ask her. After we wed, Miguel was given a job in Houston. Texas." She smiled at nothing. "America. It was a good opportunity for him. He said he could not refuse it, though I did not wish to leave my mother. We moved when I was heavy with Gerald. I did not see Mama again."

Oh, crap.

She shrugged, opened the refrigerator, and brought out a salad in a big wooden bowl. Setting it on the counter, she scattered the chopped peppers onto the lettuce bed. Five slices actually made it inside the bowl. The others were liberally spread across oven mitts, recipes, and a pen that said "True Health" in red letters.

"It is ready," she said, and striding into the dining room, she deposited the salad onto the table. "Bring the margaritas."

After that it was a gastronomic orgy.

I ate food I'd never heard of. Food I couldn't pronounce. Food that tasted like sunlight and happiness. The conversation ranged like wildfire.

Finally, Rosita leaned away from the table, propping an arm across the back of her chair. I had no idea how much she had eaten. But the margaritas were almost gone. She filled my glass with the dregs. It seemed impolite to refuse.

"So you had not met Salina before her death," she said.

"No." I sipped my drink and took the plunge. "In fact, I had never even heard of her."

She stared at me for one long moment, then shook her head, her expression sad. "Do not feel bad for this. Gerald, he does not like to speak of her."

"Why is that?"

"She was..." She leaned forward, stabbing her elbows onto the table. "I do not like to speak ill of the dead, but...Salina Martinez could not cook worth two beans."

"Well..." I cleared my throat. "I'm not exactly a maestro—"

"And..." She shrugged. "She was a whore."

"Literally?" It occurred to me in that moment that perhaps I should quit drinking, but Rosita was already laughing and motioning me toward the living area with a bottle of wine she'd pulled out of some crevice.

"So far as I know, she did not charge for her services," she said, and seating herself on an overstuffed chair, she dropped her sandals and curled her feet up under her. I sat close by, on a couch the color of a papaya. "Besides . . ." She shrugged and sloshed some Chablis into a pair of glasses. "She did not need the money. She only needed . . ." Her lips curled and her eyes were aflame. "What was not hers."

"Such as?"

She leaned back, took a deep drink, and watched me. "She did not truly want my Gerald."

"What do you mean?"

"She was not interested in him." She made a flitting motion with one hand. She wore five gold bangles on her right wrist. Her arms were firm and brown. "He was but a . . . How do you say it? A step of stone."

"A stepping-stone?"

"*Sí.*"

"To what?"

"Bigger things." She lifted a shoulder. Wine bobbled. "The Senate? The White House, perhaps?"

"The—?"

"They were all steps of stones. And eventually they would all come to know the truth. But Miguel . . ." She snorted. "He was too vain to believe it."

"All who?"

"Surely you do not think the Riveras were the only men she took to her bed."

"I hadn't really thought about it."

"Well, I cannot say the same, Christina. I have had a good deal of time to think on it." Her eyes narrowed. "To wonder why me. Why *my* family. But I see now that every man with a *pene* and a couple of pesos had their time with her."

"Ummm..."

"You have heard of Benjamin Weber?"

I shook my head. It wasn't as simple as it should have been.

"He is an aide to the president."

Holy crap.

"And Danny Hohl. He is barely off his mama's teat. But that did not matter to her."

"Danny—"

"His papa's money and his mama's brains. Not to mention Robert's support."

"Robert?"

"Peachtree. You met him, I think."

"The Texas guy?"

"*Sí*. His name was well known when he played the baseball. That is why Miguel first met him. It makes him feel important to know those who are famous. And the famous, they are often..." She shook her head and scrunched her face. "Like the puddle who pretends to be the ocean."

"Shallow?"

"*Sí*. Shallow. But Robert is different. A good man. He treated Danny as his own since his papa's death. Took him into his home. They never had a son of their own. Dottie doted on Danny something fierce, I am told. Washed his clothes. Cooked his favorites. Baked lasagna, cocoa cookies. She is not so good in the kitchen as I, but she is not so very bad. And perhaps their generosity was not all for the boy's good, *sí*?"

"I don't know Danny."

"Ahh, but you must. The handsome boy with the dimples. Surely you saw him. He has a face like Saint Michael come to earth."

Ken, I thought. *Of Ken and Barbie fame.* "The blond kid?"

"It is said he is a genius in the laboratory and will quadipple our fortunes once he settles in."

"Was he with a woman with legs up to her— *Our?*" I said.

She shrugged. "It is, as they say, a big boys' club."

I thought for a moment. "*Old* boys?" I guessed.

She laughed. "*Sí.* They are that. Old boys who share their stocks and their floosies."

"Is Jack a club member?"

She stared at me, making me realize I'd said the words out loud. "My Gerald is a good man."

"Is he . . . ?"

Her brows lowered as I searched for words.

"I mean, yes, of course he is . . . a good man . . . but I was wondering, is everything okay?"

"Okay?"

"After last night. I was afraid—"

She waved a dismissive arm. Bangles jingled. "Graystone is a thorn in the side, but all is well."

"He wasn't reprimanded, then?"

"Leighton Kindred loves him like a son." She scowled at her own thoughts. "Loves him as a son should be loved."

I made a pretty safe stab in the dark. "Not like your husband loves him."

"A pair of plastic breasts were always more important than his own flesh and blood."

"So things have never been easy between—" I began, but just then her words sank in. "She had a boob job?" In retrospect, I realize that might not have been the most pertinent question, but at the time I was sure my lack of focus wasn't due to the amount of alcohol in my system. I wasn't drunk. In fact, I felt surprisingly lucid. There's just something really fascinating about the idea of someone cutting themselves open and sticking bags of saline in their chests.

"Her breasts, they were more real than the rest of her," she said, eyes narrowed. "She could seem as sweet as honey. But inside she was like the acid. I knew it from the moment I saw her. Even as a little girl. She never cared for Gerald. She only used him."

"For what?" Okay, maybe my speech had lost a little polish, but I was sure I was a long way from belching jingoistic tunes.

She rose to her bare feet. Her sun-fire toenails were decorated with tiny daisies. She retrieved my bottle of champagne and approached me. I shook my head, but she was already pouring. I drank. I don't like to be rude.

"As you may know, things have never been easy between my husband and my son."

I couldn't help but notice that she failed to refer to her ex as her ex.

She shook her head. "I prayed to Saint Nicholas of Myra that they would bury the ax, but the blood of our ancestors, it is hot. And the two of them, they were jealous."

"Of?"

"In the beginning?" She shrugged. "Of me. Of my time. Miguel did not care to be placed second even for the care of his own child. And Gerald and I were very close."

"Mother's complex," I said.

"What is this?"

"It's when there is a strong bond between mother and son." I was coherent enough to refrain from mentioning the sexual overtures often associated with the relationship. Go me.

"Yes." She nodded. "My Gerald opened his heart to me. While Miguel . . ." She made a face. "He thrives on secrets. And . . ." She shrugged. "He always had the eye for other women. Many women. Salina, she worked on his campaign. My husband, he thought her sweet. But I knew." She snorted. "I knew even before my Gerald began seeing her. I warned him. But men . . . even the good ones, they are sometimes the fools, are they not?"

I drank. "No shit. So you think she was interested in him just because of the senator."

"She knew of Miguel's vanity. Understood it in the place where her heart should have been. What a conquest it would be for the old man to take a woman from the young, *sí*?"

"But she planned to marry the senator. Didn't that mean—"

"Huh!" Fire sparked in her eyes.

That usually didn't happen to eyes. Maybe I should quit drinking, I thought, and took another swig. "She wasn't going to marry him?"

"Why do you think she is dead?"

"I've been sort of wondering that."

"Because she was the liar and the whore."

"But—"

"Listen to me, Christina, for this I have learned." She leaned toward me conspiratorially. "A man will accept a liar. And he will accept a whore. But only if she is his whore."

"You think she was boinking..." The shrink and the cocktail waitress seemed to be duking it out in my churning brain. "You think she was unfaithful?"

"It was her nature." She leaned into the cushy back of the chair. "People cannot fight their natures. Salina, she would have cheated on the Christ himself if given the chance."

"And the senator found out."

She drank. "He is a man. But he is not entirely stupid. And he is not forgiving."

"You think he killed her." My words were little more than a whisper. The room went silent. We watched each other, eyeball to eyeball, unspeaking for several seconds, then, "But he was on a plane." My voice was raspy.

She raised her brows. "Was he? Are you so very certain of that?"

"I checked." And may go to jail if the truth got out.

She looked surprised, then laughed. "Sí, you would do just that, would you not, Christina? But things are not always as they appear. Take my Gerald, for instance. He appears strong, sí? Sure of himself. Of his own worth."

I didn't answer. My mind felt spongy.

"But inside..." She sighed and put her hand to her

chest. "Inside, he is the small boy. Miguel's harsh words crushed his self-respect. Nothing was good enough."

"Yeah." I nodded, head wobbling. "That's common. Men want to live victerous . . . victrous . . . vicar . . . They want to live through their sons," I said. "Can't allow them to fu—" I caught myself. "To fail, to be less than perfect."

"*Sí,*" she said, then watched me. "Tell me, Christina, how is that you met my Gerald?"

She'd interrupted a sip. "What?"

"I told you the story of Miguel and me. Perhaps more than you wished to know. *Sí?*"

I laughed. It ended on a snort.

"Tell me," she said.

In some dank corner of my mind, a woman with a stick up her butt, or perhaps someone with a Ph.D., suggested I employ a bit of diplomacy. The cocktail chick mocked her. "Bomstad attacked me."

"Bomstad?"

"A client."

"Ahhh." She nodded. "And my son, he came to your rescue, *sí?*"

"Kind of." I stopped the glass halfway to my lips. A little sloshed over the side. "How did you know?"

She shrugged. "It is the gift." She drank, scowled. "Tougher laws. It is what we need here in this city, yes?" I nodded noncommittally, not unlike my years at the Hog. "Where I come from, the father of the girl would have the privilege to cut off his *pelotas* and feed them to her hounds."

"I was houndless at the time," I said.

She nodded, smiled a little, eyes gleaming. "You are

good for my Gerald. Now, tell me, how did he save you from this bastard?"

Maybe, thought the cocktail girl, a bit of diplomacy wouldn't be completely unmerited. After all, I wasn't entirely certain she didn't plan to kill me with a corkscrew and roll my saturated body into the street. But, in point of fact, her Gerald had shown up like a bad dream and accused me of killing the man who tried to rape me. He'd then escorted me home, taken my shirt, and tested a stain to see if it was the perpetrator's blood. I had been certain her Gerald was a nutcase. Currently I thought he might be a nutcase with a really great ass.

"He is a good officer of the law, *sí?*"

I gave it some judicious consideration, 'cuz despite the fact that he drove me crazy, he'd kept me alive. And on more than one occasion, actually. What should this tell me about my lifestyle? *"Sí,"* I agreed. And that morning I hadn't even known I was trilingual. I drank some more. Couple more glasses and I'd be fluent.

"And a jalapeño in the bed, yes?"

Some kind of noise escaped my mouth. I can't really say what it was. *Argwew* maybe.

"After all, he is Latino." She shrugged, laughed. "And he is my son."

"Mrs. Rivera—" Even the cocktail chick was uncomfortable. And she had once fended off six biker dudes and an amorous pig simultaneously.

"Please." She sounded utterly offended. "Do not call me by Miguel's mother's name. I am Rosita."

"Rosita, I don't think we should be discussing—"

She made a *pfft*ing noise and waved her hand. "Christina,

I have but one son." She drank. I did the same. I try to be a good guest. "Surely you see that I want nothing but happiness for him."

"Uh-huh."

"And a man . . ." She made a fist and narrowed her eyes. "A true man . . . cannot be happy without a woman at his side."

I gave that some sagacious thought while simultaneously dumping a little wine on my lap before righting my glass. "You think?"

"It is truth."

"He was married before, huh?"

"*Sí.*"

"Was he happy then?"

"Tricia." She sighed and shook her head. "She was a fine girl. But she was not . . ." She scowled as if searching for the proper word. "She was not one to make a man's blood run hot."

"Really?" I had met Rivera's ex-wife under rather odd circumstances. Let me just say there was a borrowed dog with an alias involved. Tricia Vandercourt was cute, sweet, and tiny as a toothpick. Meeting her had made me feel like a lumberjack with bad hair. Come to think of it, she had been the very antithesis of Salina. And yet, years after his divorce, Rivera was, once again, involved with the hot Hayek look-alike who had surely wounded him on more than one occasion. Did that tell me anything about life, or did it simply imply something about boob jobs?

"While you are . . ." Rosita paused, watching me. "Tell me the truth, Christina. Does he not make your heart gallop in your chest?"

"Well, yeah, but usually that's because he's accusing me of murder," I said, and remembered about diplomacy a second after the words left my mouth.

"He accused you of the murder?"

"A couple of times, actually." Whoops. Wasn't going to tell her that, either.

She nodded, thinking. "And yet you want him. I can see it in your eyes."

She stared at me. I had the good sense to look away.

But she nodded knowingly. "So why are you here with me, instead of with him?"

"He accused me of murder," I repeated. Damn it!

The *pff*ting sound again. "He does not mean it. He only longs to keep you at a distance. For he knows he is not safe with you."

"Safe?"

"He has been hurt by those he loves, Christina. He is afraid to risk his heart yet again."

"You think so?"

"Trust me on this. I do not have many years of schooling, but men—men, I know."

"I have a buttload of schooling."

She shrugged as if it were a fair trade. "A wise vaquero does not let a fine stallion run wild for long, Christina."

I stared, mind slogging along. "Am I the wise vaquero or—"

"Do not let this one get away, Christina," she said, looking a little peeved at my ignorance. "There are not so many good men left. You know this, *sí?*"

"I got it embroidered on a pillow."

She laughed. "The Rivera men, they will make you

want to kill them. This I know. But it is that fire that makes the nights warm, yes?" She drank. "Miguel..." She shook her head. "He is a cheating son of a wizened whore, but he can make a woman weak in the knees."

"I'm not sure I want weak knees."

She looked surprised. "What is it you want from a man, then?"

"I'd prefer it if he didn't wear my underwear."

I think she gave me a strange look. "I admit that there are things about American men that I do not understand."

"You and me both."

"Gerald will not wear your underwear."

"It's a plus."

"But he will look good in his own, huh?"

"Yeah." I gazed morosely at nothing in particular. "But shouldn't there be more?"

"More?"

I leaned forward, holding my bathtub-size drink in both hands. "Don't you want someone to engage your intelliction...intil...to share his deepest thoughts?"

"I have found that a man who shares his deepest thoughts does not often have *culata* hard as a Spanish onion."

I felt suddenly deflated. "Good point."

"And, too, how deep can a man's thoughts be?"

I nodded and drank.

"Christina, you are woman of business, *sí*?"

Right at that moment I wasn't quite sure.

"You have patients and friends and...What is the word? Colleagues. You have colleagues, *sí*?"

"*Sí*."

"And with them you can engage the intellect, yes?"

"Ummm . . ."

"Must you be engaged while in your bed also?"

I was pretty sure there was a mistake in her logic, I just couldn't seem to ferret it out from the muzziness in my head.

She seemed concerned by my silence. As for me, I've found silence to be the least of my worries.

"Do you not find my Gerald sexy?" she asked. "Do you not burn for him?"

I opened my mouth, searching hopelessly.

Three knocks sounded from the front of the house, nearly launching me from my chair. "Someone's at the door."

"*Sí.*" She did not move. "That will be young Manny with the brandy. But he can wait. It will teach him patience. You did not answer my question."

"Listen, Mrs. Rivera—"

"Rosita."

"Rosita, sex isn't that important in the big—"

"Not important? What do you say?" She looked appalled. "Do you not feel the fire when he touches you?"

She stared at me. My mind roved back to the time in my vestibule when I'd found myself straddling her son like a junkyard dog. The sound of his ripping shirt was still loud in my head. "There might be a little fire," I admitted.

She watched me for a moment, then smiled. "So you do lust for my Gerald."

"It's not lust . . . exactly."

"Then what is it?"

"It's—"

"Christina," she warned.

"Okay, I lust!" I snapped. "I lust. Holy crap, I can't sleep at night thinking—"

A noise sounded in the doorway. I glanced up. And there, not twelve feet away, stood Jack Rivera, dark, brooding, and lusty as hell.

16

She may be an old flame, but she's still smokin'.

—Michael McMullen, to the
woman who would soon be
his ex

_M_Y STOMACH DROPPED. I sucked in air. The room was as silent as death, and for one hopeful second I thought I was going to faint.

"Gerald." His mother sounded euphoric. I felt like barfing. "This is the wonderful surprise. I was not expecting you."

He was staring at me, eyes dark with suspicion and anger. "What the hell's going on here?"

My cheeks felt hot, my stomach was doing some complicated knot work. I tried to speak. Nothing happened. I'd rather run naked through the frickin' Getty Center with a watermelon on my head than have him hear the words I'd just spoken.

"Gerald Rivera, you watch the language," Rosita scolded.

I felt him pull his gaze from my face. But it didn't do any good. I was pretty sure he'd already singed my eyebrows. "What's she doing here?" he asked.

Mrs. Rivera had risen to her feet, and even though her head didn't reach his chin, she was a formidable force. "I asked her to come," she said. "Invited her." She took a step toward him. A little of the wind seem to sail out of his sails. "Into my house. My home."

He shuffled his feet.

"What are *you* doing here?" she asked.

He looked at me, then away. Anger shone in the depths of his devil's eyes, but there was something else there, too, something that had been showing in men's eyes for as long as they had mothers. It looked a little like fear.

He drew a deep breath, settled his gaze on Rosita, and ignored me. "I need to talk to you."

But her hackles were up. "About what?"

He didn't shift his gaze, but I could feel his attention turn toward me. "Now's not a good time."

"Whatever it is you have to say, you can say it now."

"Not with her here."

She shook her head. "I taught you better . . ." she began, then slammed into a barrage of Spanish.

He countered with a tide of words just as confusing.

I stared like a besotted pumpkin.

The voices jolted to an abrupt halt, but the combatants were still glaring.

I cleared my throat.

"Well . . ." I gave Rosita an ingratiating smile. It hurt my face, which still felt hot. "Thank you for your hospitality, Mrs. Rivera, but I should be getting home."

"What?"

"The hell you should."

Both of them spoke in unison with the ringing of the doorbell.

"I'm going home," I said, and rose to my feet. My head spun off into space. The floor jittered.

Rivera laughed. The sound echoed like a bell in my cranium. "You're drunk off your . . ." He shifted his gaze to his mother, gritted his teeth. "What'd you give her, Mama?"

"Gerald, you shame me!" she scolded. "What is the matter with you? We had dinner. That is all."

Rivera's expression was deadpan. He can do deadpan like nobody's business.

"We had some wine," she said finally, and waved dismissively. The doorbell rang again. She made her way toward it, speaking over her shoulder. "Not so very much. But perhaps you are right, sí? Perhaps you should drive her home."

"No!" The word escaped before I could grab it back.

Rivera turned toward me with a scowl.

I laughed. I'm not so great at deadpan, but I'm hell on wheels when it comes to maniacal. I stumbled a little, trying to keep my feet under me. They seemed kind of bendy. "I mean . . . no." I cleared my throat and refrained from closing my eyes. My head was swirling. I thought I heard him swear, which was confusing, because I was pretty sure his lips never moved. "That won't bed necessary."

"What?" He and his identical twin to his left seemed to speak in unison.

"Be," I corrected, not exactly sure which one to address. "That won't *be* necessary. No need to trouble yourself."

"Just some wine, my ass," he snorted. "Come on."

"I can drive," I said, but maybe the last word sounded a little more like "dwive."

I made a beeline for the door. It wavered like a shimmering palm tree, but I managed to keep it in sight. To my surprise, a man stood beside it holding an amber bottle by the neck. He didn't seem to be either one of the lieutenants.

"Hullo," I said.

"It is too bad you must leave, Christina," Rosita said, fuzzily appearing beside him. "Manny has finally arrived with the brandy for the jubilee of strawberry."

I tried to formulate some kind of response but my stomach beat my lips to the punch. It gurgled dramatically. I toddled outside and braced myself against the wall. The stucco felt rough and blessedly solid against my palm. The air caressed my face, rejuvenating me. I straightened my back, hurried my step . . . and toppled forward. I squeaked in surprise as the cobblestones rushed up toward me, but suddenly the pavers were yanked away. The world was set aright with confusing abruptness. I glanced to my left. It seemed that Rivera was holding my arm. My biceps protested beneath his deadly grip, but in my magnanimous mood, I gave him a grateful smile.

I think he swore in return. I know he tugged me toward

the street. I stumbled along beside him like an inebriated duckling.

"Let me go." I don't really like being treated like an inebriated duckling. I gave my arm a dignified yank and almost fell off my feet. But I gritted my teeth and tried again. "Let me go!"

He turned toward me. "Over your dead, fermenting body," he said, and hauled me over to the passenger side of his Jeep. "Get in."

I gave him a condescending glare. We were eyeball to eyeball. He had a face that could make a virgin cry. I'd been a virgin once. Celibacy was my *new* friend. "I'm perfectly capable of diving...*driving*," I said, and miraculously finding my keys, I toddled toward my car. Somehow, he beat me to it and plopped a hand on the little Saturn's roof, barring the door. His arm was pressed against my breasts.

I faced him again. The muscles of his arm scraped across my nipples. They seemed to think it was cold outside.

But his skin felt warm against me, and he smelled like Hugh Jackman in heat. Granted, I'm not really sure how Jackman smells when he's in heat. But I'm pretty sure it'd be like that. Rivera leaned in. I couldn't help but catch my breath...pray...close my eyes. The last one was a mistake. The world spun. I teetered off balance a little.

"Fuck," he said, and bending down, he lifted me off my feet, strode around the bumper, and plunked me into the Saturn's passenger seat. I tumbled onto the emergency brake, protesting all the way.

By the time he got in I had almost dragged myself upright. It was pretty dark in the car but I could still see his glare. Would probably see the damn thing in my dreams.

I propped myself rigid against the seat. Pride may goeth before a fall, but it's better than the alternative.

I'm not sure how he got my key, but suddenly he was shoving it into the ignition. In a second we were tooling along while my stomach did a tango in my roiling gut. I opened my window, hoping for enough air to keep all my contents inside.

Silence screamed around me. I kept my eyes drilled into the windshield. Dignity was mine. I wouldn't obsess about what he had heard me say. It didn't matter. I didn't care what he thought. He was a cretin anyway. And maybe a murderer. Oddly enough, that last thought made me feel a little better. Yes, I was trapped in the car with a murderous cretin, but at least I didn't care what the murderous cretin thought. I would go home, throw up, forget about him, move on. I raised my chin.

"So what were you talking about?"

"What?" I snapped my attention toward him. A little too fast. I took a steadying breath, remembering dignity, and that ralphing eats the lining of one's esophagus. "I beg your pardon?"

He stared at me. "What were you talking about?" he asked, but slower this time, as if he were waiting for my brain to get back from its sabbatical.

I gave him a stare. I was trying to look dignified, but I'm afraid my pupils might have been staring in opposite directions.

He gritted his teeth. "With Mama," he explained.

"Oh." Well, I certainly hadn't been talking about how hot he'd look in his underwear. That would have been wrong. And just damned weird. I was holding my breath. I let it out carefully, lest I forget to start up again. "Not much. She asked me to dine with her." The air felt good against my arm and face.

"Did she?"

"Yes. She's very gracious." I turned back to stare through the windshield. Cars zipped by on the . . . whatever the hell road we were on. For all I knew we could be flying to the moon. "I have to admit I'm surprised." I didn't look to see if he was glaring at me. Odds were good. "Genetics," I muttered. "Go figure."

"You saying I'm not gracious?"

I gave him a smile. I'm pretty sure half of my mouth was still functioning. "Yes, Lieutenant, that's exactly what I'm thaying." Damn it! "Saying."

He smiled back. He looked like a Doberman guarding a hot dog. But maybe that was just the Chablis talking . . . or the champagne . . . or the tequila. Holy crap.

"So you were just two girls getting together to shoot the breeze?" he surmised.

"And eat."

"Ah-huh." He concentrated on the road ahead. Vehicles were zipping past, leaving red streaks of light in their wake.

"She's an excellent cook."

"Always has been."

"And I like her house. It's homey and—"

"God damn it!" he swore, and jerked the Saturn onto

the left shoulder. A sixteen-wheeler whizzed by, missing my elbow by an inch.

"Hey," I shrieked, and yanked my arm inside.

He was already leaning toward me, eyes glowing like a wolf's in the surreal lights cast by an oncoming SUV. "What did she tell you?"

I huddled against the door. "What?"

"You're barking up the wrong damned tree, McMullen," he warned, and grabbed my wrist.

"I'm not barking at all." I'm afraid my voice may have squeaked, but I didn't bark, so I was pretty damned happy about that.

"What did you think she'd tell you?" He seemed to calm a little, but his body was tense, his eyes smoking. Really, I think they were. "That I'd been jealous of my old man all my life? That I killed Salina in a fit of passion?"

"Passion?" I was pressed against the passenger door like lunch meat gone bad. "No. You're not a passionate kind of guy. Never rash or . . . or . . . violent?" The last word kind of sounded like a weak-assed question.

He stared at me, almost laughed, eased off a few inches. Shook his head. But suddenly his eyes struck me again.

"God damn it," he said, but his voice had lost all emotion and in the stillness between rushing cars, I was pretty sure he'd gone beyond the purgatory depth of anger and sunk lower. "God damn it, McMullen. She's my mother."

I swallowed, not following, shaking my head.

"You want a coldhearted killer? Is that what you want?"

I shook my head harder, but he wasn't really listening.

"Then try the old man."

I stopped in mid-shake. "What did you find out?"

"She was baking cookies," he said.

"What?"

"Salina. She was baking. Like she didn't have a care in the world. Dishes half-washed. Water in the sink. The crime photos..." He drew a breath, carefully controlled.

"I thought you weren't supposed to be investigating the case."

"Yeah?" His eyes snapped. There was something untamed and desperate in his eyes. "Well, she wasn't supposed to die, was she?"

"Listen, Rivera, I know you cared about her. Maybe you even feel responsible, but—"

"Cut the shrink crap!" he snapped. "And stay the hell away from Mama."

"She asked me to—"

"She's got nothing to do with this. Do you hear me?" He tightened his grip on my biceps. "Nothing."

"I didn't say she..." I began, but just then a rogue thought shambled groggily into my brain. "Is that why you went to her house? To check her alibi?"

A muscle jumped in his jaw. He leaned closer. "She doesn't need a damned alibi."

"Because she's your mother?"

"Because she's innocent."

I jerked my arm away. "Then why the hell do you think you have to protect her?"

He glared at me, silent for a second.

I was breathing hard. "Christ, Rivera, you're acting like a moron."

Something traveled like lightning across his face, but he shut it down.

I watched him, mind grinding rustily. "Worse. You're acting like she's guilty."

The car went silent. My mind was sweating, and at that moment I realized that a functioning brain might have come in really handy about then.

"What'd she tell you?" His voice was a monotone.

I gave up trying to analyze him and glanced toward the highway, wondering if I could make it across without getting squashed by a passing motorist. I knew my odds weren't good, but at that precise moment, it didn't really matter, because the truth was, I would rather have taken my chances with a speed-happy commuter than admit we'd been discussing how he'd look in his underwear. Crap. I'd rather tell him she confessed. "She said men are idiots."

He glared at me a moment, then leaned back, rubbed his eyes, and chuckled. "Yeah," he said. "Yeah. Well . . ." He blew out a breath, watched the traffic stream by. "She'd know, wouldn't she?"

I drew my first clear breath since I'd seen him standing in his mother's doorway. "How are things at work?"

"Work?" He snorted, then shrugged. "They're great. Just dandy."

There was sarcasm in his voice. And fatigue. And possibly the suggestion that he'd like to toss me out of the car and put tire tracks over my head.

"I was afraid you'd get in trouble." I watched his face. He hadn't shaved that day. Either that or he was part wolf, which I'd kind of always suspected. He was wearing a blue, western-style shirt with snaps. It was rumpled. As were his blue jeans. I gave a mental scowl. "You know . . . after last night."

His hands tightened on the steering wheel. A red Maserati zipped by at about five hundred miles an hour. I wondered if the cop in him wanted to slap on a blue light and chase it down the road or if he was too busy working on the tire tread fantasy.

"Someone called nine-one-one," he said, and glanced at me from the corner of his feral eyes. "Any idea who that might have been, McMullen?"

I swallowed, shrugged, and refrained from saying anything that would get me eaten. "There were a lot of people there. Could have been anyone."

He nodded, but something about his stillness suggested he wasn't buying it.

"People were scared," I said.

"Yeah? How about you? Were you worried about me?"

"He had . . . I heard he had a gun," I said, not wanting him to know that I'd been there, that I'd seen them fighting, that, in fact, I had been afraid for him.

But maybe he was better at analyzing people than an inebriated cocktail waitress from Schaumburg, because his face softened the slightest degree. "I can take care of myself, McMullen."

"So did the captain put you on the case?"

His face was devoid of emotion. "Yeah," he said. "Yeah. I'm on the case."

"What'd you find out? Are there clues? Was there DNA?"

"You taking up forensics between clients, McMullen?" he asked. His smile was sardonic, his tone dismissive.

I raised my nose toward the Saturn's ceiling. I'd always liked my high horse. "I think I have something of a stake in this."

"Leave it alone," he warned.

But I was on a roll. "Your mom said Salina—"

He jerked his gaze toward me.

Maybe I was drunker than I'd realized. I kind of hope so. The alternative is that I was dumber than a box of rocks.

"What exactly did my mother say about Salina?"

"She said that..." I paused. He had that hungry wolf look in his eye again. "She said she was a beautiful woman."

He stared at me a moment, then laughed and scrubbed his hand across his face. "God, McMullen, you are one piss-poor liar."

I was surprisingly offended by his opinion, which may have said something about the state of my sobriety. "Am not."

He shook his head and rested it on the cushion behind him. "Mama hated Salina from the moment she laid eyes on her."

"Oh?" I tried to sound innocent. It's not my best act. "Why is that?"

"Sali could pull in the men," he said. "But women..." He sighed. His eyes looked tired. I wondered if he hadn't been sleeping again. I wondered if he'd always called her "Sali," with that soft, wistful voice that made him seem strangely vulnerable, strangely young. "Women generally wanted to kill her."

"Did one?"

"What?"

"I mean.., not your mother, of course." I tried a chuckle. Whoa, Nellie. "She's a saint. But do you think a woman might have actually killed her?"

"Damned if I know. Coroner's looking at a couple dozen possibilities. None of 'em make sense. He's not even sure yet if it *was* murder." He seemed a million miles away suddenly. "Neighbors saw squat. Not a car, not a visitor. Nothing suspicious. But if I could get another look at the crime..." He snapped his gaze up. "Fuck me," he said. Snorting at himself, he put the Saturn in drive and pulled back out into traffic. "Half a lifetime on the force and I'm singing to a nosy shrink like a fuckin' choir boy."

"I'm just curious," I said, all innocence.

"And I'm Batman," he countered, and laughed at me.

"The hell you are," I grumbled. I don't like to be accused of murder, and I don't like to be shut out. But being laughed at makes me mad as hell.

He glanced my way.

"Bruce Wayne had a soul," I said.

He raised one brow. "You think I don't have a soul, McMullen?"

I thought it might have been wise to keep my mouth shut. But maybe I should have thought of that before guzzling ten gallons of tequila.

I gave an eloquent shrug. See, eloquent, I was sobering nicely...and thinking. If there were no problems at work, and he was officially on the case now, why couldn't he get a look at the crime scene? And why the hell did he seem so haunted? Yeah, a young woman he'd cared about was dead, but he was a doer, a shaker. If he could do and shake, why did he look like last year's corpse? "Question is, what does Captain Kindred think?" I asked.

"He thinks you should keep your nose out of it." He skimmed me with his eyes. Heat seared me. "Along with your pretty ass."

He said "ass," but I resisted giggling. Maybe I was still a little bit drunk. "You've still got your badge, then?" I pressed.

"In my pants pocket. Wanna see?"

"I'm drunk, not stupid," I said.

He laughed. "They're generally one and the same, sweetheart."

"Not this time."

He grinned.

My hackles rose. "Worse luck for you, Rivera."

He wheeled right onto Opus Street. I tipped wildly toward him, falling facefirst into his lap.

"Looks like my luck's improving."

I scrambled to right myself. "Pervert."

"Yeah," he said, and pulling up to my curb, threw the Saturn into park before catching my gaze. "But you still lust for me."

"I do not—" I began, but at that moment I remembered my exact words to his mother, and I knew he had heard them.

I felt the blood drain from my body, felt my feet go numb. Maybe I tried to think of some pithy put-down. Maybe I struggled for a denial, but in the meantime my fingers were fumbling for the handle. The door popped open. I half fell, half leapt onto the sidewalk. I heard him call out after me, but I was racing along my crumbled concrete.

The car door slammed, his footfalls sounded on the walkway behind me. But I was inside my house and locking the door in record time.

"Open up, McMullen," he said. I leaned my forehead against the door and prayed for divine intervention. I heard him jiggle the doorknob. "Let me in," he said.

I gritted my teeth and closed my eyes. "Go away."

I thought I heard him chuckle. "If you let me in, I promise not to talk about how you've got the hots for me.

"Or the fact that it's been . . ." I heard him rest a shoulder against the far side of the door. "How long has it been for you, McMullen? Ten years?"

My stomach cramped. I bent double and stumbled toward the bathroom. Four seconds later I was paying homage to the porcelain god. Ten minutes after that I was passed out on my bed, drunker than a freshman and blessedly dead to the world.

17

Absence makes the heart grow fonder, but tequila makes it so she don't give a shit if she's fond of you or not.

—James McMullen, *who is really only astute in comparison to his brothers*

*H*OW WAS—" Elaine stopped mid-sentence when she glanced over the desk at me. "Holy cow, Mac, are you all right?"

"Shh." I tried to hold my head on while I said it.

She rounded the reception desk. Her progress sounded like a charging herd of rabid rhinos. "What happened?"

"Tequila." I was pressing on my right eyeball with the heel of my hand. It might have looked strange, but I was pretty sure the damned orb was going to pop out, and no one wanted that first thing in the morning.

"Tequila?"

"Chablis."

"Sit down."

I eased into the proffered chair. "And I think . . ." It hurt to wince . . . or live, and thinking made me ache down to my personal aura. "I think there might have been some grog."

"I thought grog went out with the thirteenth century."

"Well, it's back."

"Impressive."

I opened an eye carefully, lest it take that opportunity to hop out. "I'm dying, Laney."

She laughed. Sometimes I forget how nasty she can be. And loud. Like a blow horn on steroids. "What'd you find out?"

"That I hate grog. I'm not all that wild about myself right now, either."

"What about Salina?"

"Nothing."

"You have to hold your eyeballs in and you didn't even learn anything?"

"No." I propped myself up straight in the chair. "That's not true." There was a small but mighty demon pounding on my cranium. "I did learn something." The alcohol was solidifying in my system, galvanizing my inebriated re-solve. "I did learn something."

Maybe I said it with a fair amount of drama, because Laney was staring at me, brows well into her hairline. "Tell me of your newfound knowledge, Sensei."

I ignored her facetious tone. "I learned to mind my own business."

"A valuable and difficult lesson."

"Yes." I stood up, resolute. The demon cracked me a

good one right between the eyes. I sank slowly back into my chair.

"Maybe I should cancel your first client."

"No." I rolled one eyeball in her direction. The other one was busy keeping tabs on the demon. "Who is it?"

"Emily Trudeau."

Emily was a Baptist minister's wife. "Oh God," I said.

Laney helped me to my feet. "Maybe you should have started praying before you drank your weight in fermented fodder." We were making our way toward my office. "You must have learned something helpful."

I stopped in my doorway, looking at her through a red veil of veins. "Look at me, Laney. Do I look like last night was helpful in any regard?"

"That which doesn't kill you makes you stronger."

"Including alcohol poisoning?"

"I can only assume."

"No." I shook my head...carefully. "You're right. You're absolutely right," I said. "This has made me stronger. Stronger and smarter."

"Good to hear."

"I'm through with Rivera."

"That's great."

"No more snooping about where I'm not wanted."

"Thatta girl."

"I've got better things to do."

"Absolutely."

"It's not like I'm some tuba-playing, drink-toting kid with—" The demon struck. I winced. "I'm a psychologist," I finished weakly. "Too good for an overbearing, macho, overbearing—"

"You said overbearing." She was pulling a bottle of liquid gunk out of my mini-fridge and pouring it into a glass. It was the color of slime, which, I thought muzzily, was the same color as the carpet my mother had installed in her living room when I turned five. If the seventies were put in a blender, that's the color they'd be. Taking something out of her purse, Laney dumped it into the glass and stirred it with a spoon she'd probably had stashed in her bra. It was metal. Laney doesn't believe in plastic.

"Rivera can get his own ass out of trouble," I added.

"He is a cop," she said, and tapped the spoon twice on the glass. The noise made my eyeballs twitch.

"Isn't he just," I said through gritted teeth.

"Cheers," she said, and giving me a salute, she handed over the slime.

$\mathcal{B}$y that afternoon I was back on track. I had again sworn off alcohol, carcinogenics, and paper that wasn't at least seventy percent post-consumer waste.

I don't know what was in the garbage Laney poured down my throat, but it must have been some powerful stuff, 'cuz I had also, at some point during the night, vowed to learn Hungarian and take harpsichord lessons.

I was pondering the age-old question of where to buy a harpsichord while being pulled down the dog food aisle behind a bicolored moose, when a pseudofamiliar face passed me.

It stopped. Turns out, it was attached to a person.

I tried to stop, too, but the moose was still on the move.

"Christina?"

I planted both heels and dragged Harlequin to a halt.
"Yes?"

"Rachel Banks," she said. "From the visitation."

I recognized her then. Maybe it was the fact that she
wore a pink Prada suit and looked as if she'd just been
pulled off a Miss America runway, not a lint ball on her
jacket, not a hair out of place.

I tried to coax my own coiffure into some semblance of
order, but I'd just spent ten minutes in the car with an animal the size of a eighteen-wheeler.

"You shop here, too?" she asked, eyeing my dog from a
safe distance.

I considered a smarmy comeback, then realized she
had a dog, too. It could have fit into the cavity of my mo-
lar and was sitting beside her like a hirsute princess.

"Yes." I reeled my hound in before he could swallow
hers whole.

She gave him a wary glance. "What does he eat? Or
should I say, whom?"

I gave her a careful smile. I felt itchy and overfleshed.

"Listen." She scowled a little, looking a thousand times
more sober than the last time I'd seen her. "I'd like to
apologize for the other night."

I would have commented, but I was busy having my
arms yanked from their sockets while trying to look
serene and in control.

"I shouldn't have said those things about Salina. She
and I were friends. . . ." Emotion flickered across her face.
It might have been regret. "Once."

"Once?" Not that I cared. I had sworn off. Remember?

She looked at me. "Long time ago."

Not too long. She'd barely reached puberty. Besides, I wasn't listening.

"Before we were both members of Jack's Club."

"What!" The word had a shitload more emphasis than I intended. She raised her perfectly groomed brows at me. Maybe because my eyeballs were popping out of my head, or maybe because Harlequin was lunging against his collar like Moby-Dick at the end of a harpoon while her dog sat like a silky little bean beside her designer footwear.

"Hey," she said. "Do you want to grab a drink or something?"

Jack's Club! What the hell is Jack's Club?

She tilted her head at me, eyes narrowed a little. "You're not in love with him, are you?"

"What? No. I'm not...What? Who are you talking about?"

She gave me a little smile. "I think we should talk."

Jack's Club? "I'd love to," I said, my voice a nice blend of pissy sophistication. "But I'm afraid—"

"Meet me," she said. "At the Quarry. On Burbank. I'll be the one with the dirt on your boyfriend."

"He's not my—" I sputtered, but she was already continuing down the aisle, fur ball sashaying sassily beside her.

I purchased fifty pounds of dog food in a haze and hoped it would last until morning. By seven o'clock I had fed the beast and showered. By 7:30 I had curled my hair and artfully applied makeup. But for no particular reason. I just like to look sharp as I lounge around in the evening.

It wasn't as if I was stupid enough to drive halfway across town for no apparent reason.

By eight o'clock I was dressed in a taupe linen sheath and pacing.

It was 8:42 when I walked through the door of the Quarry.

I found Rachel instantly. She was drinking something clear. I didn't think it was Sprite.

"Christina," she said, and gazed at me with bird-bright interest. It wouldn't have been necessary for me to schlep drinks for half a decade in order to tell she was getting sloshed. "You didn't have to dress up for me."

"What? Oh this," I said, barely glancing at my most expensive ensemble. "No. I had a meeting."

"On Saturday?"

"Psychotics never rest," I said.

She raised a needle-thin eyebrow. "So you *are* dating Jack," she said.

I meant to object, but just then a waiter arrived.

"What can I get you?" He was cuter than a pile of puppies.

"Do you have organic tea?" I asked.

"This *is* L.A." he said, tone bored.

"How about . . ." I paused, trying to think of a beverage that wouldn't make me wish I were dead. "Jasmine."

"You got it," he said, and turned back toward the bar.

Rachel gave me a look. "Organic tea?"

"I'm cleansing."

She laughed. I'd heard Laney talk about cleansing a dozen times. No one laughed at her. Men drooled and women called their personal trainers to ask why the hell they weren't cleansing. "Good God," she said, "you're never going to be able to climb the Rivera family tree that way."

Jack's Club? I thought crazily, but I leaned back in my chair, looking regal and unconcerned. "I'm afraid you got the wrong impression," I said. "Lieutenant Rivera and I aren't—"

"Whole damn family's nuttier than baklava, but he's Houdini between the sheets, isn't he?"

My mouth was still caught on my denial and soured up like I'd taken a double shot of lemon juice. "I beg your pardon?"

She sipped her drink. It looked like Absolut. I'd never seen anyone drink it straight before, and working at the Warthog had offered me the opportunity to see quite a lot. Folks having sex doggie style under the tables, for instance. That was a staple.

"Jack and I . . . we never meshed." She shook her head, glanced up. "He wasn't into politics. Couldn't play tennis worth a damn. And half the time he'd show up looking like he'd been running marathons in his sleep. But get him in the sack, and hold my calls." She blew out her breath and laughed, but it sounded funny, like she might rather be crying. She cleared her throat. "How'd you meet him?"

I didn't squirm. I was too busy trying to figure her out. The shrink was on the job. "As I was about to say," I said, "we're not dating. We're just—"

"Dating?" When she laughed this time there was a little more feeling behind it. "God, no. We weren't dating, either. It'd be like playing chess with a breeding stallion."

"Breeding—"

"Better equipped for other things," she explained, leaning toward me.

The waiter arrived carrying my tea. I thanked him. "So Salina," I began when he was gone. "Did she . . . play chess with breeding stallions?"

"She'd play with anything if it was a means to an end. Or had an end with means." She laughed. The sound was hollow.

"So Rivera was just a stepping-stone?"

She studied me for an instant. "Rosita tell you that?" she guessed.

I blinked. "Rosita who?"

"Oh, please. Don't play a player." Did that mean she had spent time with breeding stallions, too? "What else did she say?"

I considered denying any knowledge again, but it seemed like I should know something about something. "Mrs. Rivera wasn't very fond of her."

"No shit?" she said, and leaned back, arm flung loosely across the back of her chair.

"Said she couldn't cook."

"Sal?" She shrugged. "She had a cheesecake recipe that would make you want to bitch-slap Betty Crocker. She baked about once a month, whenever she was ready to break up with some moony sucker. Balm for their weepy wounds or something. Or maybe her way of saying she was just the girl next door and had to follow her heart. Man, she could work them, could read men like a deck of cards. Knew what they liked, what they were hiding, what drove them mad." She drank. "I learned from the best."

I shook my head, trying to pretend I was dumb as a doorknob. It wasn't real difficult.

Leaning forward, she propped her elbows on the table. "Sal, she knew the value of sex."

Could one be struck dead for speaking poorly about the deceased? I squirmed a little and took a chance. "I heard she wasn't actually paid for it."

She grinned. "She got her pound of flesh one way or the other."

"How do you know?"

"Gossip is like mother's milk in the world of politics. You must know that."

"Just organic tea for me," I said, raising my glass. "New Year's resolution."

She narrowed her eyes, drank. "I bet you drive him crazy."

I tasted my tea, straight up. No sugar. Made me thirsty for paint thinner. "Him?"

"He doesn't like to be outsmarted. Makes him angry." Her eyes glowed. "And when he's angry . . ." She tilted her head back a fraction of an inch, as if imagining. "Not everyone's got a pair of working handcuffs, you know. And when—"

"Listen!" I cleared my throat and lowered my voice. "I appreciate you inviting me here, but I think you've gotten the wrong idea. Rivera's an attractive man, but—"

"He didn't kill her."

"What?"

"He might hang for it just the same, though. Depends how the cards fall."

"What are you talking about?"

"I admit"—she leaned across the table, expression suddenly earnest—"a few years ago, I would have been judge, jury, and executioner, but . . ." She scowled, shook her head. "Now . . . I've aged. Mellowed."

She looked about as mellow as a hand grenade.

"What changed?"

She paused a moment. "Let's just say there were lots of people standing in line to kill her. Rivera . . ." She gazed at her drink, as if she could see things that weren't there. Come to think of it, after that much vodka, it was pretty likely. "He would have been way toward the end."

"Who was at the front?"

"That's the question, isn't it?"

"Where were you?"

She laughed. "In D.C."

"When did you get into town?"

She leaned toward me, eyes bright. "I can see why Rivera hates you."

"I—"

"Don't get me wrong. It's not an insult. He'd never get serious about a woman he couldn't hate."

"Did he hate Salina?"

Her lips quirked into a parody of a smile. "There was a time."

"But no more?"

She shook her head.

"Is that why you think he didn't kill her? Because he didn't hate her?" And if that was the case, what did that say for my own longevity?

"That and pride."

"What?"

She drank, raised her empty glass to the waiter, and turned her attention back to me. "He's too damn cocky to kill her. Wouldn't give her the satisfaction."

"Ummm . . ."

"Christ!" She snorted a laugh. "She was screwing his old man. You think that didn't get his dick in a twist? Back in the day, it drove him crazy just thinking she might . . ." Her voice trailed off.

"Thinking she might what?" I asked.

She shrugged. For a moment I thought she'd remain silent, but Absolut is not a great speech inhibitor. "When they were engaged . . ." She paused. "Shit, it seems like a hundred years ago. He must have been . . . what? Twenty maybe. Eyes like a fucking forest fire." She chuckled at her own fanciful thoughts. "Anyway, there was a rumor."

I waited.

She drew a deep breath and fiddled with her straw. "A rumor that she was sleeping around."

"With whom?"

She laughed, waited, then, "His old man."

What a tangled frickin' web. "Was it true?"

"He seemed to think so, and I guess it doesn't matter anymore." She shrugged and narrowed her eyes. "She did it eventually anyway, didn't she?"

"Is that what broke them apart? The rumor?"

She was silent for an instant. "That? No. Actually . . ." Her face looked pale, kind of stretched tight. "I think he might have been more upset for his mother's sake than his own."

"How'd she handle it?"

"Rosita?" She grinned and made a sort of salute with her glass. "Now, there's a woman who knows how to hate."

"Enough to kill?"

She tilted her head, noncommittal. "If she did it, it's going to put Jack in a hell of a spot, isn't it?"

"How do you mean?"

"He'll have to choose between his mama and his badge."

"You think he'd cover it up?"

"She's his mama. He's Latino."

"Still . . ."

She sat up straight, eyes bright, staring at me. "Good God! You don't know him at all."

"We're just—"

"You really haven't slept with him?"

"As I said—"

She laughed, mouth open. "You really haven't."

I gave her a prissy look. "There are others I haven't slept with, too."

"Touché," she said, and finishing her vodka, she watched me over the top of her glass before setting it on the table.

I refused to squirm under her perusal. "What about the senator?" I asked. "Was he in love with Salina?"

"If you're asking if he killed her . . ." She shrugged, accepted a fresh drink with a tipsy smile. The waiter moved away. She watched his ass, sighed, turned back to me. "You really haven't slept with him?"

"No." I felt a little like slapping her, but I refrained and wondered if I would regret my phenomenal restraint later. "What about the senator? Do you think he's capable of murder?"

"Sure." She shrugged. "But I don't think he'd let Jack take the fall."

"There's bad blood between them," I reminded her.

She raised a brow at me as if I were too stupid to breathe. "How would it look if the good senator's son murdered their mutual fiancée?"

She had a point. "Not good?" I guessed.

"I knew you were smart."

"You make him sound a little cold-blooded."

She breathed a laugh and drank. "Boa constrictors are cold-blooded, honey."

She almost said it with admiration, making me wonder if she was in the habit of lying down with snakes. "Who do you think was at the head of the queue?"

"It was usually the one she just screwed over who wanted to kill her most."

"But she's been with the senator for over a year, hasn't she?"

She made a face. "Are you from the Midwest or something?"

"I don't know what that has to do with—"

"You think she was faithful to him?" she asked, dumbfounded, as if the idea were ludicrous.

"Holy crap." I felt a little breathless.

She laughed.

"Who was she sleeping with?"

She put her glass down. "Like I said, I've been in D.C. Didn't keep track of her affairs anymore." She studied her drink, lips tight. "And Miguel didn't say."

"You kept in touch with the senator?"

She ignored the question and narrowed her eyes a little. "But Danny Hohl is awful pretty. Just the kind of boy toy Sal would enjoy."

"Hohl? The Ken doll?"

She laughed. "So you noticed him, too."

My mind was grunting beneath the weight of the conversation. I shook my head, trying to clear it. It was patently unsuccessful. "Did the senator know she was unfaithful?"

Her fingers tightened on her glass. "It's possible."

I was missing something. "But love is blind?" I probed.

"While lust is merely deaf and stupid."

"Who was Salina's latest beau?"

"Beau?" She gave me a squishy smile.

"I have a Ph.D.," I said.

She laughed. "I have a master's from Harvard. Sal and I went there together."

"Harvard." Damn. I hated being impressed. "Where'd she get the money?"

"She got a full ride. God, she was smart. Could have done anything if she hadn't . . ." Her voice broke.

My ears perked up. My voice dropped a few decibels. "Hadn't what, Rachel?"

"She should have stayed away from the men. They just used her."

I watched her face. I'd seen that expression a thousand

times in the quiet confines of my office. It was remorse, haunting and cold. "Why'd you start the rumor?" I asked.

"I don't know what you're talking about."

"The rumor about her and the senator," I said, and she started to cry, low and muffled and filled with a decade of regret.

18

In fifty years it won't matter if he's handsome, ugly, or dumb as a post. Just try to find someone who don't make you want to shove a pitchfork up his nose.

> —*Ella McMullen, Christina's paternal grandmother, on connubial bliss*

I DON'T LIKE to use labels," I said.

"That means yes." Bruce Lincoln was, without question, the best-looking client I had ever had. In fact, he might be the best-looking fantasy I'd ever had. Of course, his physical looks didn't matter an iota. I'm a professional. Still, when he smiled, my salivary glands always felt a close kinship to Pavlov and his drooling canines. But then, they do the same thing for hot fudge. So maybe my response training was skewed. "You think I'm a sex addict."

I straightened in my chair and crossed one leg over the other. I was wearing Givenchy panty hose. If I don't splurge on ice cream I can afford them and still fit into something smaller than size jumbo. "Do you want to be a sex addict, Mr. Lincoln?" I asked.

My tone was as soothing as hell, but in actuality, I was still reeling from Saturday night. When I'd gone to meet Rachel, I'd thought she wanted to vent her spleen. Turns out, she'd wanted to confess. Not to murder, unfortunately, but to sabotaging Rivera's engagement to her best friend. Seems he'd dropped Rachel for Salina. So she'd started the rumor that Salina was sleeping with Rivera's father, watched their relationship crumble, then cleverly managed to dam up her guilt for more than a decade. But guilt has a way of seeping through the tiniest cracks.

I should have that little piece of wisdom framed and hung above my desk.

"No." Mr. Lincoln jerked to his feet. I jerked, too. I'm not a jumpy person by nature, but the last six months hadn't exactly been smooth sailing. Lately, when someone stands up, I find a dead body. "No," he said. "I don't want to be a sex addict. I want to marry Tracy."

I nodded and tried to concentrate, but thoughts of Rivera and Salina kept disturbing my peace. How had he really felt about her? Last time I'd seen him, he'd looked haunted and haggard. Did that mean he still loved her? And what about Rachel? She'd implied that her relationship with him had been purely physical, but normal people don't try to ruin someone's life because of a casual affair. Of course, I've never met anyone normal.

"This your husband?" Bruce Lincoln had picked up the photograph on my desk. The man in the portrait was in his forties, tan, fit, and almost as handsome as my client. I had named him Ryan.

"No, it's not," I said, and forced myself to focus. "What is your definition of an addict, Mr. Lincoln?"

He shrugged, frowned, set the photo back. If I didn't love Ryan with my whole heart, I'd get rid of that thing. "This a quiz?"

"Yes."

He smiled. My salivary glands kicked up. Sorry, Ryan.

"An addiction," he said, "is a compulsive psychological need for something that is habit-forming."

"Do you need to have sex with the checkout girl at Starbucks?" We'd been discussing her for three weeks now. Apparently, she had "eyes like diamonds." Please!

"That depends where I am in the sequence of events," he said, and sat back down, crossing his right ankle over his left knee.

The movement reminded me of Rivera. And maybe there were other similarities. Maybe Rivera had the same problem Bruce Lincoln did. Maybe they were both sex addicts. It certainly sounded as if the lieutenant had had his fair share. More, if what Rachel implied was true.

I'm not proud of the fact, but I had called Solberg after I'd gotten home from the Quarry. It had been two o'clock in the morning. Blessedly, he had been alone—groggy, but alone. I told him I needed to see the pics the cops had taken of the senator's house.

He'd spouted some gibberish about prison and life sentences and cell mates who are bigger than fishing boats. I had then reminded him of the first time we'd met at a bar called the Warthog. He had propositioned no less than twenty-three women that night and had finally left with a girl who could bench-press an ox. The words "Big

Cheese" were tattooed on her left biceps. Maybe Laney would be interested in such charming anecdotes.

I was expecting the pictures soon. Maybe they would help me tie up the loose ends. Or at least locate the ends. Rivera seemed to think the crime-scene photos would help him prove that Salina had been murdered—and that he was innocent. Or maybe he wanted to get ahold of them because he was afraid they would incriminate him. Hmm, something to think about.

"What do you do?" Bruce Lincoln asked. Putting both feet on the floor, he leaned forward, elbows on knees.

I sat in silence for a moment, partly to give him time to consider his own question, but mostly 'cuz I'd spaced out and had no idea what he was talking about.

"Come on," he said. "I had a fucked-up childhood. My old man split. Mom spent every night . . ." He paused, expression somber. He was an aspiring actor. "Truth is, I don't have any idea how a good relationship's supposed to work. I could use some pointers. How do you keep the beast at bay?"

"I keep my pants zipped." I realized almost immediately that I shouldn't have said that. After all, I don't get the big bucks for sharing practical good sense. I get paid to spout ten-dollar words with penny-apiece meaning, but I was a little distracted.

Still, he grinned at me. "Oh, come on, you're young, attractive. What do you do?" he asked again. "When you're . . ." He nodded toward the picture on my desk. "When he's not around and you're . . . lonely."

Well, I thought, *when my favorite picture wasn't nearby, I usually go with a nice pastoral scene. Maybe framed in teak* _and angled just so_. I had other methods for when I was horny. Methods that sex addicts like to talk about in lieu of the actual deed.

I steepled my fingers and looked him in the eye.

"How do you think Tracy would feel if she knew you were prying into my sex life for your own perverse reasons, Mr. Lincoln?" I asked.

His face went ashen. His shoulders slumped. "I'm sorry," he said, and he looked sincere, but then, he was an actor . . . and a man.

City and state, please."

I tangled my fingers in the telephone cord and closed my eyes.

"What state, please." Even the recording sounded peeved.

"California," I said. "Los Angeles."

"Just a minute, please."

Within thirty seconds I had a phone number scrawled on my electric bill. After that, I paced to the freezer, took out some frozen common sense, and ruminated on why I shouldn't make the contemplated call.

Two pounds later, I replaced the carton, took a deep breath, and dialed the phone again.

"Hey!" someone yelled. Music was blasting like nuclear explosives in the background.

"Yes, hi," I said, "is Danny there?"

"What?" The shouter on the other end of the line might have had an English accent. Then again, he might have been stoned out of his mind. Or both.

"Daniel," I said, raising the amps. "Is he there?"

"This Cindy?"

Uhhh . . sure. "Yeah," I said. "Do you know where he is? I haven't seen him around for a while."

"Hey!" He screamed the word, supposedly to the world at large, but managed to siphon most of the volume into the receiver. I leaned back, trying to save my ears. "Anyone know where Danny is?" In a moment he was back on. "Don't know for sure," he said. "Could be at the library."

Library? What library? My mind was churning. "At U— here on campus?" I asked.

"Yeah, studying again like a right wanker probably. Say . . ." His words were slurred, but then, it was Tuesday night at UCLA. "Give him a shag, will ya? Get his nose out of a book for a minute."

"Sure thing," I said, and hung up before I felt the need to tell him to shut his dirty little mouth. Apparently, I wasn't getting any younger.

It took me an hour to talk myself into full stupid mode. Then I dug through my closet and came up with a pair of worn jeans. They had holes at the knees and looked like they'd had a run-in with a sandblaster. Perfect. I dragged them on, noted the condition of my legs through the holes, and peeled them back off. Then I shaved my knees, donned a push-up bra, two camis, and a flouncy top in concession with the current layering craze.

My nerves were hopping by the time I reached the cam-pus. Broad as a wheat field, its mood vacillated between modern sculptures and turreted architecture from another era. Gargoyles scowled down at me from lofty cornices and fountains ran backward. No kidding.

I kept my eyes open for future stars. According to the brochures, Dean and Monroe had matriculated at this institution, but it was impossible to differentiate between megatalent and Joe Schmo. Everyone was beautiful at UCLA.

The interior of Powell Library was no less spectacular than the grounds. I passed checkerboard floors, towering pillars, and grand wooden staircases. It beat the hell out of Schaumburg Tech, which boasted one battered stop sign and a snowbank as its focal point.

Daniel, aka Ken doll, was in the main reading room on the third floor. He glowed like a homing beacon, beach-blond hair glimmering above a chaotic smattering of handwritten notes.

I had no idea what I was going to say. Good sense suggested that I turn around and march home, but sometimes good sense and I can go weeks on end without so much as a "What the hell" between us.

I picked up a determined stride and paced past him, faltered, turned back, and stopped beside the table where he was studying. "Danny?" I said. "Is that you?"

He glanced up. His expression was thoughtful, his mouth pursed. His lips were an odd meld of Oliver Twist and Casanova. He was already gathering up the papers. I tried to inconspicuously speed-read, but all I saw was some lopsided molecular diagrams and printing that would fit on a grain of sand. In less than a second, he'd shoveled the papers beneath a tattered pocket folder.

"Christina McMullen," I said, and thrust out my hand.

He took it with some misgiving, but he was too polite to tell me to get lost and leave him to whatever was going on in his head.

His handshake, however, was noncommittal. His young Republican act needed some work.

I drew a deep breath and made my face sad. "I saw you at . . . at Sal's visitation," I said.

He looked introspective for a moment, then, "Oh, sure. So you knew her?" His voice was cultured.

"We were coconspirators." I paused, gave a sad little laugh, and wondered wildly what we might have coconspired on. "Back in the day." Maybe he wouldn't ask.

"Coconspirators?"

Damn. "Can I . . . ?" I indicated the chair across from him with a flip of my hand. Oh so casual. Like I wasn't breaking all kinds of social and moral stipulations. "Can I sit down?"

He nodded. His gaze was sharp. "Did you know her from the campaign?"

"No."

He stared.

"Harvard," I said, grasping wildly at the few straws Rachel had cast my way. "We almost blew up the chem lab there."

His eyes narrowed. "A political science major doesn't require chemistry."

"Don't I know it." No. "Old man Eddings about had a cow." Had a cow? Did they still say that? "But Sal . . ." I chuckled, reminiscing, crazy as a loon. "Well . . . you know how she was."

"No." He shook his head. "I mean, I thought I did. But I never thought she'd go that far."

I gave him my concerned look. "What do you mean? How far?"

He eyed me, shook his head, leaned back.

I scrambled for mental footing. "Far enough to marry him," I guessed.

"The senator's an okay guy, I guess," he said. "Was a friend of my father's. And Peach thinks he walks on water. But I mean . . . shit . . . he's old enough to be . . . a friend of my father's."

And he was just about young enough to be her son, but that little nugget of truth didn't seem to offend his sensibilities. "Creepy as hell," I said. "I told her that, too."

"Yeah?"

"We shared a tube of lip gloss for two years. After that you can pretty much tell a person anything. But Sal . . ." I sighed, winced at my own performance. "She didn't need any makeup. She was like—"

"Dark sunshine," he said.

I turned my gaze back to him. There was something in his tone. "How long have you been in love with her?"

"Me?" He laughed. Was the sound a little off? A little breathy? "We dated for a while, but . . ." He shook his head.

"That must have been while I was in Seattle."

"Two years ago almost."

"Why'd you break up? It seems like you'd be perfect together."

"Salina and me?" He laughed. "No. Too different. She

was politics down to her bone marrow and I was . . . well, I've been called a tree hugger, and worse. Even by old Peach."

My mind was scrambling. "Robert Peachtree?"

"You know him?"

"Just by reputation. He doesn't share your concern for the environment, I take it."

"The forests are just a place to store lumber to him. But they've been good to me. Him and Dottie. And she can cook. Except for the cocoa cookies." He shuddered. "Never wanted to make her feel bad, though. Never want to make anyone feel bad." He lowered his brows. "Maybe that makes me a weenie. But the cops still questioned me about Salina's death."

I gave him an incredulous expression. It's kind of like my "No way" look but not so out there. "They don't think you had anything to do with her death, do they?"

He shrugged. The movement was stiff. "I told them to look closer to home. Then Rivera himself comes and talks to me."

"The senator?"

"His son. The lieutenant. Came to my house. I told him I wanted to see a badge, but he said he just wanted to talk, off the record. You know what that means."

I shook my head. I felt a little cold.

"He got his ass suspended."

"Are you sure of that?"

"Are you kidding? You know what kind of ego it takes to become a cop? They'd give their kidneys for an excuse to flip open their badges. And Rivera's one of the worst.

Cocky as hell. But she left him, you know . . . for his old man. He couldn't take the embarrassment."

"You think he killed her?" My voice sounded hoarse.

"He was there, you know, at his old man's house, the night she died."

"I didn't know."

"The cops, they're closing ranks, saying it was natural causes. Peach asked around for me. Cardiomyopathy's their latest guess." He snorted in disbelief. "Maybe if she had congenital heart problems or coronary arterial disease, but Salina was as healthy as the proverbial horse. Hasn't had so much as the sniffles in years."

"Geez." I felt sick to my stomach. "You sound like a doctor."

He frowned.

"You're not a doctor, are you?"

He glanced to the left and slouched lower in his chair, the quintessential hipster. "I try not to spread it around here."

"You're joking."

He didn't say anything.

"You must be what . . . twenty?"

"Accelerated courses," he said, and sighed. "Peach and his cronies are dying to get their talons in me, but their projects . . ." He shook his head. "A cure for baldness? I mean, please. But if I keep them happy, they'll donate to the cause and I'll have time for some real work elsewhere."

"Such as?"

"We're losing a hundred thirty-seven *species* every single day. Not to mention one and a half acres of rain forest a second. That's where the money should be going. Wilderness restoration, not hair restoration. Nature holds a million medicinal secrets we've barely even begun to think about."

I refrained from blinking stupidly.

"And it's not just America. It's everywhere. The Amazon. It'd blow your mind if you knew. All the beauty. The potential. The loss. We've sent a team over. Lucky bastards." He shook his head, eyes bright. "The data they bring back. The samples." His mind seemed to be racing ahead of his words.

I remained silent, trying to keep up.

"Overpopulation." He scowled at his own thoughts. "People don't realize the immensity of the problem. We're encroaching on the wild places. And the lower the education, the higher the birthrate. Eighty percent of third-world countries can't afford decent contraceptives. They won't use condoms." He opened broad, capable hands in an expression of frustration.

"You're developing a birth control pill."

"Not a pill." He leaned toward me, intense, young, ridiculously good-looking. "A supplement. Like a vitamin. No side effects. It's a wonder drug. Women can take it without their husbands even knowing they..." He paused, laughed at himself, settled back again. "Sorry. Do you believe I came down here to relax? Mom said you only live once, so you might as well do it while you're young."

"So you met Salina here?" I asked, steering him carefully back on track.

"I thought at first that she was too stuffy. But..." He

tilted his head. Ken doll with a thousand-watt smile. "I was wrong. We had a lot of fun while it lasted."

"I miss her already," I said, and let the guilt wash over me and away like low tide. It's a gift, given to me by my Irish heritage and carefully honed through years of Catholic school. "When was the last time you saw her?"

He shook his head, thinking. "At least a year. Probably more. But Rivera still acted like I was as guilty as sin."

"The senator or—"

"The cop," he said, narrowing his eyes at my ignorance. "The one they found unconscious on her floor. But she got in a few good shots. Salina wouldn't go down without a fight."

"You do think he killed her."

He said nothing.

"But I heard there were no wounds."

He gave me a "You may actually be dumber than shit" look. "You think a Neanderthal like Rivera needs a Glock to kill a hundred-pound woman who threw him over for his old man?"

"I thought she didn't start dating the senator until long after she and the lieutenant were—"

He snorted. "Why do you think they broke up?"

So even he had heard the rumor. Not only heard it, *believed* it. Then again, maybe it was true. Maybe Salina had slept with the senator more than a decade ago and never gotten over him. "So he found out she was sleeping with his dad."

He nodded.

"But that was a long time ago."

"Yeah, but now the old man's going to marry her, shoving the whole thing in his face for the rest of his life. Christ, he'll have to tell his children that Grandpa stole his girl. If he gets over the trauma enough to ever copulate again."

I shook my head, feeling sick and a little disoriented. The truth was a twisted bed of snakes, impossible to untangle, even if I was stupid enough to try. "Wouldn't he take revenge on his father instead of—"

"Maybe he still plans to."

I felt my blood run cold. I was shaking my head. "That's crazy."

"It's a crazy world."

"Then how did he kill her?"

"You stop breathing, you stop living, Christina."

"You think he strangled her?"

"Strangulation is a crime of fierce passion. On the ecological and emotional scale, cops are just above the hyena."

"But there were no bruises."

"Who told you that?" he asked, eyes narrowing a little.

"I mean . . ." I refrained from clearing my throat. "At the visitation. It was an open casket."

"There are all kinds of ways to hide the bruising."

"You mean makeup and—" I began, but he suddenly reached out and took my hand.

I jumped like a virgin.

"We'll all miss her," he said.

"Yeah, yeah. She was . . . a good friend." Lame. "A good listener."

"Do you need someone to listen?" he asked, and squeezed my hand.

"Well..." I shifted uncomfortably. Was he coming on to me? And if so...*why?* "Sometimes...you know... Sometimes we all do."

"It's hard when a person we care about dies. Makes us remember our mortality. Makes us realize how alone we really are." He tilted his head, an animated Dr. Ken. Holy shit. "I'm an okay listener. Want to get a cup of coffee or something?"

"What?"

"Or we could just talk if—"

"No."

He raised his brows. Maybe a lot of people don't say no to Dr. Ken, at least not in that "I'm about to pass out" kind of tone.

"I mean..." I gave him a weak-assed smile and tugged my hand out of his. "Thank you. I'm flattered."

He smiled. If he was one-dimensional, you could have stuck him directly onto an Abercrombie & Fitch bag. "I wasn't trying to flatter you, Christina. I was just trying to be a friend."

"Well, I..." I jerked to my feet. "I'm sorry, I have to get home."

"Home?"

"To my husband...and kids."

His eyes widened. "Kids?"

"Five. Five kids. Tell me when you get that contraceptive perfected," I said, and fled.

19

In this town, a successful marriage is one that lasts
longer than ice.

—*Elaine Butterfield, whose*
parents were wed before
the dawn of time

LANEY?" I poked my head inside her apartment. For
reasons unknown to the average L.A. denizen, she doesn't
lock her doors. Maybe it's because every male between
Chatsworth and Laguna Beach would give his eyeballs,
and probably other types of balls, to protect her.

"Mac?" She came around a corner wearing a gray jogging suit and carrying a pair of scissors.

"Hey. You busy?"

She motioned me inside. "I just finished cutting Jeen's
hair."

I closed and locked the door behind me. Call me paranoid. "Doesn't he have a trillion dollars in the bank or something?"

"Only half a trillion."

"Enough to buy a hairstylist, then."

"But where would he keep her?" she asked, and took in my holey-kneed ensemble. "What's up?"

"Oh." I resisted doing the throat-clearing thing. "I was just spending some time at the library."

She made her way into the kitchen, where she found a broom in a closet the size of a peanut shell and began sweeping up the smattering of hair left behind by Jeen's head. I've found more in shower drains. "Which library?"

"Powell," I said, and nonchalantly lifted an unidentifiable object from a basket on her kitchen table. It might have been a fruit. Or possibly a small alien.

"At UCLA?"

I nodded, all casual.

She gave me a look. "You know there's a library not ten minutes from your house, don't you?"

"I was doing some specific research."

She raised one brow. "Regarding a client?"

I felt my face get hot. I'm all for flexible truths, but lying to Laney is like spitting on the pope. "Ummm . . ."

"Babykins," said Solberg, emerging from the bathroom down the hall. I put my back against the wall, hoping to fend off a hug. J. D. Solberg was unforgivably forgiving. "What are you doing here?"

"I was just—" I began, but Elaine cut in.

"Lying to me," she said.

"What?" He glanced from her to me, looking bemused—his best expression.

"I am not," I countered, but my defenses were weak.

"Really?" She put away the broom and faced me. "What exactly were you researching, then, Mac?"

I scowled at her. "Deviant behavior."

"Of college students?"

"Do you know a more deviant group?"

She watched me. "So," she said finally, "was he in love with her?"

"Who?"

"The poor kid you went to grill about Salina."

"I didn't . . ." I began, but she had already propped a fist on a practically nonexistent hip.

"Damn it, Laney." I sounded whiny even to myself. "I hate it when you know stuff."

"You promised you were going to stay out of this."

"I know. I know I did, but . . ." I paused, and collapsed into a straightback chair beside the little alien. "What do you know about strangulation?"

Laney stared at me.

Solberg's eyebrows popped into his hairline. It was a reach. "You think she was strangled? I didn't—"

"No," Laney said, jabbing a finger at me. "No, you don't, Mac. Not again." Her eyes were as bright as a bonfire.

"Listen. It's probably nothing," I said. "I'm just curious."

"Curious? First you're curious, then all of a sudden guys with too much testosterone are shoving you into Cadillacs and breathing garlic on you."

I tried to argue, but Laney has a fabulous memory for detail and just hearing the words made me feel nauseous.

"I know." I slumped forward. "But I . . . What am I going to do?"

"About what?"

"What if he did it?" I whispered.

Her gaze was stuck fast on mine. "If he did it, Mac, it's got nothing to do with you."

"But he—"

"Sometimes we just fall for the wrong guys."

"She's fallen for a guy?" Solberg chirped.

"Sometimes. Sometimes?" I rose to my feet with a snap. "Holy crap, Laney, *all* the time. I could start a club."

"Not all the time."

"Who, then?" I asked, throwing out the gauntlet.

"Eddie Friar."

"He's gay."

"But he's nice."

"He's gay!"

"Okay. Fine." She sounded miffed that I would take such a small offense into consideration when regarding my love life. "Jay Bintliff."

"Lived with his brother."

"What's wrong with—"

"*Slept* with his brother."

"No kidding?" Solberg chimed in, but Laney was undeterred.

"Robbie Going."

"Stole twenty bucks out of my underwear drawer."

"You keep money in your—"

"Zach—" Laney began, but I was already giving her the evil eye.

"Please," I said, and sank back into my chair.

"What?" Solberg was all but hopping from foot to foot. "What about Zach?"

Elaine was scowling. "Hey," she said suddenly. "There's the guy in Norwalk."

"The guy that changed my flat?"

"Yes."

"I never saw him again."

It looked like she was going to continue, but I think I'd exhausted her optimism. She dropped to her knees and took my hand in hers.

"It's not you, Mac. It's them."

"All of them?"

"Yes."

I looked away. "I just thought, you know, this once, maybe..."

"He accused you of murder."

"I know, but he's—"

"And now *he's* a murder suspect. It's not a good trend."

I caught her eye, slumped back in the chair, and laughed. "You think?"

"What...? Who...?" Solberg sucked in a sudden breath and came up with the next best thing to cursing. "Jumping cockroaches. She's got the hots for Rivera?"

I ignored him. "I don't know what's wrong with me, Laney."

"Nothing. Nothing's—"

"Chrissy, babe, you're crushing on—"

"Jeen," Elaine interrupted, patient as a monk. "Could you please make us some chamomile?"

He looked from me to her to me, then, "Sure. You bet,"

he said, but he was grinning like an inebriated ass when he turned away. "Rivera and Chrissy sittin' in a tree . . ."

I closed my eyes and refrained from killing him, not quite so monklike.

"It'll be okay," Laney said.

"I didn't even know they'd been engaged."

"How could you?"

I shrugged. "Hire a PI?"

"You're going to investigate every man you date?"

"The number of potential dates is decreasing in direct proportion to my ice-cream consumption," I assured her. "I don't think it's going to be that hard."

She laughed and settled back on her heels. "What'd you learn tonight?"

"Nothing. This kid, a plugged-in Ken doll, had a fling with Salina, but it's been over for years."

"Who is he?"

"Daniel Hohl."

"Hohl?" Solberg turned from the stove with a snap. "Of the carpet empire Hohls?"

I stared at him, then at Laney. She shrugged.

"There are carpet empire Hohls?"

"Well, carpets, computers, pharmaceuticals, politics. They got their fingers in half a dozen pies. They could buy and sell NeoTech, and me with it."

If only. Buy him, stamp him, and ship him off to Istanbul.

Laney scowled. "You think this Hohl guy might have had something to do with Salina's death?"

"I don't know. He says he moved on. And I saw him with some blonde with legs up to her cheekbones . . . which are way the hell up there." My own cheekbones are even with my mouth. I rested the back of my head on the top of the chair and didn't mention the fact that Hohl had seemed to be coming on to me. Flattering, in a surreal sort of way. "He thinks Rivera's guilty as sin. On the other hand, *Mrs.* Rivera is convinced the senator did it. And all the while, the police seem to be saying Salina died of a heart problem of some sort."

She scowled. "I thought the senator was on a plane."

"That didn't seem to alter his wife's opinion. Said things aren't always what they seem, or something like that."

"Well, she's right there."

"True. But generally, when it seems like someone's on a plane, he's really on the plane. I called and checked. He was on the plane."

"Or someone who looked like him."

"What are you...?" I dropped my jaw. "What's that called? When they find someone to—"

"Body double," Solberg supplied, not moving from the stove. Laney doesn't have a microwave. Something about depletion of nutrition. Or maybe she just likes to give Nerd Boy something to do.

"How hard would it be?" I asked.

"I was just speaking metaphorically," she said, and shrugged. Solberg trooped out of the kitchen and handed her a wooden bowl. She thanked him with a smile, took a few grainy-looking nuggets, and passed it on to me. I tried a sample. It tasted like navel lint. I took a handful.

"How hard?" I was scowling and munching. Navel lint's not all that bad if you eat it fast.

She didn't respond.

"Rivera thinks she intended to leave the senator."

"Okay, but so what? People leave people all the time. They don't usually . . . kill them by natural causes."

"I didn't say it made sense, but if . . ." The brain waves were really snapping out impulses now. Must have been the lint. "Say the senator did get a body double . . ."

"Which is ridiculous."

"In Hollywood?"

"This is megacool," Solberg whispered.

"If he did have one, do you suppose he'd be, like . . . an actor?"

"Mac—"

"Could the senator have hired an actor?"

"I guess it's feasible."

"Would he use the same kind of talent agencies you do?"

"This is crazy."

"Don't you know that agent guy? What's his name?"

"Bud Freidman?" Solberg supplied.

For a moment Laney almost looked peeved.

"Yeah," I said. "Didn't he want to nominate you Queen Goddess of the Universe or something?"

"Mac—"

"Laney." I cut her off before she could start the speech about not wanting me to die again. "Rivera did not simply hit his head and pass out. That's asinine. Something happened. I just want to find out what it was."

"Okay," she said finally. "I'll check into the body double thing. But you have to promise that when I come up empty, you'll drop it."

"Of course."

"I mean it, Mac. Promise me."

"I love you, Laney," I said.

"What about me?" Solberg asked, putting his hands on her shoulders.

"You," I said, staring at the two of them together—Beauty and the Geekster—"have obviously made some kind of ungodly pact with the devil. I want nothing to do with that."

"Thank God love is blind."

"That's the second time I've heard that this week."

"When was the first?"

"Ummm," I said, remembering Rachel and the fact that I had promised to keep my nose clean. "I think I said it in my sleep."

"So where was Hohl the night she died?" Solberg asked.

"Who else have you been talking to?" Laney said suspiciously.

"I'm sorry. Jeen was talking," I said, and turned solicitously to Solberg. "What did you say?"

"This Hohl kid. Just 'cuz he's good-looking don't mean he's innocent."

"How do you know he's good-looking?"

"Saw him once on television. He's like some kind of boy genius."

"What was he doing?" I munched. "On television."

He shook his wobbly head. "Research for some big-ass—sorry, big-butt drug company."

"For a new contraceptive?"

"Can't remember."

"Can you find out?"

He opened his mouth. I thought I saw the word "cell mate" forming. I raised one brow and emitted the thought *"Big Cheese."*

"Sure," he said. "No problem."

20

In the movie business, the ones we call lucky are usually those idiots who are just too damned stub born to take no for an answer. Come to think of it, the movie business is kind of like life.

—*Bud Freidman, talent agent*

I RECEIVED THE PHOTOS of the crime scene via e-mail sometime before I returned home. Solberg had sent a lot of them. My little computer droned grumpily under the deluge, but I diligently thrashed through them.

There wasn't much to see. No blood, no weapons, no masked men looking guilty. Just a walk through a big-ass house—oh, and one dead body. I studied Salina's corpse thoroughly, but if there were clues, I couldn't see them. I'd been right about her skin. It was perfect, not a bruise to be seen on her throat or elsewhere.

As for the house, it was tidy, expensively furnished, but cozy. The kitchen was the only room that showed any disarray. Cookies cooled on a wire rack. A couple of flow-ered plates stood upright in one sink, while a few more soaked in the other. A blue rubber glove drooped be-tween the two. A stemmed glass showed a crescent of red lipstick. Flour was sprinkled across the counter, and three lone chocolate chips lay beside a basket of fruit.

I was still thinking about the chips when I reached work the next day.

"Good morning." Elaine was unusually perky. I mean, she's usually perky, but that morning, she looked like a lit-tle songbird just popping out of its shell. Her happiness made me feel a little insecure, since I'd left her alone with Solberg the night before. In some dark corner of my way-ward mind, I probably knew the two of them were doing more than holding hands, but I didn't let myself think about it on an empty stomach. Which mine was. I'd got-ten up late and had to rush off to the office. Elaine looked like she'd had a good fourteen hours of sleep, done her yoga, and been kissed by the happy fairy.

"Morning," I managed.

"I have some news," she said.

"Yeah?" I dropped my purse onto the chair and un-buttoned my jacket. "Good news or—" But suddenly my mind went cold. Premonition loomed like a nuclear cloud. I turned, blinking at her through the chilly fog. "Laney, tell me you're not pregnant."

Her eyebrows did that funny little quirky thing they do. "Holy crap, Mac, what's wrong with you? Did you visit Mrs. Rivera again?"

"No. I . . . No," I said, and took a steadying breath as I drew off my jacket. "Sorry. What's your news?"

"I'm pregnant!"

I tried to scream, but this was one of those calamities that defies all kinds of normal responses. I stood gaping at her, frozen in horror.

She stared at me, happy as a hundred-dollar bill, then, "Geez, Mac, I'm kidding. I'm joking. Here." She hurried around the corner of her desk and grasped my arm firmly above the elbow. "You'd better sit down."

I did, levering myself into the chair like a dementia victim. "You're joking?"

"Of course I am. It's still too early to be sure."

"What!"

"Still joking."

"I hate you."

She laughed. "Wouldn't it be great, though? Can you imagine what Dad would say?"

"That a woman should not lie with the beasts of the fields."

She ignored me. "Maybe we'll have a son who looks just like Jeen." Her expression was goofy. She'd obviously gone mad. "We'll name him after you."

"Jesus," I said.

"No, Christopher. Christopher Jeen Solberg."

"You were such a nice little kid." I stared at the wall behind her desk, still hazy. "I remember it well—buck teeth, scraggly hair. Ugly as sin, sweet as a dumpling."

She laughed.

"Honestly, Laney, I don't know why you got so mean."

"It'll come to you," she said, then, "So, good news or bad news first?"

I was beginning to get the feeling back in my hands.

The thought of Solberg procreating always makes me go numb. The thought of him procreating with Laney makes me want to crawl into my refrigerator and never come out. I felt discombobulated. "Good . . . no, bad . . . Good!" She was staring at me like I'd lost my mind. But what did she expect? "How bad is the bad?" I asked.

"Oh, for heaven's sake. Jeen got some information about Hohl," she said.

"And?"

Standing up, she lifted a file from her desk and handed it to me. I flipped it open. A grainy photocopy lay at the top of the pile. I skimmed the article, but my attention was really snagged by the photo. It was Daniel in front of a cluttered white board, his face emitting scientific zeal as he addressed an enraptured audience of supergeeks. Peachtree was standing off to one side, looking proud and leaning on a thick, silver-knobbed cane.

"There are other photos," she said, "but Jeen was having trouble getting them to you via e-mail." Because my computer was still pouting. "So he just printed them."

I flipped through them. There were several of Salina. More of Daniel. He looked damned good in formal wear. A banner that read "True Health" was draped above the heads of the revelers. I glanced up. "Is this the good news or the bad news?"

She scowled. "I'm afraid it's only going to encourage you to do more of your life-threatening snooping."

"Ahhh. So what's the good news."

She drew her shoulders back dramatically and straightened to her full height. Then she turned with haughty slowness to stare at me in regal retrospect. I stared dumbly back, but suddenly it hit me.

"Holy crap!" I could barely breathe the words.

Her eyes were gleaming. Her mouth trembled a little.

I stumbled to my feet. "You got the part."

She curled her fingers against her mouth and nodded, eyes misty.

"You're Xena."

"They said I was perfect."

"Oh, Laney." I pulled her into a hug. "You *are* perfect. You are." I shook my head. "I just . . . This is . . ." I paused, stunned to silence as I pushed her to arm's length. "You did it."

She nodded, eyes damp.

As for myself, I was crying full out. "I can't believe it."

"We're supposed to start filming next week."

"You're kidding."

"On Tuesday."

"I'm so . . ." Overwhelmed. "I am so proud of you."

"What are we going to do?"

"Do? Oh, I don't know." I rolled my eyes and cackled a laugh. "Turn them down?"

"What about my job here?"

I gaped at her. "What about it?"

"You need a receptionist."

"Oh, no," I said, squeezing her arms. "You're not going to feel bad about this." I leaned forward, staring into her eyes. "This is why you left sunny Chicago."

"I know, but we'll be filming in Oregon."

I felt momentarily stunned. She wouldn't be here every

morning to pull me out of the pit of myself. "Well, that's only . . ." Half a continent away. "Not so far."

"You're the greatest, Mac," she said.

And I laughed. "Geez, Laney, I'm so happy I could kiss you!"

I couldn't tell if she was laughing or crying. "You say that to all the girls."

I pulled her in and kissed her on the lips just as the door dinged behind me.

We glanced at it in unison.

"Mrs. Trudeau," Laney said.

The church lady glared at us, backlit by the glass door.

"You're here bright and early."

Her lips were pursed, her eyes squinty. "I have a nine o'clock appointment."

It wasn't yet 8:45.

Laney smiled. "She who rises with the sun rises with God. That's what my father always said."

"Your father . . ."

"A Methodist minister," Laney said, and gave Mrs. Trudeau another thousand watts. "He would appreciate your punctuality."

"I try to be on time." She was giving me the evil eye, but her heart wasn't in it. *It's almost impossible to be really nasty when Brainy Laney turns on the charm,* I thought. And in that moment I realized the truth. Everything wasn't all right. I couldn't live without Elaine.

*T*welve hours later I was already finished for the day. Determined to ignore the funk caused by Elaine's looming departure, I'd offered to take her out to celebrate, but she hadn't informed Jeen of the impending life change and thought she should do so soon.

I didn't tell her how much it meant to me that she'd told me first. I also didn't tell her I was pretty sure I would be unable to function without her behind the front desk. What a brave little soldier I am.

By the time I reached home I felt like I'd been charged with high treason and faced a firing squad. There were two overdue bills in my mailbox, an oversized dog on the counter, ears flattened by the ceiling, and a message from Mom on my answering machine.

I shoved the bills in a cubby I have for things I hope to forget about, coaxed Harlequin off the counter with a chunk of green cheese, and listened to the message.

Holly was due to deliver in three months. So far, she still refused to marry Pete. Which impressed me no end, since having a melon-size being growing in your belly has to put a lot of pressure on a girl as far as husband-finding goes. Then there's Mom. She could put pressure on a rock.

In fact, she had called to say that if I didn't tell Holly to marry Pete posthaste, well, I was just going to have to live with my conscience.

The entire message made me sit down and think. I mean, ten years ago, she would have had a lot more ammo than a guilty conscience. Please. I had a shitload of more interesting stuff to feel guilty about.

The fact that, despite my love for Laney, I was feeling a little bit depressed by her success, for instance. She'd finally gotten her big break. And that was great. But it seemed sometimes that life was speeding by, leaving me in its dusty wake. Laney had made her dreams come true, Solberg had gotten Laney. Even my brother Pete was progressing. True, troglodytes tend to procreate like champions, and any imbecile with a functioning brain cell and a couple good swimmers can spawn, but still . . .

No. I rose to my feet, cleared my dishes . . . well, dish . . . and gave myself a firm talking to. I had a good career, a nice house, and I was seeing someone. Well, okay, my career involved pretty much doing the same thing I did as a cocktail waitress—listening to people's problems, sans the tips. My septic system was plotting world domination, and the guy I was seeing was a possible murderer.

So there might be better things to do than slurp down a hundred thousand calories and ruminate on my brother's ability to procreate. Such as sleuthing.

Three hours later, I had no proof of Rivera's guilt or innocence. I had Googled Daniel Hohl. There was a shit-load of stuff about him. Some of it simply echoed what I already knew. Some of it was about his environmental efforts, some about his work with needleless medications. In January he had spearheaded True Health, a small but avant garde nonprofit company that had attracted some of the brightest minds in the world. He was a scientist, a doctor, a fiancé. My mind stopped and spun backward. He was engaged? I clicked to the photo. I wasn't sure, but I thought his engagee, Cindy Peichel, was the same girl I'd seen at Salina's visitation. Pretty, blond, leggy. So why the hell was he coming on to me? Was I getting close to something . . . or was he just a man?

"Cindy Peichel." I said the name out loud, then on a whim did an Internet search for her. Nothing came up besides her noteworthy engagement. Daniel Hohl was Boy Wonder, son of Mr. and Mrs. Boy Wonder. *She* was, well . . . an employee of the State of California.

Nothing much else was revealed.

I scowled at my screen. That was strange. I mean, Hohl came from a family that seemed to have one degree of separation from God himself. Surely he wouldn't just marry a nobody. She had to have roots, and probably a buttload of money.

Or maybe she was some penniless hick from Elkhorn, Alabama, who had taken on a false identity, seduced him, and planned to steal his family fortune. Maybe she'd killed Salina. Believe me, stranger things have happened.

Then again, maybe he was actually marrying her for love.

I glanced at their engagement photo again. They were as pretty as poetry. As pretty as Rivera and Salina would have been together, fighting crime and making babies.

I sighed. My mood was taking a belly flop. I thought about Holly and Pete and the little troglodyte-to-be.

Depressed, I stood up. Harlequin thumped his tail against the floor and lifted his head. I stroked his ears and stared at the phone. It scowled back at me.

"Listen," I said, "it's not my fault my brothers are cretins. I mean, against all odds, Holly's no fool. What am I supposed to do about that? Tell her to suck it up and marry some nimrod who made me eat sheep droppings as a kid? Hey, so baby's not going to inherit the revered McMullen name. Big deal."

Harlequin dropped his head and rolled up big sad eyes.

"Oh, for crying out loud," I said, and dialed the phone.

21

There isn't much a pan of warm brownies and a glass of milk won't fix. Unless it's low grain prices. Or poverty. Or the national debt. I guess there are a few things, but nothing you have to worry about right this minute.

—Mavis McMullen, Chrissy's
favorite aunt

QUESTIONS NAGGED ME. Was Hohl correct? Had Rivera been suspended? And if so, how would he cope? He was a cop through to his soul. It was more than what he did. It was what he was. A small child grown, needing to find value despite his father's disapproval. Maybe it's what we all were.

Holy crap, I was philosophical, but the memory of his haunted eyes disturbed my sleep, making me jittery and restless. The week had slipped away from me. Saturday morning dawned gray and uncertain. I fought for good sense, lost, and finally called Rivera. He didn't answer.

I glanced around, feeling disoriented. My little house

was dirty, I had laundry piled up to my chin, and if I didn't go jogging soon, my fat molecules would eat my lungs. But I turned back to my desk and spent the morning alternating between the Internet and the phone.

I knew I shouldn't. Told myself the same.

But a couple of things kept bothering me. If Danny Hohl hadn't seen Salina in more than a year, how did he know she never got the sniffles? And if he was engaged, why was he holding my hand? And how the hell was I supposed to believe that a man, any man, would lose interest in Salma Hayek?

By noon I finally hit pay dirt. At 1:25 I was chugging down the 5 toward the Los Angeles Zoo and Botanical Gardens. I admit it was no coincidence that that's where Cindy Peichel worked. Two hours of slogging investigation had told me as much.

Ponytail stuck through the hole of a Dodgers baseball cap, I hurried down blacktop walkways and wound my way past the ATM machines and choo-choo train. A group of kids in party hats were hopping and screaming and crying in front of the flamingo pond. A little girl dressed all in pink seemed to have a lollypop stuck in her hair. Grape, I think. Danny Hohl's work in contraceptives had never seemed more important.

The World of Birds show had already begun. I climbed up the bleachers and sat among a few dozen other zoo-goers. Down below, two guys were holding large, angry-looking predators on their gauntleted wrists.

"But perhaps most spectacular of all," said a disembodied voice, "is the golden eagle."

A bird the size of an SUV swooped out of nowhere,

dove low over the gasping crowd, then flew a high circuit in the metal gray sky.

The voice chanted about wingspan and thermals. The bird dipped and soared, then swooped back over us to land with a flourish on a strategically outstretched arm.

It wasn't until that moment I realized a woman had joined the guys on the woodsy stage. She was somber, tall, tan. It took me a minute to be sure it was her. Cindy Peichel. Fishing binoculars from my earth-friendly cotton bag, I studied her with the rest of the mesmerized mob.

She looked somewhat older through the glasses. Fine lines crinkled the corners of her eyes and the beginnings of a single crease showed between her brows, as if she'd spent some time gazing at distant horizons.

Her hair was the color of Cousin Kevin's wheat fields and her stance was straight. At the visitation I had only seen her from the back and had assumed she played Barbie to Daniel's Ken. Now I wasn't so sure. Barbie looked like she might be able to handle herself in a street brawl.

"With your help we can save these wonderful creatures," she was saying, and maybe it was just rote, but there seemed to be a certain amount of zeal in her voice. "For ourselves and for generations to come."

The threesome remained onstage for a while, displaying the grouchy predators to the *ooh*ing audience. As for me, I'd come prepared. Keeping an eye on the bird folk, I slipped behind a wooden building, removed my jacket and cap, and popped them into my bag. Pulling the binder from my hair, I sauntered toward the Zoopendous Center, gazing at nothing in particular through my binoculars.

It took almost fifteen minutes for Peichel to emerge from the aviary. I followed at a safe distance, pausing now and again to pretend to read a placard.

She finally stopped at a brightly colored food stand, paid for an order of fries, and sat down at one of the umbrellaed tables. I stood in line and pretended to study the menu. She didn't seem to be going anywhere too fast. The line moved along. I ordered an ice cream parfait with hot fudge and peanuts so that I wouldn't look conspicuous. What a trooper.

Then, juggling the plastic dish and my bag, I skirted her table and stopped.

"Excuse me," I said.

The crease between her eyes deepened a little as she glanced up at me, and I could see now that freckles were sprinkled across the bridge of her nose. She wore absolutely no makeup. That could only mean one of two things: She'd had to rush off to work that morning, or she was the bravest woman I had ever met.

"Yes?"

"Hi." I reached out, still fumbling with the bag and laughing a little at my own ineptitude. I may be as batty as hell, but I was becoming a kick-ass actress. If Laney ever needed pointers... "I've seen you at the aviary several times. I try to come at least once a month."

"Oh." She wasn't the type who felt a need to smile for social acceptability. Which didn't seem quite appropriate for her stage persona. So perhaps it was her environmental fervor that had helped her land her current job. Or her fiancé's clout. "You enjoy the birds?"

"They're wonderful. Awe-inspiring, really. So beautiful."

"Yes, they are."

"I think we may have met before. I volunteer at the Northridge Nature Center from time to time."

My ice cream was beginning to drip. I made helpless motions with my hands.

"Have a seat," she said, still somber.

"Thank you."

"So you work with Chip there?"

I glanced up, deer in the headlights. Who the hell was Chip? Or *what*? I took a spoonful of heaven, but wasn't able to appreciate it fully, what with Eagle Woman gazing at me. "I don't get there nearly as much as I'd like."

She was neglecting her fries. "You should make more time," she said. "They have a good program there."

"Don't I know it. But my company is on the verge of a big—" I made air quotations. "—hair restoration breakthrough, and I'm working overtime—"

"Hair restoration?"

"Yeah. Sharpe Pharmaceuticals. They're treating the introduction of this product like Christ's second coming. Like the planet's biggest problem is follicular failure. Don't they know we're losing one hundred and thirty-seven species a day?" I was chanting Hohl's words to her, reeling her in with our common bond. Maybe.

She was watching me closely. My nerves felt like they'd been bleached and hung out to dry. I couldn't even guess what she was thinking, so I shoveled in some calories.

"Well, that's two things we have in common," she said.

I wiped ice cream off my hand. "You're a messy eater, too?"

Her lips quirked up the slightest degree. "My fiancé works for Sharpe. Not on hair loss. Improving contraceptives mostly. The funding is for human use, of course, but it could be a huge boon to the veterinary industry, too. Less danger to the handler. Less stress to the animal. It's only a small step from there to its use on exotics."

I'd been right. She was a zealot. "That's fascinating," I said. "What's your fiancé's name?"

"Daniel Hohl."

"Danny?" I gave her my surprised face. "I thought he was . . ." I stopped the spoon halfway to my mouth, eyes wide. Move over, Meryl Streep.

"What?" Her tone was level, her expression unchanged.

"Nothing. I'm sorry." I didn't have to will myself to blush. I was sweating like a fat quarterback. "What a coincidence," I mumbled, and shoveled in ice cream.

"What were you going to say?"

"I just . . ." I shoved my spoon into the parfait and fidgeted. "I just thought he was still dating Salina Martinez when she . . . when she passed on."

She was watching me. I shifted my eyes away, but every twitching fiber in my being was testing her reactions. Was she tense? Angry? She could stare down an eagle in full flight. How the hell was a mere cocktail chick turned shrink supposed to know what she was thinking?

"What made you believe that?" she asked finally. Her tone was reserved. She was leaning back in her chair, almost casual, but not quite.

"Nothing. I just always thought . . ." I squirmed in my chair. "They were such a . . ."

"A beautiful couple?"

"I'm sorry." I really was. Possibly the sorriest creature on the planet.

"So you saw them together?"

"No." I avoided her eyes. "I just saw them . . . separately, and thought, you know . . . Oh God, I'm so sorry. Danny seems like a perfectly nice guy. I didn't mean to cast suspicion." But I had, of course. I was no better than Rachel Banks, except I was trying to ferret out a murderer. Just doing my civic duty. Or was I simply trying to prove I couldn't possibly have fallen for a murderer? Was I willing to sacrifice this woman's future to ascertain that fact? It looked like it. Then again, if she was truly in love, she wouldn't let silly innuendo ruin her relationship. It would probably make their bond stronger.

Holy shit, I was obviously in need of professional counseling.

"When did you see them?" she asked.

"What?"

"When were they together? What were they doing?"

There was an edginess to her voice now, but was it smoldering fury or fresh-cut rage? Was it killing emotion or passing curiosity?

"I'm sure he's much better off with you," I said.

She stared at me, assessing. "I'll be sure to ask him if he agrees," she said. Her voice was clipped. "He's meeting me for lunch."

"I didn't mean—" My mind clicked in. "Here?" I asked.

"He tries to stop by on Saturdays. He's very thoughtful

that way." Her left hand was gripping the arm of her chair. Did the knuckles look white against the dark metal? "You should stay and say hi."

"Sure," I said, and making the bravest and most desperate move of my life, spilled the parfait into my lap. It soaked my T-shirt and seeped with chilly justice into my jeans. "Oh." I stumbled to my feet. "Oh, no."

She was still watching me with those osprey eyes. "I have a clean set of clothes in my Jeep if you want to change."

"No. No. I'll just . . . I have to get home anyway." The ice cream slid down my pants and plopped onto my shoe, leaving two peanuts beside the zipper. "Ohh." It sounded like I was going to cry. I wasn't that far off. My feelings for ice cream run deep. And ruining someone's chances at happily ever after isn't that great, either. "Well . . ." From the corner of my eye I thought I saw a tall blond Ken doll moving through the smattered crowd. "It was great meeting you."

"Again," she said.

"What? Oh . . . yes." I was already moving away, face burning, leaving the ice cream where it lay, melting morosely on the concrete. "Again. Good-bye."

I rushed into the mob and popped around the corner of the treetop terrace, mumbling prayers and curses.

From across the way, a red ape pointed and chuckled.

"Ms. McMullen?"

I jerked around, squawked like a macaw, and froze, shirt sticking to my belly like flypaper.

"What the hell happened to you?"

I looked up. An elderly gentleman with a cane and cowboy hat was watching me.

"Robert Peachtree," he said. "Peach to my friends. We met at the visitation. I would shake your hand but . . ." He indicated my stickiness and gave me a big old Texas grin.

"I had a little accident."

"I can see that. What are you doing here?"

"Just . . . Just visiting the . . ." I glanced to my left. The ape was still laughing. "The monkeys. How 'bout you?"

"Oh, business." He wore sandals with socks, but his ginormous belt buckle was firmly in place. "Always business. I was hoping to catch up with Danny. Daniel Hohl. You know him?"

"Hohl? Danny Hohl?" I shook my head, still wiping ineffectively at the ice cream and lying for all I was worth.

He scanned the crowd. "We got a deal in the works, gonna make a bushel of money."

"So . . ." I calmed myself and took a stab in the dark. "No more baldness?"

He looked surprised. "Now, who told you 'bout that?"

"I keep my ear to the ground."

He laughed. "Quick as a wink I'll have more hair than them apes. But Sharpe Pharmaceuticals is about more than that." Taking his hat off, he ran his hand through the few wisps that had survived past his prime. "Near as that is to my heart. Hey, have you given any thought to my offer?"

"Offer?"

He chuckled. "I'm gonna take that as a no. But you should think about it, young lady. Sharpe could offer you a bunch."

I quit wiping to watch him with raised brows. "Why me? I'm not famous. I'm not even a doctor."

He shook his head. "I ain't the kind to care how many fancy titles folks have collected." He pursed his narrow lips and stared at me. "I'm a good judge of people, can tell stuff just to look at 'em. And I know this much just by lookin': You'd do the job, all right." He nodded. "You're what I like to call dirt smart."

The ice cream was beginning to dry. Dust from the walkway had adhered to the goo, making the fabric stiff. I cleared my throat. "I think you mean dirty."

He laughed. Digging his wallet out of his back pocket, he pulled out a card and handed it over. "There's the number for my ranch." He pointed to a row of digits with a fingernail yellowed by time. "But here . . ." He shifted to another set of numerals. "We got us a little place in town. You can reach me there. Come by and talk to Dottie and me sometime."

"I would love to, but—"

He held up a hand. "I know what you're gonna say. You're doing fine on your own. You modern gals." He shook his head and grinned. According to one of my Internet scavenger hunts, he'd been a looker in his day. A looker and a lightning-quick shortstop for the Houston Astros. Dottie had found herself a keeper. "You remind me of my Anna. Independent as a mustang. But everybody can use a few more bucks in their woods, huh?"

"Ummm . . ."

"Just give me a call sometime. Better yet, you stop by next Saturday. In the afternoon sometime. Dottie'd love to fuss over you."

"Okay." Even though I was flattered, I had no intention of stopping in. But the drying ice cream was beginning to itch. I was ready to beat a hasty retreat. "Thank you."

"Thank *you*," he said, and stumped happily into the crowd.

22

I been a little cranky since that house fell on my sister.

—*Grandma Ella, who didn't have a sister*

ON SUNDAY we ran an ad for a receptionist in the *Times*. Laney was nervous about it. But I assured her everything would be fine. We live in L.A. Twenty-four hours from now we'd have her replacement, an international supermodel who performed brain surgery on the side.

That night we dined at the Gardens restaurant in Beverly Hills, where the patrons didn't seem to be tempted to abscond with the silver and the desserts are high caloric enough to make a grown woman cry. It was my treat.

By eight o'clock I was stuffed to the eyeballs. Laney had eaten a plate of something that may have been plucked off a Swiss hillside and marinated in lemon juice, but I didn't ask what it was. Instead, I raised my champagne glass. She was actually sharing in the toast. "To you," I said.

She clicked her glass against mine and smiled. "I still can't believe it."

"Tell me all about it."

"I don't know anything yet," she said, but Laney's not knowing is nothing like anyone else's not knowing. She talked for fifteen minutes about actors I'd never heard of with terms I didn't know. It made me kinda melancholy. My little girl was growing up.

"How did Solberg take the news?"

She shrugged, glanced at her flute, and swished her drink a little. I think there might have been more than when the waiter had first poured it. "Okay."

"Okay as in he's happy for you, or okay as in he cried like a baby?"

She glanced up. "He didn't cry . . . like a baby."

"Just a little bit, then?"

"Hardly at all."

I resisted laughing. It wasn't that hard. I felt kind of close to tears myself.

"I think he's afraid I'm going to meet someone else." She sighed, set down her glass. Our waiter, tall, dark, and earnest, appeared in a heartbeat, asking if all was well. Was the champagne satisfactory? Was she feeling okay? Would she run off to Vegas and be his teddy bear? It had been like this for over a decade. If Laney looked unhappy, the male half of the population went into crisis mode. What would it be like when she became a star? She gave the server a smile and sent him away. His knees held up under her attention. "How could he think I'd want someone else?"

I returned my attention to the matter at hand, then set my wineglass down and looked at her. "Are we talking about Solberg?"

She gave me a "Who else?" expression. Apparently, she hadn't noticed our waiter had a chin dimple deep enough to drown in . . . while her boy Solberg made you *want* to drown. "Well . . ." I began, but she stopped me with a glance.

"I'm really happy for you," I said.

She smiled, nodded, fiddled with her glass. "What about you, though?"

"What about me what?"

"Come on, Mac, the police are calling Salina's death accidental. Why can't you do the same?"

I shrugged, drank, thought of the seventy-six men who had come and gone before Rivera. "You didn't hear back from that talent agent yet, huh?"

She took a drink of champagne. An actual sip. I watched her. She didn't meet my gaze. "What talent agent?"

"The one you were going to call to see if the senator had—" I stopped when I recognized her expression. It was the same look she'd had at thirteen when she'd confessed our experimental smoking to her father. And while confession might indeed be good for the soul, her declaration hadn't been a real boon for me. I became guilty by association . . . or by the fact that it was my idea, my money, and my cousin who had made the purchase. It was also, as I recall, me who was forced to smoke a full pack of Camels in one sitting. It had been the best part of my day. "Laney?" I said.

"What?" Her tone was a surefire meld between innocence and defensiveness.

I felt the air leave my lungs. "Holy crap," I said, "he has a double."

"Listen, Mac, I don't know that for—"

I felt numb from the waist up. "He hired a double . . . some guy to take his place on the plane. Which means the senator was—"

"We don't know any of this."

I stared at her. My lungs felt icy. "What *do* we know?"

She blew out a breath. "Bud said there used to be a guy in the business who might fit the description."

"What description?"

"Tall, Hispanic, handsome. Similar to Senator Rivera."

"What's his name?"

"I don't know."

"Was he working as a body double on March third?"

"I don't even know if he's still alive."

"You don't know or you won't tell me?"

"Let it go, Mac."

"Do you think the police know about him?"

"They're calling it natural causes."

"I need to talk to him," I said.

She opened her mouth as if to speak, but I beat her to the punch.

"What if the police are wrong? Or covering up?"

"You're jumping to—"

"What if the senator killed her?"

"Then that means the lieutenant didn't. We could have a party."

"But his father did? Is that any better? What would that do to Rivera's psyche? He's already half crazy. And what if the senator didn't do it? Then who did?"

"Maybe the LAPD is right. Maybe no one did."

I gave her a look.

She scowled back in angry defense.

"Do you have his address?"

"Whose?"

"Phone number?"

"I don't know what you're talking about."

"Laney—"

"Is it so bad that I want to keep you alive, Mac? Is that so terrible?"

"I can't just bury my head in the sand, Laney."

"Want to be cremated instead?"

"You're being—"

"What? Protective? Yeah, I am. And you know why? 'Cuz I care about you. And I'm not going to be here to look after you once the filming starts, Mac. What if something happens? What if you're right and you do something stupid?"

I wanted to tell her that I wasn't going to do anything stupid, but I'm not that good at lying.

"I've got to know what happened," I said.

She didn't respond.

"You know I do, Laney. Think about my track record."

She was still scowling.

"Jay Bintliff," I said.

Her scowl deepened.

"I told you he shared a bed with his brother. What I didn't tell you is that he—"

"Here," she said, and tossed a scrap of paper at me.

I read it out loud. "Julio Manderos."

"Are you happy now?"

"Do you know where I can find him?"

"Who?"

"Would you like me to tell you what Jay and his brother did on Saturdays when—"

"Strip Please!" she snapped.

I raised my brows at her. "I beg your pardon?"

"It's a dance club. Okay?"

"Like . . . ballet?"

"Yes." Laney isn't usually prone to sarcasm, but tales of my past dates sometimes make her kind of irritable. Go figure. "Absolutely. Every Friday night they perform *Swan Lake* to an audience of thousands."

"Friday—"

"Damn it, Mac!"

I stared aghast. Laney was swearing. The apocalypse had arrived, and I intended to take all the necessary precautions, like covering my head with a newspaper, but just then I saw the tears in her eyes.

I felt every man in the room bare his teeth.

"I don't know what I'd do if something happened to you." Her voice was low and earnest. But not quite low enough. The menfolk had perked up their ears.

I shifted my attention to the right. The waiter was hovering. If he thought I had made her unhappy, I'd be lucky to survive the evening. I reached across the table and took her hand.

"Listen, Sugarcane." It was a pet name from years past, but it failed to make her smile. "You don't have to worry about me."

She turned her hand in mine. She has a grip like a road mender. Yoga's a funny thing. It looks like you're just sitting there upside down with your foot in your ear, but . . .

"Well, I do," she said. "I love you, Mac."

I thought I saw the waiter's eyes widen a little, but he didn't look discouraged. What is it with men and lesbians? The prospect of seeing two guys together is about as appealing as exfoliating with battery acid. Shouldn't a normal, thinking man feel the same about girl on girl? Shouldn't a well-adjusted . . . Ahh, screw it.

"I'll be fine, Laney," I said.

"You're not going to that place alone."

I shook my head, but my brain was already spinning out wild possibilities.

"I mean it, Mac. You wait until I can go with you."

"To the Strip Please." My tone may have been less than believing. Laney gets embarrassed during a TV kissing scene. "What would your father say?"

"He'd say you're an idiot," she said. "And I'm going with you."

"Geez, Laney, a curse word and an insult. I—"

"You're not going alone." She sounded honestly pissed. The waiter stepped closer. And he wasn't smiling. Could be when he wasn't dressed like a hovering penguin he was bouncing folks out of places like the Strip Please. I almost laughed at the idea, but he was pretty big . . . and oozing testosterone from every pore.

"Okay," I said.

"But I won't be here on Friday ."

"Maybe I could go with..." I was being cautious, lest the waiter/bouncer swing me out of the restaurant by my hair. "...someone else?"

"Who?"

"Someone...armed?"

"Jeen could go with you."

In concession to her obvious concern, I stopped the insult before it reached my lips. "Thanks, but..." Turns out I had nothing to say in lieu of something rude.

"Who, then?" she asked.

"I don't know yet."

She opened her mouth, but I interrupted before she could suggest Daffy Duck or Elmer Fudd. "But I won't go alone."

"Cross your heart and hope to die?"

I winced, thinking that both of us had come too close to the death thing not so many months before. "I cross my heart," I said.

23

It ain't a party till someone ends up naked.

> —*The only debate all three*
> *McMullen brothers ever*
> *completely agreed on*

SENATOR!" I gasped the word. It was a drizzly Monday morning. He was standing on my stoop, dressed to the nines. I was dressed for a jog and maybe throwing up afterward. Harlequin was decked out in his usual and didn't mind delaying our run for a minute to sniff the senator's crotch.

"I understand this is unorthodox," he said. "But I was on my way to the airport and thought I might stop by to make certain you are well."

"I'm fine." And *he* had a body double. What the hell did that mean?

"I saw you at the visitation talking to . . . well, talking to several people, in fact I hope they did not upset you."

"No. No. Everything's fine."

"My son can be . . ." He sighed. "Difficult. And Ms. Banks . . ." He paused. "Please do not get the wrong impression. She is a talented, intelligent woman, but perhaps she bears some resentment that colors her perspective."

My arms were getting sore from holding Harlequin at bay. My brain had been sore for weeks. "Resentment toward . . . your son?"

"He was very young when he dated her. Perhaps he was less than sensitive when he discontinued their relationship," he said, but he had paused just a moment too long before answering and my mind had finally clicked a couple puzzle pieces into place.

"Or resentment toward *you*?"

He tilted his head and gave me the shadow of a smile. "Perhaps she feels some bitterness by association alone."

"Or because you slept with her just to make Salina jealous?"

For a moment he was absolutely silent, then he spread his hands in a gesture of defeat. "She was at a fund-raiser in D.C.," he said. "I had not seen her for some years. It is no excuse, this I know, but Salina and I were having difficulties at the time."

Holy crap! He was like a five-legged dog in a mosh pit. "Was it Rachel who told you Salina was seeing someone else?"

He drew a deep breath, looking suddenly older. "I loved Salina. That you can believe."

I watched him. "Did you know, Senator, that is the one statement most commonly made by abusive men?"

"I did not kill my fiancée." His eyes looked earnest and solemn. "But perhaps it was my philandering that caused the death of any chance of a happy marriage. I am willing to take the blame." He raised his chin like a martyr ready for the blaze. It made me want to slap him upside the head. "God knows, I made mistakes."

You think? I scoffed, but I was lucid enough to keep the words to myself.

"But please, Christina, do not judge me too harshly." He gave me a sliver of the charismatic smile that had gained him a seat in the Senate, and probably a place in a hundred women's beds. "I would not want the lady who may be my future daughter-in-law to think poorly of me."

I raised my mental brows. What was he trying to do? Bribe me with his son? Or was it his own fortune he thought I might find appealing? I glanced toward the street. His Town Car stretched halfway to the bank. Okay, it was kind of appealing. "What was your business in Boston?" I asked.

"I beg your pardon?"

"When Salina was killed," I said, "you were on your way to Boston, weren't you?"

He was silent again, perhaps wondering how I knew. "Wellesley, to be specific."

"What were you doing there?"

He watched me in silence for a moment, then, "There is a progressive pharmaceutical company breaking new ground out East. They wished for my opinion since I am a major shareholder."

"Breaking new ground on balding scalps?" I asked.

He smiled again. "I am impressed, Christina. Truly I am."

Uh-huh. So they were all in bed together—Hohls, Riveras, Peachtrees. But what, if anything, did that have to do with Salina? My mind was spinning, but I kept my tone light, lest he know I was ferreting out his secrets like a rat terrier. "So will we be eradicating the awful baldness epidemic in the near future?"

There was laughter in his eyes. Once again, he looked handsome and confident and mildly amused. I found myself hoping that when I died I left someone behind who was better at this mourning business than he was. "We shall see."

"No promises?"

"Not just yet, no. But in truth, I had another reason for stopping by this morning."

"Another reason?" I braced myself.

"It concerns my son."

"What about him?"

His expression was solemn again. "There has been some trouble."

I was holding on to the doorjamb. "What happened?"

"He is not injured."

I drew a careful breath and eased my grip on the rotting wood. "What, then?"

His lips curled up a little. "Christina, I cannot tell you how it warms my heart to see that you care so—"

"What the hell happened?" I snapped.

His brows shot up. "They took Gerald's badge."

So Hohl had been correct.

"Not many know of this. Captain Kindred is keeping it as quiet as—"

"Why?"

He shook his head. "There may be several reasons. Officer Graystone alleged that Gerald attacked him the night of Salina's visitation."

Holy crap. My gaze wandered dizzily down the street.

"But you need not feel guilty about calling nine-one-one."

I snapped my attention back to his face.

"You see, you are not the only one who has little-known information, Christina."

"I didn't mean to—"

"Cause trouble for him? No, I am sure you did not. But Gerald . . ." He closed his eyes for a second. "He is difficult to understand at times."

I nodded dumbly.

He smiled, his face grim. "He broke into my house."

"What?"

"I was not there at the time. I am certain he was searching for clues," he added quickly. "Attempting to determine what happened on that dreadful night. But there are others who believe he may have been trying to destroy evidence."

"Holy shit."

He reached for my hand. I was in a haze and let him take it. "So you see, my son needs you now more than ever. Please, you must do what you can to put his mind at ease. I am certain a woman of your quality knows just how to do this."

I stared at him, boggled. Was he talking about sex? Or was that just the way *my* mind worked?

"It has been a pleasure seeing you again," he said, skimming his thumb across my knuckles. Then he walked away, straight as a pool cue, and maybe as guilty as hell.

I agonized over the senator's words for days, but I didn't call Rivera. Maybe I was a chicken shit, but what was I supposed to say? *"Hey, pal, heard you've been suspended from the job that gives your life meaning. Sucks, huh?"* It didn't sound great. Besides, my mind was reeling. Why would Rivera break into his father's house? If it was merely to prove his innocence, wouldn't it have been practical to simply ask his old man for admittance? Despite what I wanted to believe, I had to accept the possibility that Rivera might be guilty. Or maybe the senator was responsible for Salina's death and was slanting the evidence against his son. Or perhaps...A dozen other scenarios chased themselves through my mind.

By Wednesday I felt certifiable, but I kept seeing clients and shuffling through the applicants who showed up for Laney's job. The most likely contender had a two-pack-a-day habit and refused to work before noon.

By Friday night I felt harried and edgy.

Eddie Friar looked Kansas clean and pretty as a pony standing beneath the glaring orange lights of the Strip Please club.

"You came," I said, and leaned in for a hug.

"Of course I came." Wrapping his corded arms around me, he gave me a quick kiss on the cheek.

He smelled yummy. But Eddie always did, even when I'd first met him just weeks after moving to L.A. Cavorting with his greyhound on Topanga Beach, he'd looked as rugged as the sculpted landscape behind him and as windswept as the waves. He'd smiled when I'd handed back the Frisbee he'd tossed out for his dog, and I'd been lost.

We'd dated for a while. Long enough to learn he loved animals, good food, and . . . oh, men. Still, I sometimes wonder if we shouldn't have tried harder to work things out, even if he is as gay as a songbird. What's sex compared to a guy who talks baby talk to a race hound and can cook like a cruise line Frenchman?

He eyed the dark door. To say this was a seedy part of town would have been overly kind. "I couldn't let you come here alone."

"It had nothing to do with *L.A.'s premier strippers,* then?" I had checked their website . . . for a while.

"I'm insulted," he said, and grinned as he leaned past to open the door for me. Call me the Benedict of the feminist movement, but I still like it when men do that. And when they touch the small of your back as they usher you along. "Then again, if we see someone interesting, we can arm wrestle for him."

"Please!" I said, managing quite nicely to sound offended. I had dated a dancer once. He'd had enough muscle to sink the *Titanic.* Most of it had been firmly packed in his cranium, sharing space with an ego the size of Mount Whitney. "What I don't need is some steroid-popping behemoth in my life."

"Oh, that's right." He ushered me inside . . . with a hand on my back. Sigh. "You have a Ph.D."

I gave him a look over my shoulder. Eddie has a doctorate in Marine Biology and a bachelor's in Zoology. Eddie could think me under the table.

"I'm just here to find Manderos," I said.

"Just dumb luck that he's a guy who likes to take off his clothes, then," he mused, but I honestly didn't know what kind of guy Manderos was. Laney hadn't exactly been a fount of information. And I'd discovered zippo about him on the Internet. Which could mean any number of things, but most probably indicated my lack of technological ability.

As for Eddie, he and I hadn't had much time to discuss things on the phone. I'd said, "Male revue," and he'd said, "I'm in." Short and . . . well, a little disturbing maybe. I mean, there had been a time I thought Eddie was the one with whom I'd share the fortune cookie of my future—smart, kind, good-looking. It was one of life's cruel jokes that we were about to sit side by side and watch a bunch of greased gorillas take off their clothes.

The place was dark, loud, and packed. We ordered drinks at the bar and carried them to one of the tiny tables placed in rows around the stage.

At ten o'clock an emcee greeted us. Ten minutes later, the first performer appeared. He was dressed as a police officer. It was a disgusting display of male exploitation that offended the fine-tuned therapist in me. On the other hand, my internal cocktail waitress wasn't quite so prissy and couldn't help wondering how Rivera would look in breakaway pants. The image made me feel itchy. By the time the fourth dancer took the stage, I felt like a time bomb, armed and ready. I squiggled uncomfortably in my chair.

Eddie gave me a beatific smile. The psychologist scowled back. The cocktail girl was busy panting.

He leaned closer. "How are you doing?" he asked.

I rolled my tongue back into my mouth like an over-heated Labrador. "Fine," I said, and took a casual sip of my margarita. Had I been thinking properly, I would have just dumped the damn thing in my lap.

We'd been discussing the attributes of the various dancers. So far, I hadn't tried to wrestle Eddie to ground . . . or any of the other guys, either, but one look at the fellow called Clifton made me wonder how much longer that kind of disciplined civility was going to last.

He was tall for a Latino, with sleek black hair that was caught at the nape of his neck and fell over the collar of his white poet's shirt. He wore a tricorn hat, buff-colored breeches tucked into knee-high leather boots, and a gold hoop in his right ear. Sail ho, maties. He was a pirate.

"What about him?" Eddie asked.

Clifton had just taken off his hat. His eyes were black as a demon's; his smile, little-boy mischievous. "He's okay," I said, and reminded myself to breathe.

The music thrummed on.

Eddie was staring at me. "I meant . . . could he be Manderos?"

Onstage, Clifton slipped his shirt off his shoulders and skimmed splayed fingers down his abs. They rippled like a washboard. *Take me, laddie, I'm dirty.*

"Rivera's double?" Eddie reminded me.

"Oh." I snapped back to business. It wasn't that I had forgotten my purpose for being there. But holy crap, this guy was buttered up like a hot cross bun. Slap a little frosting on him and he'd be a diabetic's worst nightmare. "I know that," I said, then scowled and looked closer. Clifton was probably about the right height, though it was hard to say for sure, what with the gyrating. Somehow he had managed to remove his boots. The breeches followed. I swallowed. He had an ass like a . . . well, like a frickin' stripper. But truth be told, I wasn't sure how the senator's ass looked with a thong the width of dental floss separating him from a night in lockup. Of course, I could imagine, but . . . I cleared my throat and tried to do the same with my thoughts. "He's too young. Don't you think?"

Eddie shrugged. "I've never seen the good senator."

I turned toward him. "What?"

He flashed me a grin. "Hey, I'm just here to keep the guys off you."

I snorted. There were a couple hundred women in there. If one of these men was crazy enough to want to get to me, he'd have to go through every last slavering one of them. "You must have seen Rivera's picture," I said.

"If I did, I don't remember it."

"Fat lot of help you—" I began, but just then the thong disappeared. He still wasn't completely naked, though. What the hell was young Clifton doing with that eye patch? My eyebrows rocketed, racing my respiration and my estrogen level. But I kept my voice steady. "He could be Rivera himself and you wouldn't—"

"I think we'll have to question him."

"What?"

I didn't bother to look at him. The eye patch was kind of mesmerizing.

"How else are we going to learn anything?"

"What about his admirers?" I asked, and nodded disjointedly toward the audience. "Most of them are younger, thinner, and drunker than I am."

"Yeah, but where are they on the desperation scale?"

I smirked in his general direction. Never turn your back on a pirate.

"I'm just kidding," he said. "I bet you can bring him over here."

"Who?" I yanked my attention from the eye patch. An influx of adrenaline had squeezed my heart up tight in my throat by the time I motioned toward the stage. "Him?"

"Yeah."

I laughed. It sounded like an ass on nitrous oxide. " 'Fraid I'm fresh out of million-dollar—" I began, but Eddie was already pressing a piece of paper into my hand.

I glanced down. It was a hundred-dollar bill. My lungs joined my heart in my esophagus. "Are you serious?"

"You're the one who thinks her boyfriend's a cold-blooded murderer. Time to find out for sure. Fish or cut bait. Shit or get off the pot. Screw him or screw him. Cut the bull or turn him loose with—"

"Okay!" I snapped my gaze to him. He was still grinning. I tightened my fist around the bill and tried to marshal my brain cells into some kind of coherent order. "What do I do now?"

He shrugged. "Beats the hell out of me."

"Tempting," I said.

He laughed. "Put it on the table and let kismet do its thing."

"Kismet?"

He nodded.

I set the bill beside my drink.

The volume picked up. Clifton was doing some kind of bumping grind and the crowd was working itself into a preorgasmic frenzy.

By the time he was standing on his hands, I felt a little light-headed.

Two tables away, a waitress wriggled through the mob, looking harried. Eddie picked up the hundred and flagged her down. She shimmied over and leaned close. I couldn't hear him over the man-thirsty mob, but when the two of them lifted their gazes to me, I was pretty sure of the direction of their conversation. I willed myself not to blush—when pigs eat Lean Cuisine.

The waitress shrugged, took the money, and moved away.

"I was thinking kismet was something a little more nebulous," I shouted. And Eddie laughed. Fifteen minutes later, the show came to a grinding, ear-shattering halt. I studied the crowd, but if the senator's body double was there, he was either female, gay, or a twenty-something stripper stuffed to the gills with steroids. The mob was beginning to dissipate and Clifton hadn't appeared to tell me how he had flown to Boston so Senator Rivera could kill his fiancée.

I stood up, feeling foolish . . . and as horny as a teenage tuba player.

Eddie grabbed my sleeve. "Where you going?"

The volume had decreased but still held a pretty good beat. "There's got to be a better way."

He snagged my sleeve and pulled me down beside him. "What about kismet?"

"Kismet, my ass. I—" I began, but in that instant, a man appeared beside Eddie. I glanced up. He was dressed in a white shirt and black trousers, but I was pretty sure I'd be able to pick Pirate Man out of a crowd for the rest of my coherent life. I took a deep breath and shrank back down. Almost missing my chair, I teetered for a moment, then slid into place.

"Hi. I'm Clifton. Patricia said you wanted to see me."

I was staring openmouthed. Eddie dug his elbow between my ribs.

"Yes. Yes, I . . . Yes," I said.

I could feel Eddie's rumbling laughter close beside me. He thrust me away a couple inches, rose to a half-erect position, and extended his hand. "I'm Eddie Friar." They shook. "This is Christina." Clifton's fingers engulfed mine but finally our hands parted. I didn't know what to do next. Speech was out of the question and I was afraid I'd get trampled if I fainted.

"Do you have a minute?" Eddie asked.

"Sure." Clifton's voice was a hormone-sluicing rumble. He took the seat across from me. I glanced at him and shot my gaze away. My face felt as hot as a radiator.

Silence misted around us.

"Great show," Eddie said finally.

The pirate was watching me with eyes like glowing faggots. I was blushing down to my short hairs, secretly living out a scene in a romance novel I'd read when I was thirteen. I don't remember the title, but it was about a pirate and a virgin. I think it was called *The Pirate and the Virgin*. Romance novels aren't always subtle. "How about you, Christina?" he asked. "What'd you think of the show?"

I tried to talk, but the scoundrel had tied the virgin to the yardarm and was torturing her with unrelenting kisses down her midline. Those pirates . . .

"Did you like it?" he prompted.

I blinked. Eddie gave me another elbow in the ribs.

"Aye . . . Aye . . ." I could feel the two of them staring at me. Was I talking pirate-speak? "Yes." I was starting to sputter a little, maybe because of the excess saliva. "It was . . ." For a while I think he'd tortured her with the nine-inch handle of a cat-o'-nine-tails. And then they'd buried his treasure. ". . . nice."

Clifton laughed. The sound rumbled around me. I felt my breastbone melt. He leaned back, hooking his thumbs behind him on the chair. The neck of his shirt stretched open, revealing a whole dumpload of tight, mounded muscle. "So, are you two married?"

I was attempting to speak, but in my mind I was trying to remember the last time I'd been tortured with anything more stimulating than the *Times* crossword puzzle. The latest had asked for a two-word phrase for a type of medieval protection. I'd tried "broad sword" more than once, in concession to Laney's current gig. Not enough letters. And actually just one word. Such academic pursuits appealed to the psychologist in me. Turning my mind away from Clifton's sword appealed to the woman who didn't want to make a damned fool of herself.

"Just friends," Eddie said.

"Ahh." The Pirate King was eyeing me again. I felt hot down to my shoelaces. It seemed outrageous that he could be interested in me, but in *The Pirate and the Virgin,* the virgin hadn't been particularly stunning, while the pirate . . . "Have you been to a male revue before, Christina?"

I swallowed some estrogen, forgot about the *L.A. Times,* and steadied my voice, my mind spinning out of control. What if the world had gone mad and he wanted to take me home? What if he didn't have protection? What if I didn't remember how to do it? And why the hell hadn't I shaved my— Eddie was poking me again. "No," I said. "No, I haven't."

"Was it what you expected?" Clifton rumbled, shifting his thigh closer to mine.

"Chastity belt!" I sputtered.

Eddie turned toward me like I'd lost my mind.

"It's a . . . it's a form of medieval . . ." I blinked. ". . . protection."

I chanced a glance at Clifton, pirate-dark and as alluring as a thousand-calorie cappuccino.

Eddie cleared his throat. "She doesn't usually drink," he said.

"Ahhh." The pirate nodded. His throat was broad above the snowy white shirt that matched his teeth. He leaned forward. His shoulders were massive. They filled my vision and would probably do so for some nights to come. If I didn't manage to die of embarrassment before returning home. "Well, Christina . . ." He took my hand in his and kissed my knuckles. "I'm happy to broaden your horizons." He squeezed my fingers. I could feel an orgasm bubbling up in its wake and braced myself against the cessation of skin against skin, wondering wildly what the hell to do next. Vainly searching my purse for a condom seemed a little obvious. Then again, leaping across the table—

"How about you, Eddie?" Clifton asked. "You been here before?"

"No. I hadn't heard of this place before Christina called me."

"Well, I'm glad she did. We—"

But suddenly my breath caught in my throat. A Hispanic man stood not twenty feet away. He was tall, mid-forties, attractive, and though his hair was black and his clothing casual, I couldn't look away. He was a young version of Senator Rivera.

"You okay?" Eddie's inquiry barely broke through my haze.

I managed to stare in hypnotized wonder. Now that it came down to it, I had no idea what to do.

Eddie tensed almost imperceptibly, but he picked up the thread. "Hey," he said, tilting his head casually to the right. "Who is that guy? He looks familiar."

Clifton turned. "Oh, that's Julio. Julio Manderos. He owns the Strip."

"Yeah?"

"Bought it for a song. Built it up from nothing. Listen, Eddie, you're in pretty good shape," he said. "You dance?"

Eddie must have responded, but I had risen like a ghost in a trance and was making my way through the milling crowd.

"Mr. Manderos?" He was moving away. I skirted two giggling girls no older than my shoes. "Julio?"

He turned. His eyes struck me. I almost stumbled back. The clothing was different. The bearing was altered. But his eyes were Rivera's.

"Can I help you?" His voice was a low, rich blend of Spanish-English.

"How well did you know Martinez?"

He watched me for a fragmented instant. Dark emotion flitted across his face, but then he smiled. "I am afraid I do not know anyone by that name." He nodded with old-world grace. "If you'll excuse me . . ."

I hurried up behind him, heart pounding. "What a terrible tragedy."

He kept walking.

"Mr. Manderos," I said, grabbing his sleeve. I could feel Eddie nudge up beside me. The pirate was a couple paces behind him. Maybe he doubled as protection, but I didn't think so. Usually men that pretty don't like to mess up all that mouthwatering muscle.

"I did not know her," Manderos insisted, turning toward me with a scowl.

"Then how did you know she was a woman?" I asked.

24

There aren't many things a man finds more appealing than loyalty. Unless it's a woman with really big knockers.

*M*ANDEROS SMILED AGAIN, but there was tension around his mouth and something else entirely in his eyes. He glanced at Eddie, past him to the room at large, then back at me. "Perhaps you would wish to converse alone in my office," he said.

Something in me suggested that I would rather swallow my own head than converse alone in his office. I think it might have been called "cowardice," or maybe "good sense." It was impossible to say. I was just coming down from an estrogen high that was burning its way through my pants.

I glanced to my right. The bouncers who hovered

near the door were big enough to wrestle dinosaurs. But seventy-six failed relationships is a lot of motivation.

"Yes. Thank you," I said, and stepped forward, but Eddie caught my arm.

"What the hell are you doing?" he whispered.

"Just talking."

He glanced toward the bouncers. Apparently, they didn't look any less intimidating from his point of view. "Then I'm talking with you," he said. I had known for some time that Eddie was one of the good guys, but at that moment his gesture all but brought tears to my eyes.

"Good evening," Manderos said, and reached past me toward Eddie.

They shook and made introductions.

Manderos nodded, his expression solemn, almost sad. "The young lady will be perfectly safe with me, Mr. Friar. If you but wait here, Mr. Corona will assure you of that." Motioning to a waitress, he asked her to fetch them whatever they wished and lifted a hand toward the back room.

I felt a little like a dead man walking. His office was decorated in ultramodern decor, in sharp contrast to the rest of the club.

"Please, sit," he said, and motioned to a love seat upholstered with red crushed velvet.

I sat.

He poured sparkling water into two tumblers and handed me one.

"I do not believe we have had a proper introduction," he said.

"Christina." I felt very somber and ultimately unhorny. "Christina McMullen."

He nodded. "I would bet much that you come from a fine family, Ms. Christina."

I didn't know how I was supposed to respond. I was in uncharted water and a little bit drunk, so I steadied my tipsy boat and said the first words that came to mind. "My mother thinks I've ruined her life. My father hasn't spoken more than five words to me in as many years, and the last time I saw my brother he left a dead rat in my freezer."

He gave me a look I couldn't decipher, something between confusion and humor, but then he took a deep breath and spoke "Mama died shortly after giving me life," he said. "She was but fifteen years of age." He paced to the window. It was blacker than silt behind the club. "I do not know who my father might have been."

I had to admit even *my* pedigree looked brighter by comparison.

"I spent some years in an orphanage." He wasn't looking at me. "Have you ever been to an orphanage in Mexico?"

"I grew up in Illinois."

"This was not such a pleasant place. I was happy when I was selected to go to a foster home." There was tension in his shoulders, a tightness in his hands. "But not so happy as Raul, the man who would put a pretty boy in his bed, *sí?*"

I suddenly felt like I was in a bad dream. Not a pirate in sight. "Mr. Manderos . . ." I don't know what I was going to say, but when he turned toward me, I stopped, words corked up tight in my mind. His eyes looked as old and sad as death itself.

"Do you believe that all sins are equal in the eyes of our Lord, Ms. Christina?"

"I . . ." I shook my head, out of words.

He smiled grimly. "The sisters at Casa de Angeles had taught me not to steal, but this man, he had much money, at least it seemed so to an orphan boy from Charcas." He drew in a hard breath. It sounded shaky. "He very much liked his tequila. When he passed out one night, I took the money I had found hidden in a boot beneath his bed. I took it all. Every peso. When I was twelve years of age I came to America."

"I'm sorry," I said. I felt foolishly pampered, horribly weak.

"But there are not many jobs for scrawny boys of Aztec descent in Waco, Texas. Not many . . ." He smiled without humor. "What is the word . . . *legitimate* jobs."

"I haven't come to cause trouble for you," I said.

He paced the room. "Why is it that you have come, Ms. Christina?"

I waited, trying to figure out how to word my response. But there was no good way to phrase the questions roaring around in my head. "I think Salina Martinez was murdered."

His body was absolutely motionless. "I have murdered no one. This I promise you."

"Can you say the same for Senator Rivera?"

He seemed to pale under the natural mocha of his skin.

"You know him," I said.

He sat down abruptly on the black vinyl stool across from me, looking temporarily stunned.

"I need to know the truth."

He shook his head, looking dazed. "I have done nothing for which I am ashamed."

I wished I could say the same. "Then tell me what happened."

"I cannot."

I stiffened my spine, turning my back on the pretty boy who had somehow made his way alone to the land of the free, only to learn that nothing comes free. "Better me than the LAPD." It was a threat. Probably not subtle. "Help me."

"Why?"

"I have a friend who . . . I know someone who is involved."

"Who is this someone?"

"Jack Rivera."

I watched him wince involuntarily.

"Please," I said. "I need to know. For me. Just for me."

He smiled. It was sadder than tears. "There are those who say that women cannot keep secrets."

"I'm not a woman." Technically that may have been a lie. And a dumb-ass thing to say. "I'm a psychologist."

He looked unimpressed.

"And a former cocktail waitress."

He scowled. "What is Senator Rivera's son to you?"

I drew a breath and shook my head. "Do you know him?"

He looked up, eyes vacant, face drawn. "We have not met."

"But you know the senator."

He was gripping his glass in both hands but didn't drink. "He is a good man. That is all I know."

"Please, Mr. Manderos, I need to . . ." I glanced toward the door, embarrassed for myself, ashamed of the world. "I would like to trust someone. A man," I corrected. "But I . . ." I shook my head. "I know I'm lucky. I come from a good . . . from a decent family. I've had a good education. And I'm smart." I felt teary-eyed. Alcohol does that to me. That and the memory of past relationships. "But the men I care about . . ." I shrugged. "They're sometimes cruel."

"Perhaps your image of cruelty and mine are not one and the same."

My throat felt dry. I took a drink. "Some of them try to kill me."

He raised his brows, probably attempting to figure out if I could possibly be telling the truth.

"What are the chances, huh?" I said, and stifled a sniffle.

"Ms. Christina . . ." Leaning forward, he set his glass aside and did the same with mine. "You seem to be a fine lady. Wise." He smiled. "Beautiful."

"I—" My voice cracked. I cleared my throat. "I just need to know." The words were no more than a whisper.

"Why?" His question was no louder. His hands were warm around mine. "What can you do? She is already dead."

"I can have peace of mind."

He smiled mistily. "Such peace is not so easy to find. This I know."

"What else do you know?" I was drilling him with my eyes, hoping against hope.

He leaned back, studying me. Silence stretched between us.

"Pornography is not so bad a life," he said finally.

I blinked at him. My eyelashes felt fat.

He shrugged. "Not compared to some. But the drugs . . . It is difficult to quit the drugs."

His meaning dawned slowly. "He helped you. Senator Rivera. He helped you get clean."

"He saved my life."

"And in exchange you became his double."

His smile was uncertain, and somehow I could imagine him as a little boy, dark eyes bright with mischief. "I won't inform the police," I said. "I swear to God. If you tell me the truth, I'll keep it to myself. I just . . . I need to know."

"At times, upon his request, I would assume his identity."

"It was you. On the plane to Boston. It was you."

He stared at me, then, "No," he said finally. "It was not."

I felt myself pale. "Then you were in the car. Near her house."

He closed his eyes. "Salina Martinez did not love him."

"You knew her," I breathed.

"*Sí.* I knew her," he admitted.

There was something about the inflection of his words. My mouth opened. I sucked in air. "You . . . *knew* her."

His smile was sad. "She was young. And demanding. And difficult. But she took a liking to me. I cannot say why, though . . ." He shrugged. "I am not yet so very bad at my former profession."

I stared google-eyed. "He *hired* you to . . . to . . ."

"At times."

"That night? The night she died?"

He looked pale and broken. "They had argued. Senator

Rivera wished for me to soothe her. I went to his house. She did not know to expect me."

"Did you—"

"I did not kill her. I swear on Mama's grave, I did not. The door was open. I went in. Called her name. She did not answer, and then I saw her." The words, once uncorked, spilled out. He swallowed, eyes haunted. "I know something of death, Ms. Christina. Perhaps I should have stayed, but I admit, I was afraid. I did not even go to her."

"You called the police."

"From a pay phone."

"Who killed her?"

He shook his head. "I have heard she died of causes that are natural."

"And you believe that?"

He was silent a moment, then, "A man of my history does not have the luxury to believe otherwise."

"You have to go to the police. Tell them the truth."

He smiled. "What are the chances they will take the word of an orphaned whore from Charcas?"

"You're innocent."

"I was an innocent in Charcas also. Raul did not care."

"Rivera believes his father is guilty."

"He is wrong. I am certain. You must tell him differently."

"I don't know differently," I said.

He held my gaze with his and rose slowly to his feet. Drawing me up beside him, he kissed my hand. "Then you must do what you must do," he said.

25

Trust is important to any relationship . . . and easier to come by if you got a picture of the guy's wife buck naked.

—*Warren Peuter, ex-boyfriend
and underwear thief*

YOU OKAY?" Eddie was at my elbow the moment I left Manderos's office.

"Yes," I said, but I felt numb and hazy as I pulled my keys out of my purse.

We made it to the car, but Eddie nudged me aside. "Go sit down."

I did as I was told, folding myself into the passenger seat and staring blankly ahead.

He locked the doors and turned on the ignition. "What happened?"

Excellent question.

"Christina?"

I looked at him. "I don't know."

"What?"

"I think the senator killed Salina."

"Holy shit! Did Manderos tell you that?"

"No."

"Then—"

"He said Miguel was on the plane and he was with Salina."

"What?"

"I think he lied."

"Why would he—"

"Loyalty."

"So you think Manderos really was in the air?"

"Leaving the senator with Salina."

"What now?"

I shook my head. "Stay a million miles away from the Rivera family?"

"But you think the lieutenant's innocent."

"I think he knows his father isn't."

He released a breath. "I thought he hated his old man."

"Yeah, but maybe blood really is thicker. Or maybe . . ." The thought made my own blood run cold. "Maybe it's money. Maybe no matter how much he hates his dad, he can't give up his inheritance." My mind was boiling. "Maybe he went to the crime scene to destroy evidence that would incriminate his father."

Eddie shook his head, confused. "You think the old man's paying him to keep him quiet?"

"Or it might be blackmail or . . . Crap." I covered my eyes with my hand.

The Saturn's little tires hummed busily along Rosemead Boulevard.

"Could be you're jumping to conclusions," Eddie said finally.

"Manderos admitted the senator had hired him that night. Why would Rivera do that unless he was planning something he doesn't want others to know about?"

"Point taken," Eddie said. "But maybe you've got it all wrong. Maybe Manderos really was with Salina."

"Why?"

"So the senator could be elsewhere."

"Such as?"

"I don't know. Maybe he's a cat burglar."

I gave him a look.

"Okay. Maybe he was cheating on his fiancée."

"Yesterday I would have thought that impossible."

"And now?"

"Men are sick."

"Yeah."

"She was so beautiful, Eddie." I sighed. "Amazing. Stunning."

"Some guys want more."

"Yeah?"

"Yeah."

"What do *you* want?"

He glanced my way. "Someone like you, but with chest hair."

I watched him for a moment, wishing things that were never to be, then leaned my head back against the cushion again. "Just my luck that you're gay."

"I didn't do it to spite you, Chris."

"You're gay, Rivera's somehow involved in a murder, and I think I spoke *pirate* to the best-looking offer I've had in a decade."

He didn't say anything. I turned toward him. "I didn't misread Clifton's signals, did I?"

"Huh?" He didn't look at me.

"Clifton. The dancer. He *was* coming on to me, wasn't he?"

"Oh . . . yeah . . . I mean . . ." He laughed. It sounded weird. "Who wouldn't?"

The car went quiet. Reality dawned by slow, painful degrees. "He made a pass at you, didn't he?"

"No!" He turned abruptly toward me. He was as pretty as a picture framed against the black glass of the driver's window.

I felt my libido take a nosedive and watched my self-esteem streak past it to ground level. "He made a pass."

"No, he didn't."

I was staring at him.

He fidgeted. "All right. He did ask if I'd be interested in seeing *Dorian Gray*."

I stared at him, unblinking, like a tree frog.

"It's a play." He loosened and tightened his hands on the steering wheel. "At the Forum. I've heard good things."

Fuck.

"But he thought you were very nice. Kind of . . . odd . . . but nice."

I remembered my pirate fantasies and considered dying. But spontaneous death isn't as easy as you'd think.

Eddie pulled the Saturn into my driveway. I was still

plastered against the seat. He got out of the car, rounded the bumper, and opened my door.

"Shoot me," I said.

"I don't have a gun. Come on," he said, and hoisting me out, he half dragged me up my heaving walkway to my stoop. Wouldn't you know it, in my life the stoop was the only thing that was heaving.

"You could poison me," I suggested. But my heart wasn't really in it.

"Forgot my magical herbs," he said. "Open the door."

"Hit me over the head until I'm dead."

"Too messy. Hurry up with the keys, will you?"

"Strangle me."

"Now you're talking. But open the door first, will ya?" he said, shifting his arm against my waist. "You're getting heavy."

"I *am* heavy." I felt the sniffles bubbling up like a sulfur bog.

"Christina." His voice was immediately contrite. He cupped my face with his free hand. I felt myself slipping toward the broken concrete. "You're beautiful. You know that."

My throat was closing up.

"And intelligent."

I sniffed.

"Kind."

"Now you're just lying," I said.

"Of course I am," he admitted, jostling me. "Damn it, Chrissy, open the door."

"I'm sorry," I said. Pulling away, I shoved my key in the lock. I punched in my security code and stood in the foyer, feeling silly and a little drippy about the nose and eyes. Harlequin crammed his nose under my hand, either consoling or wanting to be consoled. Maybe both.

Eddie was staring at me. "Are you okay?"

"No. Yes!" I blew out a breath. "Please." I waved a floppy arm at him. "Take my car home, will you? I just . . . I'm really sorry to drag you into this."

"It's no problem."

"Yes it is. It's just . . . my life. . . ." I was feeling teary and stupid. I should never drink, not under threat of death. I forced myself to brighten. "Did I tell you Laney got the lead in a TV series?"

"Elaine Butterfield?"

I was going to cry. "Yeah. Isn't that great? It's a . . . huge break for her."

He didn't look very happy. Maybe he was going to miss her terribly. Maybe he'd been her best friend since fifth grade and thought he was worth something by the simple virtue of being her friend. But maybe that's me.

"But she's going to be staying in L.A., right?"

I cleared my throat. "Sure. Well, some of the time. But they're filming—"

"I'm going to stay the night," he said.

I looked at him through fuzzy eyeballs. "You're still gay, right?"

"Gay as you are straight."

"That's . . . ." I remembered the pirate. It's damn hard to forget a good pirate, even if he did proposition your nicest male friend. ". . . disappointingly gay."

He had the most beautiful smile on earth.

"You don't have to babysit me," I said.

"Babysitting?" he scoffed, and let Harlequin out in the yard for a run. "You kidding? I'm dead on my feet. I just don't want to drive home."

"And don't patronize me."

"Okay, I like to babysit. You know what those kids get paid these days?"

"Go home, Eddie," I said, but he had already wandered into my walnut-size kitchen.

"Nope." He started rummaging in my freezer, brought out the ice cream, dredged up two spoons.

I helped myself to one. We dug in together. "My couch will kill your back," I said around a mouthful of Mango Explosion.

"No it won't."

"I'll be fine."

"You're such a hard-ass," he said.

"That's not what you implied earlier."

He laughed, leaned a hip against my counter, watched me, spoon empty. That's probably why his ass *is* hard. 'Cuz he could live with an empty spoon.

Tapping the cover onto the ice cream, I tucked it into the freezer and padded over to the couch. Eddie took the seat across from me, elbows on knees, watching.

"What are you going to do now?"

"I don't know."

"How much do you like this Rivera guy?"

"I hate—"

"Honestly," he interjected.

Interjected. Good word.

I sighed. "Half the time I hate him."

"And the other half?"

"His other half looks pretty good."

His eyes smiled. Such pretty eyes. I should have known he was gay the first time I looked at him. "Maybe his efforts to protect his father are noble."

"And maybe he killed her himself."

"Could be he's perfectly innocent in every regard."

"If there's one thing I know for sure, it's that Rivera's not perfectly anything."

"Is he capable of killing?"

I thought for a moment, lost track of time, leaned back. The world was getting sleepy. "Maybe we all are."

"Under the right circumstances?"

I shrugged. Eddie could discuss philosophical nothingness for hours. I was pretty sure I had another thirty-two seconds in me. I can always sleep, but when I'm tipsy it's pretty much mandatory.

"Go to bed, Christina."

"Eddie?" I dragged my eyes open. The task was tantamount to self-imposed brain surgery.

"Yeah?"

"You ever get lonely?"

"You're drunk, honey," he said.

"You know how long it's been since I've been..." He seemed to be lifting me from the couch. I tried to make it easier for him by wrapping my arms around his neck but my limbs were kind of watery. "You know."

"I *don't* know." He huffed a little under my weight. But he'd said I was beautiful... and a hard-ass, so he was probably just out of shape.

"Intimate," I said.

He pushed the bedroom door open with his shoulder.

Luckily, I hadn't made the bed, so there was no need to pull back the sheets. Good thinking on my part. He set me on the mattress and sat down beside me. The light from the living room softened his face, like a rugged angel. "Are you using 'intimate' as a euphemism for sex?"

"I thought they were one and the same."

"Uh-huh."

I dragged my eyes open and flopped my right arm above my head. "You mean the nuns were wrong?"

He didn't answer. When I turned he was gone. But in a minute he was back, Harlequin at his side. "Move over," he said.

I tried.

He rolled me onto my side like a Vienna sausage and stretched out beside me. Harlequin grunted onto the mattress on the other side.

"I suppose you think it's easy for a gay guy."

"Oh, please." The words were a little slurred. "You were just propositioned by a pirate."

"You're hallucinating."

"He looked like a pirate. Had an eye patch."

"But not on his eye."

"Lucky, frickin' eyeemabob...thing...th..."

"And now you're mumbling," he said, and wrapping his arm around me, he pulled me close. "Sleep tight, honey."

He didn't have to tell me twice.

26

Yeah, world peace would be all right, but what about a day off and a slab a ham the size of my head?

—Chrissy's dad, a down-to-earth chap, but not necessarily someone with whom to discuss the complexities of the cosmos

MY NOSTRILS TWITCHED at the smell of bacon. My pirate rumbled a laugh as he bent over an open flame. His chest was bare except for the bandoleers that crossed his sun-darkened torso. There was a scar on the right side of his mouth and—

"You alive in there?"

I opened my eyes. There was no pirate, but Eddie was waving a platter of bacon in front of my nose. I sat up, said a brave good-bye to Bandoleer Guy, and took a strip. It was golden brown, fried to perfection, not microwaved within an inch of its life like some people were wont to do.

Wont...I am wont to ravage you, lassie. Okay, maybe the pirate wasn't completely gone.

Harlequin sat mesmerized beside the bed, watching the platter as if it bore the crown jewels...or bacon.

"Don't give him any," Eddie said. "We already had a bowl of oatmeal."

I eyed the dog. He eyed me back, head tilted, ears cocked. He knew he looked cute that way. "He eats oatmeal?"

"And the bowl it's served in. I was going to make you a quiche," Eddie said, and sat down, "but then I remembered you were from Chicago, so I just fried up some fat."

I didn't rise to the bait, unless the bacon was the bait, in which case I was jumping like a fat trout at daybreak. The second piece was just as good as the first.

"How's your head?"

I shrugged, assessed, chewed. "All right."

"And I see your stomach's okay."

"I will survive," I said, gazing dramatically into his Everclear eyes. "Ohhhh, as long as I know how to love—"

"Please don't sing."

It was a leftover joke from when he'd first told me he was batting for the other team. The gay team. I cleared my throat and slowed my chewing.

"Thanks for staying," I said.

"No problem."

"I'm not usually such a baby."

"I know."

I fiddled with the bedsheet and debated eating another five hundred grams of saturated fat.

"Did I tell you Pete's girlfriend is pregnant?"

"Pete?"

"My moron brother."

"The one I met last Thanksgiving?"

I nodded, tried to resist the call of bacon, failed, munched. "Moron number deux. Holly's due in June."

"Wow. They getting married?"

I leaned forward, trying to get the kink out of my shoulder. He dragged my pillow up and plumped it behind me. I leaned back with a sigh. "I was sure they would. I mean, he's been married about forty-seven times. What's wrong with forty-eight?"

"He's a good-looking guy."

"He's a troglodyte."

Eddie shrugged, set the platter on the mattress, and gave Harlequin a stern look. Somehow it worked. "A good-looking troglodyte."

"Mom thinks it's my fault they haven't already made a nest in a charming little bungalow just down the street and named their firstborn after her."

"How's that?"

I glanced out the window. "It might be because I told Holly not to marry him."

"Mothers!" he scoffed.

"But the depleting ozone layer . . . she thinks that's my fault, too."

"The oil companies told us it wasn't the carbon fuels." He tapped his forehead with his palm. "I should have listened."

"She likes to call me Saturday mornings to remind me that I've ruined the world as we know it."

"The ice caps *are* melting."

"I was just trying to help. I mean, we have to put a beer can on Pete's shoe to get him to tie his laces. What kind of father forgets to tie his laces?"

He didn't say anything.

"So I just suggested that Holly . . . give it some thought, maybe make a few suggestions, see if he's willing to bend, to grow up, to prove himself. I didn't think she'd listen. I mean, if she's foolish enough to get herself knocked up by the dumbest . . ." I paused. Sighed. "I was just trying to help." I sounded like a teenybopper in a poor script. "But now I think, maybe . . ." I didn't quite manage to complete the sentence.

"You're afraid you did it out of spite."

I glanced up, appalled. "I am not."

"You're afraid you're jealous."

"I am not jealous of my infantile brother who—"

"Who's going to have a baby, make a family, have a life."

"Yeah, well . . . life sucks," I said, and dropped my skull against the headboard.

He laughed. "You could call her up and tell her what a great guy Pete is."

"Did I tell you about the sheep droppings?"

"I believe he made you eat them on your cousin's farm in North Dakota."

"He left a dead rat in my freezer at Thanksgiving."

"I think I'm in love," he said, and stood up. "Come on. I've got to get going, and you stink. On your feet, take a shower, call your mom."

"I'd rather shove marbles up my nose," I said, but I

shuffled out of bed. The bacon was gone. There was no reason to remain.

"I tried the marble trick once when I was three. It's not that great." He put Harlequin outside and sauntered into my office. "Hey, who's the doll-faced boy in these pics?"

I glanced out of the bathroom and was just able to see him past the door frame. He had the photos Solberg had printed fanned out beside the rubble on my desk. "Name's Daniel Hohl," I said. Closing the door most of the way, I undressed behind it. Leaving my clothing in a heap, I struggled to turn my robe sleeves right-side out.

"Of carpet empire fame?"

"Has everyone but me heard of him?"

"Probably."

I looked in the mirror. One glance suggested it would be foolhardy to do so again anytime soon.

"Brains and money and . . ." I could hear him shuffling papers. "Holy cow. He's pretty even when he's scowling. He still look like this?"

I stuck my tongue out at my reflection. Shrugging into the robe, I cinched it tight. "Pretty much. Why?"

"Why?" More shuffling. "Geez, it's like the land of good and plenty. Who's the gorgeous chick with the Spanish dude?"

"What Spanish dude?" I asked, but Eddie had abandoned the photos and returned to the bedroom to retrieve his wallet. He straightened just as the phone rang. Premonition wafted through me.

"Don't answer that," I said.

He grinned, tripped past me, and picked up the receiver. "McMullen residence."

I stopped, dumbfounded, watching in horror.

"Eddie Friar," he said. He was Mr. Congeniality. "Is this Mrs. McMullen?"

I was shaking my head and making rapid slicing motions at my neck.

"I'm a friend of Christina's. I hear congratulations are in order."

Even from across the room I could hear her question.

"Pete's going to be a father, right?" He listened, nodded. "Well, I'm sure Chrissy didn't mean it that way. She's always telling me wonderful stories about her and her brothers. Picnics on her cousin's sheep farm, that sort of thing."

He smiled at me. If I still had the rat I would have shoved it down his pants.

The volume on the other end of the line picked up a little.

"Perhaps she was using reverse psychology in an attempt to convince Holly to marry him," he suggested. "She is a therapist. And very bright."

Silence. He raised his brows at me.

My mouth had frozen.

"Well, thank you, but no. We're just friends. I dropped by to make her breakfast."

"I'm not here." I couldn't even hear my own words. "I'm jogging. Tell her I'm jogging."

"What's that? Oh, sure. She's right here. It was very nice talking to you, Mrs. McMullen," he said, and handed me the phone.

I gritted my teeth at him and mouthed the worst swear

word I could think of. He laughed. Damned gay guys. "Hi, Mom," I said.

He kissed my cheek and headed for the door. "I've gotta go. Call me later."

"Who was that?" The harsh glare of Mom's criticism had dulled a little under the light of Eddie's charisma.

I wasn't that easy. "I thought he told you."

"I mean, what's he doing in your house at this hour of the day?"

I took a deep breath. It had been like this since the beginning of time. My brothers could prowl the neighborhood like hot-blooded tick hounds, but I was supposed to be as pure as popcorn salt—apparently until the day I died or got married, whichever came first. It was probably the reason for my early promiscuity. Well, that and the fact that Marv Kobinski was a champion kisser. No, seriously, I think he won awards.

"He likes to cook," I said, and dropped into a slat-back chair. "He made me breakfast."

"What'd he make?" Her voice was suspicious, happy to catch me in a lie.

Eddie waved from the open door, still grinning. I slapped a hand in his general direction and turned away.

"Bacon," I said.

"Bacon! That stuff will kill you."

I closed my eyes. "You made bacon all the time when we were kids."

"That was for your father. And your brothers. Men can digest food girls can't begin—"

"Listen, Mom..." I snapped my eyes open and turned

toward the door, searching for an escape. I really didn't think I could bear to hear the men-can-eat-whatever-they-want speech. "I've got to get—" But at that moment my lungs collapsed.

Jack Rivera was standing in my doorway, looking as long and mean as a smoking pistol.

27

You are the perfect woman, a magical blend of beauty, intelligence, and spirit. Without you, my life is nothing.

*—Ryan Blackhawk, the good-
looking, but fictional, guy
in Chrissy's picture frame*

I GLANCED TOWARD my office, remembered the photographs, the gossip, the secrets. My fingers curled involuntarily into the fabric of the robe near my throat. Rivera stared at me, eyes smoking.

"Chrissy!" Drill sergeants have nothing on my mother.

"I've got to go, Mom." I could feel my hair standing on end, reaching for unsuspecting strangers like Medusa's infamous snakes. There was dried spittle on my cheek. It cracked when I moved my lips. Maybe, I thought hazily, Eddie wasn't really gay. Maybe he simply couldn't see himself spending the rest of his mornings with a drooling slob. But turning to men just to get rid of me . . . that was kind of a complicated ruse. So perhaps he was only trying to spare my feelings. Eddie was a nice guy.

"Who's the boy toy?" Rivera asked.

I jerked my mind into submission.

Rivera nodded toward the door. He was closer now. I could feel the heat of him in the soles of my feet. I curled my naked toes around the wooden dowel on my chair and held on like a discombobulated spider monkey.

"Is someone else there?" The drill sergeant was getting angry.

"No!" The thought of my mother and Rivera communing in any manner made my mind skitter around like a kid on a sugar high. "Just . . . No."

"Let me talk to Eddie again." Her voice was rising.

My brain was starting to sweat while swear words and apologies popped out of my eyeballs like zits on a tuba player. "Eddie's gone."

"I heard a man's voice."

My fingers felt numb against the receiver. "It's the TV."

"This time of day?"

"Listen, Mom . . ." I was thirty-three years old—thirty-three—but I was groveling like a spanked whelp. "I have to get to work."

"Work! It's—"

"I'll call you tonight. Promise," I said, and slapped the receiver into the cradle.

Rivera stood no more than eighteen inches away. His eyes were deadly dark, his clothes rumpled, his body language hushed. The lull before the storm. "You should have let me talk to her," he said. The light in his eyes was bright enough to read by. It might have been laughter. It might have been anger. Note to self: Learn to read the light in Rivera's eyes.

"What are you doing here?" My voice was wondrously casual. As if I wasn't considering the fact that he might have killed his ex-lover in a fit of jealousy. As if two red-hot guys crossed paths at my door every day of the week. As if I hadn't been digging around in his personal life. As if I hadn't been prying into his family's affairs. God help me.

He lifted one corner of his mouth. The scar at the right twitched up in a piratical manner. I curled my fingers tighter against my throat. Good thing I wasn't a virgin or he might have to torture me.

"I was worried about you," he said. "Just thought I'd stop by on my way to the station."

But according to his father and Daniel, he'd lost his badge, which meant he wasn't going to the station. Which meant he was lying. Why would he be lying? "I'm not on the way to the station," I said.

He gave me a half-assed grin. And despite it all—the lies, the suspicions, our glowering history—I felt my hormones sizzle. He turned toward my office. His jeans rode low on his hips, hugging his thighs, caressing his—

Holy crap! The photos!

"Rivera!" I didn't shout his name, but I didn't exactly whisper it, either.

He looked over his shoulder at me, eyes dark and steady, almost bored.

Why bored? Why? He knew something. What did he know? That I'd been snooping around in his life? That I suspected his mother . . . if not of murder, at least of sleeping with the liquor guy, who couldn't have been out of diapers for more than a year? That I have an abiding interest in pirates?

"I think you owe me an apology," I rasped.

He turned slowly, facing me. I got to my feet. I wanted to die with my boots on. Shit, I'd forgotten my boots. Maybe I could run out and buy a nice pair of Guccis. One last splurge.

"An apology?" he said. My breath was coming hard. He seemed to suck all the oxygen out of the air. Like a Hoover, only with a better ass.

"I was just . . ." I managed to keep my eyes from darting toward the office. "Dinner was your mother's idea. I was just trying to be . . . social."

His brows rose the slightest degree. The scar twitched. "So you weren't snooping."

"No!" God, no. Dear God, no.

He took a step closer. I refrained from stepping back. I also refrained from ditching the robe and wrapping my limbs around him until he bleated like a lost lamb. What the hell is wrong with me? "And you haven't been snooping since?"

My skin felt clammy. "What are you talking about?"

He smiled and rested a hip against my table. It was as lean as a slab of filet mignon, and he was staring at me. Maybe he was wondering if there were bats in my hair. Or maybe he liked the "I'm possessed by demons" look. You don't know. "Where were you last night?"

"What?" I sounded like a chipmunk. They're cute.

"Last night," he said. He could drill holes with those

eyes. "You go out or did you and sugar baby have your own party here at home?"

"Sugar baby." I laughed, but inside, my mind was spinning like *The Exorcist* chick's. How much did he know? How much did he guess? How much did I want to dive into the ugly carpet beneath my feet, or sink my teeth into his lower lip?

"We, ummm . . ." Maybe Rivera had come by last night. Maybe he knew I'd been gone and was just toying with me. That seemed like something he would do. "We went out for a while."

"Yeah?" He tilted his head lazily. "Anywhere special?"

"No." I cleared my throat and settled back into my chair, casual, and oh so not nervous. My left knee popped out between the edges of the robe. His gaze shifted to it. My lungs collapsed. It would only be a short jump from gripping the chair to being coiled around him like a Slinky.

"No dancing?"

"Dancing?" I heaved a laugh. "Why would you think—"

He eased into the chair next to me and reached out. My breath hitched up hard in my throat. His hand brushed my thigh and skimmed along the silky fabric of my robe. My legs threatened to fall apart. True, last night's show may have been a shameful display of male exploitation, but that didn't mean it wasn't effective as hell.

"Remember last time you lied to me, Chrissy?" he asked.

My esophagus was dry. Other places weren't quite so arid. His fingers trailed along the border of my robe, down the length of my thigh.

"When the two guys in the Cadillac kidnapped me and threatened me and took my purse, which I left on the floor when I escaped?"

"Yeah, that time."

I shook my head. I couldn't take my eyes off his fingers. "It's a little blurry."

"Remember the screaming and the shooting and the you almost getting killed?"

His fingers were dipping toward the inside of my knee. I was pressed back into my chair, breath held, lungs like Goodyear blimps.

"Maybe we should try to avoid that this time," he said, and slipped his knuckles against my bare skin.

I shivered, took one shuddering breath, and held it. He slid his hand toward my torso. I watched it like a cobra. God in heaven, that felt good.

"Chrissy?" His hand stopped. He was looking at me. I could feel his attention on my face. Was he waiting for a response? Would he not move his damned hand unless I answered?

"But last time . . . last time . . ." I licked my lips. My tongue felt heavy. ". . . Elaine was . . ." His fingers were moving again, stroking gently. Holy crap, it couldn't be more than eighteen inches between his hand and my crotch. How damned long could it take him to get there? "She was in danger."

"Maybe you're in danger this time."

Was that a threat or concern? And shouldn't a trained shrink be able to tell the difference? Maybe if the shrink would quit panting like a greyhound.

His gaze burned my face. His hands felt like black magic against my thigh.

"I'm . . . I'm fine," I breathed.

He stared at me. "Then who's in trouble?"

"No . . ." I began, but his fingers slid a couple more inches. My head jerked back like a ragged-assed puppet's.

"What's going on, Christina?"

"Nothing." I sounded possessed.

His fingers skimmed across my panties. I think I screamed, and suddenly he was on his knees. His hands scooped beneath my robe, pushing it aside. His fingers felt like voodoo around my ass, pulling me close. His mouth was inches from my O zone.

"I don't want you hurt again," he rasped.

I shook my head.

He kissed me, just above the elastic. I croaked something indiscernible.

"What were you doing last night?" He kissed me again, lower this time.

"Dinner. Just dinner." Somehow my fingers had become curled up in his hair.

His grip tightened on my cheeks. "I didn't know they served meals at the Strip Please."

For a second my mind froze, then I was scrambling backward, feet, hands, knees, elbows, everything flying. The chair bounced off the wall and toppled. Rivera caught it in one smooth move as he rose to his feet.

"You were following me!" I rasped. What was he afraid I'd learn?

His eyes were midnight black. "What the fuck were you doing there?" His voice was low and soulless.

"What do you think I was doing there?" I was spitting like a cat and raised my chin. Heroic under fire. His gaze crackled like lightning down my midsection and stopped at my crotch. I reached down to drag my robe together, hands shaking like wind socks in a hurricane.

"Looks like the boy didn't do a very good job."

He took a step toward me. I took a step back. My knees weren't all that steady, either, but at least they were together.

"I don't know what you're talking about," I said.

"What'd you have to pay him, McMullen?"

"Screw you!" I snarled.

And suddenly he was on me, his body pressed tight against mine, his hands plastered against the wall behind my head. "Only if you tell me the damned truth," he said. I could feel his erection brush like lightning against the big O. "Why'd you go to the club?"

"No reason."

"Who'd you talk to?"

"No one."

He pressed against me. "Too busy with other things?"

I closed my eyes. "Yes." If he wasn't a police officer, what was he? Enraged? Desperate? Dangerous?

"Whose things?"

I licked my lips. He watched the movement. I think he'd quit breathing.

"Christ, McMullen, if I'd known you were that desperate, I would have dropped everything." He captured my shoulders, ran his hands down my arms, pinning them to my sides. "Including my pants."

I was breathing hard now, rasping like a freight train. "You're all heart, Rivera."

"Not quite," he said, and pressed against me again. My robe had surrendered. His erection felt like a baseball bat against my belly.

"Get off me," I growled. My internal shrink told me to say something clever to pacify him, but the back of his shirt had become twisted up in my fingers, and the cocktail chick had thought of others ways to calm him.

He dropped my arms, and for one hideous second I was terrified he would do as told, but suddenly his hands were on my waist, sliding upward, bumping over my ribs until he was holding my breasts in his palms. His thumbs flicked across my nipples.

The world exploded. "Damn you!" I hissed, and crashed my mouth against his.

It was all over then. No coherent thought. Just scrambling. My robe was gone, pooled on the floor. We were slipping on it, skittering toward the bedroom. His shirt released his arms and hung from his waistband. My fingers bumbled at his belt. He shoved them away, but it didn't matter. He knew what he was doing. His erection popped out, big and hard, and plum tight between the teeth of his zipper.

I think I may have taken God's name in vain at the sight of it. But suddenly we were in my bedroom. No more need for curses.

He backed me toward the mattress. Our lips met, teeth grazed, breath hissed. My buttocks hit the bed. It groaned beneath me. I fell back and lay down, stretched out on the cool sheets. My breasts felt heavy, my skin hot, but not as hot as his gaze, searing on contact.

He straightened slightly. His body was pretty damned beautiful, dark and hard and lean.

"You're not drunk this time, are you?" His voice was a husky snarl of masculinity.

I managed to shake my head.

" 'Bout damn time." He stepped forward and slipped on something, then dropped his gaze to the floor. And suddenly I knew I was doomed. I didn't immediately know why, but I could feel the chill like a cold Chicago wind whistling around the corner of my life.

I felt him freeze. He bent down, lean muscles flexing along the bend of his arm. I tried, but I couldn't manage to lower my eyes in the direction of his. Somehow I knew what he was looking at. I just knew.

Eddie hadn't left Solberg's file in the office after all.

When Rivera straightened, he had a half-dozen damning photos in his hand. The world was eerily silent, and then, quietly, almost reverently, he said, "Sali. Damn, she was pretty, wasn't she? Bright. Funny." He shuffled the grainy pictures, still staring. A muscle jumped in his jaw. "Almost invincible." His eyes looked crazy dark. "Almost."

I don't remember pulling the sheet over me. But it felt cold against my skin.

"So what do you think?" He lifted his spooky gaze to me. "Did I kill her? Or was it Mama?"

I drew a careful breath, wondering if maybe it would be my last.

"Either way, it's nice of you to decide to fuck me," he added.

I wrapped the sheet around me, stepped off the bed. Our bodies were inches apart. I could feel the heat of his chest sear mine. Anger had replaced the void left by passion. "Get out," I said.

"Have you figured out how I did it yet?" he asked.

"Leave me alone." I tried to brush past, though I don't know where I was going. He caught my arm, but destinations are limited anyway when you're wearing a toga and gorgon hair.

"There were no bruises, Chrissy. No signs of a struggle. No DNA." His grip tightened like a vise. He gritted his teeth. "No fucking witnesses."

I strained away from him.

He gave me a crooked grin. "But you're not buying any of it, are you? Not Christina McMullen, Ph.D. You're still betting on me, aren't you?"

I didn't move away, didn't move at all. Barely breathed. "You didn't kill her," I said.

"Yeah?" he said, and squeezed a little closer. "What makes you think so?"

"You didn't care enough," I said. "You don't care enough about anyone."

He eased up a little on my arm and pulled away half an inch, curious. "Is that your professional analysis? Is that what you think? People only kill if they care?" He ran his free hand through his hair and chuckled. "And they gave you a license to peddle that crap?"

Anger mixed with indignation and turned cold. He could insult my morals, my hair, or my mother, but it really pissed me off when he took swipes at my career. "You saying you're guilty, Rivera?"

He shrugged. The movement was stiff, his fingers hard. "Doesn't matter now that the boys in tox finally got their shit together."

I waited, mind churning. He didn't continue.

"What are you talking about?"

He dropped my arm and shrugged, but his movements were stiff, jerky. "There was a gas leak."

"What?"

"In the kitchen." He nodded once, eyes narrowed. "The oven."

I hissed in surprise and half shook my head. "That's what killed her?"

He laughed. "What's the matter, Chrissy? Hoping for something juicier? You can call the captain if you like. He'll corroborate my story. Hell, call Graystone, if you want."

My mind was reeling. "If there was a leak, why didn't it kill you?"

He propped a hip against the wall. "I left the front door open."

"But . . ." My brain was sputtering over facts and suppositions. They were all half-assed at best, but nevertheless, there was something wrong here. I could feel it in the soles of my feet.

"But what, darlin'? This is good news. Now you can fuck me with a clear conscience instead of worrying that you might be screwing a—"

"It smells."

His brows rose. "What?"

"Gas smells."

"Wrong again, Chrissy love. It's odorless."

"But they add something. Just so this sort of thing doesn't happen. They add a scent. Just—"

"It was a small leak."

"Still—"

"Damn it!" he snarled, hands fisted. "Tox says it was the gas!"

He watched me from inches away, eyes sparking.

As for me, I felt strangely calm. "And you believe them?"

He laughed. The sound was grim. "Fucking right I do. So I guess I'll have to admit that dear old Dad is innocent. And I'm a . . ." He raised a brow. "What am I, Chrissy? Just a guy who wants to live out his adolescent fantasies of retribution. Wasn't that what you said? Wasn't that the shitty line you fed me?"

"You're an asshole," I said, and sweeping the sheet in front of me with dramatic flare, I stepped away.

He was in front of me in a heartbeat. "And you're still horny."

I looked him up and down. "I'll get over it," I said.

He took another step forward. My throat convulsed. Other stuff pulsed. Literally pulsed. I could feel my heart beating between my legs. Weird. I've been called an uppity broad, but I'll tell you what, my body is a slut down to my toenails.

"Want me to help you with that?" he asked.

I laughed. It sounded more like a croak. "Over my dead body."

"I don't do that, remember? Guys in tox verified it." He reached for me. I slapped his hand. He snarled a grin. "So you won't have any need for that dewy-eyed little boy toy you brought home."

"Eddie's twice the man you are." I was slipping back into elementary school, but it was too late to retract the words. Next I'd be calling him names and giving him purple nurples.

"Yeah?" He pressed up against me. "Eddie who?"

I almost spit out his name, but contrary to popular opinion, I'm not completely brain-dead. I drew my tattered dignity around me and gave him a look.

He looked back. I had some cleavage showing, and most of one leg. He looked for quite a while. "Give me his last name." His eyes were glowing. The muscles in his arms and chest bunched. My heart pounded like a jackhammer. "I'll just have a talk with your little friend," he said, and reaching up, pushed my hair away from my face. I didn't swoon. "Make sure he's treating you right."

I laughed. The last time he'd talked with one of my "little friends," things had gone weirdly awry. And if there's anything I've figured out in the past decade or so, it's that I can ruin perfectly good relationships all by myself. "I wouldn't tell you his name if you tortured me with a cat-o'-nine tails."

He gave me a weird look, snorted, and turned away. "Never mind," he said, "I'll just go to the club and ask around."

I grabbed his arm. The sheet slipped and a nipple popped out. His scar jumped. I dragged the toga back up. He did the same with his eyes, except slower. Harlequin whimpered at the door . . . I think.

"Please." I'm not sure why I was down to begging.

Maybe it was for the little Mexican boy who'd made his way to the land of the free on stolen pesos and terror. And maybe I should have told the cops what he'd told me, but I couldn't. Not yet. Not while I remembered the look in his eyes. "Don't."

He watched me. Waited.

"Eddie's a friend," I said finally. "Nothing else. We just . . . we were just bored. Heard about the Strip Please."

His lips curled up in a half-assed parody of a smile. "You were in there half the night, McMullen. I would think you would have had time to get your rocks off before coming here."

He'd been watching, waiting. He was playing with me . . . again. The idea made my blood boil. "What were *you* doing, Rivera, sitting in the corner, living out some forbidden fantasies?"

"Decided to bring Travolta home, live a few fantasies of your own, did you, McMullen?"

I didn't say anything.

He pulled his arm free, turned away. "I'll give the other stripping stud muffins your regards," he said.

I ground my teeth, debated for a fraction of a second, then blurted, "He's gay." The words ripped through me like a kidney stone.

Rivera stopped dead in his tracks. I closed my eyes, steeling myself against the fallout. I could feel him turn toward me, could feel him draw nearer, almost touching.

When I opened my eyes, he wasn't exactly smiling. His expression was too stunned, as if he'd just captured a fairy and couldn't quite believe his good fortune. "What'd you say?"

In that moment I would have given my left boob for a pocket stocked with Mace. But the sheet was damnably short on pockets. Long on tails, though. I tried, with quiet dignity, to pull it up my shoulder, but it was caught on something. So I sniffed instead. "You heard me," I said.

He tilted his head. "Your lover is gay?"

He made my teeth hurt. "Eddie's not my lover."

"Because . . . he's gay?"

"What is it, Rivera?" I asked, conjuring all the hauteur possible with snake hair and a bedsheet. "You prejudiced or just jealous?"

He stared at me for an instant, then he threw back his head and laughed.

I glared at him, blood simmering. He continued to hee-haw like a wild ass. My temper perked up a notch, trip-ping toward the boiling point. I tried another tug at the sheet. But it was stuck fast . . . beneath his feet.

The beautifully balanced justice of the situation struck me with silent bliss.

I stared into his eyes. He stared into mine, still laugh-ing, and then, ever so slowly, I unraveled the sheet. It fell away from my boobs with silky disregard, slithered down my belly, and pooled gracefully at my feet. Rivera's jaw dropped like a rock.

And in that instant, in that beautiful nip of time, I reached down and yanked the sheet with all my blood-boiling might.

I watched his eyes go wide, watched his arms begin to flail. For one terrible moment I was afraid he might recap-ture his balance, but then he fell, windmilling backward to land with a solid *crack*.

I didn't give myself more than a couple of seconds to enjoy the view. Then I turned and sprinted toward my bedroom.

He snatched me to a halt before I reached the door. I swung around, drew my arm back, and slammed the heel of my hand into his eye.

He stumbled backward.

"Shit."

We said the word in unison. I was covering my mouth. He was covering his eye.

He lowered his hand first. The area around his iris was no longer white, but crisscrossed with a hundred scarlet tributaries.

"Holy crap, Rivera—"

"Not bad," he said. "But remind me to teach you how to strike with your elbow."

"I'm sorry."

"Yeah." He nodded. "Me, too." He dabbed at the corner of his eye with his thumb. It was seeping. "I think you might be driving me crazy."

Okay, I'd just popped him in the eye and I was standing there naked three feet from my bedroom door, and I might have been considered a little defenseless, but I was still mad.

"I can recommend someone for that," I said.

He chuckled. It sounded tired. I wondered when he'd slept last. Something dark and lonely shone in his eyes. Was it fear? Confusion? Guilt? Shit, I had no idea. But, oddly, at that precise moment, it didn't matter. I stepped forward, wanting to touch him, to be touched. But he backed away.

Silence whispered like a draft between us, then he turned, walked away, and closed the front door behind him. Harlequin barked. I imagined him jumping circles around his fallen hero. I remembered the haunted look in Rivera's eyes when he'd seen the pictures, the look of trust slashed.

I sighed, feeling guilty. But what the hell was I supposed to do? Had he expected me to accept the fact that he may or may not have killed Salina Martinez? Should I have dabbed on some lip gloss, grabbed my handbag, and headed off to Spago to score a glimpse of Jennifer Aniston?

I didn't work that way.

Tripping over the fallen sheet, I stumbled into my bedroom and flopped onto the mattress.

Photos lay scattered across the floor. A picture of Daniel lay on top. He still looked sharp, but angry as he gazed at . . . Salina?

My mind clicked over. I snatched up the image, staring, google-eyed. Was that Salina in the crowd? Were they together?

Jumping to my feet, I raced bare-assed into my office, grabbed a magnifying glass from the drawer, and aimed it at the paper. The image was tiny and indistinct. The photographer had just caught the edge of her profile, but it was Martinez. I was certain of that. She was wearing a slim, sweeping evening gown. Her sleek hair was piled up above her elegant, swan-smooth neck, and her hands were gloved. One rested on the chest of a tuxedoed man. His hair was dark, his face hidden. But hers was just visible, and the expression, even half-hidden, was one of absolute adoration.

I felt myself pale as tiny puzzle pieces clattered into place.

"Holy crap," I breathed. "Those guys in tox are morons."

28

Life's funny. Sometimes it's your oyster, and sometimes you're its bitch-slapped man-whore.

> —*Zach Peterson, Chrissy's
> former beau, who really
> was a man-whore. Really.*

ROBERT PEACHTREE LIVED up in Santa Clarita, where there's still enough room to breathe. But I couldn't appreciate the view. My nerves were stretched as tight as Laney's longbow, my fingers gripped the steering wheel with white-knuckled intensity, and my stomach felt queasy and uncertain. Maybe my mother had been right, maybe women weren't supposed to eat pure fat first thing in the morning. I considered stopping for an orange juice to straighten out my blood-sugar level, but couldn't force myself to take the time.

I knew what had happened. All I needed was a little corroboration.

It took me over an hour to reach Peachtree's property. The house was the size of a baseball field. The driveway wound around it, ending beside a copse of persimmon and poplar. I parked between it and a black BMW and got out.

The sun was warm against my skin, but I still felt chilled as I rang the doorbell. Facts and rumors and suppositions ran through my head like raw sewage.

Peachtree himself answered the bell. He was wearing shorts that showcased saggy knees and blue-veined lower legs, but had still donned the traditional straw hat and ten-gallon buckle. "Ms. McMullen," he said, and reached out with a leather-clad hand to shake mine. His grip wasn't strong. The other hand looked a little shaky on the head of his cane. "Excuse my appearance. I was just helping Eldwardo with some work outside." He looked thrilled to see me and shuffled back a little, holding the screen door wide. His socks were pearly white where they showed through the open toes of his leather sandals, and somehow it was that sight that made my uncertainty swell like a river. Someone loved him enough to wash his socks. And he loved, loved Daniel Hohl like a son. "But I'm happy as a clam that you've taken me up on my invitation. Welcome, welcome."

"Mr. Peachtree." I felt a little breathless. "Thank you for seeing me on such short notice." I had called him less than two hours before, giving myself enough time to shuffle through the photos, both Solberg's and the crime scene's. My heart was pounding.

"No problem. No problem at all. Come in. Please." He waved me inside, then took off his hat and gloves and tossed them onto a wooden bench. He looked smaller without his nod to the Old West. The house rambled away. To my left, I saw an office decorated in rich browns and forest greens. To my right was the dining room, table neatly set for eight. A bottle of Chardonnay stood at the corner, a corkscrew beside it, its handle pewter and shaped like a rattlesnake. Like all the rooms, the great room we were standing in was vaulted and rugged.

"Have a seat." He waved to a trio of leather chairs arranged around a wagon-wheel coffee table. Against the left wall there was a fireplace. Nights can get cool so close to the mountains. "Or we could sit outside by the pool, if you like."

"No." I settled into a chair, feeling light-headed with my own soaring sense of knowledge. "This is fine."

"Good. Good." He glanced out the window and scowled. "If you'll excuse me just one minute."

"Of course."

Stumping toward the deck door, Peachtree opened it and stuck his head out. In profile, his neck looked long and scrawny, like an aging turtle's. Guilt spurred me. This was going to hurt him. "That's great, Eldwardo. Don't worry about the magnolias. I watered them yesterday. But you'd best see to Mrs. Peachtree's flowers, or there'll be hell to pay when she gets back."

I didn't hear Eldwardo's answer, but the old man chuckled a response, waved, and returned to me.

"So . . ." He stumped past again, heading to a side table near a couch the size of Montana. "Christina McMullen . . ." He did a fair Gaelic impression. "Is that Scotch or Irish?"

"Irish as mutton stew," I said.

"Well..." He poured himself a Scotch and raised the glass. "There's nothing wrong with that, is there now?"

"Not a'tall," I said, playing along, impatience tap-dancing on my nerve endings.

"You want a nip, then?"

"It's kind of early in the day, but sure, why not?" I had unraveled the mystery.

"That's the spirit." He poured me a hundred thimble-fuls, then made his laborious way back toward me.

"Thank you." The glass was as heavy and clear as... well, crystal.

He nodded, then sighed as he sank into a chair not far from me. The cushions groaned. "So, lassie, you'll be wantin' to know more about my offer, will you?"

I had been intentionally vague on the phone, merely saying that I was ready to talk. I cleared my throat. "I'm flattered you'd consider me," I said. "But actually, I came by to discuss something else entirely."

He stuck out his lower lip and narrowed his eyes, not comprehending.

"It's a matter of some importance." I drew a deep breath and plunged. "It's about Daniel Hohl."

"Danny Boy?" His scowl deepened. "What about him?"

"He works for you. Is that correct?"

"I'm no fool," he said.

It was my turn to look bemused.

"Danny's smart as a firecracker. I wasn't going to have him working for my competition. Don't get me wrong. I love him like a son. But even if I didn't, I'd a found a way to convince him to work for Sharpe."

"How about for True Health?"

"What's that?"

"True Health. He does a considerable amount of work for them, too, doesn't he? Research, that sort of thing."

He shook his head and drank. "Danny does what he wants on his own time."

"Even if it involves murder?"

The old man drew himself up with righteous indignation. "I don't know what the hell you're hinting at."

"Daniel said it was over between Salina and him. That he hadn't seen her in over a year, but that wasn't true, was it? Even after his engagement to Cindy, he was still seeing Salina. I found a picture of them at a fund-raiser for True Health."

"I don't know what you're talking about."

"True Health is a new company. Not more than six months old. They're working with experimental drugs. Plants from the Amazon. That sort of thing."

"He's a pioneer. All the great minds are. So?"

I nodded. "I saw a picture of Salina and Daniel at a True Health function. He lied about his association with her."

He snorted and waved a hand at me.

But I continued, on a roll. "His fiancée didn't know about them. Maybe no one did. But Cindy was willing to believe my merest suggestion. Woman's intuition maybe. He'd told her other lies, about being uninvolved with hair restoration. It made me wonder why."

"Danny's a good boy." His brows were low, bushy over eyes that were suddenly teary. "I won't have you slathering up his name."

I set my Scotch on a nearby table. "She wanted to end it, didn't she?"

He looked from the glass to me. "You're crazy."

"She was in love with someone else, so she wanted to end it. She baked cocoa cookies for him, just like your wife used to do, only she was planning to say good-bye. But Danny's used to getting what he wants. And he wanted her. Isn't that right?"

"I don't have to listen to this," he growled, and shakily turned away.

Guilt and exhilaration sluiced through me in a powerful blend. My head felt light. I grabbed the arm of my chair.

He turned back toward me with a scowl, anger and caring chasing each other across his creased features. "You okay?"

I straightened. "I'm fine, Mr. Peachtree," I said. It might have been a little bit of a lie. My hands felt shaky. "But it's time for you to face the truth. I wanted to talk to you before I went to the police." And I wanted him to tell me I was right.

He glared at me. "Blast it, girl, you're pale as a ghost. I'm not going to be explaining to the missus why some gal swooned on her favorite wool rug. I'm getting you something to eat," he said, and shambled off, but he was back in a second, grumpily handing over a plate with a trio of cookies. Dottie's revered cocoa treats. I picked one up and looked at it.

"Now's not the time to be worrying about your weight, girl. Eat it before you keel over."

I took a bite and waited for the euphoria, but it wasn't as good as I'd expected, and then, suddenly, like a reel from an old movie, I remembered Daniel's admitted aversion to them.

I stopped, mind whirring slowly to a halt. The world was quiet. "They weren't his favorites," I said.

Peachtree was watching me like a spider, head pulled tight between his bony shoulders.

"They're yours." I jerked to my feet, propelled by the power of the truth. The floor tilted beneath me. "Holy crap! She was going to leave *you*. *You* were in love with her."

"Couldn't leave things alone, could you?" he asked, and stepped toward me.

I backed away. My chest felt tight. "You killed her," I said. "With a drug too new to be detected."

He grinned. It didn't look so harmless anymore.

"But..." I tried to shake my head, remembering the crime photo of the glass imprinted with Salina's lipstick. The world shifted. "I didn't drink anything. Hardly ate..." I darted my gaze to the cookies he'd offered.

He chuckled. "That Danny's a genius, ain't he? Developed stuff that'll absorb right through the skin. It's hardly nothin' but a damned plant extract."

I looked down at my hands. They felt disconnected. My vision wavered. "It was on my glass?"

"Don't work real good on smooth surfaces. But on leather—"

I jerked my gaze back up. "Your glove."

"Has a latex lining. Stuff has a kick like a mule if you get it on your skin. It'll make a damned fortune. You just got a middlin' dose, but you're feelin' it, ain't you?" He chuckled. "Topical anesthesia. It'll do some good, too. Damn doctors, always poking around for a vein like I'm a fuckin' lab rat. Just rub a teensy bit of this on the skin and I wouldn't feel a thing. Numbs you clear down to the bone. 'Course, if you get too much . . ." He grinned. He was stalking me, shaking his head. My legs felt like noodles beneath me. I was only a few steps from the deck door. From help. "You pretty gals. You think you run the world these days. Sali . . ."

I backed into something, fumbled around it, gasping for air, for sense. The world seemed cloudy.

" . . . she was a beauty." He snorted. "Morals of a tiger shark, but pretty as the sunrise. Slept with every man-whore in town. It's a shame."

My fingers touched something. It felt indistinct as it came away in my hand. Nothing but a pillow. A pillow. I hadn't gotten past the couch.

" 'Cuz I woulda given her the world."

"You were sleeping with her, too." I stumbled around the end of the couch. The floor slanted up to meet me. I fought the incline.

He laughed. The sound ricocheted off my ears. "There wasn't much sleepin' done when she was in the room. Hell, she's been draggin' Danny around by his pecker ever since the beginning. Ever since we started making some real money. Thought he might quit her when he became engaged, but . . ." He snorted. "Sali, she's like a drug. Can't just say no. And we was all about to make a bundle of cash. She liked to stay close."

I shook my head. The room shifted erratically. *"We?"*

"Had us a good thing goin'. Sali, too. Stood to make a fortune on that hair goop. There was some cancer in the test animals, true enough. But cancer . . ." He huffed a snort. ". . . it's in the air these days. Don't mean nothing. Miguel, though, he was being difficult. Wanted more testing done. Getting all high and righteous. And after all the shit he pulled with his aides and such. Hell, his own son won't hardly talk to him." He shook his head. "Family's everything. Kids these days, they don't know that. Divorce everywhere you look. But I guess that don't matter to you no more. Anyway, Sali—she could have brought Miguel around. Only all of a sudden she wanted to come clean. Start fresh, she says."

I remembered Salina's adoring expression, her hand resting on a dark-haired gentleman's chest. "She was in love with Julio. The senator's double. She was in love with him."

"The drug's undetectable," he said, as if I hadn't spoken. "Stops the lungs if you get too much. Tricky that way. Danny'll figure out how to make it work for us, though. But why am I telling you? You must have figured that out. Smart girl like you." He scowled, scrunching his face. "Smart girls, takin' jobs from men. Blackmailing men. That's what you had in mind, wasn't it? Blackmail. I knew the minute I saw you talkin' to Danny's girl at the zoo."

"You saw me."

"I'm old but I ain't blind. Or stupid, neither. I know folks. Can read 'em like a book. I knew you was trouble the minute I laid eyes on you. Was hopin' you wouldn't cause no ruckus, though, seein's how you had your hands full with Miguel's boy. But then I checked into your past." He shook his head. "Nosy broad, ain't you? Can't—"

"You can't kill me." My voice was raspy. "Too much of

a coincidence. Salina...now me. They'll figure it out. Rivera—"

"Sali thought she could just pull up stakes and take off. But hell, she knew everything. Got her hands on some reports. Figured out there were problems. That gal could get a man to confess to murder." He giggled at his own pun. The sound echoed eerily in my rocking brain. "Besides, there wasn't no reason not to tell her. Wasn't like she cared if half the country croaked. But all of a sudden she wanted out. I went to Miguel's house to change her mind, but she wouldn't budge. In my heart, I knew she wouldn't." He shook his head. "Like I said, I know folks. So I brought the stuff with me." He curled his paper-white fingers as if he held the drug in his hand. "I hated to do it." For a moment his eyes looked distant, almost dreamy, then he laughed. "She fucks like a hungry whore, but money talks."

"You wore her rubber glove." I yanked my gaze from his fingers. "The mate to the blue one in the photo. I thought it was Daniel at first. But his hands were too big. You wore her glove to avoid fingerprints."

"I helped her with dishes. Like one of her New Age pansy boys. But I didn't wear 'em just for fingerprints, lass. That's where you're wrong. The drug don't absorb through rubber."

"You put it on her glass."

"On her glass." He chuckled. "*In* her glass. Didn't want to take no chances."

"She drank it."

"Girl could empty a fish tank and still be desert-dry. And that stuff is potent when taken by mouth. Had you drunk your Scotch like a good girl, you'd be dead as my elephant-hide boots." He shrugged. "It'll be a little slower now, but we'll get the job done."

"What about Rivera? He'll—"

"Rivera? Miguel's boy?" He laughed. "I saw him pull up the drive that night. Looked just like his old man when he stepped out of his car." He shook his head, reminiscing. "All earnest and righteous. Sali, she'd hit the floor just minutes before. I was just riggin' the stove so's L.A.'s finest could find a convenient cause of death. They get testy when they're baffled. And this stuff of Danny's is a puzzler."

"You hit Rivera. Knocked him out." I could see it now. Could see him standing behind Rivera. Not Daniel, but Peachtree. Damn. A little late and kind of important. "With your cane. The heavy one I saw in the picture."

He laughed. "Folks think I'm done for. But I still got some starch in me. Felt like ol' times. Swingin' for the bleachers. Gerald, he was just turning toward her. In a big rush. I was behind the wall. Plenty of room. He dropped like a rock. Thought for a minute he might be dead, but it's just as well he wasn't. Miguel would probably have raised holy hell."

"What about Salina?" Keep him talking, and keep breathing. Really had to keep breathing. "Senator Rivera wasn't attached to *her*?"

"She was plannin' to leave him. Hell, she'd always been screwin' someone else. I knew it all along. I suspect he did, too. Hard to love a gal who's crushin' your balls in both hands. Easy to kill 'em, though."

My knees buckled. I straightened them with a snap. "They'll figure it out," I said. "They'll know."

"You think I'm an idiot? You think I'm gonna leave you lying on my deck for the crows to pick at? Naw. I'll shove you back in your little car. Take you down that windy road, let you run into a tree. It'll be terrible sad."

"Eldwardo." The name came to me in a blast of lucidity. If I could just make it outside. "Your gardener knows I'm here."

The room boomed with his laughter. "I don't know no Eldwardo. We're alone here, little girl. Just you and me."

"I heard you—"

"Talk to someone who ain't there? Yeah, you did. Thought you could outsmart me, didn't you? Come here, asking questions. All innocent. All sweet. But I can smell a tramp a mile off. Just like Sali." He shook his head. I had stopped moving without knowing it. I stumbled back into motion, almost hit my knees.

"I gave her the moon. Woulda given the sun and the stars, too. Just had one little favor. One thing."

"I can't breathe," I said.

"I know. It's a shame. That's what she said. *'Can't breathe. Can't breathe.'* Well, then she should have talked to Miguel, shouldn't she? Should have told him to keep things quiet. A little bit of cancer in the lab rats. Well, men ain't rats, are they? But Miguel said he was going public unless there was more testing done. She coulda changed his mind. Once she spread her legs, ain't no man could keep his head on straight."

"Help me." My knees hit the carpet. The impact shattered my system, cracking against my lungs, sparking memories through my oxygen-starved system. "Rivera!" I screamed. The word was a harsh croak.

Peachtree froze in his tracks. "What the hell are you playin' at, girl?"

"He's here." My lungs were giving out for good.

He glanced out the window. "There's no one here."

My mind was off-kilter. "Of course he is. He always is. Rivera!" I screamed again, and staggered to my feet. The room spun. I closed my eyes. "Every time someone tries to ..." I was falling again. My shoulder hit the floor. I rolled onto my back. "When someone tries to kill me."

I could feel Peachtree bending over me. I was by the fireplace. I could see the variegated brick, the hearth, the tools.

"Lying little bitch," he snarled, but suddenly my fingers closed around the poker. I swung it with all my might.

He shrieked and stumbled back, holding his ear.

I scrambled to my feet, but my legs were numb. I fell, half crawling, half running toward the door.

"Rivera!" I shrieked, but something tangled in my hair and I was yanked off my feet.

My head cracked against the floor. Peachtree was standing over me. Blood was oozing from his ear, but the poker in his hands stole my focus. It was raised above his head.

"Bossy bitches. Gotta make life so damned hard," he rasped, and swung.

I rolled sideways. The poker scraped across my back, but I was already scrambling away on all fours. The dining room table was ahead of me. I scurried between the legs of a chair, got stuck at the hips. His hand grazed my back, snagging my waistband. I shrieked and reared up. The chair went with me. Then I was falling, careening over backward, the chair on him, me on the chair. It cracked in two.

He was cursing. I wished I had so much breath to waste. He tried to grab me, but splinters of wood were everywhere and the table was in sight again. I galloped beneath it on hands and knees I couldn't feel. He roared after me, trying to snatch my feet. But I was safe for a moment, gasping for each painful breath, fighting the haze that pulled at my mind.

His face appeared not three feet away, peering at me.

"Come on out of there, girl," he said. He was breathing hard, too. "We'll talk."

"Talk?" My voice sounded like sandpaper on concrete. "You think I'm crazy?"

"Crazy." He wiped the blood from the side of his head, then straightened, maybe to save his back. "Crazy like a fox. Crawl outta there now. Listen, I know when I've been beat. We need another smart cookie on staff. We'll cut you in."

"You'll . . . cut me . . ." I croaked.

Peachtree chuckled and bent again. And in that instant I remembered the table setting above me.

I reached up, felt something against my fingers, and yanked it into my lair.

"In my day, women weren't—" he began, and then I struck, stabbing with all my might. My weapon turned out to be a corkscrew. It sank into his foot, rattlesnake handle quivering between the straps of his sandals.

He shrieked. I spun around, striking my head on chair

legs and scrambling for the far end. Freedom. The door. I knocked the last chair out of my way. I could hear him coming for me, cursing, moaning, stumbling, but I was almost there.

And suddenly the sky fell. I was slammed to the floor, my lungs pinned beneath the weight of the world. In some dim region of my mind maybe I knew he'd planted a chair across my back. Maybe I knew he was crushing the breath from me. Maybe I knew he was stepping on the chair, forcing the last gasp of breath from my lungs.

But at that moment the door flew open. The weight left my back. I managed to lift my head. Rivera stood framed by the sky behind him, expression darker than hell, legs spread, hands holding a gun. My first thought was that I should get me one of those. My second was that he looked kind of like a pirate.

"Gerald . . ." Peachtree's voice shook. "I'm glad you're here. This woman—"

"Move so much as a finger and I'll blow your fuckin' head off," Rivera growled.

There was the sound of running feet. "Rivera!" someone yelled. "Lieutenant! Put the gun down."

"I would, Captain." Rivera's voice was low and steady. "But maybe we better make sure Peach here doesn't kill Chrissy first."

There was some cursing. A couple snapped questions. After that I'm not sure exactly what happened. Somebody yelled. Something about paramedics. Some running feet.

The chair was lifted from my back.

"McMullen."

I could hear Rivera's voice, but it did indeed sound like it came from the end of a long tunnel.

"Damn it, McMullen, open your eyes."

I did. Funny, though, I'd thought they were already open. Rivera's face looked pale and fuzzy, except for his left eye. That was bloodshot and surrounded by skin the color of a bad banana.

"You're the most beautiful girl in the universe, and very possibly the smartest," he said.

Or maybe that's not what he said. I've never been sure about the side effects of those drugs. My lips moved, but nothing came out.

He yelled something to the hazy mob behind him, then leaned close, ear to my mouth. "What, honey?" I was in and out of consciousness. But I really think he did call me honey in a voice gruff and soft, like he cared that I was dying. "What'd you say?"

It took all the strength I had, but I managed to speak. "Damn, you're slow," I croaked.

29

A balanced diet and a brisk daily walk will help keep
you healthy, but there's nothing like a good-looking
young man with a nice butt to hep up your cardio-
vascular system.

—*Sister Nina, Holy Name's
most scandalous teacher*

IT WAS DARK in my world. I blinked to make sure
my eyes were open. A green light blinked back at me.
Hospital. Alone. I tried to reconnect with the days past.
There'd been a lot of screaming again. Not so much running. More crawling. I took a deep breath. It hurt my
lungs, but I didn't feel like I was going to pass out. A fa-
vorable sign. I vaguely remembered an ambulance ride.
Someone had checked me in. Nice of them. Still, it would
have been even nicer if that someone had stayed around a
while. Laney was already on location. I wondered foggily
how much time had passed.

"What the hell's wrong with you, McMullen?" Rivera's

voice came from the end of the bed. I lifted my head. The darkness shifted erratically. I laid my head carefully back down and smiled at the ceiling.

"Well . . . I can't breathe very well. Feels like someone's sitting on my chest. My head hurts." I paused to take inventory. I imagined it was a good sign that I could remember the word "inventory." "My knees sting. My back is sore—"

"Are you a fuckin' nut job, or what?"

I didn't jump right in on that one, wanting to give it the sagacious consideration it deserved, but fell asleep instead. Might have been for the best.

Sometime later, I awoke with a start.

"Told you he wasn't guilty," I grumbled. I could feel crusty drool on my cheek. I glanced around, hoping Rivera hadn't noticed.

"Mac?" Laney was beside my bed. Seemed like she was holding my hand. I noticed that there were two bouquets of spring flowers and a stuffed Eeyore along one wall. The room remained relatively stable.

"Told him his dad wasn't guilty," I rasped.

"Are you okay?" Her voice sounded squishy.

I scowled. "Is someone sitting on my chest?"

"No."

"Not so bad, then," I said. My words were slurred. "But my head still hurts and my back aches like a son of a—"

A tall figure approached from my right. I jerked my gaze in that direction. A little too quick.

"Senator!" I said, and tried to straighten my hair. A tube protruded from my right hand and disappeared past the edge of the bed.

"This is Julio Manderos," Laney said.

"Oh." I felt like a stroke victim, but probably looked more like someone who'd had an unhappy meeting with a lightning bolt. "Sure." My hospital gown was twisted uncomfortably around my waist. But it was probably too late to look sexy anyway. Maybe I'd go for coherent. "Hi."

He smiled. His expression was as sad and gentle as I remembered. Taking my pierced hand carefully in his, he caressed my fingers. Belowdecks, a little conductor sat up with a jolt *Hey, there's some good-looking guy stroking our knuckles. Respiration, quit lollygagging. Endocrine, get cracking.*

"You look beautiful," he said.

I glanced desperately toward Laney. "Not dreaming," she murmured.

I nodded uncertainly and turned back toward Julio.

His eyes crinkled endearingly at the corners. "And you are incredibly brave."

I turned toward Laney.

She gave me a "Could be true" shrug.

"Kind." Bending over the bed, he gently kissed the tender skin beside the needle. *The conductor cracked his baton over Endocrine's head.* "And very, very wise."

Laney raised a brow and tilted her head. I decided to ignore her from there on out.

"I called your office. Your secretary said I could find you here." He looked sad again. If his eyes were any more expressive, he could save his mouth for things more important than speech. "I came by to apologize. Had I been half so noble as you, your head would not ache as it does." Reaching out, he skimmed his knuckles across my brow. "I am sorry. I should have told the police that which I knew, but I was too much the coward."

I cleared my throat. "There wasn't much you could have done."

His eyes smiled again, thoughtful and wise. "Not so much as you, I suspect. Still, Salina was my friend . . . in a manner of speaking." I didn't ask what manner. He drew a deep breath. "I did not love her as she deserved to be loved. As every woman deserves to be loved. But I should have done what I could to find her killer. Instead, you have taken the burden upon yourself." He had returned his attention to my hand, stroking the scraped skin. "Poor brave child."

I squirmed a little. The conductor was aces at his job. "I'm not exactly a child, Mr. Manderos."

He laughed. The sound was sweet and low, like the little packets of sugar substitutes. "That is good to know, Ms. McMullen," he said, perching carefully on the edge of my bed. "Good indeed, for I was hoping I might call on you from time to time."

"Call on me?" My voice squeaked. I cleared it and tried again. "Call on me?"

"Perhaps we might have dinner together from time to time."

"You're still conscious," Laney said, reading my mind.

"Certainly," I said. "I'd like that."

Leaning forward, he kissed my cheek. He smelled like kindness and sunlight. "Thank you, for being that which you are."

I watched him rise to his feet. The room shifted with him. I glanced at Laney

She laughed. "Go to sleep," she said, and I did.

Eddie Friar stopped by the next day. He looked like a caramel sundae. Good enough to eat. I refrained, which, considering the hospital food, was no small feat. A wooden basket with fuzzy chicks sticking out of a bunch of foliage had joined the flowers, and there was an array of colorful cards.

"How are you feeling?" he asked.

"My back hurts, and I can't stay awake more than ten minutes at a time. My butt is getting sore, and I'm starting to hallucinate about ice cream."

"No pirates?"

"Just one."

He laughed and dropped a book on my stomach. *The Princess and Her Pirate,* by my favorite author.

"Eddie," I said, feeling a little teary-eyed. Probably from lack of sugar. "You do love me."

"You bet your sore ass I do," he said, and dropping into a chair, he put his feet up on my bed.

We'd been talking for a few minutes about the vagaries of the human psyche—in other words, the fact that it was just plain bad luck that people kept trying to kill me—when Cindy Peichel walked in. She was carrying a peanut fudge parfait and not smiling.

"Hi," she said.

I sat up a little straighter, took the offered treat,

introduced her to Eddie, and waited to see if she was one of the many who wanted me dead.

"Go ahead and eat," she said. "I was in a Thai hospital for a week after an accident with an elephant." She sat down in the only available chair and stretched her mile-long legs out in front of her. "Lost five pounds and the will to live before they'd let me back with the herd."

I was munching peanuts and slurping ice cream. "You went back?"

"There are only about fifteen hundred of them left in the wild there. Less than half what there were only twenty years ago."

"Sorry," I mumbled. It's hard to talk while sucking in ambrosia.

"I'm not sure it's your fault specifically."

"I'm sorry about some other things, too."

She seemed to consider that for a moment. "After I confronted him, Daniel admitted he'd been cheating on me."

I wondered if she'd been holding some kind of tranquilizer gun when she'd done so, but the thought was vague.

"I'm sorry," I said again.

She nodded. "So you don't really work for Sharpe, huh?"

I shook my head, chewed, and swallowed. "I'm a psychologist."

"A psychotic or a psychologist?"

I choked on a peanut and hoped rather wildly that Eddie would save me if she tried to kill me.

"Just joking," she said, her face absolutely solemn. "Danny's pretty broke up about Peachtree. Shocked. You know, after we heard what happened, read the article, saw your picture in the paper. I put a couple of facts together. Found out you were here." She nodded. "I just came by to thank you."

I gave another feeble cough. "For?"

"I don't like lies."

"Sorry again."

"I meant *his* specifically."

I nodded, still feeling badly about my part in the fiasco. "Daniel seemed like a nice guy."

"Other than the fact that he was screwing someone else?"

"Yeah." I winced. "Other than that."

She exhaled quietly, slumped back in the chair, and watched me. "In most ways he's extremely intelligent. Articulate. Environmentally conscious. He'll do some good in the world." She looked thoughtful.

"So you're staying with him?"

She laughed. It was the first time I'd seen her do so. "So I'm going to let him *live*. Stay with him? You kidding? I'd rather be run over by a herd of pachyderms."

"You would know."

She looked at me. The expression almost seemed fond. "Finish that up," she said, "so I can recycle the dish."

I did as ordered. She stood up. "I owe you one," she said.

"One broken engagement?"

"Something like that." She took the plastic dish before I'd had a chance to lick it out, and reached for my hand. I gave her my untubed one. Which was a good thing, because she had a grip like a mountain gorilla. Okay, I'm just guessing.

"How you feeling now?" Eddie asked when she was gone.

"Am I dreaming?"

"Not yet."

"Anyone trying to kill me?"

"Not so far as I know."

"Feeling pretty good, then," I said. "Kind of sleepy."

He stood up, kissed me on the forehead, promised to return, and left me to my pirates.

When next I awoke there were three dozen roses residing in a fat earthenware vase beside my bed. Someone was fussing with the arrangement. She turned.

"Christina." It was Rosita Rivera, looking extremely well groomed and perky. I considered trying to mess with my hair, but there wasn't much motivation and even less hope. "You are well, *sí?*"

"*Sí.*" I tried to sit up. She helped me. Her hands were warm.

"I was very worried."

"I'm fine."

"Robert Peachtree." She shook her head, scowling. "The one man I thought wise enough to keep his *pene* to himself, huh?"

"Go figure."

"*Sí.* Go figure." She sat down in the chair closest to me. "I did not know about the rats with the cancer, Christina. This I promise you."

I nodded again. "I don't think many people did."

She grinned. "In truthfulness, the men I see these days will not have to worry about the baldness for some time."

So young Manny was indeed her lover. I gave myself a mental high-five. Right again.

"My Gerald has been worried to sickness about you also," she said, cutting my self-congratulations short.

I could tell when he called me a fucking nutcase, I thought, but decided not to mention it to his mother.

"He blames himself."

"Alpha personality," I said. "He likes to be in control."

"And you are not the one to be controlled, *sí?*"

I sighed. "Maybe in this case, it wouldn't have been so bad to listen a little."

"He wishes to protect you."

"I guess so."

"He cares a great deal. But he is like the small boy yet inside, and afraid to show his feelings."

"You think so?"

"I do. A small boy inside, but a hunk of burning love on the outside, *sí?*"

My face was already hot before he stepped through the door. But this time I wasn't surprised by his entrance. My hair was greasy and the hospital gown was twisted around my neck like a noose. Murphy's Law ordained his imminent arrival.

"Gerald," Rosita said joyously. "We were just now speaking of you." Her smile dropped away. "What happened to your eye?"

He turned his dark gaze on me. The eye itself looked okay. But the skin around it had sprouted some pretty spectacular hues, like magenta and puce.

"Tell me the truth," I said. "This time I'm really having a nightmare, right?"

He grinned. My stomach coiled up. He turned back to his mother. "What were you talking about?"

"How you are a hunk of burning love." She touched his face with gentle fingers.

"I didn't say that," I said. "Not even in the nightmare."

He laughed, squeezed his mother's hand, and stepped toward the bed. "I brought you something," he said, and passed over a pamphlet. It was a schedule for self-defense classes. I opened it up and glanced down the list.

"I have to work," I said. Besides, I was too tired to think about moving.

"Are you fishing for private lessons?"

I snorted and stared at his eye. "Looks like I can kick your—"

But his mother was already clapping her hands. "That is the marvelous idea. Gerald would be the perfect one to teach such a thing. See his eye, he was most probably in a fight with a lord of drugs or perhaps the boss of mobs."

I didn't say anything. He laughed. "How are you feeling?"

"You should have told me not to get involved," I said.

"I'll remember that in the future. And maybe—"

Someone stepped into the room. We turned toward Senator Rivera in unison. Everyone stopped breathing.

"Ms. McMullen." He gave me a nod. His voice was low and formal. There was a Styrofoam take-out box in his hand. I was just glad Cindy wasn't there anymore. There's nowhere to recycle that Styrofoam crap. She probably would have killed us all.

I cleared my throat and wished I could do the same with the tension. "Hello, Senator."

"Miguel," he corrected, and stepping past Rosita without a word, stood opposite his son. His back was very straight. "I was out of town on business, but I came as soon as I was able," he said, and handed over the box with a slight bow. "It is tiramisu. Gennaro made it especially with you in mind."

"That's very kind of you."

"No." He shook his head. His expression was sad. "It was kind of you ... to prove my son innocent."

I watched him for a moment. "You never really thought he was guilty."

He raised his brows, managing to look surprised and amused all at once. "I did not say I did."

"But you implied it ... subtly, but absolutely."

He shrugged. "You are an extremely intuitive young woman. I cannot control your thoughts."

"You wanted me to think you doubted him. To feel that I had to prove you wrong."

He laughed. "Perhaps I should have—"

"You sorry, fucking son of a bitch!" Rivera was all but spitting, fists clenched as he leaned across my bed. "You put her up to this?"

They faced off, the senator regally affronted. "I did no such thing. She was concerned. As was I. We—"

"You think she's a damn pawn? Someone—"

"You underestimate both her abilities and her intellect."

"She could have gotten herself killed."

Rivera Senior shrugged. "It was your task to prevent such a thing, was it not?"

"Shame on you, Miguel!" Rosita hissed. He spared her a glance. Perhaps there was some guilt in it.

"I should slap your sorry ass in jail."

"For what?" the senator scoffed. "Trying to save your job, ridiculous as it might be?"

"Ridiculous!" The word was a growl.

"You could have been anything you wanted. I have given you every opportunity."

"You gave me the determination to be nothing like you."

"Gerald, please," Rosita murmured.

"Well, that is good, then, for you do not measure—"

It was then that I put my hand to my throat and pulled in a loud, ragged-assed breath.

The three of them turned to me in terror.

"McMullen!" Rivera was leaning over me, gripping my hand. "Jesus, McMullen, are you all right?"

"Breathe slowly." The senator's face was taut with concern. "Try to relax."

I dragged in another dramatic breath, holding my throat and motioning them closer.

They leaned in, listening hard.

"You're acting like children," I said.

They straightened in unison, identical expressions of surprise blooming into anger.

"Fuck it, McMullen, don't ever—"

"You," I said, rounding on Rivera. "You wanted to believe your father was guilty. While he believed in you enough—"

The accused made a sound of denial, but I went on, louder now.

"And *cared* enough to try to prove your innocence, all the while knowing you would never appreciate his efforts."

"It is true," said Miguel. "You have forever disregarded—"

"And you," I said, spearing the elder Rivera with my glare. "You need to reevaluate your life. You're not a young man anymore. The clock's ticking, buddy. If there are people you truly care about, you sure as shit better figure out a way to prove it."

He straightened with regal aplomb. His lips tightened and then he turned and walked out.

The room was silent. I felt a spear of regret and guilt, but in a second he reappeared.

"Rosita." His voice was low, his expression solemn. "I have not yet eaten. Would you, perhaps, wish to join me for lunch?"

She raised her chin and her brows in haughty unison. "I'm meeting Manny in but a few—"

I cleared my throat, loud and authoritative. She glanced at me. I shifted my gaze from one man to the other, then settled it back on her.

"I suppose I can spare a few minutes," she said.

They left together. Not arm in arm, not singing love tunes, but not spitting at each other, either.

"I suppose you think you're clever," Rivera said.

"Hardly." I scowled. "He took my tiramisu."

"Serves you right."

"You two are idiots," I said.

"Is that your professional opinion?"

"Yes."

"I suppose you have a perfect relationship with your mother."

"Well..." I said, and snorted out a breath. Truth be told, I *was* feeling pretty clever, and kind of powerful. "At least we manage to conduct ourselves with a modicum of maturity."

"Do you?"

"I've learned through the years that one cannot—"

"Chrissy!"

I jerked my eyeballs front and center, but my mother was already rushing toward me.

I made some kind of noise, like *"Ackk."*

"Chrissy. What have you done? I called your house. No answer. Elaine said you were in the hospital. I caught the first plane out here. There were two kids yelling in my ear the whole way. Some people don't have any idea how to raise—"

"You must be Mrs. McMullen," Rivera said. There was a smirk in his tone.

"You knew she was coming," I said, but my voice was almost inaudible, drowned out by screaming acne and the *oompaa*ing huff of a tuba.

"Who are you?" Mom asked, eyes narrowed, and Rivera laughed.

Unconsciousness never looked better.

About the Author

LOIS GREIMAN lives in Minnesota, where she rides horses, embarrasses her teenage daughter, and forces her multiple personalities into indentured servitude by making them characters in her novels. Write to her at lgreiman@earthlink.net. One of her alter egos will probably write back.

If you enjoyed Lois Greiman's
Unscrewed, don't miss the next
mystery from this
"dangerously funny"* author.

Look for

Unmanned

Available now from Dell Books

Read on for a sneak peek!

*Janet Evanovich

Unmanned
Lois Greiman
On Sale Now

Honesty is for folks who don't know how to lie good.

> —*Chrissy McMullen's*
> *fifteenth boyfriend, who*
> *was actually more honest*
> *than most*

*M*CMULLEN," RIVERA SAID. I was juggling a stiff slice of pizza, a cell phone, and ten million irate commuters when he called—an average Tuesday morning in L.A.

"Yeah?"

"Sorry about last night." He had said he would drop over after work, but he hadn't shown up. Still, he didn't sound sorry so much as angry...and borderline psychotic. If I had a nugget of sense the size of a germ cell I would have drop-kicked our so-called relationship into the distant memory bin long ago, but Rivera's got an inexplicable appeal. And a really great ass.

"No big deal," I said.

There was a moment of impatient silence, then, "You're pissed."

I gnawed off a chunk of coagulated mozzarella and glared through the blob on my borrowed windshield. The weatherman had failed to predict an early-morning bird poop deluge. "I don't get pissed."

"It couldn't be helped." He sounded irritable and a little distracted, but I wasn't too thrilled, either. This was the third date he'd missed in as many weeks.

"Yeah? An emergency with another ex fiancée?" I asked, and immediately knew I should have kept my mouth shut. Intelligent silence isn't a new idea . . . just a good one.

"You jealous, McMullen?" he asked.

"Please," I said, but it's difficult to sound haughty while masticating.

He laughed.

I bit my tongue. Literally and figuratively. "Listen, Rivera," I said. "It's good of you to call, but I have to get to work by—"

"I'll come over tonight."

I balanced the pizza on my purse and gunned the snappy little Porsche past a late-model Caddy. "I'm afraid I'm otherwise engaged this evening. I'll—"

"Be right there!" he yelled, ineffectively covering the receiver, then said to me, "Around eight."

My smile was beatific. A shame it was wasted. "As previously stated, I'm afraid I'll be unable to—"

"I'll bring Chinese."

I felt my salivary glands tingle at the thought of Asian

delights, but I infused my spine with pride and the memory of a half dozen broken dates. "That's very considerate of you but—"

"Don't bother dressing for dinner," he said. His voice was low and smoky.

"Listen..." I began, but he had already hung up. I stared blankly at my phone until the blare of a car horn yanked me back to reality. Jerking the Porsche back into my chosen lane, I classily resisted returning my fellow commuter's early-morning salute and snapped the phone shut.

"Don't dress for dinner," I snorted. Like he could just sweep me off my feet with a little white sauce and testosterone. Like I had nothing better to do than wait panting by my door for him to show up with those sexy little take-out boxes from Chin Yung. Like I was desperate!

By the time the low-fuel light clicked on, I had inhaled the pizza and worked up a full head of steam. I swiveled into the nearest gas station, selected a fuel choice that wouldn't require a third mortgage, and dragged a windshield scraper from its receptacle near the paper towels.

Standing there in my silk suit and classy but secondhand sling backs, I scraped ineffectively at the Porsche's windshield. The car wasn't mine. It had been loaned to me by a height-sensitive little myope who was dating my best friend and former secretary, Elaine Butterfield. Laney had recently morphed into the Amazon queen— long story—and left to film a pilot in some remote area of the Calapooya Mountains. Thus I was left with her rightfully insecure beau and a long string of secretarial applicants who could neither type nor, apparently, think. I dared not be late to work, but there was one particularly large blob directly in front of the driver's seat. It was the color of ripe eggplant, and I was out of washer fluid. Murphy's Law had struck again.

"Here. Let me help."

I turned toward the gentleman who had appeared near my left elbow. He was six feet tall in his scuffed work boots and held a windshield scraper in his right hand. Blue fluid dripped from the netted sponge.

"Unless you need to prove your independence or something," he added. He wore round, gold-framed glasses over aquamarine, heavily lashed eyes. I have four eyelashes. Two on each side. Men always have superior lashes, despite a butt load of Maybelline and feminine insecurity. Coincidence or Murphy's Law? You be the judge.

"I have a strangulation hernia from carrying salt down to my water softener," I said.

He studied me, head tilted, hair thinning a little on the top. "Screw independence?" he guessed.

I nodded toward the windshield. "Knock yourself out."

He did so, not literally, leaning over the hood and sawing with vigor. His blue jeans rode low on narrow hips and there seemed to be zero fat molecules hanging around his waistband.

Turning the scraper, he squeegeed off the excess water and moved around to the other side. His T-shirt had been washed to a soft, olive green that set off the tight flex of his triceps.

"Thank you." I was trying to put the irritating memory of Rivera's Asian bribery behind me, but I was still feeling fidgety and a little flushed. "You can leave the rest."

But he was already applying the sponge to the passenger side. "I'd rather commit murder."

My nerves cranked up a little. Maybe it was the fact that I was late for work. Or maybe it was the mention of murder. Murder makes me kind of jumpy lately. "What's that?" I asked.

"Leaving a car like this dirty," he said, and grinned at me over the sparkling windshield. "It'd be a heinous crime."

I studied him more closely. "Are you an attorney?"

"No." He laughed. He had an intelligent aura about him, so I suppose I should have known better. "You?"

"A psychologist."

He nodded. "If I had a Porsche I'd swaddle it in bubble wrap and stow it in a climate-controlled garage."

Maybe I should have informed him then and there that the car wasn't mine, that my own vehicle was just above lumber wagon status, and that I had made more per annum as a cocktail waitress than I did as a licensed therapist, but my vanity was feeling a little bruised. "I'm fresh out of bubble wrap," I said, and checked my watch. It was 9:52. My first client was due to arrive in eight minutes, and leaving Mr. Patterson with my current receptionist, the Magnificent Mandy—her choice of sobriquets, not mine—would be tantamount to cutting my psychological throat. "And functioning garages."

"Tell me you don't leave it out in the elements," he said, stroking the cobalt hood as if it were a cherished pet. He was kind of cute in an honest, disarming sort of way.

"L.A. doesn't have any decent elements," I said.

Dumping the scraper back into its receptacle, he

rounded the bumper. "You from Minnesota or something?" he asked.

"Chicago."

"No kidding? I grew up in Oshkosh. Wisconsin," he added.

I nodded. "Land of the Packers and baby overalls?"

"That's right," he said. Wiping his hand on his jeans, he stretched out his arm. "Will Swanson." His grip was firm but gentle.

"Christina McMullen," I said.

He gave me a smile. Little wrinkles radiated from the corners of his eyes. "You miss the cold?"

"Almost as much as I miss acne."

"Yeah." The smile fired up a notch. He nodded toward the interior of the gas station. "Me and my brother just moved down here a couple months ago."

"Movie script in tow?"

He laughed at himself, ran his fingers through his hair. "Guess everyone has one, huh?"

"Not at all," I lied. "I met a guy just the other day who doesn't write anything but poetry."

"Haiku?"

"Free verse."

He grinned. "We're doing carpentry work to pay for an overpriced apartment in Compton."

Thus the nice forearms.

"Say . . ." He tilted his head again. His hair was straight and a little too long. "You're short one garage. I'm short on cash, maybe we could help each other out."

"I'm afraid my cash isn't very long, either."

"We work cheap." He scowled as he glanced at the scrap of paper he'd just pulled from his back pocket.

"Sorry. I guess Hank has our business cards, but I can write down my number if you're interested."

He *did* have nice arms. I'd spent money for worse reasons.

He was already scribbling with the nub of a pencil he'd pulled from his jeans. "Are you any good?" I asked.

He nodded, then grinned, hunching his shoulders a little. "Actually, we suck."

Funny. Self-deprecating. Cute. Rivera was irritating, conceited, and dangerous. Hmmm.

My phone rang from inside the car. I opened the driver's door.

"Call me sometime," he said.

I gave him a smile as I slithered onto the Porsche's buttery seats. And for a moment I almost felt sexy.

By two o'clock sexy was but a distant memory. By six-fifty, I couldn't even remember what the word meant. I felt tired and kind of dirty . . . but not in a good way.

The phone rang in the reception area. I waited for the Magnificent Mandy to pick it up. She didn't. I answered on the fifth ring.

"L.A. Counseling."

There was a moment's hesitation before the phone went dead. I put the receiver back in the cradle, at which time my so-called employee poked her head into my office. Her face was heart-shaped, her hair short and dyed the color of lightning bolts.

"Should I have answered that?" she asked.

I tightened my hand on the phone and refrained from lobbing it at her head. "That might have been nice."

"Even if it's after six?"

I gave her a serene smile. "If it's not too much trouble."

"Oh no." Her eyes were bubble-bright behind glasses with little stars at the peaks of the black frames. I had hired her because of the glasses, thinking they made her look smart. I've made other, equally idiotic decisions, but not in recent memory. "No trouble. That's what you're paying me for, right?"

"I thought so."

"You look tired. You have a hot date or—"

Her question was interrupted by the doorbell. She glanced toward it, thinking hard. Maybe it was easier with her mouth open.

"Perhaps you should see who that is?" I suggested.

She nodded snappily. "Good idea." Her platform shoes tapped merrily across my carpet and onto the linoleum. Her tights were popsicle pink. "Hello."

"Hi." The voice sounded familiar.

There was a pause which Her Magnificence failed to fill.

"I have a seven o'clock appointment."

No response, but I recognized the newcomer's voice. Mrs. Trudeau. She'd been a client for some months now. I had a feeling she found me shallow and unprofessional. I'd spent a good deal of time trying to convince her otherwise.

"I called yesterday to reschedule, remember?" she said.

There was another pause, then, "Oh crapski," Mandy said.

I plunked my head onto the desk and refrained from crying.

It was eight-fifteen when I turned onto the 210. Despite a good deal of self-loathing, I was nervous about Rivera's impending visit. I needn't have worried though, because when I pulled the Porsche up in front of my little fixer-upper, his Jeep was nowhere to be seen.

Harlequin met me at the door in a series of whines and wiggling spins, thwapping me with his tail at regular intervals. Harlequin is the approximate size of a minivan. He's bi-colored and droopy-eyed. If I liked dogs, he would be at the top of my Facebook list.

"No Rivera," I said.

He cocked his boxy head and grinned at me, showing crooked incisors as I kicked off my sling backs and hobbled into the bathroom.

"Probably best anyway," I said, locking the dog in the hall as I used the toilet. He whined from the other side of the door. "I have a lot to do." And exciting things they were too—carpet shampooing being the most titillating.

Straightening my skirt, I scowled at myself in the mirror above the sink and remembered that wisdom comes with age. I was looking pretty wise. Washing my hands, I sighed, then wandered into the hall to arm the security system.

The doorbell rang just as I was about to touch the key pad, and I jumped despite my placid nerves.

Harlequin barked and circled ecstatically. He loved Rivera almost as if the scowling lieutenant were human.

"Steady," I said. Maybe I was talking to the dog.

Taking a few deep breaths, I put on my cool face and opened the door.

"Congratulations, Rivera. You're hardly late at—" I

began, but my words withered as I recognized the wind-shield man. He stood on my crumbling steps, hands shoved into his back pockets, eyes sincere behind his wire-rim glasses.

"Will Swanson," he said and gave me an embarrassed grin. "From the gas station?"

"Oh. Yes."

Strong as a bulldozer, Harlequin squeezed past my leg to slam his nose into Windshield Guy's groin.

"Holy crap!" he said, backed against the stucco. "What is that?"

"Sorry. Harlequin, come!" I ordered. I might just as well have told him to dance the mambo. He paid me not the slightest attention. But after a couple more snuffles, he sneezed twice, then galloped loose-limbed down the steps and made a mad circle around my abbreviated yard.

Windshield Guy watched, eyes wide behind the wire-rims. "Is it . . . a dog?"

"Maybe," I said. "What are you doing here?"

"Oh." He looked surprised. "I'm sorry." Embarrassment amped up a notch. "Weren't you expecting me?"

I may have blinked. It was the most intelligent response I could come up with.

"I called your office."

I waited.

"Asked if it would be okay to stop by. Your secretary gave me your address," he added quickly.

I wished like hell I could believe he was lying, but I'd known Mandy for a couple of weeks now. The girl made Gatorade look like Einstein.

"Oh shit," he said, and blushed, backing away. "She

didn't tell you I called. You probably have company. I can . . . I'll come back later."

"No." No company. No Asian ambrosia. "How'd you get my phone number?"

"The yellow pages. L.A. Counseling. Christina McMullen, Ph.D." He was blushing again. Kind of sweet, but when I glanced onto the street, I felt my suspicions fire up. Maybe they're innate. But maybe the attempts on my life had had an adverse effect on my naturally optimistic nature. "Where's your car?"

"I'm sorry. I've made you uncomfortable." He backed down the steps. "I'll let you get back to what you were doing. Give me a call sometime . . . if you want to."

Suspicions. Maybe this was why I was sans five fat babies and the ubiquitous minivan. "No. This is fine." I followed him down the steps. "Did you . . . want to take a look at the garage?"

I turned left, giving him time to recover.

"I thought your secretary would have told you to expect me."

"The Magnificent Mandy doesn't like to be conventional."

He laughed, sounding nervous. "Hank needed the truck. I took a cab over. Cost me an arm and an ear."

I immediately felt guilty. I mean, yeah, I did need a new garage, but I was a little more interested in how his forearms flexed when he cleaned windshields. "Listen, Will, I don't know if I can afford—"

"Shit. I'm sorry. I don't know what's wrong with me." We'd reached the corner of my garage. It canted toward the south as if fighting a stout nor'westerly. He glanced down Opus Street. There was no traffic this time of night. "I didn't mean it like that. Man, I'm terrible with hot—" He paused, flustered.

My ears perked up . . . along with my self-confidence. "What were you saying?"

We made eye contact. The sun was setting, casting a rosy glow over the ensuing night . . . and my mood. He shuffled his feet. "Hank can charm the socks off pretty girls. But I . . ." Another shrug.

I remembered our conversation at the gas station. It had actually been rather witty. "I think you do okay."

"You kidding? I'm sweating like a greased pig. Of course, in Oshkosh they find that sexy."

I laughed. He exhaled sharply, stared at me for a moment, then turned nervously away. "So this is the alleged garage."

I gave it a jaundiced glance. I'd once parked Solberg's Porsche in it. He'd threatened litigation. "Can it be saved?"

He made a face. "Are you religious?"

"When I have to be."

He tapped a rotted board with his foot. "Now's the time."

"I'll buy a rosary."

He glanced at me. "You're kidding. You're Catholic *and* beautiful."

Our gazes locked again. "Am I going to have to pay extra for the flattery?"

"We don't see a lot of girls like you in Oshkosh," he said and took a step toward me.

I should have stepped back, but it wasn't as if Prince Charming was waiting in the wings. Hell, Rivera wasn't even waiting in the wings. Still, my nerves were jumping. Nice girls don't make out on the first day. Of course, it had been about a decade and a half since I'd considered myself a girl. And the rules are less stringent for aging women who have been inadvertently celibate for twenty-one months, two weeks, and six days.

"Thought my heart was going to stop when I saw you across the parking lot," he said, and stepped a little closer. He smelled kind of woodsy, like fresh-cut timber.

Harlequin galloped around the corner of the garage, chasing nothing.

"Would have sold my kidneys just to see you smile."

Things were heating up rapidly. "Listen, Will—" I began, but then he kissed me with mouthwatering sweetness.

"I'll leave if you want me to," he whispered. "Or—"

He froze, glanced at the street.

"Or what?" I whispered, but suddenly something popped.

"Fuck it!" he swore, and lurched behind me.

Another pop. I spun toward him, numb, disoriented, and *sure,* absolutely *certain* someone wasn't shooting at me. Not again. Wood sprayed into the air. I screamed. He shoved me forward. I fell onto my knees. A bullet whizzed through my hair. I dropped onto my belly, chanting Jesus' name.

And it must have worked, because the night went silent. My heart was beating like bongos against the dirt. I lifted my head a quarter of an inch. No pinging.

Behind me, something whined and suddenly I felt sick. Sick and shaky.

"Harlequin." I turned on scathed hands and bloody knees.

Will Swanson was sprawled on the ground in front of me. Eyes staring, hand slack around the pistol that lay beside him.